Trails to Heaven

Trails to Heaven

Stuart Wavell

ROBERT HALE · LONDON

ISBN-10: 0-7090-8188-X
ISBN-13: 978-0-7090-8188-3

Robert Hale Limited
Clerkenwell House
Clerkenwell Green
London EC1R 0HT

2 4 6 8 10 9 7 5 3 1

Typeset in 9¾/12¼pt Revival Roman
by Derek Doyle & Associates, Shaw Heath
Printed and bound in Great Britain
by Biddles Limited, King's Lynn

CHAPTER 1

*T*HE THREE HUNTERS *climbed through ice fog for an eternity of pain, hearing only the soft crunch of their mukluks and the whisper of falling crystals, until the shrouds of mist twitched apart to disclose an alarming vision. They ducked down behind a crest, their hunger forgotten.*

Searing back the rime cold of late winter, spring had miraculously touched this broad amphitheatre in the Small Cloud Hills, carpeting its floor with purple saxifrages and filling the air with the delicate perfume of bay rosemary. Within the apparition, movement snagged the men's gaze.

As far as the eye could see, a caribou herd darkened the land. As plump as rain barrels, the large deer milled gently as they cropped the tundra's mosses, their hides glinting in the sun.

The eldest hunter darted a glance at his two sons, reading their alarm at this enchantment. Their thin limbs were tensed, strung for flight.

They have no understanding, the father thought.

Inuk Charlie laid a hand on his younger son's arm and nodded to the other boy, Isaac. As one, father and son rose to their feet.

In a practised motion, the old man lifted the antlers and skin of a deer's head, hefting their weight in one hand. With the other, he grasped a small bundle of whalebone pegs. By imperceptible degrees he and the boy advanced towards the herd, Isaac treading in his father's footsteps and carrying a scoped rifle horizontally in each hand.

Both men wore tight caribou leggings and a strip of white skin around their foreheads. Similar markings adorned Inuk Charlie's wrists. At measured intervals he rubbed the pegs against the antlers in a movement peculiar to the caribou. Father and son took care to raise their feet simultaneously before setting them down abruptly in the manner of their prey.

The effort of this discipline, compounded by hunger, led Isaac to stumble against his father. The pair froze as the herd raised their heads to study the interloper short-sightedly, but under Inuk Charlie's skilful manipulation the caribou head dipped as if to lick its shoulders and attend to other needs. The herd relaxed.

They infiltrated the mass of caribou until Inuk Charlie, judging the moment to be right, reached behind him and felt a smooth rifle stock pushed into his hand. Then, in a synchronized movement, father and son put their backs to the sun and thumbed off their safety catches.

The crashing sound of the guns' release mechanisms, amplified by the surrounding hills, rooted them to the ground like a thousand shouts of accusation. Paralysed, they saw the herd around them transfigured into a snarling horde of scaled creatures that advanced with deadly purpose.

'Run,' Inuk Charlie commanded.

Dropping his rifle, the old hunter dodged into an aisle between the beasts' clamorous ranks. His legs, as heavy as stone, threatened to betray him. Then he was through and retreating into the familiar world of snow and ice. He ran down a deep couloir of firm snow that thudded with the reassuring footfalls of his two sons pounding in his wake.

'Father, wait,' a voice implored.

Inuk Charlie glanced behind and shrank back.

Two pairs of disembodied legs, clad in his sons' deerskin mukluks, staggered down the slope towards him. Isaac's boots stopped in front of him.

'Please, Father, take us home,' his son's voice beseeched.

The old man sat down heavily. The monsters' roars filled his head and he saw their dark shapes blotting out the sun.

The howling of sled dogs woke Inuk Charlie. A note of savagery had entered their cries since his last lucid spell. Skewers of cold lanced through every joint in his upper body. Hunger cramped his gut and a terrible weariness fogged his brain. The odour of putrefaction in the tent told its own story.

I am alive, then, he thought.

Inuk Charlie's gummed eyelids parted reluctantly to admit a distressing tableau. His gaze fell upon four naked legs, frozen solid and still sheathed in their deerskin mukluks, stacked unceremoniously beside the tent's entrance. He had been too weak to carry them beyond the reach of the dogs and now their vile stench filled the tent.

The limbs' owners, his sons, lay inert beside him under thick caribou rugs, their faces darkly contused with poisoned blood. He had taped a feather to each of their chins to check they still breathed. Between long intervals the vanes continued to flutter.

He thought about the failure of his vision quest. Like other skilled hunters who dreamed the location of their prey in sleep, Inuk Charlie had often drifted from the familiar topography of fjords, hills and ice into a mystical realm that had acquired its own reality over the years. Some hunters drew maps of these spirit journeys, charting the trails to Heaven so they would find the route when they died. Inuk Charlie had willed himself to pursue such a path in the sprawling cartography of his unconscious mind, hoping to escort his dying sons to the other world. The thread of a promising route had gleamed tantalizingly amid a tangle of paths, but it had led back to this stinking tent.

It was an old man's dream and he chided himself for presuming that death's final cadences could be cheated. The truth sat like a boulder on his chest: the malediction that had fastened upon his family demanded further increments of pain. His stoical spirit, tested so many times, quailed at what lay ahead.

Inuk Charlie's face cracked in anguish. Frostbite and gangrene were a hunter's constant companions, harrowing yet essentially inconsequential and even perversely welcome. The pain signified that you were alive. Only death was painless.

But he had never encountered such a virulent infection. Rather than advancing from the extremities, this pestilence had struck his sons in the upper legs, heralded by a loss of feeling in those limbs. Within two weeks, dark bands of suppurating lividity had cleaved the legs from groin and hip. Their legs had literally fallen off.

'Kill me,' Isaac had pleaded.

He could not. His own legs were numb and useless but they had been spared these involuntary amputations. Somehow, the trio continued to survive.

He would have to fetch help. Inuk Charlie glanced around and took an inventory. He rejected the Coleman stove, his rifle and snow saw. He could carry little, for the heavy sledge was no longer an option with only four dogs. They were all starving.

Yet there was meat, a pile of meat. The rank smell of the walrus was driving the dogs mad. It sat like a malignant beast at the end of the tent, wrapped in its original skin. He had located the carcass buried under rocks to guard against bears' predations. It was his cousin's food cache, but Kaymayook was recovering from a stomach operation and had no compelling need of it.

Finding the meat had seemed providential. Animals simply refused to allow themselves to be taken. Each seal hole proved deserted, each fishing net came up empty. Even *nanuq*, the wanderer, had vanished from his haunts among the towering pressure ridges of the seaway. In desperation, Inuk Charlie had cut around a caribou footprint with his knife and reversed the frozen cast, praying to his *iriraq* spirit to make the herd return.

Isaac and Matthew tore into the chunks of butchered walrus meat, not waiting for it to thaw. In the ensuing days of famine, the men savoured the walrus's lean consistency and ungreasy fat. Its life-giving broth renewed hope after each day's disappointments.

After five dogs had lain down and died in their traces, Inuk Charlie and the boys had eaten their transport for a fortnight. Another four dogs had disappeared into the cooking pot and the four spindle-shanked survivors were their only hope of fetching help. Men and dogs were reduced to chewing the sled's bindings – rope cut in a long spiral from the skin of a bearded seal. This scant nutrition was washed down with melted ice chipped from the solid lake beneath them.

'Tough old tooth-walker, you are killing us,' Inuk Charlie growled. 'Now you can save us.' Disrespect for the dead animal's spirit could incur no worse horrors than they had already suffered. Inuk Charlie shuddered at the recollection. The meat was bad. Realization had dawned with the onset of headaches, nausea and a tingling in their legs.

Too late, he had pinpointed the cause. Deeply embedded in the walrus's thick hide, its point concealed in a knob of bluish gristle, he found the rusted head of a harpoon. He examined it closely. It was of an unusual design from another age, stamped with an interlocking motif he did not recognize. What stopped his breath was the dark stain of infected tissue around the entry wound. The poison was now in their blood.

The hunters were 140 miles from home and *Nunaniuqtl*, the earth-maker, had not relented. They began to starve on the ice sheet.

Inuk Charlie pushed away the rugs. '*Ajurnamat*. It can't be helped,' he murmured. His sixty-five winters had taught him that all life was a hardship to be overcome by action. He would make a last, supreme effort. He rated his chances poorly; so much would depend on the dogs.

Fastidiously, he inspected the seams of his furs and boots, making repairs with a sharp awl and sealskin twine. Rolling over, he wrestled the walrus hide clear of its stinking burden and bent it into the shape of a cylinder. A drag sled had no rigidity but Inuk Charlie counted on smears of surface melt water stiffening the skin as it rode over the ice.

It took him four hours, sewing the seams tight and trimming the excess with an *ulu* blade. Inside the funnel, he carefully packed a cocoon of rugs. Talking to himself, he fixed a hood above the opening and sewed strong loops of bearded sealskin at each side. For good measure, he lined the bottom with polar bear pelt for its slippery resilience. He grunted. He had a sled. Then he fell asleep.

When he awoke, resolve nearly deserted him, but the sight of his sons, still hovering between life and eternal sleep, stabbed at him. On all fours, pulling the drag sled through the tent flap, he crawled outside and blinked in the glare. The chained dogs were excited but recalcitrant. He spent a long time talking to them, invoking the familiar names of people in Snowdrift until he was satisfied by their laughing faces that they understood his purpose.

Fixing the dogs' traces in a fan hitch taxed his draining strength. Inching into the coccoon was much more difficult. He could not move, except to press his mitts together and offer a prayer to the Christian God. Then he took a deep breath and summoned the bear cry that would electrify the dogs.

'*Kawwwwk!*'

CHAPTER 2

IT WAS A FORTNIGHT before Easter, and winter retained its implacable grip on the land. A frigid gust from the bay's thick ice sent chimney
smoke eddying around the church spire and along Snowdrift's unpaved
streets. Ice rimmed the silhouettes of skinning frames and caribou antlers
poking through the snow beside wooden cabins. It was 20° below, yet the
village slumbered warmly in its dream, mantled in a fresh cowl of snow and
cradled in a sweep of cliffs.

In the freezing updraught of the cliffs' teetering walls, a raven wove patterns
in the air. A distant sound, amplified by the snowy walls, caught its attention.
Far out on the radiance of the ice sheet, a blaring object signalled its approach.

Jack Walker's office was a standard Arctic prefab of steel, housing two
rooms, a toilet and a garage workshop that throbbed with heating pumps for
ten months of the year but admitted no natural light. He sometimes thought
the absence of windows was designed to keep the real world at bay and the
Wildlife Service's officers hunched like drones over their paperwork.

Jack contemplated the polar bear skin arrayed on the floor. Blood matted
the yellow fur. He thought of the intelligence that had once inhabited it.
Working close up to bears always brought a rush of emotions. Beyond fear
and awe, he was conscious of an almost human quality that eluded the
scientific notations of his ledgers. Thought and guile were woven into bear
tracks; when working a pressure ridge for seals, the spoor was always on the
down-wind side; a nose print on a skim of ascending ice told another story.
He had observed bears employing eight distinct methods of hunting seals.

The fur was smelling up the room and Jack glanced at his watch impatiently. Turning back to the computer, he wrote: *The conclusion that only 2%
of the habitat is suitable for the birthing lairs of Ringed Seals implies compet-
itive predation between native hunters and polar bears. Of the 162 seal lairs
inspected, 24 were excavated by bears prior to the arrival of seal hunters.
While not an excessive proportion, this suggests the potential for encounters
and conflict.*

A slight understatement, he thought. In his manor, 500 Eskimos were
outnumbered by 2,500 polar bears. Which was higher in the food chain, he

9

wondered? Men hunted bears and bears hunted men. It was never clear which was the prey.

Keying in the date to the report, he registered its significance. It didn't seem like a year since he had returned to Snowdrift. He had kept a low profile, cautiously testing the air like one of those perplexing tundra plants that survive weather extremes by being frozen one moment and thawed out the next. Gauging the warmth of his welcome in Snowdrift was a trick that still eluded him.

Jack understood the villagers' polite reserve. The teenage oddity of distant memory had returned Janus-faced, bearing a peace officer's powers and the unpopular wildlife statutes. A person's character can change a lot in thirteen years. In Inuktitut custom, strangers were observed patiently until constant traits emerged. White people, fickle and ever changing, were seen as wilful children who required two or three years' study before any firm conclusions could be reached. Jack's diffident manner hadn't helped.

The outer door crashed back. Showtime.

Allowing a minute for the ritual boot stamping, Jack found the visitor in his outer office. A thickset Inuk of advanced years, wearing a frayed denim jacket and storm trousers, bent forward to give critical study to two official wall posters, each depicting an identical polar bear. *Curl up. Play possum!* one advised in English. *Fight back!* instructed the other in triangular Syllabic script.

'A difficult choice. Which was yours?' Jack enquired in Inuktitut.

Lukie Suvvisak, a primordial throwback whose looks had not been improved by more than sixty freeze-ups, directed a baleful gaze at the wildlife officer from beneath jutting brows. His deeply set eyes glinted darkly like flat buttons.

'I killed it for meat.'

'And not the fur?'

Jack led Lukie into his office and squatted beside the bearskin. The pelt was worth at least $1,500 at auction, he reckoned, but perhaps Lukie had planned to settle for half from one of the traders that plagued the community. Inserting two fingers into the holes made by a .22 Magnum, he looked at the hunter quizzically.

The Inuk made an impatient movement. 'It was wounded. I thought it best to kill it.'

'You heard the judge yesterday: shooting a denning bear is unlawful.' Jack intoned the words patiently.

'I did not know it was female.'

'Ah, gender confusion.' Jack nodded sympathetically.

Lukie began folding up the bearskin. 'The judge said I could keep it,' the hunter growled.

'Just don't sell it.' Jack wondered if the old bastard recognized him as the boy who had saved his life. Improbable on two counts, he reckoned. Lukie had been snowblind and drunk when Jack came across him freezing to death a day's journey from Snowdrift. The Inuk's dogs would have run him home unaided if they hadn't been drunk as well. Someone had seen Lukie and the dogs slurping up dregs of communion wine thrown out by the Catholic mission. Jack was ten years old and had known what to do, building a small snow house and placing moist tea bags over Lukie's eyes. He left without receiving a word of thanks, returning home a day late to a tongue-lashing from his stepfather, Aglukark.

Lukie was still sailing close to the wind, except that now the case against him was cut and dried. Lukie and his nephew, David, had come across a polar bear den in a snow bank some forty-five miles from Snowdrift. According to the Crown prosecutor, David fired a shot over the den to flush out the bear, whereupon Lukie placed a shot nearby. The bear put its head out of the den and quickly withdrew. Another shot from Lukie brought it out. Seeing the bear was wounded, Lukie administered the *coup de grâce*.

Judge Edwina Browne had given him a slap on the wrist and ordered the unrepentant hunter to endure Jack's recitations from the Wildlife Act.

That was fly-in justice, Jack reflected. A ten-seater Piper Cherokee had disgorged the judge, two attorneys, a clerk, a stenographer and an interpreter. The law they enforced had grown out of an agricultural society, with fixed ideas about property, sexuality, children and policing that were totally alien to Inuit who had been nomadic hunters as recently as the 1960s.

Jack had to admit that the animal quotas imposed arbitrarily on each village were a poor substitute for the Inuit's traditional limits on hunting, set by their understanding of each species' sustainability. Official targets were based on inaccurate estimates that bore little relation to local circumstances. Yet most Inuit were law-abiding, concealing incomprehension and resentment behind polite smiles.

One evening sufficed for the defence lawyer to confer with half-a-dozen defendants accused of crimes ranging from joy-riding snowmobiles and glue-sniffing to break-ins and domestic violence. Meanwhile, Judge 'Culpability' Browne knitted a garment of perplexing dimensions in the hotel lounge. One day of court and the circus was gone in a belch of aviation fumes.

Jack sat down and swung his feet on to the desk. 'Next time there'll be a thousand dollar fine and you could go to prison for six months. That's the law.'

'*Qallunaat* law. We are in our land now.'

He had a point, Jack conceded, studying the hunter's sullen expression. The law of the *qallunaat* – white men – still held sway in the newly established Inuit homeland, a territory of two million square kilometres carved out of Canada's eastern Arctic. Nunavut, or 'Our Land', was still wrestling with the problem of adapting catch-all legislation to local custom. The bottom line was that a native could kill any animal in self-defence or for subsistence. What interested the law was the value of the hide.

And the lower jaw, he reminded himself. Lukie had brought it in a green plastic bag. 'Just leave it in the workshop,' he instructed. Every bear hunter was compelled to surrender the jaw for scientific analysis in exchange for $35. The samples provided scientists with a wealth of data on age, contaminants and diet. As a convicted man, Lukie had to forfeit the $95 rewards separately for ear tags, lip tattoos, rump fat, liver, skin and hair. Now the bear's gender was beyond dispute, he would also forgo $35 for a baculum, the penis bone.

The phone rang. Jack nodded to his departing visitor and took the call. It was Jim Elias. The stout sergeant rarely ventured outside his warm RCMP office at the end of town. He sounded rattled.

'You still covering search and rescue, Jack?'

'Service with a smile,' he said guardedly. In most other communities, Wildlife had relinquished emergency services to the Mounties but Snowdrift lagged behind, as in so many other things. Jack took a deep breath. 'Who is it?'

'Inuk Charlie was picked up in a drag sled. He's down at the nursing station. He says he had to leave his sons at Stanley Point when they got some kind of infection.'

Jack recalled the family. Both sons had records for domestic violence and alcohol related break-ins. The old man must have prescribed a spell of clean living out on the ice. It was the only effective cure the elders knew for welfare sickness.

'What kind of infection?'

Elias fumbled the message and started again. 'He says their legs came away. Just rotted at the groin and fell off.'

'*Jesus!*'

Jack ordered his thoughts. Stanley Point was a pimple on the uninhabited east coast of Somerset Island, 130 miles distant. The site was less than half-an-hour's flying time from Resolute Bay, the High Arctic's transportation hub, which had a full-time doctor, he recalled.

'How sick is Inuk Charlie?'

'He's lost the feeling in his legs, but he can still count all his toes. His dogs dragged him in a skin sled to McBean Bay, where John Anayoak found him. He says he could eat a whole caribou.'

Inuk Charlie was eating with grim determination when Jack seated himself beside the clinic bed. The old hunter, his spider-webbed features darkened by exposure, crammed his mouth from saucepans of food arrayed on his bed-stand. Winnie, his wife, passed him a steaming mug of seal broth to moisten his palate for the next culinary onslaught.

'I told them to take away the white man's junk,' the old man remarked, seizing a hunk of boiled venison in his teeth and attempting to saw off a piece with the hospital knife.

Jack passed him his own clasp knife. 'I heard you were running in the Midnight Marathon this year, Grandfather, but it's a funny way to train.'

Hearing the tongue spoken, the old man managed a wheezing laugh. 'Yes, funny.' He shook his head dazedly. 'I've been all over hell without a map.'

'Tell me, Grandfather.'

Haltingly, between mouthfuls, the harrowing saga unfolded. When Inuk Charlie finished, he sagged back on the pillow and looked at the officer from the Queen's land. This *qallunaat* had been a difficult child, he recalled. What had the people called him? 'Never-cries'. A bad business, his parents' deaths. The young man's expression reminded him of something.

'There was a black cloud over that walrus.' Inuk Charlie waved the knife upwards. 'It followed us everywhere. Even when I was breaking my head inside that tooth-walker's skin I could see the cloud straight above me. I thought, "What am I doing? Now I am in its stomach". The dogs knew: it's why they never stopped. They were running away from that black cloud.'

Jack marvelled at the Inuk Charlie's resilience. The old bird was indestructible. The last three days must have seemed like being pulled backwards down an endless flight of stairs.

'Grandfather, I'm going to take that walrus skin into custody and lock it up.'

Inuk Charlie grinned weakly. 'Then you must lock this up, too.' Reaching inside his shirt, he took out a bullet pouch containing a heavy object and placed it in Jack's hand. It was the walrus harpoon blade.

Jack found the clinic's temporary director, Susan Taggart, a stern Scottish nurse on loan from Coppermine, in a corridor. 'Doctor McPherson promised to fly over from Pond Inlet tomorrow,' she reported. 'He said it doesn't sound like simple gangrene or trichinosis, but I'm doing tests.'

The nurse appraised Jack discreetly. He had the squared-off hardness that put her in mind of French Legionnaires she had seen jogging beside her hotel on a Corsican holiday, an impression reinforced by his sage uniform and closely cropped hair. But there the similarity ended. A thinker's brow, high cheekbones and humorous green eyes invested him with an unfathomable air. A hungry angel, she thought, studying his hollow cheeks and dark stubble. She guessed he must be around her age, 28.

From her office, Jack made two calls to Resolute, commandeering a doctor and then an equally reluctant charter pilot for a rescue mission the following day.

CHAPTER 3

H E CROSSED TOWN on foot, skirting treacherous ice glazes and snowmobile ruts that led past the hamlet office and Northern Store. The warmer days had almost emptied the village, beckoning families down the fjord where there were plentiful seals and good birding.

Jack cut down a steep track that led to the hunters' and trappers' shack, a distressed wooden building canted towards the shore. A chorus of howling grew louder. Looking down on the bay, he counted eight chains of sled dogs staked out on the ice. Funny, he thought, when he was a kid there had been four dog teams. Now there were fourteen, thanks to trophy hunting.

Three waves of bad air engulfed him as he shouldered into the cabin. A nauseating assault by rancid pelts and acrid tobacco smoke was overlaid by boiler fumes that stung his eyes and caught in his throat.

Six guides, all Inuit hunters, were ranged around a table. Their boss, Jonas Hainiak, diminutive and dapper in a white jumpsuit, stroked his thin moustache while he pored over a large aeronautical map held down by a chipped ashtray and a long skinning knife.

Jack had the feeling he had walked into an argument. He fished a cigarette from his breast pocket. 'Well, are you ladies all powdered up for your illustrious clients?'

Jonas wandered over with a lighter. 'Every sports hunter I ever met was an asshole,' he grumbled. 'Damn waste of meat, shooting a polar bear just to stuff it.'

Jack's cigarette, spotted with gun cleaning oil, spluttered and died. 'No, they're pussycats. Two days of eating frozen fish and they'll want their tummies tickled.'

The hunters chuckled. They were hardly the A-team, Jack thought. Benny, in his early 50s, had only one eye. His dead socket served as a permanent warning against using a rifle to break the ice shackles of a food cache: a stone chip from the bullet strike had taken his right pupil. Joseph, a gaunt figure a few years younger, had lost a lung to TB – an occupational hazard for hunters who had grown up inhaling oil fumes under canvas. Robbie, his brother, suffered from a permanent limp since losing three toes to frostbite.

A gunshot wound disfigured the craggy features of Simon Inuksaq, a Pentecostal lay preacher and the group's natural leader. Jack noted two youngsters, Paulie and Dale, late recruits as drivers. Paulie had a squint.

Between them, he reckoned, they would be hard put to muster a single school certificate and more than a few grammatical sentences of English. Yet this ragtag crew ranked among the world's pre-eminent hunters, operating cheerfully at the margins of human endurance.

Jonas picked up the skinning knife and critically examined its wickedly curving blade. It was one of a Portuguese consignment the Hunters' and Trappers' Association was offering to hunters at concessionary rates. Not one had sold: hunters who butchered animals on the ice and in boats required knives with buoyant cork handles. The batch ordered by Jonas had wooden handles and didn't float. The oversight said much about the Inuk's land skills.

Jonas laid the blade down in disgust. 'OK, we've got four clients flying on Wednesday morning. Three men and a woman who won't leave until they've got a polar bear each. You can bet they'll want running hot and cold water out on the ice. Remember that billionaire? He wanted to sue our asses.'

The client was listed as the ninth richest man in the United States. 'Mr Harry' had parked his customised 737 at Resolute and carried a briefcase stuffed with thousand-dollar tips. The falling-out had arisen over the client's insistence that his bathtub accompanied him on the trip and that it was filled every night. Somehow it had tipped off a sled and disappeared into an ice crack.

Jack smiled at the memory. 'Well, we did offer to compensate him in meat.'

Reminded of the purpose of his visit, he unhooked Inuk Charlie's bullet pouch from his shoulder and extracted the rusted harpoon blade. He laid it on the table.

'You heard what happened to Inuk Charlie? He took his cousin's walrus cache because his sons were starving and he reckons it poisoned them. The walrus was carrying this lump of iron in its hide. The harpoon didn't kill it, but the iron probably contaminated the meat. It must have rotted in there for years. I'd be interested to know who the harpoon belonged to.'

The guides regarded the harpoon blankly. He knew what they were thinking. For all the banter, he was a peace officer dedicated to monitoring hunting quotas and upholding the Wildlife and Fisheries Acts. Jack was not as strict as his predecessor – in the past year he had brought only three prosecutions – but the Wildlife Officer's word could result in a heavy fine. Anything said here could unwittingly implicate someone else. What if the walrus's claws and tusks had been sold illegally? Every able-bodied man in Snowdrift hunted for food and none was immune to such temptations.

He reassured them in Inuktitut. 'This is a medical matter. If we know how long the animal was carrying the harpoon, maybe it will help the doctors to treat Isaac and Matthew.'

The guides relaxed fractionally. Simon Inuksaq picked up the harpoon blade and hefted its weight dubiously. With a pocket knife he began scraping off some of the rust to study the entwined design beneath. 'It's not from around here,' he pronounced eventually.

The piece of metal went from hand to hand around the table until it came to Benny Illuitok, who held it up to his good eye. 'Mmnn.' As though savouring a tasty morsel, he inclined his head in recognition. 'I think maybe I've seen something like this before. I was staying with my wife's folks in Greenland one time, maybe twenty years ago. I saw one like this in a house. Or maybe it was a museum. I don't remember.'

Jack frowned. Greenland? Could the walrus speared in Greenland have swum to north Baffin Island, a distance of 250 miles? It was theoretically possible. From a microlite he had observed walruses migrating in the open pack ice to distant wintering grounds. But usually their movements were restricted to shallow coastal waters where they could dive for clams. The deep, yawning expanse of Davis Strait seemed inconceivable.

'Maybe that harpoon was like iron pills. Gave him extra strength,' he prompted.

'And the runs,' Jonas added, closing the subject. He turned back to the map and began to rehearse the logistics of the bear hunt.

Jack studied his old classmate affectionately. Jonas took his duties seriously as the hamlet's economic development officer. With diplomas from Toronto and Montreal, he could have written his ticket to any job in the old Northwest Territories. Instead, he had flown back to Snowdrift, married his childhood sweetheart and settled in for the long haul. Jack's own return had been more circuitous.

In the past year, Jonas and Jack had joined forces to develop the Hunters' and Trappers' Association as a profitable concern. Tomorrow's polar bear hunt would bring $45,000 in fees directly into the community, Jack calculated. The fund was held by the HTA, in which every village hunter was a stakeholder. The ten-day operation was fraught with potential cock-ups: no wonder his friend was edgy.

Jonas beckoned him to the table. 'OK, it's time for Jack Walker's quick 'n' dirty lecture.'

The guides hammered on the table.

'Gentlemen, please,' Jack reproved. Then, speaking in dialect, he explained that most of the problems the guides were likely to encounter would be cultural misunderstandings. 'The clients are mostly old and it is good to show respect for elders. Normally you would never feed an elder or handle his clothes, because that is to belittle him. These men call themselves serious hunters, so you would never suggest where they should look for animals.'

Jack had their attention. 'But you are thinking in Inuktitut. These *qallu-naat* are not going to feel shame if you treat them like little children. They'll whine unless you constantly feed them. They'll cry with cold if you don't give their hands a friendly squeeze from time to time. They'll pee in their pants if you don't help to unbutton their clothes.'

Paulie raised a hand. 'Are you saying we should undress the woman and squeeze her when she looks cold?'

Jack joined in the laughter. 'Only elders. But you're getting the idea. Treat them like dirt and the happier they'll be.

'And don't forget,' he added, wagging a finger, 'everyone's a meal out there.'

The hall clock showed 10.33 p.m. when he pulled off his sealskin boots and climbed the stairs to his study. Jack's house was Snowdrift's only two-storey structure, set on elevated ground near the shoreline and affording a grandstand view of the ice sheet. At last he permitted himself to shiver, standing by the window and gazing out at the bay's frilled skirts and soaring pressure ridges as the house's warmth invaded his body.

The spectacle of the blue icescape always held him in thrall. Beyond the circular bay with its narrow inlet stretched the convulsed span of Victoria Sound, a fjord studded with locked icebergs and buttressed by 1,000 ft walls. Outsiders found the scene austere and forbidding, but every feature had a name and a story linked to Inuit history. The land was an old friend, a provider that their fathers and forefathers had known. The Eskimos, the animals and the land were caught in an elaborate drama.

A movement caught his eye. Two miles out, backlit by the fjord's pink cliffs, a fourteen-dog team was ghosting fast across the solid platform of sea ice. Simon Inuksaq would not stop for brew-ups until he reached the base camp in eleven hours' time. The lay preacher was driven by a force that invariably put him at the top of Jack's hunting ledgers. Born on a whaling beach before the advent of public housing in the 1960s, legend had it that the infant had fallen off a rock and been scooped up by a narwhal, the small whale known as the unicorn of the sea, and clung to its long tusk as he was gently deposited on a rocky strand.

Jack turned away, summoned by the weary sigh of his fax coming to life. Allowing for the machine's sluggish workings, he set a kettle to boil and returned to the window. In common with the rest of the house, the sitting-room bore the solid, inexpensive stamp of the old Hudson's Bay Company, the cracked covers still preserving the soft furniture in clear plastic.

Their retention was a sign of his uncertainty about the community's welcome. It still pained him that his return had been greeted with the question, 'How long are you staying?' As if he was another *qallunaaut* on a short-term posting that would nudge his career towards the white men's heaven, an executive job in the south.

The fax disgorged a closely typed letter bearing the august coat of arms of a British newspaper. He read a few lines. Irritated by their unctuous tone, he let the sheet fall into a bin. Returning with a mug of tea, he retrieved the letter and began to read it carefully. It was an invitation to write a critique of ultra-Darwinism, one of several quasi-academic battlefields on which he won honours. Jack's mocking rhetoric, allied to a facile command of detail, had put several celebrated noses out of joint.

These days the notion of serving the media's agenda filled him with distaste. As a young Oxford lecturer with an axe to grind, he had served them well, until he realized the futility of explaining the ethos of hunter-gatherers to a nation convinced that all Eskimos still lived in igloos and the Arctic was perpetually covered in snow. He had become an entertainment.

Exchanging the academic life for a more rooted existence had been designed in part to avoid such blandishments. Jack had retired from the world in order to join it. Memories of his childhood in Snowdrift had tugged at him since his English boarding-school, a place full of displaced souls like himself, and suddenly the urge to return to the Arctic became compelling.

Of the limited job options – teacher, social worker or Mountie – the Royal Canadian Mounted Police seemed to offer the answer. His qualifications and dual nationality were accepted with alacrity, yet he overlooked the capriciousness of officialdom. A two-year posting to Yukon cured him of his childhood fascination with red uniforms and funny hats. Dawson City, a place of bar-room fights and drunken truck drivers.

A research job in Fisheries had been his passport back to Baffin Island for six months before his transfer to its sister organization, Wildlife, opened the way back to Snowdrift. There were aspects of the past he hoped to resolve, but he had never been able to formulate them consciously. Why did a murderer return to the scene of his crime?

In waking hours he was at ease in the solitude of his mental hinterland, a ream of knowledge spun from observation and practical experience. Familiarity with the daily lives of hunters provided him with insights that pierced the flabby theorizing of academics.

Yet his exile seemed to encourage the flood of appeals for book reviews, polemical articles and commentaries on global warming. He was appalled – and secretly gratified – that e-mails and faxes made nonsense of his withdrawal to the borders of the civilized world.

He remembered the harpoon and withdrew it from the leather pouch. Balancing it in his hand, he sipped from the mug and felt the tea's warmth course through his body. It was a fixed blade, not an Inuit toggle design, he noted. Eskimos relied on tiring a walrus rather than killing it outright. Once buried in the animal's thick hide, the Eskimo version was designed to detach from the shaft and swivel at right angles to its rope tether, creating a secure attachment.

As a small boy he had been taught to fear walruses as much as bears. The lesson had been hammered into him by his stepfather. A walrus could hook a tusk over a boat's gunnel and pull it down, or erupt through a foot of ice. On land it had the grace of a three-legged elephant, but was capable of ferocious bursts of speed.

He recalled stories from his childhood. In the old days, Eskimo hunters paddled in the currents close to shore, looking for walrus herds asleep on ice pans. Creeping onto a nearby floe, they chopped holes in the ice and secured harpoon lines to the solid base before hurling their missiles at a single animal. Rolling into the water, it soon tired of fighting the ice floe, allowing the hunters to move in for the kill.

Rifles had not rendered such weapons obsolete. Harpoons were still used to hunt seals or tow a walrus through the water before lifting its one-ton bulk onto the ice. The Eskimo solution employed the principle of the block and tackle, creating a mechanical advantage that hoisted the huge animal up the six foot wall of the ice edge.

Jack traced the outline of the imprinted design with his fingernail, trying to locate where the barbs had been welded. Padding downstairs in his socks to the utility room, he rummaged in a toolbox for a tangle of wire wool and a scrap of medium-grade wet-and-dry paper. He held the iron blade under a running tap while he worked methodically on the bloated scabs of rust until the emblem on one face was clearly revealed.

Simon Inuksaq was right, he concluded. The blade's interlocking motif, crudely executed yet conveying subtlety, was not of local origin. He found himself thinking of Scotland. Unbidden images of an excavation, plagued by midges and mud, ran through his mind.

A tic fluttered on his cheek. Norse? The Vikings had settled in Greenland for several hundred years before disappearing mysteriously. He tried to recall their westward expansion across the Atlantic, visualizing a colour map. Hungry for land, they had island-hopped from Norway to the Shetlands, the Faroes and then to Iceland, which became a major base until a few adventurers sailed further west to plant settlements in Greenland.

Confirmation that the same Norse explorers had discovered America, mounting an expedition from Greenland, had sent a shockwave around the world four decades before, Jack recalled. Yet he had read nothing about them visiting Baffin Island.

In Jack's ten years in England, the pervasive ignorance of Britain's history had at first perplexed him until he came to recognize this amnesia as a liberating mechanism that helped to explain the country's constant reinvention. So he was not surprised when mention of Baffin Island prompted only blank looks. To the Victorians it was a land of boundless promise known as Meta Incognita when Martin Frobisher, an irascible adventurer from Yorkshire, set off in 1576 with the nation's cheers ringing in his ears as he sailed down the Thames on his epic journey to find the North-West Passage. Queen Elizabeth I had waved to him from her palace at Greenwich.

The farcical aspects alone might have engraved the story into legend, like King Alfred burning the cakes. Believing he had found the fabled short-cut to the Orient, Frobisher sailed into a giant inlet of Baffin Island, where he discovered something infinitely more valuable – gold. He mined 400 tons of ore and loaded it aboard his ships, to discover on his arrival that it was the mineral pyrites, which looks like gold but is a worthless mineral only suitable for paving roads.

Baffin Island did prove to be the eastern gateway to North-West Passage, although all-year ice in some sections ruled out its early promise. Carved by glaciers and ice from rock a billion years old and separated from the North American mainland by only fifteen miles, it counted as the largest island in Canada's archipelago. Only nine small communities, mostly Inuit dependent on subsistence hunting, dotted a land mass almost twice the size of Britain.

As he stared at the blade, a thought struck him. Three hundred years after Frobisher's humiliation, Europeans returned in force to slaughter bowhead whales, wintering on Baffin Island's east coast. Could it be an old whaler's harpoon? The connection seemed as improbable to him as a Norse link. And yet, he thought, the weapon had not materialized out of thin air. Only a chain of extraordinary circumstances could account for its presence.

His bookshelves ran the length of his study. He liked the volumes' pristine look and their smooth, untrammelled touch. His collection on Greenland amounted to eight books, of which he selected two. It took him ten minutes to find what he was looking for. The Norse design was almost identical.

His Polaroid camera took longer to locate. It was in a dry chest where he stored his shotgun and tranquillizing kit. Improvising a camera stand from a chair with the seat removed, he shot seven photographs of the harpoon before he was satisfied with the results. Gently waving the prints until they dried, he fired up his photocopier and made an enlargement.

Then he began to compose a letter to Professor Patrick O'Connor. If the Vikings had sailed to Baffin Island, Paddy would want to know. The Dublin archaeologist was one of three top experts on Norse and Anglo-Saxon history. He was also Jack's friend and the mentor who had lifted him out of his desultory studies at Oxford by teaching him that scholarship could be fun. The weeks of discomfort as a team member of Paddy's digs in the north of Scotland had been among the happiest of his life.

It was nearly midnight when he fed the A4 sheets into the fax. In Oxford it would be about 7 p.m. he calculated.

CHAPTER 4

PATRICK O'CONNOR WAS late. The Woodstock Road was closed for resurfacing work at Wolvercote roundabout, paralysing traffic on the Oxford by-pass and putting three-quarters of an hour on the drive from his home in Kidlington. Adding hobnails to the boot of fate, it was snowing. The professor judged road works and weather to be the principal curses of England, closely followed by piss-poor beer.

Normally he would have added being spied on by speed cameras – Oxfordshire's zeal was almost Nazi in this regard – but his diversion through Summertown spared him a particularly sadistic concentration.

He nudged the Volvo into his usual space in St Giles. Neither the doctor's card on his dashboard, which manifestly belonged to his wife, nor his illegal parking cone, had ever been challenged. Something about the Irishman's short, stout figure and his quizzically penetrating look, reminiscent of the actor Cyril Cusack, kept traffic wardens at a respectful distance.

A small plaque bearing a skull logo and the legend 'Dublin Viking Project' was the only embellishment on the outer door of his office. A project of the distant past, it had laid the foundations of his reputation and he kept the sign as a talisman.

The professor closed the door and took off his coat. He could smell Alta Rica coffee. 'Odette?' he called. Hearing a muffled response, he selected a path through an orderly maze of plastic file bins to find his deputy scowling at a computer screen.

Seeing him, her face lit up with amusement. Odette Blanchard's effulgence of brilliant teeth and laughing eyes, which happened to be smoky indigo, always entranced and perplexed the professor.

'Ne'er cast a clout till May is out,' he recited. 'Why does it always snow in April?'

'Until May *blossom* is out,' she elaborated. 'Paddy, there's snow on your roof.'

And fire in the grate, he reflected, absently brushing flakes from his wispy hair. No one called him Paddy nowadays, not even his wife. It was a

21

mystery to him that Maeve O'Connor had taken a hand in securing Odette's appointment as his site supervisor. The girl had a model's tall and willowy figure, with fabulous breasts and a look that could set a man's trousers on fire.

Odette had been one of his brightest PhD students, with her own clear ideas on Viking expansion and much else besides. Her intuition for bones and stones put him guiltily in mind of Mary Leakey, whose finds in Tanzania's Olduvai Gorge had underpinned the legend of her husband, the great Louis Leakey. On several occasions, Odette's discerning eye had transformed an unpromising site into a dig for victory.

These attributes were not lost on Maeve O'Connor. Paddy's wife was a clinical psychologist who recognized Odette Blanchard as a class act who brought a rigorous cheerfulness to a dig; yet the girl's archaeological skills did not extend to reviving old fossils like Patrick. So for the past two years Odette had brought order to her husband's affairs.

Odette poured Paddy a coffee and watched him warming his hands on the mug.

'Good news first,' she announced, tapping a thick envelope. 'Utrecht has done the business.'

'Good, good.' He tore off the envelope's sticky binding with clumsy fingers. Six weeks for a radiocarbon dating must set a speed record, he mused. The Van de Graaf Laboratium had processed eighteen samples of burial mound deposits. Their age would help to identify bone samples from a Pictish site in Orkney with promising signs of Viking occupation. Scanning the calibrated dates, the professor sniffed fiercely like an asthmatic rodent.

'I think we're home and dry,' he muttered. 'There's this extra difficulty regarding the effect of a marine diet on C-14 dates derived from bone. We'll just have to get a reading on the proportions in the collagen.'

He glanced up. 'Bad news, you implied?'

Odette's expression was pained. 'Something a little bird told me. A gentleman of my acquaintance has a sister on the Arts and Humanities Research Board. She has her ear close to the panelling and it looks as if we're stuffed on funding in Iran.'

The professor flushed. 'Has the Foreign Office put their hounds on to us?'

'Who knows? Maybe we just left it too late. Funding applications were meant to be in by January.'

Paddy scratched his head furiously. Would the Americans cough up? Probably not, if the Brits were playing silly buggers. Perhaps he'd been naïve.

Odette took the coffee mug from his hand. 'I nearly forgot, there's a fax for you. I put it on your desk.'

She watched him wander distractedly to the kraal of tables that defined his working area, reminding herself that she had hitched herself to a bright star. In the world of archaeology, Paddy was a big man with an international reputation and an Irish passport that, allied to his genial charm, opened doors all over the world.

He gazed at the two fax sheets of A4 blankly, his thoughts still on Iran. Seeing Jack Walker's signature at the end, his face lit up. He tried to focus on the letter, which appeared to be a complicated story about a Norse harpoon. He carefully folded the fax and tucked it in his jacket pocket: he would read it at lunchtime. By then he had forgotten it.

Jack's office stood beside the landing stage of the Hudson's Bay store, long since defunct and a bitter-sweet reminder of the fur-trading era. The hamlet had been built on three terraces fronting the bay, and he rode his snowmobile along the highest ridge.

A small Bell Jet Ranger helicopter was parked on the ice below. It looked like good flying weather.

The garage door was open and he rode up the ramp into his workshop. Levi Eghelok, his assistant, was sawing through an aluminium boiler to fashion a curving base plate that would add several inches to his snowmobile windscreen.

Jack greeted him cheerfully. 'Great idea, suits of armour. Time we had a change of uniform.'

Levi grinned and jerked his chin towards the inner door. 'He's eating your doughnuts.'

Waldo, a giant of billowing rotundities, was seated at Jack's desk. He had consumed the entire packet of doughnuts and was draining the last of the coffee. The long-faced Czech pilot gave a good impression of a moose crammed into a flying suit.

He reached up and shook Jack's hand. 'There's one or two problems and I've gotta gas up. Give it two hours?' He waved an arm towards the outer office. 'You've got a visitor.'

Jack poked his head around the door. A lean Inuk of middle years, his hat folded in his hands, sat patiently in a wooden chair. Jack recognized the man as Marcus Kilabuk, an old-time hunter. A fortnight previously Marcus had called by to claim an advance on two wolf skins, each worth $600 as parka trimming. It was department policy to make such advances against the likely price of skins at auction in Montreal. Eliminating the delay staked hunters for the next trip and spared them the temptation of selling to unscrupulous traders.

Jack beckoned him into his office. '*Ilali*. Take a seat, Father. Coffee?'

Kilabuk shook his head and looked steadily at the *qallunaat*. 'I knew

your father. He got me a job at the mine, one time. He was a kind man. He
came to my outpost camp a lot of times.'

Jack nodded. Such pleasantries, while inevitable in the village where he
had grown up, still filled him with misery and shame. It was no secret that
his father had blown his brains out. Nor were his reasons for doing so.

'What can I do for you, Marcus?'

The hunter glanced down at the cap in his hands. 'I heard about Inuk
Charlie. They said you got the harpoon. You think maybe I can look at it?'

'Sure, I've got it right here.'

Jack fetched his satchel and handed over the piece of iron. Marcus
squinted at its dull surfaces and gave a nod of confirmation.

Jack leaned forward. 'Where did you find it?'

Marcus's account began two years previously with a spring journey that
wove across rubbery sea ice and climbed into the foothills above Victoria
Sound. April was the seal-hunting season, when caribou had not yet
acquired their summer fat. 'Thin, but tasty,' he remarked. His wife was
insistent they needed meat to entertain guests and he learned of a small
herd in the mountains.

He told his wife he would take a look. No hunter tempted fate by
announcing his intention to catch animals, however likely the outcome.
Instead, he murmured, *'Angunahuarniaqara'* – 'I'll give it a try.'

Marcus was lucky: he downed three caribou in two shots, one bullet nail-
ing two females. He was doubly fortunate in that flat terrain had permitted
him to approach the carcasses by snowmobile, saving him the backbreaking
work of butchering them on the spot and carrying the quarters on his shoulders.

'I tied them on my sled.'

Jack nodded encouragingly, undisturbed by this profligate slaughter. Any
surplus meat would be shared. 'What did you do then?'

The butchering was best done on the fjord ice, so Marcus had descended
with his load and, on impulse, headed up Victoria Sound to the natural
haven of Ituquvik.

'You know it?'

Jack nodded. 'The Place of the Old People' was an idyllic spot, next to
a stream, where nomadic groups had once left the elderly and infirm before
undertaking arduous expeditions in the year's hunting cycle. Jack remembered playing in Ituquvik's ruins long ago, half-convinced the place was
haunted.

'I picked a place out of the wind and made some tea. Then I went for a
walk. When I came back, the head was gone.'

Jack frowned. 'Someone took a caribou head?'

'Just cut it off. I never seen anything like that. First off, I didn't recognize the tracks. They went right past the weir to a pile of rocks. It was a wolverine den. Those *qarvik* jammed the head right down in the stones. Then I saw the harpoon next to it.'

Tactfully, Jack refrained from enquiring what had happened to the wolverines. It was a fair bet they ended up as parka hood trimming.

'So what did you do with the harpoon, Father?'

By Marcus's account, he had fitted the blade to a shaft and kept it as a spare in his sled. A few weeks later, when the sea ice was breaking up, he was marooned on a small floe with his snowmobile and sled. A four-foot lead of open water separated him from a larger pan. Leaping the gap, he had used the harpoon to chip a hole in the ice pan, to which he secured a rope. Hauling on the line from the smaller floe would draw him to the stable platform.

He was about to take the strain when the floe tilted alarmingly. It took him several moments' confusion to discover the cause. A walrus had planted its tusks on the floe edge and was attempting to haul itself out of the water. Marcus was sent skidding across the ice pan into the sled, which threatened to drag the snowmobile over the side.

'One wave came up on the ice and I was slipping in the water. The animal thought to kill me. My rifle was tied down by the grub box, so I threw the harpoon.'

Marcus clutched his side to show where the missile had struck, then let his hand fall expressively.

'He went straight down. I saw him once more, swimming. Then he was gone.'

'Thank you, Father. You've helped a lot.' Jack saw him to the door.

He now had a connected chain of evidence. Marcus had found the harpoon two years before and then lost it several weeks later when spearing the walrus. Despite the harpoon blade lodged in its skin, the wounded creature had survived until about six months ago, when it was shot by Kaymayook, who had stashed it under rocks against a rainy day. The food cache had seemed like salvation to Inuk Charlie and his two sons, promising respite from their starvation but poisoning them.

Jack had reservations about Marcus's killer walrus story, but his account was plausible enough. Under the subsistence quota system for each village, Snowdrift's allocation was ten walruses a year although trading the ivory tusks was forbidden. Self-defence was a legitimate excuse for exceeding the quota. Stranger things happened at sea.

One thing was clear: the Viking connection started at the Place of the Old People.

CHAPTER 5

OUTSIDE THE NORTHERN Store, an Inuit woman loaded her three children on to the long seat of her snowmobile. Jack gave her a hand hitching her box of groceries to the back. She smiled her thanks and shot off. He caught a friendly wave as the hamlet's water truck trundled past. An effort had been made to clear the wooden steps of ice, but he placed his feet carefully in climbing up to the store's heavy outer door.

The supermarket retained something of the Hudson's Bay Company trading era that he remembered. To a child's eye, he imagined, it still had the air of an Aladdin's cave – a cornucopia of rifles and bullet boxes in glass cases, a selection of deadly knives, racks of parkas, gloves, hats and thermal underwear, rows of white mukluk boots, rubber boots and fancy seal *kamiq* boots, trimmings of wolf and fox fur. Jack wandered down a food aisle, stacking flat boxes of groceries on his left arm and pausing to inspect the astronomical meat prices displayed on the refrigerated units. The fruit counter boasted a single bunch of four small, mottled bananas. White man's junk. The only reminder of the store's original purpose – a hatchway for trading furs – was boarded up.

The deputy manager, a southerner, caught him at the checkout as he was paying Ruth Inuksaq, Simon's sister. 'I guess this is goodbye, Jack. I'm shipping out tomorrow. Yeah, I know, it's only been a year, but I can't take another winter. The darkness gets to you.'

Jack walked home and watched the end of the 9 a.m. CBC news without taking anything in. The southerners' wars in Iraq and Afghanistan held little interest for people in the High Arctic, other than increasing their distrust. Over the decades the Inuit had been led to expect attacks from the Japanese, the Russians and now Al Qaeda. Many remembered strange explosions in the sky during the 1960s, when the Mounties had warned people to stay inside and then instructed them to bring in any unusual metal objects they discovered.

He lay down. Sleep often eluded him at night, when he was compelled to mount watch over his disquieting thoughts. What had the deputy store manager said? *The darkness gets to you.* Taking daytime naps was also a childhood habit dictated by the availability of animals and firmer travelling surfaces at night. Time was a meaningless concept in seasons of perpetual light and darkness.

He reached out and clicked on the metal HF radio beside his bed. It was a standard two-way Spillsbury set, switched to an open frequency, which crackled and then blared out a cacophony of excited voices. In a quick-fire exchange of conversation, Jack could make out a hunter's delirious account of sighting a two-horned narwhal at the ice-edge in Lancaster Sound. A single ten-foot ivory tusk, twisting from the small whale's upper jaw like an overgrown tooth, could fetch several hundred dollars. A rare double set might buy a new snowmobile, although the value had to be weighed against the significance of the narwhal's appearance. It was a propitious omen.

Another voice broke in, complaining about the fishing catches at the far end of Victoria Sound, eighty miles distant. The previous night's pale moonlight had evidently inhibited the movement of arctic char beneath the lake, causing the speaker's indignation that only three had swum into his ice nets. Someone announced that people who wanted meat could help themselves to his spare seal on the dock.

Jack turned the volume down and listened to the comforting whisper of voices as he drifted off to sleep. He had the old dream. Despite his subliminal vigilance, its setting could assume a variety of beguiling permutations before he could close the horrific images down. This time he was walking beside the rugby field of his boarding-school towards the beech forest that lined the hillside. The unfamiliar yet intriguing scents of trees, intensified by the heat of an English summer's day, often drew him to this path.

In an eye blink the scene shifted. Figures burst from the tree-line, firing guns at the small army around Jack. Someone pushed a crude rifle into his hands and he took aim, noticing it had no bolt or firing mechanism. He experienced a hunter's satisfaction when his first shot toppled a distant rider from his horse, but then the fighting was close around him and he fired from the waist into a threatening shape.

It was a woman, who cradled a child with one hand and cupped the other over the bleeding wound in her stomach as she gazed at him with shocked reproach. He recognized the anguished features of his mother. Spotting his stepfather behind her, he ran forward and swung the rifle with savage joy at Aglukark's head, feeling the butt connect with jarring force. He grasped the barrel for the killing blow that always eluded him.

Jack pivoted out of bed, struggling to clear his brain. It was a practised manoeuvre, now involuntary, but never quick enough to escape the mortification that followed. Thankfully, something else was calling for his attention.

The phone. For half a minute a distant voice swam through miasmas of guilt and self-loathing until Jack made out the brisk tones of Patrick O'Connor.

'Jack? Are you all right? Have I chosen an inopportune moment?'

He turned off the HF radio and pressed his head to the wall.

'That's all right, Paddy. Just getting into my swimming costume. It's sunbathing weather up here.'

Paddy's laugh intensified the pressure in his head. 'Same old Jack. How are you now? Weren't you a Mountie in Yukon or some such? And now you're working in Snowfall?'

He reproached himself for not going into more detail in his Christmas cards to Paddy and Maeve during the past three years. His debt to them deserved no less than keeping their relationship in good repair.

'Snowdrift in Baffin Island,' Jack corrected.

'Ah yes, I can picture it on a map. Well, I'm thinking of Baffin Island as the rhinoceros shape that's practically touching the North American mainland across a narrow stretch of water aptly named the Fury and Hecla Strait. If memory serves, your village of Snowdrift must sit on the rhinoceros's secondary horn not far from Lancaster Sound. To think the British spent four hundred years up there looking for the North-West Passage only to find it was an impasse. Rather like the Irish question, really.'

Jack massaged his forehead. 'You got my fax, then?'

Paddy's sonorous brogue was tinged with regret. 'A Viking spear from Greenland, you think? Well, now, it's quite possible. The blade motif appears to be in the Mammen style, which is quite remarkable in a way. It's the same interlaced pattern you find in Norse art between about AD 860 and, say, AD 1020. A Norse blade would be quite a find, but in historical significance not worth bean.'

'Paddy, I thought you said the Vikings went on shopping expeditions to Baffin Island and Labrador.' Jack could imagine Paddy scratching his balding pate in exasperation.

'Well, of course, any eejit only has to look at a map to see how easy it would be. By sea, the Norse settlements in Greenland were much closer to North America than their trading port in Norway. But if the poor dears were frightened of crossing open water, the wind and currents would carry them around the coast of Baffin Bay.'

His headache was lifting. 'So why isn't this harpoon of any significance?'

Paddy snorted. 'Trade goods! That's what my esteemed colleagues chant every time a Norse fly-button or coin turns up in North America – the Eskimos must have brought them from Greenland. Well, I ask you!'

Jack had to admit the objection did not seem logical. 'If the Eskimos could travel backwards and forwards between Greenland and Baffin Island, why couldn't the Vikings?'

Paddy exhaled noisily. 'If I ever gave tongue to such heresy they'd put the thumbscrews on me, Jack. We must prostrate ourselves before two great articles of faith. Article one: that the Norse in Greenland learned nothing at all in the way of travel technology from their Eskimo neighbours. Article two: that the only settlement the Vikings ever established in North America was the Vinland base in Newfoundland. Lily-livered cowards that we know the Vikings to be, they took fright at the first shower of native arrows and scurried back home, never to return to Vinland or North America. Anything else is wild speculation, inviting a visit from men in white coats.'

For a long beat, the warm voice of his old mentor wafted Jack back to their collaboration on vacation digs in Scotland and the Shetlands, until an expectant silence pulsed down the line. He felt mild relief that the matter was laid to rest.

'So I can forget about the harpoon?'

'For now, yes. But promise me one thing, Jack: if anything else of the sort turns up you'll let me know immediately.'

The conversation tapered off amid expressions of mutual regard and a quick word from Maeve. A wave of affectionate reminiscence was already smoothing away the searing images of his dream. Jack felt the inordinate gratitude of all orphans towards strangers who dispensed kindness not as a duty, but as a boundless commodity. The O'Connors had offered themselves as his surrogate parents, yet they had been rebuffed by his deeply watchful reserve. Under Maeve's gentle probing, he had confided more about his background to them than anyone in his life – without reaching the point where lies began.

Paddy and Maeve were probably discussing his abridged story now; it was not one they were likely to forget. Jack tried to imagine how the conversation might go. They would recall that his father was a Cornishman, an engineer and geologist who worked at the mine ten miles from Snowdrift. His wife was much younger, a pretty girl and apparently a bit of a shrew.

The mining settlement had some rough types, so the Walkers had rented a house in Snowdrift and, when Jack was old enough, sent him to the village school. Then the embarrassing bit: his father hit the bottle and his mother ran off with a local man, taking Jack to live in a permanent outpost camp. It seemed the fellow was some kind of healer.

He could recall Maeve's pained expression when he had recounted the next cascade of misfortune. Jack's father had shot himself in the head. For the next nine years, the boy had lived the Eskimo life with his mother and stepfather until fate intervened once more. On a springtime journey, the family were camped under a cliff when fierce winds had dislodged tons of snow on the crest, burying the tents.

Only Jack and his younger stepsister had escaped to raise the alarm, but the depth of the avalanche had hampered rescue attempts. During the thaw two months later the body of his mother was found, cradling her one-year-old child. The boy had evidently survived his mother long enough to chew parts of her face in hunger. The body of Jack's stepfather was not recovered, although there was evidence to persuade the coroner that it had been dug up and eaten by polar bears.

For the thousandth time Jack weighed the story for plausibility, probing its weak points for flaws.

The story's darkness had lifted in the last chapter: at the age of fifteen he was whisked over to England by an aunt, his father's spinster sister, who pulled a few strings to get him into a public school in Surrey. And then, by diligent study, he went to read anthropology at Oxford, where his unwelcome insistence on an allied course in archaeology brought him to Paddy's attention.

Perhaps, he decided, the saga's sheer awfulness made it seem credible to others. He had passed judgement on his own soul long ago. He looked at his watch. Waldo would be hitting the sky in ten minutes.

CHAPTER 6

THE POLAR BEAR was in turbo mode, loping across the stretch of flat ice and casting glances over its shoulder at the giant insect that droned in pursuit. Each time the helicopter lined up for the shot, the bear jinked away and circled back to its cubs, roaring defiance at its tormenter twenty feet above.

'Let's try it lower and faster,' Jack prompted.

'You want me to give it a haircut?' Waldo grimaced at the controls. He was chewing something.

'Her,' Jack corrected. 'It's a mother.'

'Damn right about that.'

Jack made an effort to remain calm. The sow was now panic-stricken and close to over-heating. Waldo had no feel for this kind of flying. His predecessor had been a shit-hot former air-force pilot who could make his chopper dance. Darting a bear from the air called for a swift approach that put the animal directly under the skid, permitting a shot down the cone of still air inside the turbulent prop-wash.

His thoughts drifted, probing the harpoon puzzle like a throbbing tooth. He recalled that in early summer, a bottleneck in Davis Strait attracted drift ice that formed a solid barrier where walruses could haul out. Norse hunters would have been compelled to steer west to remain in open waters. Eventually, they would have sighted Baffin Island.

Waldo began another lumbering run and Jack lowered his rifle one-handed beside the fuselage. The trick was to pop the bear in the back of the neck or the thick muscles of the front shoulder. He could not risk hitting it in the stomach, which could perforate the bowel, or even worse in the ribs, which might puncture the lungs.

He squinted into the freezing airflow: despite his polarized mirror shades, the ice beneath was a confused blur. *Christ!* They were only fifteen feet from the surface.

'Too low!' He glimpsed the bear immediately ahead.

Waldo reacted a split second too late, pulling back on the controls. As the

31

nose lifted, the rear of the skid dipped.

Time slowed to a series of freeze-frame elapses. The bear turning to face the chopper. A snarling malevolence rising on its hind legs from a crouch to its full eleven-foot stature. The apparition swiping at its attacker. The machine lurching as two powerful arms clamped on the right-hand trailing skid.

'Keep her steady!' Jack yelled. Any attempt to rise would tip the craft over.

'It's pulling us down!' Waldo shouted.

Another careening lurch.

'Bear aboard!'

Suddenly its ferocious head appeared below Jack and a huge arm groped towards him.

It was trying to hook him out of the window.

The rifle felt like a lead weight in his hand. With dreamlike slowness he inched up the barrel for a snapshot until he felt the stock kick into his shoulder.

Reacting as if stung, the bear loomed upwards and roared into Jack's face, its fetid breath frosting over his sunglasses instantly.

He was blind.

Then the chopper surged and the shaking subsided.

Jack yanked in the rifle and flipped off his sunglasses. He looked down. The bear was ambling unsteadily towards its cubs. After a few more paces it sank wearily to the ground. He glanced at Waldo: the pilot's long face was jumping.

'No passengers! I told you, no free rides!'

Jack's heart thumped in his chest. 'Start thinking free meals, Waldo. You'll dine out on this story for years.'

He forced himself to think: if all the drug was expelled from the dart he had three-quarters of an hour to do the bear.

'Can you put her down about a hundred yards off?'

Waldo selected a sheltered stretch of ice for an inelegant landing. 'I guess I'll stay in the cabin,' the pilot grunted. He unwrapped a chocolate bar.

Jack reloaded the gun, using a rod to push the dart halfway down the barrel. Much as he disliked the idea of shooting one of the cubs, they might defend their mother with display charges that could become over-exuberant. It was a painful deterrent: the dart was effectively a heavy three-inch bullet carrying a half-dose of Telazol that was expelled by a detonator on impact through a steel needle.

He grabbed a medical bag from behind his seat and opened the door. Stepping down on the ice, he took his bearings. A light, chilly breeze stole the edge off a fierce sun. Around him, the shattered icescape of Prince Regent

Inlet extended into infinity. Violent winter storms had created havoc with the seaway's frozen surface, ripping open great leads and slamming them back together with momentous force to create pressure ridges that soared thirty feet into the air. Blue lights pulsed in ice blocks the size of houses.

At his approach, the cubs skittered away: they were fairly harmless year-lings, he saw. Two year olds were a different matter – they could tear you up badly. Their mother was lying on her side, the dart lodged in her upper shoulder. Whistling tunelessly, Jack shifted the bear's head away from the sun and began a familiar routine. Satisfied the dart was fully voided, he squeezed ointment into the animal's open eyes to prevent dehydration and extracted a radio collar from its plastic bag.

With difficulty, he secured the white harness around the bear's neck and reached into his medical bag for pliers. Gently easing open the animal's jaws, he made a quick inventory of tooth wear, wrinkling his nose at its rancid breath. Seal buffet.

A small redundant pre-molar came out smoothly. Good choppers, he noted, slipping the bloody tooth into a sample bag. Working around the animal's bulk, he clipped the end of a claw from a rear paw and took hair samples from the back of a leg.

Last, he inserted a small gadget and tattooed a serial number inside the lip. He had misgivings about contaminating such an important source of meat. Jimmy Okadlak had put it succinctly: 'Think how you'd feel if you found a pubic hair in your hamburger.'

He was steadying a tape measure between the bear's nose and the tip of its tail when he heard Waldo's shout. The pilot gestured to his headphones. Jack glanced at his watch: another fifteen minutes before the bear awoke. He made a guessed notation of the sow's tape weight and, gathering up his equipment, he gave the bear a pat. 'Good luck, Doris.'

Waldo registered exasperation. 'That was Resolute. They got pissed off waiting. Message is Inuk Charlie's boys didn't make it. They've been dead for days.'

Jack had been expecting it, but was surprised by a tug of emotion. 'That's a shame. The old man deserved better.'

He thought for a moment. He had counted on tagging six bears today but Waldo's flying skills made that a forlorn hope. There was another pressing matter he could always pass off as official business – the wolverine den where Marcus had originally found the harpoon. Paddy had not discounted its Viking provenance but merely pointed out the difficulty of proving the Norse had brought it from Greenland. Perhaps the site would yield more compelling evidence.

'Let's call it a day. Think we can fly up near Cape Hooper? There's some-thing I have to check out.'

Jack showed him on the map. The pilot's studied nonchalance barely concealed his relief. 'All the same to me. The government's paying and we've got two hours' flying time.'

'That's where the Eskimos left their old folks?' Waldo asked. 'Looks kinda barren.' Perhaps contemplating his own premature retirement, the pilot took comfort in another Snickers bar.

Below them in bleak monochrome stretched a limitless expanse of ice and tundra, relieved by the harsh lines of deep canyon walls buttressing fjords and distant mountains. The scene looked eternal, but a few clicks of the time vault would soon release another spectacle of open water and variegated brown hills. Then it became one of the wonders of creation.

The miracle always thrilled Jack. Spring sunshine was already sparking the genesis. A golden-brown coating of algae was forming beneath the thick sea ice, releasing an explosion of plankton, krill and gastropods. Soon the waters of Lancaster Sound would teem with millions of fish and a multitude of seals, both prey to polar bears stalking the floe edge and the moving pack ice. Walruses would come to dine on the biggest scallops in the world. Then larger beasts would arrive.

In a few weeks' time, more than 55,000 narwhal would swarm north through open leads in the eastern Arctic to their summering grounds. They would be joined by thousands of beluga whales, nearly a third in North American waters. Their fluting harmonics would blend with calls by giant bowhead whales, once almost extinguished by whalers. For a few weeks, Lancaster Sound became the richest marine mammal environment in North America.

From the air, Jack could appreciate why Eskimo nomads had chosen Ituquvik. Strategically, it lay at a crossroads between several hunting grounds, sited near the confluence of Lancaster Sound, Victoria Sound and Britannia Inlet, one of the world's largest fjords. He gauged the short distance from the abandoned settlement to a fifty-mile-wide floe edge extending across the mouth of the fjord, where Eskimos hunted narwhal and beluga in late spring.

A little further distant, he could see the stippled pack ice of Lancaster Sound, the eastern entrance of the North-West Passage.

'Summer was the worst time for them,' Jack remarked.

Waldo shot him a glance. 'Let me guess – no air-con?'

Jack laughed. 'The whale hunters went off and made camp for the season: if the whales didn't turn up, the group starved,' he said. 'Leaving the weak behind was an act of charity.'

The helicopter began to descend rapidly.

'OK, I'm going to put her down on that patch of sea ice, so you'll have to walk,' Waldo apologized. 'Don't be long – there's weather headed this way.'

Jack ducked under the lazy rotors. Before him loomed sheer 1,000 ft cliffs, their upper faces striated with geometric bands and uniformly weathered buttresses. As a child he had gazed at these castellations in awe, conjuring Aztec temples and Indian war parties in his mind. Even now, Jack caught himself searching for smoke signals.

The Eskimos' ancestors had found a deep fissure in the rock wall, undetectable from the fjord except on a direct approach. Behind the entrance, glaciers had sculpted a gently shelving valley cleaved by a rippling stream. At freeze-up, its outflow had buckled the fjord ice, creating a steep bank that Jack climbed with difficulty.

Marcus Kilabuk had found the harpoon here, so perhaps something else would be lying in plain sight.

Cresting the brow, he paused to contemplate a picturesque scene. Much of the recent snow had been blown into drifts, exposing the stream as a ribbon of dull copper winding up the valley floor. On either side stood the ghostly outlines of sod houses, now reduced to skeletons of driftwood and whalebone spars. Jack recognized a ring of small boulders, placed at a respectful distance, for securing tents.

He tried to recall the salient details of Marcus's story. The hunter had left his sled and gone for a walk, probably to relieve himself, returning to find the caribou head gone. Then he had passed the weir. Jack crossed to the mouth of the stream and looking down through the ice he could make out the crystal bumps of large stones, positioned to trap migrating arctic char. He could visualize the aged community fishing between summer's first break-up of the ice and early September, when the last fish entered the rivers to make their way to freshwater lakes before winter tightened its vice.

Marcus had said he followed tracks from the weir to a pile of stones. Jack scoured the ground carefully. Wolverines mostly frequented boreal forests and were rarely seen on the Arctic islands. He wanted to forgo the privilege, recalling a cabin destroyed by the marauders in Yukon.

A flicker of movement registered in his peripheral vision. Turning slowly, he noticed a faint line of tracks leading to a freestanding column of rock. He squatted, frowning. The spoor was similar to a wolverine's, but smaller. A tiny cub? With measured tread, he approached the rock. Again he sensed a movement, snake fast. A piercing cacophony of shrieks and yammering sent him reeling backwards. To his horror, a five-headed hydra appeared in a crevice, hurling bolts of sound at him and darting out with deadly menace.

'Bloody hell, weasels!' Jack was too shocked to laugh. The mother and her four offspring made a convincing impersonation of a mythological beast as they continued their reproach.

He walked around the rock, studying its bricklike pattern of weathering. At its base, a slab had sheared away, leaving a wide crack. His eye fell on two lines of small bones, perfectly aligned.

Jack stood stock-still. He felt numb, ambushed by the past, and tried to thrust away the scene that began to materialize in his mind. He saw a boy and a girl in an apple crate, the bones ranged in front of them. They were the shoulder knuckles of seals, taken from a cooking pot. Small children played with them in games of make-believe, arranging them in lines of sled dogs. He and Soosie had fashioned the harnesses from wire and thread.

Suddenly impatient to leave, he settled for a cursory search, wishing he had obtained more precise directions from Marcus. The most promising area was a promontory to the left of the stream. Here a solid ramp of flat rock led up to a pile of boulders, surmounted by a tall outcrop of rock.

Reassured by the absence of wolverine tracks, he paced along the rocks. Experimentally, he tried to move one: it was locked fast with ice. When he shoved the next, it shifted. Putting his weight behind it, he rolled it aside and saw it partially obscured a hole. Inside, there appeared to be a rudimentary tunnel. He could see wisps of dark brown and tan fur clinging to the sides. Wolverines. He could faintly detect the coyly mingled smells of animals and urine, but the occupants were long gone.

Jack thought the entrance might just admit his head and shoulders. In for a penny, in for a pound. He was wearing an old bush jacket, impervious to ill treatment. Among the junk in its pockets he found his pen torch. The bulb was weak, but produced a glow.

He had to prise away a sharp stone before he could fit in comfortably. The tunnel was short, curving into a hollowed-out area just beyond his vision where the wolverines had performed a prodigious task of excavating the rocks and fill.

Jack noticed that the right wall of the tunnel was flat, as if the animals had encountered solid rock and burrowed in another direction. Playing the torch along the rock surface, could see a slot about eight inches long. It appeared to be deeply indented and perfectly rectangular. He removed a glove and ran his hand along it: the edges were sharp. Straining forward, he could make out crude chisel marks in the stone.

He stared at the groove. He could recall no such feature in the ancient Inuit sites he had visited or read about. A bell was ringing in the recesses of his mind. What? A page in a book. Then pain. He became aware that his back muscles were clamouring for respite. He pushed backwards, encountering resistance. He was stuck.

Jack relaxed, taking shallow breaths. Still curious, he redirected the torch to illuminate the den partially. Reaching forward, he groped around the corner of the small cave. His hand encountered rock, splinters of bone and a piece of stiffened hide. He rolled a tuft of soft fur between his fingers. The White Rabbit? Beneath the fur his hand closed on a hard object that felt like a large collar stud. The Mad Hatter's? Expelling his breath and using the rock groove as leverage, he eased himself out.

He sat on a rock and lit a cigarette, the smoke searing his lungs in the dry air. Abstractedly, he gazed at the mound of impacted rocks beneath his boots. It was the den spoil ejected by the wolverine tunnellers, he realized. Marcus must have stood on this spot and seen the harpoon among the detritus.

He began to attack the ground's hard surface, striking down with the toe and heel of his Ski-doo boot. After five minutes he had only sweat and blisters to show for his exertions. Removing his jacket, he cast around for a heavy stone to break the ice seal binding the mound. His third attempt shattered the crust enveloping a flat rock and several more blows exposed a finger-hold at one end.

The small slab pivoted up easily. Jack pushed it to one side and peered down but the presence of more rocks beneath proclaimed the futility of the task. His eye was caught by a thin edge of bone nestling between two stones. Intrigued by its symmetry, he removed a glove and probed for it, but the object was too deep and eluded his fingers. Remembering his Swiss Army knife, he slid out a pair of tweezers recessed in the handle. The prongs were tiny and had to be bent back to accommodate the sliver of bone.

He withdrew the object carefully. A comb. Amused, he turned it over in his hand, recognizing the bone as antler. Unusually, it was double-sided, with teeth protruding in both directions and although sections of teeth had broken off, the majority remained intact and surprisingly rigid. The comb appeared to have been constructed from a number of thin rectangular pieces, filed into teeth and clamped together between two central backing plates of horn.

'Curiouser and curiouser,' Jack murmured. He rubbed the backing plates between the finger and thumb of his gloves, locating five small bulges equally spaced along the comb's length. Unlocking his knife blade, he gently shaved away flakes of grime. The backing plates were incised with two neat parallel grooves along their length and three groups of triple grooves in the centre. Five metal rivets, reduced to blackened blobs, held the comb together.

Jack shook his head slowly, trying to sort out the thoughts cascading through his mind. He had seen many pictures of combs like this: he had even handled one at the finds office of a student dig in the Shetlands.

Combs were the most common artefacts found in Viking Age towns and graves.

The harpoon and now the comb. He rummaged in his pocket and found the collar stud. Beneath bulbous encrustations it was an iron rivet, he realized. A ship's rivet? He looked around, appraising the site with new eyes.

Had the Vikings sailed here from Greenland and for what purpose? A spark flared in his memory: the slot in the tunnel wall. In his mind's eye he could visualize the reference on a page. Norse long houses had slots for benches around the walls. They were integral to the construction of turf and stone-built houses in Iceland and Greenland.

He drew back a dozen paces and studied the rock face. The boulders occupied a natural fault about fifteen feet wide. The ice rang like iron as he ran across the stream and looked back. It fitted: the water channel, the stone ramp and a natural enclosure. He was looking at a slipway leading to a boathouse. The implications unfurled in his mind.

CHAPTER 7

IN THE NIGHT, foxes had left a monument to their artistry. The caribou was too old to outrun the wolves that had playfully hamstrung its back legs before leaving it trembling on the ice, where surface water froze to its hoofs. Foxes had moved in to excavate its living body from the rear, finally abandoning the hollow carcass on the bay ice. It still stood upright.

A walker, Jack thought. A walker was a male driven off from the herd and destined to wander alone. The epitaph of Jack Walker?

The gruesome spectacle was overlooked by the windows of the Tuugaalik, Snowdrift's only hotel, an uninviting wooden structure whose outer hall was lined with parkas and embellished by an ancient wind factor conversion table. The push-bar delivered a crackling shock of static as Jack shoved through a wall of dry heat.

In the dining-room, a group of newly arrived construction workers, all southerners, were dismantling piles of waffles and steak. Sam, the manager, acknowledged Jack with a grunt.

A burst of laughter erupted from a group seated around a low table in the lounge. The trophy hunters, Jack guessed. He had filled out their hunting licences after checking their paperwork was in order and their fees paid. He was here to deliver them. Four guides sat with Jonas on a bench, observing their merriment impassively. The hunting party comprised three men – two Americans and a burly Frenchman, the film director – plus a pneumatic blonde who must be his personal assistant, along for the ride. Poor girl, he thought. At 30° below, the film director's good wife could rest easy at home.

Jack took out the hunting licences, pretending to check the names as he studied the three men. He could read them like a book: committed trophy hunters all, they would be wealthy men who had bagged the Big Five and hired the best taxidermists to enshrine their bravado. It was like a religion to them. Now each craved the ultimate prize, the head and skin of a great white bear.

The elder one, a scrawny Californian in his mid-sixties, was in full flow,

39

recounting his exploits in Africa. 'We're halfway home when this croc comes back to life. I got six niggers, a guide and myself, all abandoned the Land Rover because of the flip going on in the back seat. It took an hour to get this thing tied down. Then those blacks didn't want to get back in the buckie.' The Californian whinnied. 'I tell you, no way they wanted any part of that action.'

The protesting scrape of a chair was lost in the group's guffaws. Jack noticed Jonas rising to his feet. 'What a crock,' the Inuk murmured, heading for the door.

Jack placed the licences on the table and addressed the elder American. His tone was polite. 'We're a bit short of crocodiles but I'm sure you'll be pleased to know we have a nigger here today. Let me introduce Benny Illuitok, one of our most accomplished guides.'

Benny had been an invisible presence at the table during the strangers' banter. He let the embarrassed silence stretch interminably, then cleared his throat. His deep, nasal voice seemed to reach them from far away.

'That's right,' he said agreeably, his single eye seeking contact with each of the sportsmen. 'Some of the American whalers that wintered down in Pangnirtung were black slaves. They sort of married with my folks. I guess that makes me a nigger, too.'

The Californian blenched. His companions stared resolutely at the table. Jack was oblivious to their discomfort. He addressed the bench of guides. 'Fascinating. Any more niggers or coons? What about the Okadlaks and the Otakiaks?'

Jimmy Okadlak shook his head slowly. 'Sorry. We're Micks.'

Sam suppressed a smile. It was an old joke.

Jack turned back to the sportsmen's table. 'I'd better give you the bad news first. The good people of this hamlet have voted to renounce the evils of drink, which means, I'm afraid, you can't buy alcohol in this hotel or anywhere else.'

He raised his hand as if to quell a chorus of groans. 'But the good news is that where you're going, drink will almost certainly result in death by hypothermia. So you're much better off without it.'

The French girl studied him with interest. 'Can we be sure to catch a bear?' she asked, innocently laying a hand upon his.

Jack withdrew his hand gently. He did not like being touched.

'Everyone gets a bear and a kupie doll,' he said. 'But no mummy bears or baby bears, please.' He tapped the hunting licences. 'One last thing. You'll be leaving in two hours. Let Simon check out your clothes and boots now. We've got caribou furs for all of you. I advise you to wear them.'

Outside, he took a breath of astringent air. The High Arctic brought out the worst in trophy hunters, he reflected. The cold frightened them: each man dreaded the voyage of discovery to his own threshold.

*

His office still smelled of bearskin and he left the door ajar while he tuned in to the HT emergency frequency, so he didn't hear the schoolgirl's tentative knock or see her enter. He looked up to find her seated before him, a pretty teenager with her arms folded across her ample bosom.

'I want to be a hunter,' she declared.

'A hunter?' Jack couldn't quite grasp her meaning.

Sighing at his slow wits, she pushed a folded leaflet across the table. It was a Wildlife leaflet offering weekend courses in land skills, he saw, part of the department's drive to familiarize schoolchildren with their parents' traditions. 'It says you will teach me how to be a hunter,' the girl said, with a sweet but emphatic smile. 'I will need personal instruction.' She raised her perfect eyebrows expectantly.

'Not a lot of women want to become hunters,' he ventured cautiously. He recognized her as Benny Illuitok's adopted daughter. She must be fifteen. Did Benny know about this?

The girl drew up her shoulders imperiously, putting an alarming strain on her white smock. 'I see, the handsome wildlife officer says women can't become hunters. And why is that? Because women have to stay at home doing all the work while men get unfair credit for killing a few animals?'

It sounded like a rehearsed speech. A scuffle outside the door gave Jack a clue to what this was about. He grinned to himself. 'Have you spent any time out on the land?'

'Oh, don't worry about that. I can handle myself very well in a tent.' The girl's meaning was unmistakable. This time he heard faint laughter.

'I see.' Jack tapped a pencil thoughtfully. 'I was thinking of the survival swims. There's always a danger of going through the ice so we have to be sure you can last in the water for a couple of minutes. Do you think you can manage that?'

The girl made a dismissive gesture with her hand. 'It is a rule of nature that women have more insulating fat than men.' She looked down demurely. 'Do you need a physical examination?'

By an effort of will, Jack quelled a rising fit of coughing and reached for his notebook. 'Excellent. I'll sign you up for next weekend. It's Rachel, isn't it? Benny will be delighted.'

Rachel's confident manner slipped. 'Oh, you're not going to tell Dad?' Suddenly she was on her feet and edging backwards towards the door. 'I'll have to give it a bit more thought and let you know.' She blew him a kiss and fled, to be greeted by a gale of schoolgirls' hoots and laughter.

When Levi looked in a few minutes later he wondered why Jack had a daft grin on his face.

*

The trophy hunters emerged promptly at 10 a.m. to an audience of small giggling children lined up in front of the hotel to watch the spectacle. Looking self-conscious in their furs, goggles and woolly hats, the tourists staggered across the slippery road with their bags and gun cases, brushing aside the guides' offers of help.

Jack nudged Jonas. 'See any bathtubs in there?'

Jonas grunted. 'How's Inuk Charlie?'

'Still eating.'

Three twenty-foot wooden sleds, each yoked to a snowmobile by a double towrope, were drawn up in line on the icy track. Hoods of curved plywood had been fixed above the double passenger seats to afford some protection from the wind, lending the transports an uncanny resemblance to prams that increased the children's mirth.

The elderly American, Baker, towered over Jonas, an angry glow blooming in his nose capillaries. 'I don't want your smelly fur,' he snarled. 'I tell you I've worn these clothes in the Himalayas and the Yukon. I want to know I can run after that bear if I have to.'

Seeing his friend's expression, Jack intervened. 'Quite right, sir. A man should wear what he feels comfortable in, especially when chasing a bear. Mind you, we once had a distinguished client who felt exactly the same way as you do. A former assistant secretary to the US Navy who had some excellent cold-weather gear, exclusively designed by NASA if I remember correctly.'

'Dead right,' Jonas said. 'He keeled straight over on the ice. Hypothermia followed by a heart attack. Transportation cost the widow a fortune. When you change your mind, there's furs in the sled.'

Without a word, Baker climbed in beside his younger compatriot. Clumsily, both men struggled to zip large duffel comforters over their boots.

Jack found the Frenchman and his mistress similarly engaged. The girl, who looked as if she had been crying, glanced enquiringly to the third sled. 'Monsieur Walker, are you coming with us?'

'It's a back-up sledge,' he explained. 'I may be dropping by in a few days when you've settled in at camp. *Bon voyage.*'

Jack and Jonas watched the procession lurch over the shoreline hummocks and snake out across the bay. 'Poor bastards,' remarked the Inuk. Jack knew his friend's deep antipathy to travelling by sled. Why anyone would pay thousands of dollars for a twelve-hour journey of unremitting hell was an abiding mystery to him. Jonas had always been a town boy.

*

The steeper roads had melted in the past twenty-four hours and people were enjoying the seasonal novelty of walking on gravel. Several greeted Jack on his stroll along the middle terrace, past the Co-op. A good number of snowmobiles were still parked outside houses, Jack noted. In a few weeks they would be clustered down on the bay ice, safe from dry land. Rocks and grit were the summer's curse, flaying a snowmobile's drive track to rapid destruction, whereas the unyielding seaways gave untrammelled access to distant hunting grounds until break-up in late July.

Prudently, Jack had mentioned his discovery to no one, other than sending another fax to Professor O'Connor. A Viking site would hold little interest for most Inuit, he reasoned. In their eyes, North America had been discovered by their Eskimoan ancestors, not the Norsemen.

Jonas's office, like its occupant, was small and obsessively neat. He shared space with the post office and the hamlet office inside a cramped local government building plastered with official posters and no smoking signs in syllabic script. Jack put his head round the door.

Seeing him, the economic development officer jabbed a lighted cheroot at the chart on his desk. 'We're running an army out there.' His expression reminded Jack of a seal surprised by a bullet.

'How many?' Jack took a seat and rested his feet on the desk.

Jonas expelled an evil-smelling cloud. 'We've got three dog teams at base camp and one in reserve. That ties down three drivers, a cook and three guys to feed the dogs. Add four snowmobile drivers and you're looking at eleven.'

'That's marvellous. Generous tips all round. Did they make it all right?'

Jonas grimaced. 'Simon called in. They got a lot of mountain wind on the Brodeur Peninsula and had to make camp. The old guy was complaining about the food, but that's to be expected. They're down on the ice now and taking a day's rest.'

'Sounds peachy.'

Jonas shook his head. 'You're not getting it, Jack. These are the last days of the Roman Empire.'

'Ah.' Jack nodded sagely. He studied his friend's worried face. Even as a child Jonas been given to melodrama. 'Does that mean we can stop wearing togas now? Mine's getting a bit draughty.'

The small Inuk scowled. 'Look, last week the community took a vote on whether we continue to allow trophy hunters to take our polar bears. Only one vote and it could have gone the other way. Next year it will. The community's gonna be short of nearly a hundred thousand bucks and the elders expect me to make it up from somewhere else. Soon we'll have to forget money and go back to bartering.'

Jack knew the figures by heart. Snowdrift had an annual quota of fifteen polar bears, of which trophy hunters had been allocated nine. Each bear represented $10,500 in sports hunting fees that were shared out among the community, but social pressures threatened to end the bonanza. Every year five or six additional young hunters came on the market, demanding the honour of killing a bear.

'Polar bear pants are a fashion item,' he observed. 'Wait until the kids discover flares.'

Jonas waved his cheroot. 'It's not just about polar bear pants or furry snowmobile seats. The hunters complain that the trophy hunters want the biggest bears. That means the oldest and mangiest males. The meat is inedible. It's a waste of the animal. That's why we're looking at the last bucks-for-bears hunt.'

There was another subtext, as Jack knew well: the community had lost patience with the trophy hunters' behaviour. The word was over-bearing.

Jack enjoyed his friend's rants: they articulated many of his own views.

Jonas stubbed out his cheroot in a small tin. 'You know what it all adds up to?'

'Yeah. But Rome wasn't burned in a day.'

'We're going broke. We need to come up with a project to screw some money out of that Nunavut investment consortium. Which is like breaking into Fort Knox.'

'I've got an idea.'

Jonas allowed himself a wan smile. 'Not the troupe of performing bears?'

'Close. In the past year I've tagged ninety-seven bears. Do you know how much the air charter costs the government? I checked the figures with Waldo. Nearly a hundred and twenty thou.'

Jonas whistled.

'Right. Now, the Lord giveth and the Lord taketh away. Even as one door shuts, another opens. Swings and roundabouts and all that.'

Jonas was mystified. 'You want bears performing in playgrounds?'

'No, we tender for the contract at half-price. We – that is to say I, with the assistance of our noble band of brothers – make the government a bargain-basement offer to dart and tag a hundred bears for a nice round sixty thousand—'

Jonas interrupted, 'Legally, you'd be forced to use dog sleds. It could take years to catch a hundred bears.'

'Wrong, dog teams are more efficient. You can move into a bear population without scaring them off and you don't have to keep returning for aviation fuel. And from a bear's point of view it's much less stressful than being chased by a chopper.'

Suddenly Jonas resembled the small boy Jack remembered, eyeing rifles in the Bay store. 'Do you think the government will go for it?'

'We'll have to dress it up with a training programme. But yes, I think it's a flier.'

'You're a genius, Jack. You coming over to dinner this evening? Lila's cooking pork chops.'

'Sorry, I can't. The coroner wants to see some of that walrus meat. Can you believe the dozy bastards left it behind? I thought I'd set out for Stanley Point this evening.'

Jonas had always been partial to meat that had sat in a freezer for months down south, Jack reflected. Most Inuit could neither stomach nor afford it. They called cows and pigs *nujuataitut*, 'the animals that do not run away'.

CHAPTER 8

'I FEEL LIKE a relic from a bygone age, Jack. This welfare baloney is ruining the Eskimos. They're taken care of from the day they're born to the day they die.'

Jack watched the old man insert the petrol nozzle shakily into a fuel can. 'Everyone's subsidized in the north, Red – natives and non-natives.' Six five-gallon jerry cans were lashed to the front of Jack's sledge and he was impatient to be gone.

Red Addams breathed into the furry back of his mitt to warm his face. 'Free housing, free flights to hospital, grants for snowmobiles, you name it and the Eskimos've got it. I remember when all they needed was a few groceries to keep them going for weeks at a time.'

Jack didn't bother to reply. Across the north, the collapse of the fur trade had consigned thousands of subsistence hunters to the dole. In Snowdrift, the lucky ones had menial government jobs. Without subsidies and the income from the springtime bear hunt, the community would go belly-up.

Red ran the fuel dump half a mile from town. Those with long memories swore his name had been a tribute to his hair: now it described the hue of his nose. Red was a Bay widower. The Hudson's Bay Company had brought him north in the 1940s and left him stranded in a rock pool of regrets. He was a *kuujjangajug*, an 'upside-down person' who had once exercised plenipotentiary powers over the lives of Eskimos. Self-government, the end of the fur trade and social changes had sculpted his whiskered face into bitter ravines.

Jack looked across the bay. It was a pretty sight. A narrow trail, the hamlet's longest road, curled around the shoreline to Snowdrift where a few lights were showing. The late sun was turning the ice aquamarine and casting long blue shadows from the stranded boats and small huts where dog meat was stored. Good travelling weather, he thought. The evening air would freeze any surface water.

Damn Waldo, he thought. The pilot's departure left him facing a three-day round trip. He took out his wallet as Red replaced the nozzle in its cradle. The old man spoke over his shoulder.

'Good news about Soosie, hey?'

'Soosie?'

'Soosie Aglukark, you know – your Soosie. She wrote to Anna Algona that she was thinking of coming back.'

'Wait a minute, Soosie's coming here?' The quick flywheel of Jack's brain seemed to have jammed. He felt winded.

Red nodded. 'Anna says Soosie's been working for social services for a couple of years in Frobisher Bay. Seems she got a diploma down south and got homesick.'

Like most old-timers, he used the original name of the island's capital, commemorating the hapless Yorkshireman. It had been renamed Iqaluit, 'the Place of Fish'.

Red fumbled in his parka for the change. He looked up, scenting mischief. 'No one told you? Anna said there's a vacancy in social services here and Soosie was thinking of applying. That's all she wrote. Wanna receipt?'

'No, thanks.' Distracted, Jack grasped the toggle-cord and fired the engine, only to stall it a second later: the sled's runners were iced to the ground. Angry with himself, he backed the snowmobile a pace and shot forward to jerk the sled free.

To breach the hummocks at the bay's edge he adopted a jockey's stance on the running boards, flexing his knees as the machine and its heavy trailer slewed and crashed across the obstacle course. At last the belt found traction on the smooth powdered runway of flat ice, and he hit the throttle with his palm. The snowmobile flew over the marbled bay, heading for the point.

Normally Jack relished the solitude and challenge of a long journey. Now an unknown dread rose within him. He was oblivious to the wind's invasion until his thumb began to go numb on the throttle.

Soosie. He had last seen his stepsister thirteen years before – half her lifetime, he realized. They had exchanged letters for a few years until it became evident they had retreated into different worlds that could not be bridged with paper and ink.

He cleared the bay and turned west around the headland, the speedo showing forty. A clear trail of furrowed tracks lay ahead, snaking along the shore of Victoria Sound, where drifts and hard ridges forced him to halve his speed. Soon the exertion of controlling the machine made him sweat inside his parka. He loosened the collar and pushed the hood back.

His aunt's generosity had not extended to his native stepsister. Jack felt guilty, but not sorry. He and Soosie were bound together by a tyranny of their parents' making. They shared a darker secret that would not easily be forgiven, even in a society that tolerated the worst anti-social behaviour. He and Soosie were halves of a binary code, posing little risk of disclosure as long as they were apart. It was a self-serving belief but still true, he realized. He would have to think about leaving Snowdrift.

He was deep in thought when he was waved down by three teenagers who grinned sheepishly and pointed to a dismembered engine that lay beside their snowmobile. He recognized two of them as Andrew Hologak's boys, Samuel and Peter. They introduced the third boy, John.

'The head gasket has blown,' Samuel announced.

Jack quickly read the scene. Confident that someone would pass by, they had thrown up a snow house and gone to search the pressure ridges for seals. Accepting their offer of tea, he ducked into the small *igluviga* and squatted by the boys' Coleman stove. The cold despondency in his guts warmed to their good humour as they debated the capricious nature of seals and snowmobiles.

It struck him as ironic that his expectations had funnelled down to a mug of hot tea in a snow house. The prospect of leaving Snowdrift was forcing a stocktaking that he had shied away from for too long. In the end, this was the only companionship he had ever wanted, among people who were compassionate and caring, and who made light of hardship.

He had learned not to make lasting judgements, but to his mind the people of temperate England lived cold, meaningless lives, while the characteristics of people in the frozen north were warmth and jollity. He remembered a question that had predominated among his English friends: how could people tolerate living like that? He had countered: 'How can people hate their home?'

One of the boys, Peter, reminded him of another teenage Inuk who had given him his first childhood lesson in geometry. Jack had been wandering in the hills behind his stepfather's outpost camp when he came upon Keegotak struggling to put down a net beneath lake ice during a blowing storm. The boy's sick grandfather lay asleep on a sled and the dogs were voicing their hunger, so Jack lent a hand to haul the heavy net the forty-yard distance between two ice holes, each the diameter of dinner plates. Keegotak was twelve, the same age as Jack but older than his years on account of his father's death three years previously. 'My father stills hunts through me and that helps,' he said.

Jack slept at their camp through the night's storm, but in the morning Keegotak was sick, too, and they retrieved only two fish from the net. The dogs were more ravenous than ever. Then the young Inuk became too weak to go on and had to lie down. 'We have to put down another net to feed the dogs. My father has told me what to do,' he reassured Jack. 'Just follow what I tell you.' His instructions seemed baffling: take a living fish from the net and tie a fishing line of twine to its tail. Then cut a third hole at an equal distance from the other two.

Later, Jack marvelled at Keegotak's elegant strategy of creating an equilateral triangle between the three holes. The fish, inserted through the new hole, swam feebly with the current directly into the net, trailing the fishing line. By hauling in the net, Jack recaptured the fish and its long leash, which now connected the new ice hole to the old one. It was a relatively simply matter to attach a rope and rig a second net between the two points. That night they fed the dogs and sat around a stove sipping fish soup. 'My father told me that hunting is eight parts effort, one part luck and only one part skill,' Keegotak told his new friend. 'But sometimes your brain helps.'

Jack was drifting. Abruptly aware of the three lads' curious stares, he realized he was forgetting his manners. He told them the story of Waldo and the bear until they clapped and laughed. Humour was a guest's most valued gift and Jack kept a ready supply.

He glanced at his watch. 'Let's see, do you need a cooking lid?' It was an old remedy. A piece of soft aluminium served as a gasket when laid on the cylinder head block and shaped with a hammer's gentle tapping.

Samuel demurred politely. 'There's a bunch of people up ahead with spares. We were thinking maybe we could hitch a ride,' he said.

'Absolutely not. No free rides.' The trio crumpled with mirth again.

The boys hauled the engine onto Jack's sled, found perches on the grub-box and waved him forward.

The tantalizing smell of warm bannock bread heralded a seal camp two miles ahead. Three families had pitched large double-wall tents on open ground overlooking the inlet. Celebrating the return of spring was irresistible after the long months of darkness. Despite the late hour, small children ran out to greet the new arrivals.

Jack grabbed a carton of doughnuts from the grub-box and strolled across to greet the boys' father, a broad-shouldered, handsome man in his late forties who gestured the wildlife officer into his tent.

'The land is waking up,' Hologak remarked, his sparkling eyes conveying appreciation of both Jack's visit and the coming of summer.

'It's been a long sleep,' Jack responded.

The tent's spacious interior was spotless and neatly divided, the communal area warmed by two portable kerosene heaters upon which rested tins of fresh bannock. Andrew's wife Sarah brushed flour from her hands and took the carton with a nod of thanks.

Hologak held out a phone receiver. 'Hainiliak's been on the radio asking for you.'

'Jonas? I saw him only three hours ago.'

'He said you would be stopping by. They're a driver short.'

Jack had to break into a conversation between two hunters to get through. He heard Jonas's voice faintly through a blizzard of solar interference.

'Jack, there's an extra client and we're a man down. Paulie injured his foot. Do you mind driving a team until I can send a replacement?'

'Sure. Who's the new client?'

'A rich nutso. He's paying way over the odds and he's chartered a plane down to the base camp. The quota can stand it and he's real hungry for a bear.'

Jack grinned. 'Let's hope it's not mutual. What happened to Paulie? I told him not to squeeze the lady client.'

'Some damn nonsense about a fox trap. Maybe it was the foxy lady, but then he'd have something else strapped in a bandage. Good luck.'

Jack thanked Andrew and made his excuses. At the entrance Sarah pressed something into his hand. It was a moist sealskin bag bulging with arctic char.

He arrived at the trophy hunters' camp shortly after 7 a.m. It was pitched in a cove set back from the convulsed icescape of Prince Regent Inlet. Four sleeping tents were ranged around a large grub tent, from which leaked a welcoming aroma of frying bacon and eggs. Some way off, four dog teams lay tethered in the pattern of their traces.

Granules of tiredness pricked his eyes. Caught by blowing snow in the mountains, he had snatched a few hours' sleep stretched beneath his sled, dreaming fitfully of Soosie and another storm.

The grub tent was stifling. He nodded to Benny Illuitok, tending the stove, and walked around boxes of provisions to take a seat beside Jimmy Okadlak. 'Clients misbehaving themselves?'

Jimmy pulled a face and swallowed a mouthful of porridge. 'They're still sleeping it off. Big kids, like you said. The old guy moaned all the way. Then he wanted to sleep outside last night. I told him he was just meat to a polar bear and I couldn't guarantee his safety. I said I might shoot him by accident. He came in pretty quick.'

Jack grinned. 'See, I told you diplomacy always works. Jesus, what is this, Benny?'

The plate Benny had placed before him was a confection of porridge, jam, peanut butter, brown sauce and cubes of *maktaak*, the rubbery skin of beluga whale.

'Didn't Mrs Illuitok tell you never to serve barbecue sauce for breakfast?'

Benny rumbled with laughter. He placed a finger beneath his blind eye in a Nelsonian gesture that expressed his opinion of his wife's advice.

Jack spotted Paulie hobbling towards him. His bandaged right foot was encased in an improvised boot of bearded sealskin. The young Inuk held a rusty leg-hold trap, complete with its clanking chain.

'The ghost of Jacob Marley,' Jack greeted him.

Paulie put the contraption on the table. 'Thought you might want to see this, Jack. Nearly broke my ankle. Good thing I had duffels, so it just broke the skin. Someone is out of date.'

Jack saw what he meant. The trap's jaws were serrated like saw blades, which made it illegal. To pacify the anti-fur lobby, his department had first tried to introduce 'humane' devices with rubber jaws, but these had not subdued objections that a trapped fox was placed at the mercy of other predators. Finally, the authorities had ruled in favour of quick kill traps that broke the animal's neck and put it out of its misery. They were expensive and heavy, with the result that another tranche of hunters had gone on welfare.

Jack flexed the trap's jaws thoughtfully. 'Anyone trapping now?'

Benny's ruined face fractured into grim lines. 'You know how it is, Jack. Some folks go trapping before Christmas, and that's it. Now you're supposed to check a trap line every twenty-four hours You catch a fox, bring him home frozen stiff, thaw him out, turn him inside out and skin him, then dry him in your house. So you have a smelly old fox fur hanging inside. What for?'

Simon shook his head in disgust. 'You might get twenty-five dollars if you are lucky. And there's not a lot of fox. Some days there's none to trap. The only guys doing it now are teaching kids.'

Jack understood their bitterness at the anti-fur and anti-sealing campaigns that had undermined native subsistence hunting in ways never envisaged by well-meaning protestors. He had given up explaining that European concerns about cruelty sprang from ritualized ideas about hunting as a recreational activity. It was a stale debate and most Inuit had moved on, but the nerve was still raw.

His main question remained. 'So who would want to go trapping in April?'

'Maybe someone who is hungry.'

Jack looked around. A large European, clad in stylish furs, stood framed in the doorway where evidently he had been eavesdropping on the conversation. The rich nutso. Jack appraised him: late forties, neatly trimmed silver-gold beard, muscular physique and a leather-tanned face dominated by a hawk-like nose and sea-grey eyes. Money and power smoked off the man.

He strode forward and took Jack's hand in a crushing grip. 'Sverker Karlsson. It is an honour to meet you, Mr Walker. I am a big fan of your writing. Did you know your articles are syndicated in Stockholm?'

'Really?' The chances of meeting a foreign admirer inside the Arctic Circle disarmed Jack for a moment.

The Swede took a chair opposite and fixed him with an intense gaze. 'Your series on hunter-gatherers was really excellent. I sent it to all my managers and instructed them to read it.'

The series, Jack recalled, was prompted by a published study of neolithic farm sites in the Near East. The paper suggested that the world's earliest agriculture had been an emergency response to severe drought, not a considered step in the glorious flowering of *Homo sapiens*. Jack had reasoned that the findings threw doubt on assumptions that industrialized society was the intended pinnacle of human achievement.

Karlsson helped himself to toast. 'You wrote that Cain was the first agriculturalist who had to kill Abel, the aboriginal free spirit. I liked that. You wanted to reconcile the two brothers in the modern world.'

'It'll never catch on.' Jack felt his irritation stir at being patronized by a stranger.

'On the contrary, I assure you. I want to exploit your message. You've probably not heard of my company, Karlsson Industries. We are a multimedia group in Scandinavia and just like hunter-gatherers we have to adapt quickly to changing conditions or die. I want to impress on my managers the need to embrace the philosophy of the hunter. You write with great clarity and precision. Can I persuade you to draft a booklet that I can circulate in my organization?'

'Sorry, I don't have the time.' Jack dismissed the idea. The man had missed the point by a mile and his proposal was a travesty.

'I would pay you well.' Exuding confidence, the Swede pulled off his Paul & Shark knitted hat and shook loose a silver mane threaded with gold.

'I'm already well paid and there's not a lot to spend it on. Money, in the vernacular of these parts, isn't worth a bucket of warm spit.'

Karlsson shrugged. 'Please think about it. Now, there is another matter that Mr Hainiliak said I should mention to you. I have a bow. Is that a problem for you?'

'A bow with arrows?'

The Swede nodded. 'It's an old design but very powerful. I'm quite proficient with it, I assure you. I have never shot a bear, but I believe a lung shot is best. The animal will drown in its own blood.'

Jack sighed. He remembered their last bowman, a hairy-arsed Texan oil worker who sobbed in cathartic relief after bringing down a bear that had bristled with shafts like a pincushion. 'Well, it's quite academic to the bear how it's killed, except, of course, it'll take longer to die in terror. It means we'll have to place you closer to the bear, with an increased risk to the dogs.

You'll have to do exactly what you're told.'

'Naturally. I want to hunt just like an Eskimo.'

As a policeman, Jack had hit men in the line of duty: now it would be a pleasure.

'Mr Karlsson, let's get something clear. The people here don't play with the animals. It shows disrespect. They kill an animal as quickly as possible, skin it, butcher it and then eat it. They believe an animal must agree to be killed. They're prepared to return the favour either in this life or the next. Are you?'

Unperturbed, the Swede did not answer but applied marmalade to his toast, a smirk playing around his lips. Jack caught Paulie's eye and jerked his head.

Outside, they were hailed by the American, Baker. 'Morning. I was dreaming of polar bears last night. I had to kick them out of bed.'

Ignoring him, the two men approached Paulie's dog team. The traces, coated with bear fat, spread out like a fan's ribs from a sixteen-foot hunting sledge. Jack mentally laid aside several hours to familiarize himself with the fourteen dogs: driving a new team was not the same as swapping cars.

'When were they fed?' Jack asked. Bear dogs needed a hungry edge.

'Last night.' Jack followed Paulie's glance to a rope, stretched taut between a harpoon driven into the fjord ice and a chipped hole, at the end of which a seal was suspended. Seawater kept the meat thawed at a constant 2°.

Paulie fussed over the dogs like an anxious mother. Jack understood the young Inuk's anxiety. The greatest danger in a bear hunt was posed not by the bear, but by the chase itself, which could veer within an inch of insanity, and inexperienced dogs ran the risk of being run over by the sled and breaking limbs.

'I'd like to train that one.' Paulie was watching the approach of the French girl in a fetching set of furs. To his delight, she stopped nearby, gazing at the fjord's spectacular pressure ridges with a look of consternation.

'It looks so empty.'

Paulie inhaled her perfume appreciatively. 'Lots of bears out there, miss, and lots of trophies. Two things are happening right now: there's plenty of seals and this is the breeding season for polar bears. The males are hunting seals but they're also hunting females.'

The girl eyed him dubiously. 'They are running after the females?'

Paulie grinned. 'They're walking them down on the big, rough ice. When the female first sees that male bear coming, she runs but he just keeps following, maybe two, three days. Being chased and being scared like that turns her on. Then she slows down and, well, they start dancing.'

The girl laughed. 'Is she hunted by more than one bear?'

'When that happens you get real bad fights. You see males all tore up, with no ears, cuts on their neck and legs.'

The girl winced and turned to Jack. 'Will we see cubs?'

He met her gaze and wondered if the bruises beneath her eyes came from lack of sleep. 'Maybe a few two-year-olds. A sow with newborn cubs usually takes them to a bay or inlet where she'll hunt seal pups. She'll avoid the males, because they'll try to kill the cubs, probably to bring the female back into season. If the bear population's too high, it's a natural way of restricting their numbers.'

'Thank you, Mr Wildlife Officer.' The girl was flirting with him, Jack realized. 'Jean-Marie says we must stay until he shoots a big bear. How long must we wait?'

Jack's reply was not helpful. 'The biggest bears are the easiest to catch but the most difficult to find.'

CHAPTER 9

THEY HIT THE big ice twenty miles across the inlet. A ferocious west wind at freeze-up in October and early November had caused dramatic multi-ridging and deep snowdrifts which now tested the dogs as they attempted to read the ice surface ahead and the intentions of their new driver. The team was excited and focused at the prospect of closing on an enemy for which they nursed an ancient hatred.

Jack found little use for his whip, a thirty-five foot length of braided seal-skin, preferring to rely on the team's finely honed instincts and their prompt response to his calls.

The majority of floes had bonded together in early March, but some stretches were moving, opening ice cracks that called for a supreme effort by the dogs. The fan-hitch formation, devised with a thirty-five foot lead trace and progressively shorter traces tapering to ten feet, kept the dogs separated while giving them the lateral freedom to launch themselves across open leads of six feet or more, the sled behind impacting on the far lip with a juddering crash.

Karlsson was proving to be a more congenial companion than he expected. On the flat stretches, when the eerie quiet was broken only by the hiss of runners and the creak of bindings, the Swede taxed him on the dynamics of ice and animal populations. Unlike most clients, for whom the hunt was a miserable experience that attained epic status only when they stood over a bleeding animal, Karlsson seemed to be enjoying himself.

It was a clear, cold evening, when the bears would be more active and moving around. In the distance they could see the hard, metamorphic cliffs of the inlet's far side and the ethereal glow of the plateau's icecap beyond. Occasionally an inquisitive seal popped up to study the interlopers and then vanished into its hole.

Jack stopped the dogs beside a twenty-foot pressure ridge and boiled some tea for the Swede. 'I'm going to take a look.'

'May I come with you, please?'

Jack hesitated. It was a tricky climb, but Karlsson looked fit.

'All right, on one condition. We have to fool the dogs. They're watching us now. If they even suspect we've seen anything they'll go berserk. So when we come down we have some more tea and act as if we're on a Sunday picnic. Otherwise we might have to walk home.'

'Understood.'

Handing the Swede a steel harpoon to steady himself, Jack slowly led the way up the tiered spur of ice, his bearded sealskin soles finding traction on a layer of granular snow. Near the summit he crouched down and rested his long spotting scope on an ice sill to glass the rough ice.

'Anything?' After five minutes the Swede could barely contain his impatience. The light breeze was chilling him to the bone. Jack did not answer. Eventually, the Swede had to strain to catch his murmur.

'A couple of females and a young male.'

Another ten minutes of exasperating silence ensued.

Jack stood up. 'There's a very large male about three miles ahead. He's hunting seals but he keeps looking forward. He knows the females are there. We'll have to circle around ahead of him.'

He closed the scope slowly, conscious that the dogs were alert to the slightest telltale noise. Speaking in low conversational tones, the two men returned to the sled.

'You're lucky,' Jack said. 'We could look for ten days and not find a bear that size.'

'How big?' A fierce light burned in Karlsson's eyes.

'I'd guess eleven feet from nose tip to the end of his tail. Now, you'd better listen to this carefully. We'll have to work our way around. I'll place you within thirty feet of the bear while he's fighting the dogs. Take your time and give it your best shot. Whatever happens, don't leave the sled. Remember, I'll be backing you up with a rifle. I'd better check out your bow now.'

Karlsson opened a long aluminium case which, to Jack's surprise, contained an elegant wooden bow. Most bow hunters favoured compounds. The Swede handled it lovingly. 'I had it specially made. It's based on the design of the only complete Danish bow from medieval times found at Hedeby. It has exactly the same dimensions, a hundred and ninety-two centimetres long and a draw weight of a hundred and forty pounds.'

'Hedeby?' Jack half-recalled the name.

'It's the famous boat-chamber grave near the Danish border with Germany.'

Jack frowned. 'It's Viking?'

Karlsson gave a barking laugh. 'For sure. Made of yew, like the English longbow. The Vikings understood the yew's unique combination of sapwood and hardwood, giving both strength and elasticity. A bow like this

could punch an arrow through a rider's armour, through his body and
saddle, driving so deep that it killed his horse, too.'

'Really.'

'Yes, most people regard the Vikings as close-quarter fighters, but the
bow was an essential weapon in their armoury, as it was for the English at
Agincourt. Of course, the favourite weapon of the Swedish Vikings was the
spear.'

'Fascinating.' At the back of Jack's mind, a faint alarm bell was trilling.

'Yes, I'm an amateur collector of Norse artefacts. In fact, I heard you
have acquired something of the sort recently. A Greenland harpoon, I
believe? I'd be interested in seeing it. It could be very valuable, in a historical sense.'

Jack's felt an icy calm. 'It's not mine to sell. It's impounded as forensic
evidence for an inquest.' The Swede had flattered him, attempted to buy
him off with a publishing contract, and was now approaching his true
quarry. He was intrigued. 'The bow is bent and drawn. Make from the
shaft.'

'Shakespeare, I believe. *King Lear?*'

'No, *Casablanca*. Why did you have to walk into my bear hunt, Mr
Karlsson? You fly halfway round the world to gatecrash our party with your
bow and arrow, then it turns out that you're not only a lifelong admirer of
my articles but you want a lump of iron in my possession. What's the story?'

Karlsson busied himself returning the bow to its case. 'Why so suspi-
cious, Mr Walker? There's no mystery. I'm a publisher with an information
network that I sometimes use to indulge my interests as a collector. I also
enjoy hunting, so my presence here is a perfect synergy.'

Jack had read the brief reports of Isaac and Matthew's deaths in the
Nunavut News; there had been no mention of the harpoon. 'Who was your
informant?'

'You know what I am going to say: a journalist's sources are confidential.
But I am still interested in learning where the harpoon was found.'

So that's it, Jack thought. 'I'm surprised your source didn't tell you.'

Karlsson raised an eyebrow. 'He didn't know. But I would have liked to
speak to Inuk Charlie before he departed.'

'He's left Snowdrift?'

'You don't know? Inuk Charlie has departed this life.'

The horror suffered by the old man and his sons revisited Jack again,
piercing him with a deep sense of sorrow. The loss of one was felt by all in
such a small community.

Karlsson had the grace to acknowledge the pain behind Jack's silence. 'I
am sorry to be the one to tell you. It seems he died before my arrival and
after you left. Apparently he discharged himself from hospital and had a

heart attack while attempting to return home.'

'Crazy old bugger.' Jack could visualize Charlie remonstrating with the clinic's staff about eating white man's junk and then crawling out into the night.

'Please, Mr Walker, let us draw a line. You have made your views about my requests quite clear and I respect your position. I apologize if I have offended you, but we Swedes are sometimes too direct. We have an appointment with a bear: should we keep him waiting?'

Jack had a dark premonition about this client.

The dogs locked onto the first set of bear tracks and would have lit their afterburners if Jack had not brought them to order by cracking the long whip along their flanks. The spoor indicated a medium-sized female that was now deep in the rough ice parallel to their smooth track.

Karlsson eyed the wilderness of jumbled ice blocks and vertiginous ridges with a hungry expression, as if sizing up a battlefield. The man seemed to have an unhealthy obsession with Vikings.

'The Norsemen were the Romans of their day,' he remarked. 'Unfortunately, their culture has been overshadowed by other stereotypes.'

'Yes, rape and pillage do seem to get a bad press.'

The Swede shook his head ruefully. 'People wilfully confuse two periods of history. There was a violent phase that lasted from AD 800 to about AD 900. Then we see a different story.'

'I've already heard it: the Vikings were tourists and traders who brought the benefits of high culture to a benighted world. They sailed out of the north armed to teeth with handicrafts and needlepoint skills. Yes, it's true they could be a decent people, but only after they'd cut everybody's throats or driven them off their estates.'

The Swede bristled. 'They were the first true marines in military history. They waged a brilliant form of land warfare and changed the shape of the globe.'

Jack couldn't resist goading him. 'Correct me if I'm wrong, but Viking military strategy amounted to relying on crude frontal attacks in which they slaughtered women, children and old men just for the fun of it. Of course, they were masters of refinement when it came to torture. They broke people's backs, strangled them and ritually drowned them. Their speciality was blood-eagling, or spread-eagling the victim and saturating him in gore by removing his ribs.'

'You are talking about the Norwegians and Danes. The Swedish Vikings were more interested in opening trade routes.'

'Oh yes, I forgot. Slaves from the Near East, wasn't it?'

After a few minutes' silence, Karlsson's tone became more conciliatory.

'It is possible that your Greenland harpoon was not trade goods, which would have profound implications.'

'Implications?'

'Yes, you see it was always assumed that trade between the Greenland Vikings and the Eskimos of Baffin Island was one way – that the Eskimos must have travelled to Greenland. Then, a few years ago a museum in Quebec decided to re-examine some items from an ancient Inuit site.'

'Do you mean a Dorset site?'

'Yes, a Dorset site here on Baffin Island. They found a three-metre strand of yarn, spun from artic hare fur mixed with goat hair. It was obviously of Viking manufacture, because the Inuit had neither goats nor the technology of spinning. An archaeologist at the museum thought the yarn was unlikely to survive such long-distance trade and it probably arrived directly on a Norse ship.'

'It seems a big deduction to spin out of such slim evidence. The Inuit didn't always travel to Greenland by the slow overland route.' Paddy had made the same point, Jack recalled.

'Of course. That is why your harpoon is important. If its provenance could be established, it might provide definitive proof that the Vikings were the first transatlantic traders.'

Jack made a mental note to swear Marcus to silence about where he found the harpoon. The Swede was on a fishing expedition the purpose of which remained unclear. The thought of this devious man discovering the wolverine site made him uneasy.

'I suspect only the walrus knows the truth. And he's gone to the great clam bake in the sky.'

They had now looped ahead of the large male and were working back, the wind burning their faces. Several times Jack instructed Karlsson to wait beside the sled while he climbed to a vantage point with his scope.

Half a mile distant, the bear was working a ridge for ringed seals. It still wore a creamy yellow winter coat, delineating its streamlined shape against the white surroundings. Frozen breath and the blood of its prey had created a death mask. It was a huge animal measuring four feet high at the shoulder and weighing 1,400 lb, Jack estimated. He was struck once again by the almost human ingenuity of its hunting skills. Always on the downwind side, it was employing a range of techniques, from stalking and waiting to breaking into dens. He could almost see it thinking.

A map of the terrain ahead was now fixed clearly in his mind. Success depended on ambushing the bear on a flat stretch and cutting off its retreat into the safety of the rough ice. The bear was moving towards such an open expanse. It was time to make their move.

Jack gathered all the dog traces into a single knot that could be slipped with one tug and secured his rifle beside him. He had loaded it earlier. Most sports hunters favoured high-powered guns with winterized scopes and Parkerized barrels, but Jack had always found a standard Winchester .30-.30 to be adequate. It nestled in its scabbard, a Yukon moose hide cover decorated with Loucheux beadwork.

'Ready?'

The Swede had buckled on a back quiver. Lips drawn back over white teeth, he stared ahead with fixed concentration, a heavy war arrow already notched to the bowstring across his knees. He nodded stiffly.

Jack ran the dogs up to an ice shelf and turned the corner. Filling his lungs, he bellowed a bear cry that sent a shiver through the dogs and produced a savage jolt of speed. Reaching forward with his knife, he cut the lead dog loose, and then released two others. The trio streaked ahead, trailing their leashes and barking like avenging furies.

The sled was flying now in a tumult of angry sound and pitching danger-ously over snow hummocks. Jack ignored an explosive crack as a knife-edge of ice sliced through a slat beneath the slewing vehicle. In the distance he could see the dogs closing on their prey.

Instead of retreating, the bear faced its attackers fearlessly, its muzzle swaying to catch their scent.

The lead dog, chosen for its strength and intelligence, circled the bear before hurtling at its hindquarters while its two companions harried the beast from the front. But the tactic of biting its backside, designed to bring the bear to bay, plainly was not working. Instead of squatting down to protect its rear, this bear ignored its tormentors and pounced on one of the snaking traces. With a shock, Jack understood its intention.

The bear walked up the leash to the lead dog, which, realizing it was at the predator's mercy, thrust back frantically. It happened in a handclap. A single swipe lifted the dog in a parabola that met the ground fifteen feet away, where its broken body sprawled lifeless. Seeing its fate, the other two dogs desperately renewed their attacks, darting at its backside with bared teeth. Again, the bear was too fast and out-thought them. Jumping on a swishing trace, it advanced slowly down the line, as if relishing the terror its approach was inducing. Another sickening whack rent in the air. The remaining dog retreated to circle at a respectful distance.

The odds were still in their favour, Jack calculated. He steered the sled between the fighting group and the bear's line of escape, although his prox-imity to the unfettered animal now gave cause for concern. With a tug of the slipknot, he released all the dogs on the bear. As the sled crunched to a halt, he turned to the Swede.

'OK, you can fire at will.'

Jack stepped away from the sled and levelled his rifle. The bear was roaring, fresh blood on its muzzle, as it whipped around on all fours to lash out at the swarm of enraged dogs. Abruptly it reared up to its full height and the dogs fell back. This is the moment, Jack thought.

A loud crack spun him around. Larsson was gripping half a bow and staring incredulously at the splintered length of wood that hung from the bowstring, together with his hopes of a bear trophy. His handcrafted Danish yew had snapped in the dry cold.

'Oh, fuck.' Jack knew it was now a choice between the dogs and the bear. The dogs were beyond recall, but it was not their job to kill their quarry, only to detain it. The bear was more likely to kill a number of them. He took a bead on its chest, mindful that a headshot would probably ricochet off its skull.

A shout distracted him. Karlsson was yelling something in Swedish and racing towards the bear, a steel harpoon held high like a javelin. Jack's concentration snapped back. The bear's chest steadied in his sights and he squeezed the trigger. Nothing. He fired again. Nothing. *Click, click, click.*

He sprinted after Karlsson.

Roaring a challenge, the Swede ran straight at the bear, drawing back the harpoon and releasing it at a distance of fifteen yards. It was a good throw for a solid steel missile, sailing true in its flight until the last moment when it dipped and struck the bear's shoulder. The harpoon bounced off.

The bear's head came up and Jack, a dozen paces behind Karlsson, felt the malevolence of its stare. Eskimo hunters warned of rogue bears that looked at you through the dogs. Such bears were apt to break through the pack and bring the fight to the hunter.

'Get down! On the ground!'

Impervious to the order, Karlsson pulled a bayonet-sized knife from his coat. Slashing the air and shouting dementedly, he advanced like a berserker of old. The bear held its ground and watched him come.

A few dogs were milling about on the outside of the fray. As one passed close, Jack seized its harness and dragged it forward.

'Karlsson, lie down!'

Triggered by the shout, the bear burst through the circle like a train and bore down on Karlsson, dwarfing the large human. Jack saw the knife go back, but the charge took the Swede unawares and he was bitten, cuffed and thrown aside like a rag doll.

Jack found himself looking into the barrels of the bear's dark eyes. Now Karlsson was out of the picture, he relaxed. Curbing a bear was like fighting bulls: you had to get close. The dog in his grasp squirmed desperately. He held it forward, his left hand clamped on its harness, feeding it to the bear. If the bear wanted him, it would have to dispose of the dog first.

Suddenly the death's head mask darted forward on the long neck, baring large canines and jagged cheek teeth.

Jack struck. His rifle whipped forward into the bear's nose, the sharp pin sight ripping the black velvet skin. The bear hissed in surprise and then roared with pain as Jack repeated the jabbing manoeuvre. Bears can withstand unlimited punishment, except to the nose and eyes. Confused, its eyes weeping, the bear was backing off. Jack reversed the rifle with both hands and slammed the bleeding snout once more with the butt.

His foot touched the harpoon. He could finish it now, he realized. But the bear had had enough. Spinning round, it fled with a deceptively fast, lumbering gait. Jack ran in front of the dogs, shouting at them to be still. To his surprise they obeyed, perhaps recognizing they had met their match.

He walked over to Karlsson. The Swede was conscious but in too much pain to talk. There were bloody puncture marks in the shoulder of his parka and his left leg appeared to be broken.

'No more hunting for you. Bad form, hounding a defenceless animal with a bayonet.'

Ignoring the injured man's groans, Jack sealed him inside two sleeping bags and a tarpaulin, leaving him lying on the ice while he rigged an aerial. It took ten minutes to raise Jonas.

'The butcher's bill amounts to three dead dogs and four that need crutches. You were right about one thing.'

'What's that, Jack?'

'The guy was a nutso.'

CHAPTER 10

'ODETTE.' PADDY'S IMPERIOUS manner usually prefaced an impossible demand. Now he was brandishing a fax at her.

'How much is there in the slush fund?'

'About thirty thou. And your publisher sent a cheque yesterday.'

'Excellent. We're going a-viking.'

She groaned. The Norse term meant to abandon usual pursuits and go in search of distant plunder. She wondered if Viking women used it as shorthand for wild goose chases.

'We?'

'I'd like you along, if you could make yourself available.' He was sniffing ferociously, always a bad sign.

'May I ask why, not to mention where and when?'

'Forget the why for the moment and concentrate on the where and the when. I'd like you to book us open flight returns two days' hence to a place called Snowdrift on Baffin Island. You'll find it in *The Times* Atlas about two thousand miles north of Montreal.'

'Yes, masterful one. Immediately.'

Several minutes of diligent research left her puzzled.

'Paddy, I've got a Snowdrift on the Great Slave Lake, near Yellowknife.'

Paddy did not look up from his attentive perusal. 'Wrong tribe. They're all Dene Indians down there. Look in the Nunavut Handbook on the shelf there. It gives all the place names.'

'So it will be cold, I take it?'

His lopsided smile resembled a leer. 'Absolutely bloody freezing.'

The old mining company had laid the airstrip on a stretch of elevated ground between Snowdrift Bay and the cliffs. An unloved wooden shed had been replaced by a well-insulated steel construction of similar dimensions that could barely accommodate twenty people standing, but Jack found himself sharing it this evening with only two Inuit passengers as he gazed at the blizzard that shrieked across the gravel runway and battered the observation window. He took it as a good omen that the flight had not yet turned back. The ticket desk at Resolute had confirmed that Patrick O'Connor was a passenger.

'Hurry up and wait.' The forlorn mantra of long-suffering Arctic travellers was uttered with weary humour by a tall, stooping man with white hair who sported a fawn European parka and patterned sealskin boots that looked too fancy in these surroundings. Putting down a medical bag and a small overnight suitcase, he shook off his coating of snow.

'Hello, Doc. Nice weather.'

Doctor John McPherson had been a fixture of the High Arctic for as long as most people could remember, a Scot whose flinty carapace belied the gentle humanity he brought to the gunshot woundings, tuberculosis cases and breech births that kept him in orbit among the northern communities.

He cast a professional eye over the ferment outside and made a swift diagnosis. 'I give it ten minutes. I'll be back in Pond on time.' He inspected Jack critically. 'That was quite a competent job you did on the Swede's shoulder. Glad the Mounties taught you something useful. Giving him an anaesthetic was quick thinking.'

Jack smiled. 'I gave him a cub's dose. It's a pity I had a syringe: I'd have preferred to administer it with a rifle.'

'Hmm. The fellow really tried to attack a bear? Must be deranged. He should be ready to ship out in a few days' time. You're bringing me rather a lot of patients, Jack.'

'Inuk Charlie? I meant to give the coroner that walrus meat.'

'Dinnae worry. I've sent biopsies to Toronto. What's your guess?'

Jack thought back to a workshop he had attended three months previously on 'northern contaminants', at which hunters and elders from every community expressed concern about the number of abnormalities found among animals. They reported changes to the colour of meat and fat in walrus, seal and polar bear. Particularly alarming was the appearance of round wounds, resembling burn holes, in the skin of seal, walrus and narwhal.

'They did an analysis of a walrus in Arctic Bay that showed a strain of flesh-eating bacteria,' he said. 'But this looks more like a case of iron poisoning.'

The doctor pursed his lips thoughtfully. 'The devil is always in the detail. Do you remember Ernie Lyall?'

'Before my time, Doc.'

'Ernie was from Labrador, but many people thought he was an Eskimo because he married a native woman and had lived the Eskimo life. He became a Hudson's Bay manager and a magistrate. Anyway, in 1948 he reported something odd at Cresswell Bay, where about ten people died after eating infected walrus meat. They had the same symptoms of loss of feeling in their legs, followed by the loss of limbs. No one got to the bottom of that one.'

The small hall was filling up. Jack spied Jimmy Okadlak, who was accompanying his mother down south for cancer treatment. Three pretty teenage mothers, babies peeking from the cradling shoulder hoods of their embroidered white costumes, conversed with a burly Inuk in a dog collar. The Revd David Kalluk caught Jack's eye and walked over.

'Can we count on you this evening, Jack?'

'I'll be late, Vicar. I've got a visitor, but maybe I can persuade him to come when I tell him about your jokes.'

'Jokes?' A moment's incomprehension gave way to booming laughter. 'Like Waldo and the bear? What a sermon that would make. No free passengers!'

Others joined in the vicar's merriment. The story had evidently done the rounds. A pressure change in the room stilled the laughter. After a minute they registered the subsonic vibration of distant engines. Jack saw that Dr McPherson's prognosis had been right: the storm had been chased away by spring sunshine.

Odette gripped the arms of her seat. The plane banked as if taking violent evasive action and suddenly she glimpsed a mountainside flashing past the wingtip. Petrified, she glanced at Paddy but he was dead to the world, pole-axed by two days of air travel and copious helpings of free drinks.

She had never seen him so animated when Jack's latest missive arrived from Baffin Island. 'This is going to put some big men's noses out of joint, that's for sure,' he muttered excitedly. 'Imagine, Vikings in the North-West Passage! They could have known the world was round, although we must keep that thought to ourselves.'

She had snatched a few hours' fitful sleep in an Ottawa hotel and then shepherded Paddy into a taxi to catch a 7.30 a.m. flight. Five hours later they disembarked at Iqaluit, where the knife slash of cold seared her face and ears. Too jaded to visit the Baffin Island capital, they had slumped uncomfortably on airport chairs until their flight was called to Resolute, where another plane, a battered two-engine propeller job, had been waiting.

The Twin Otter began to dive. Simultaneously, sharp explosions sounded in the cabin. Odette looked around wildly. Across the aisle, an Inuit businessman smiled reassuringly. At last, Paddy surfaced from sleep, snorting like a startled warthog. Checking his seatbelt, she spoke with quiet deliberation. 'I think it's an emergency landing.'

Paddy squinted out of the window. 'Nonsense, my dear. Twin Otters are indestructible and their pilots are gods. There's a handkerchief down there and we're about to land on it.'

The plane connected with the ground like a sack of potatoes, bounced twice on its huge tundra tyres and swung around perilously close to the end of the gravel runway. The businessman helped her to retrieve a bag from the overhead locker. She towered over him.

'What were those bangs?' she asked.

The Inuk pointed to a box, marked 'Crisps', lashed down at the rear of the cabin.

'The pressure was too much for the bags.'

'I know the feeling.' Bitter cold had entered the open rear door like a thief, snatching her warmth away as she followed Paddy down the aisle. Like her, he was wearing a sheepskin coat, but his rotundities seemed impervious to assault as he marched across the gravel, exclaiming at the spectacle of sheer cliffs, flat-topped mountain and distant blue ice sheet that dazzled them.

'Will you look at that, now. Have you ever seen such a pretty sight?'

Odette had to agree. She had supervised digs in locations as diverse as Scotland and the Middle East, yet this pristine setting had a scale and grandeur beyond human imagining. It was heart-stoppingly beautiful. She was possessed by the odd sensation of being an intruder in God's dream. But, Jesus, it was bloody cold.

Then she was roasted by the oven blast of the tiny airport terminal, where Paddy introduced her to a tall young man in an olive parka. Jack Walker's hollow cheeks and green eyes were arresting. He seemed faintly disconcerted to see her, yet mustered a reassuring smile and went off to field the luggage.

A thousand details competed for her attention – the delicate fur edging of parkas, the elegance and fine stitching of sealskin boots, the grace of the young women with babies, the reddish tinge of people's skin, sometimes burnt almost black around the pale outline of goggles. Her mental images of chubby Eskimos struggled to adapt to the neat, compact people in the room. Several smiled welcomes at her, yet there was no overt deference in their attitude, rather a sense of confident purpose. They seemed incredibly . . . focused.

At Jack's summons they made a swift transfer to his antediluvian Land Cruiser, inside which a heater fan was roaring. 'I'll find some lighter clothes for you both. We're having a bit of a heatwave at the moment.'

Paddy leaned across the wide seat to make himself heard. 'It's really good to see you, Jack. Now, in the matter of accommodation, what's to be done? Can we book into a hotel?'

Odette caught a flicker of discomfort in Jack's quick glance.

'The hotel's bursting at the seams; there are only twelve rooms and most people have to share. I've a spare room – that's to say two rooms – if you don't mind dossing.'

Odette stopped listening and sat back to study the rows of small, cosy-looking wooden houses, each fitted with a heater fuel tank and covered by snow. The contrasts intrigued her – a huge parabolic communications dish next to an ancient sod house, a fire station opposite a ramshackle Hudson's Bay store, and caribou antlers poking through the snow. A group of well-muffled infants on a plastic toboggan slid down a terraced slope, pausing at the bottom to wave at the car. A keening noise drew her eye to the bay, where lines of chained dogs greeted an approaching snowmobile.

The Land Cruiser halted. 'Here we are. You go straight in and I'll bring the bags.'

Odette examined Jack's two-storey house. It had once been painted blue, but had now weathered to a flaky duck-egg patina. The front porch steps, encrusted with icy snow, led to a wooden veranda occupied by a long-neglected barbecue stove. Beyond an unheated porch, filled with heavy implements and suits of fur, she entered a warm hallway lined with fabric parkas and cluttered with boots. Bending down to remove her own, she glimpsed a utility room packed with domestic machines and an outsize boiler that thumped and groaned.

'Paddy, you'll do yourself an injury.' He was wrestling with his boots and puffing like a grampus.

Jack preceded her up the stairs, carrying their heavy cases with ease. Not bad, she noted, seeing his shape outlined in refracted sunlight. At the landing, the view through the sitting-room drew her to the window. The immense, blinding void reduced her to a speck of insignificance and she stepped back, trying to imagine the glacial forces that had carved out such a savage landscape.

Turning around, she was struck by minimalist ornamentation in the room, which seemed to have just come out of mothballs. The stout armchairs still bore transparent plastic coverings. On the walls, Jack had given pride of place to a framed print of Raoul Dufy's cheerful cartoon *Le Casino de Nice*, flanked by smaller exhibition posters from the Grand Palais and the National Gallery. A selection of soapstone carvings shared a ledge with two small pouches, one decorated with Bushman beadwork, the other with a distinctively Asian pattern. Curious, she picked up the African pendant and was enveloped in cloud of heady scent reminiscent of patchouli. Inside, she glimpsed a caked yellow powder of crushed plants. The contents of the second pouch smelled strongly of sweet hill tobacco, transporting her back to a Cambodian trip. She smiled at the neatness of the idea: scent was the most powerful trigger of memory, so what need for souvenirs? She looked up to see Jack inspecting his fridge contents in a kitchen alcove.

'I hope you're hungry. Does anyone find the thought of caribou too repulsive?'

Odette did, and found herself apologizing. 'I'd really rather not, if you don't mind.'

'No problem. Tagliatelli and salad OK? Good. Caribou steak for Paddy. I'll show you to your rooms and dinner will be served in twenty minutes. Bathroom's along the corridor. This one's yours, Paddy. And here's the presidential suite.'

Odette saw at a glance the room must be Jack's. Neat stacks of books lined the walls and a pair of Indian snowshoes peeped from the top of a cupboard. Otherwise it was depressingly bare, although she noted the bed's creamy white duvet cover with approval.

'I'll fetch some fresh sheets.'

'Where do you sleep?'

She watched something flit across his face. 'The living-room sofa's fine,' he reassured her.

'You weren't expecting a woman, were you?' It was a reflex action to challenge this self-possessed man. Odette Blanchard was professionally adept at detecting flaws in beautiful objects.

'No, but we can't have you bunking up with Paddy, can we?'

'I don't see why not. It wouldn't be the first time.' She was gratified to see the look in his eyes, then he shrugged and closed the door carefully behind him. She grinned impishly. Technically, of course, it was true. More than once rain had forced her and Paddy to share a tarpaulin with a group of snoring archaeological students.

Dinner was an exuberant affair as Jack and Paddy vied to cap each other's stories, further enlivened by a bottle of pink vermouth that, to Odette's surprise, tasted divine. Jack was explaining why most people feigned abstention.

'Drink's ruined a lot of Eskimo communities, so every few years the hamlet holds a plebiscite on alcohol. Here they voted for controlled distribution, which means you can't buy booze in a store and you need approval from a local committee to import it. The freight charges are reckoned by weight, so most people order the hard stuff.'

Paddy interrupted. 'Why do people pretend they're teetotal – they don't like sharing?'

Jack laughed. 'Not with burglars. The few crimes here are mostly alcohol-related. People like to leave their doors open in case friends drop by, but they know the temptation of booze can prove too strong for youngsters. So they tell everyone they're on the wagon.'

Odette was mystified by Jack. While he was speaking, his intelligent face came alive with humour and self-mockery, then fell into a stone-like repose, his gaze preoccupied by another dialogue scrolling behind his green eyes. Sometimes, the faintest ripples of emotion crossed his face so quickly they seemed like her own imaginings. Stranger still, when he posed questions to her, his eyes seemed to be asking other questions. It was a not unpleasant experience: he was just different, she decided.

Jack was also resolving a puzzle in his mind. Once or twice Odette had dropped a Latinate word with a perfect French pitch that drew her mouth forwards in a moue and gave the lie to her Hampstead vowels. She had a small mole above her top lip, he noticed. A French parent, probably her mother, would explain the faint olive patina of her skin and the classic bone structure that would endure until old age. He detected an emotional maturity that set her apart from Oxford contemporaries who were still living an extended adolescence, although perhaps his joyless background made him judge them too harshly.

It was interesting, he thought, that she had chosen to work in the arcane field of archaeology when her beauty would open up better paid and more glamorous jobs, as if she had taken a decision to not to allow her looks to define her life. The odd defensive tick in her manner suggested she had not altogether succeeded. He guessed she was a solitary woman who lived with a cat, which some men would think a shame, but he found it somehow reassuring.

She was saying something to him. 'Why is drink so important?' she demanded.

It was a question southerners always asked and Jack gave his stock answer, which wasn't altogether true. 'It isn't, in this community. You can't be a hunter and a drunk without making mistakes, and most men in this village hunt for their food. The problems start when people can't hunt or they fall into the welfare trap. You see a lot of that in the south. Travelling on the land gives you a blast like nothing else; take it away and drink is the only thing that comes close.'

By mutual consent, no one broached the purpose of their visit, agreeing to leave a plan of action until the following morning.

'I must join the fairies, Jack.' Paddy yawned massively.

'Of course, you both must be knackered. Look, I have to pop out for a while, but you'll find bath towels in your rooms. There's constant hot water; coffee and tea are always on the stove. Please make yourselves at home.'

'Where are you going? Can I come too?' The words were out before Odette had considered them. Her body clock was out of kilter, confused by shifting time zones and the light outside. She wanted to walk off her long incarceration.

Jack hesitated. 'It's just a chore. But sure, be my guest.'

*

Outside, her dreamlike state intensified. She felt snugly warm in Jack's spare parka, looking out through the narrow aperture of its elongated hood. Twirling snowflakes hatched a village scene out of Dickens. Hard snow crunched satisfyingly beneath her borrowed caribou boots.

'Do the Eskimos really have a hundred words for snow?' An idiotic question, but one way of breaking the ice, she thought.

Jack was hefting a large leather case he had described as equipment. He glanced at her, as if noticing her height for the first time. 'The answer's yes and no. There's only one word for snow, *aput*. Inuktitut's a compound language like German, so the word's bolted on to descriptions like powdery, sticky, slush, sleet and so on. A hundred words may be an underestimate.'

Odette was used to reading men's vibes but Jack was transmitting neutral signals that seemed to blank out whatever thoughts he might be having. Stealth technology, she thought. When they had been greeted by three pedestrians, she realized they had joined a small procession converging on a large building. Through a cloud of steam shrouding the entrance she could see a score of parked snowmobiles.

Half-a-dozen teenagers were smoking in the outer hall. After depositing their coats on pegs, Jack murmured to her. 'Duty calls. I may be gone some time, as the man said. Don't feel you have to stay. Just follow the track home and let yourself in.'

She followed him obediently through a pair of heavily insulated doors and then stood rooted to the spot by a blast of country and western music. The hall was packed, an outer ring of Inuit crowded around a central area where old folk and children were dancing to a record. Apart from teenagers in leather jackets and swept-back hair, everyone seemed to be smartly dressed and enjoying themselves hugely.

An Inuk in a dog collar parted the throng and shook Jack's hand, nodding to Odette. 'Glad you could make it. Now we can get the show on the road.'

Throwing a wry look at Odette, Jack disappeared into the crowd. She slipped into an empty seat by the wall, bemused and slightly dazed. Several minutes later he reappeared on the stage with a button accordion strapped across his chest. She put a hand to her mouth. So much for the equipment. The clergyman tapped the mike and raised a violin and together they launched into a boisterous Scottish square dance which soon stirred couples to take the floor.

Odette shook her head. Eskimos and Scottish dancing? It was like straying into the nether world of Raymond Briggs's *The Snowman*. For another hour the music soared and couples twirled, until she heard Jack's name being called. Others took up the cry, some glancing at her with friendly grins. Oh hell, they think I'm his girlfriend, she thought.

With a good-natured show of reluctance, Jack was prevailed upon to swap his accordion for a guitar. A three-piece band shuffled into place around him. After a whispered consultation, he stepped up to the microphone and began to sing *Blue Moon of Kentucky* with a relaxed exuberance that surprised her. Crew-cut backlit in a halo, he seemed to be enjoying himself, in a rather matter-of-fact way.

A wave of exhaustion took Odette unawares. Feeling dizzy, she crept out and found her parka.

She awoke at 3 a.m., checking her watch against the sunlight that streamed through the curtains. The bedroom was sweltering and she felt dehydrated. Cracking open the window proved as counter-productive as opening a spaceship window: the cold streaming in passed the heat rushing out.

Wrapped in a dressing-gown, she stole towards the kitchen. At the threshold of the living-room she paused, puzzled by a whispering noise. It came in spurts of sound, like a radio transmission. Detecting excited cries and laughter, she recognized the hubbub of an HF squawk box, evidently set to an open channel.

Entering the room, she saw Jack, fully dressed, leaning beside the window. His gaze was fixed on the far distance, where the bay met the fjord. He was motionless, his expression closed and intense. She backed out silently.

CHAPTER 11

'WELL NOW, I think it's safe to say these are congruent with Viking objects found in Greenland.'

A slight trembling of Paddy's hands belied his cautious pedantry as he caressed the artefacts before him. Jack had retrieved the den hoard from his office safe and the items now lay spread out on the kitchen table among the remnants of breakfast.

Simon Inuksaq, who had dropped in to see if they needed anything, drank his coffee thoughtfully.

Odette thought Jack looked none the worse for a sleepless night. Her simple thanks for the evening's entertainment had drawn a non-committal smile. Pressed to explain his musical skills, he had remarked that many youngsters in the north learned to play the squeezebox.

Like a magpie with a piece of coloured glass, Paddy cocked his head excitedly over the medieval collar-stud. 'Without any shadow of doubt this is an iron rivet, which is a good indication that a Viking ship landed here. If Jack's site is indeed a boat or repair yard, we might expect to see lots of these clenched nails with roves, or washers. The Vikings built their ships with overlapping planks that were pinned together with masses of these. The joints were caulked with hair or moss soaked in resin to render them watertight.'

Paddy held up his next exhibit, the comb. 'Beautiful. This is one thing that every Viking possessed and was always losing. They really were quite a vain people. Even when they were about to lop off people's heads they still found time to groom their flaxen locks.'

'Oh, balls, Paddy.' Odette took the comb and indicated a gap of missing teeth. 'They wore out their combs grooming for lice. The floor samples I've collected are full of them. I bet this comb was thrown away.'

'I stand corrected. Man's old friend *Pediculus humanus*. Now, see the geometric pattern here? The same basic designs are found across the Viking world. They must have had cottage industries churning out combs.'

Odette inspected the horn surface closely. 'Pity there's no runic script saying "This belongs to Olaf".'

'Or Helga,' Paddy added. 'Think what it would mean if women had been on the voyage. Impossible, of course: Baffin Island was too barren for settlement. No, we don't want to find any runic script, the experts will fight over it like dogs over a bone. Wrong grammar, wrong period, blatant forgery and so on.

'But I think this one is flying under false colours.' Paddy ran a magnifying glass slowly along the harpoon blade. 'The one thing we know about the Greenland Norsemen is that they don't use harpoons. They take seals and walruses with clubs and spears, which is greatly less efficient than Inuit techniques. No, this is a spear.'

Paddy laid the blade on a catalogue page depicting Viking spearheads of similar configuration, but more slender and tapering. 'Now, to the Vikings spears were weapons of status, like swords, and many were decorated and pattern-welded, like this one. The difficulty here is that most were much longer, up to two feet in some cases. They were socketed into ash shafts between six and nine feet long. Which suggests that this one has been scaled down, either for a specific purpose or several roles.'

Odette ran a finger over its heavily pitted surface. 'Why would they bring such weapons to Baffin Island?'

Simon cleared his throat politely. 'Our ancestors left us stories about the first *qallunaat*. They weren't very friendly.'

Paddy brushed breadcrumbs from his trousers. 'This touches on the most important aspect – the business of motive. The Norse enjoyed hostile away-games, but we mustn't discount the possibility of hunting. The Viking economy in Greenland is heavily dependent on trade with Norway. We know they travel a short distance to Disko Island to hunt walrus for ivory, which they sell as a luxury item. Walrus hide rope was the strongest available. We also know they go on dangerous excursions to the Nordrseta hunting grounds in the far north of Greenland to gather the fur and hides of polar bears, seals, caribou and arctic foxes.'

The scholarly affectation of projecting the past into the present tense amused Jack, who voiced his own theory. 'I wonder if an animal population crash forced them to look further afield.'

'Please explain that, Jack.'

'We've seen the same phenomenon here. The elders say it goes back a long way. One unseasonal shower of rain that freezes the ground at the wrong time of year can have repercussions all down the food chain, from lemmings and owls to foxes and wolves. The same goes for marine mammals. Sometimes dogs spread canine distemper to seals and you end up with polar bears dying of starvation. The upshot is that hunters must find alternative supplies elsewhere, or they die too. It was the same for the Vikings.'

Paddy inclined his head gravely. 'That calls something to mind. The Greenland Norse have a fatal weakness that creates a hunger gap at the end of winter. They blithely ignore the Inuit techniques of seal-hole hunting, so they are restricted to only two species of migratory seal that can be caught on the ice. Hence they are denied the common ring seals that are available throughout winter.'

Jack saw the connection. 'So they must have prayed for the arrival of harp seals in the springtime. Any disruption to the migration would have put them in difficulties.'

Paddy sipped his coffee judiciously. 'All right, starvation is as powerful a motive as any. But let's not forget good old-fashioned Viking curiosity. The decoration on our spear suggests we are looking at circa AD 1000, when the Vikings are credited with discovering North America. They have been settled in Greenland for only about twenty years and are sniffing out their surroundings. They sail south-west to a place they called Vinland, but what can be more natural than assessing the potential of their close neighbour, Baffin Island?'

Odette interrupted. 'I thought they did, and wrote it off as a dump.'

Paddy blinked ferociously. 'You're thinking of the Greenland Sagas, written about three hundred years after the events they describe. It's true they make uncomplimentary remarks about Baffin Island, but only in the context of other expeditions to North America that had a much more ambitious purpose.

'Baffin Island is first mentioned by a Norse sailor called Bjarni Herjolfsson who is blown off course in about AD 985 and makes a landing in Newfoundland. Trying to return to Greenland, he sails up the coast of Labrador until he reaches Baffin Island. Without bothering to make a reconnaissance, he concludes that it is "a land good for nothing".

'The next attempt is made fifteen years later by the epic hero Leif Eriksson, who decides to perform Bjarni's voyage in reverse. This time he determines to make a cursory inspection of Baffin Island. Climbing up on a windswept plateau, he can see distant mountains capped with ice. The intervening land, he says, is "like one stone field". He concurs with Bjarni's negative assessment, naming the place "Helluland", or "Land of Flat Stone". Then he sails south to a forested land he calls Markland – probably Labrador – and on to Newfoundland or beyond, where he discovers a verdant land which he names Vinland. The rest is history. Leif Eriksson is acknowledged today as the true discoverer of North America, four hundred and fifty years before Columbus.'

Odette laughed. 'He really discovered Canada. It doesn't sound quite so grand.'

Paddy concealed his irritation by attempting to remove a speck of butter from his glasses, succeeding only in smearing it on the lens. 'Yes, Newfoundland is in the modern political construct of Canada, but in geographical terms Vinland was a historic landfall on the North American continent. Like Baffin Island, Newfoundland is a Canadian island separated from the continental landmass by only a few miles of water.'

Abandoning his glasses, Paddy squinted at his audience intently. 'The point is this. A Viking site here would be like finding the Holy Grail that disbelievers have always said was impossible. Wrong place, too remote, too barren. Yet geography suggests to all but the blind that the Vikings made their first landfall on the American continent in Baffin Island.

'The expedition to Vinland, over a thousand miles longer than the journey here, has a specific mission to locate commodities precious to the expanding Greenland population – timber and pasture for their livestock. Manifestly, Helluland-Baffin Island possesses neither, but it may have other virtues.'

Odette prompted him. 'Such as?'

'Hunting we've discussed. Then there is iron, of which Greenland is in desperately short supply. And last, but not least, the route west.'

Jack topped up their coffees. 'The North-West Passage?'

'Well, Jack, let's not get into the realm of wild speculation until we've visited the site. Hold one thing in your minds: the Vikings had very keen noses. They followed the trade routes to Byzantium and Russia and brought back wealth beyond the dreams of avarice. Now, when their western expansion took them to Greenland, a wave of Eskimoan migrants from northern Alaska was travelling along the North-West Passage towards them, possibly stimulated by trade with the Vikings themselves.'

Simon interrupted. 'Excuse me, I didn't go to school. Why did southerners want to sail through the North-West Passage?'

Paddy pinched the bridge of his nose and closed his eyes. 'Baldly stated, it was a short cut from the Atlantic to the Pacific across the top of North America. Its eastern entrance, facing Greenland, is Lancaster Sound. For British traders it would have reduced the distance between Europe and the Far East to under eight thousand miles. I use the conditional tense advisedly, because it is never free of ice, and therefore too dangerous to shipping. After four hundred years of searching for it, that came as something of a disappointment.'

'So they built the Panama Canal instead?' Odette interjected.

'Quite so. But there is unproven evidence of a prolonged warm period at this point in Viking history. The North-West Passage could have been relatively clear of ice.'

'And you think the Eskimos showed the Vikings where to go?'

A certain testiness crept into his reply. 'We must tread carefully here.

The accepted view is that Norse and Eskimos hold each other in mutual contempt most of the time. Vikings refer disparagingly to the native people they encounter as *skraelings*, synonymous with "weaklings", even though the Eskimos are not averse to attacking them on sight and giving a good account of themselves. This partly explains the presence of our spear, for reasons of self-defence.'

Odette was still puzzled. 'If the British spent four hundred years searching for the North-West Passage, how did the Vikings find it in only twenty?'

'That's quite simple. Look here.' Paddy unfolded a map showing the east coast of Greenland and Canada's northern islands. 'The North-West Passage proved such a tricky problem to the British because the poor dears were approaching the problem from the south, getting hopelessly confused by this maze of islands. The Greenland Vikings, on the other hand, only had to sail north-west or follow the coast around to arrive in the mouth of Lancaster Sound.'

Released, the chart curled up with a snap. 'Enough. When do we see this site of yours, Jack?'

Jack hesitated. 'I can leave in a couple of hours. It's a ten-hour return journey, which in practical terms means an overnight stay. But there's a tiny problem: I can only put my hands on one four-man tent.'

Odette pursed her mouth at the implication. 'Man being the operative word, I suppose? Perhaps you'd prefer me to stay behind to do your housework, or paint the outside?'

'That's really kind. I think a bright green would be nice.' He caught the angry flash in her eyes and raised his hands. 'I was going to say that we can rig a tent curtain and observe all the proprieties. Besides, you'll have more security in our tent.'

She snorted. 'From burglars, I suppose?'

'No, bears.'

'What sort of place have you brought me to, Paddy?'

A storm had scoured drifts from the ice on the fjord's eastern side, allowing Jack to open the throttle along the smooth stretches. Most of the Arctic was polar desert, characterized by almost cloudless days. This was such a day, a painting of azure blue and white with ochre smudges of land.

They travelled in fast stages. Jack halted the sled every hour to brew tea, keeping a discreet eye on Paddy and the girl to gauge their resilience. The Irishman's experience in Greenland was helping him through the brutal phase of acclimatization. Odette worried him more. Her long, slender figure betrayed little, if any, insulating fat.

He watched her running to keep warm, surprised at her lithe quickness beneath his fur parka and heavy wind-proof trousers. Occasionally she paused and stamped the surface, as if testing the five-foot-thick platform of ice beneath her.

She jogged over to inspect him chipping ice with a heavy knife, lifting her sunglasses to present a dubious expression.

'It's sea ice, isn't it?'

He dropped another shard into the kettle. 'That's right, but don't worry. The salt's leached out and it's quite pure.'

Odette began jogging on the spot. 'I can't get my hands warm.'

He stood up. 'Take your gloves off.'

She gave him a look of playful disbelief. 'Two hundred years ago that would rate as ungentlemanly.'

'It is two hundred years ago here. Better take your gloves off.'

She obeyed, her eyebrow a comma of scepticism.

Jack pulled off his mitts and gripped both her hands. They were ice-cold and disproportionately large, he noted, watching relief blossom in her eyes. It was a courtesy hunters had performed for him many times in his childhood. They stood in silence, locked together in the strangely impersonal heat transfer for a full minute until she gave a powerful squeeze of gratitude and broke the grip.

'You're burning hot. How do you stay so warm?'

'Early morning swims. Well, no, the cold's a bit of a fraud. The air's so dry that twenty below feels like minus five to people who live here. In winter it can fall to minus fifty, which really hurts. To answer your question, people heat up by eating frozen fish and seal meat. It's like jump-starting a car: your temperature shoots up by five degrees.'

Odette's attempt to conceal her distaste was almost comical. 'You eat frozen seal meat?'

'Certainly. We call it yum yum.'

Instead of responding, she explored more diplomatic ground. 'This jacket feels marvellous. I feel as if I'm going to the opera. Is it arctic fox?'

Jack knew he had been thrown a grenade but he was tired of dissembling to appease southerners' consciences. Mischievously, he pulled the pin. 'No, it's polar bear. I shot it myself.'

'How could you?' With an involuntary gesture, the girl stroked the coat's long guard hairs, as if comforting Jack's innocent victim.

'Quite easily. He came into town scavenging last summer and ate Sami Itorcheak. When Sami came out of his house, the bear was hiding under the porch; it came up behind him and whacked him. We found half of his body near the municipal dump.'

'So you shot it?'

'Popped him through the eye. I didn't want to spoil the fur.'

'That's awful. I suppose you ate it then?'

'There was talk of a feast, but people felt it would be like eating Sami.'

Without a word, the girl turned and jogged back to join Paddy.

Jack dumped three teabags into the boiling water. His lapse surprised him. He disliked being touched, yet he had held the girl's hands without a moment's thought. That way lay humiliation and grief. Yet something more than heat had passed between them. She possessed a heightened quality of femininity that beauty alone cannot confer. He liked the tension between her cool indifference and the stricken look that flared sometimes in her eyes. Disciplined to patrol the narrow corridors of his exclusion zones, he was nevertheless reminded of possibilities that were denied him.

He called out, 'Anyone for tea?'

CHAPTER 12

THEY REACHED THE Place of the Old People after five hours. Gunning the engine in bursts, Jack towed the sled gently over the steep bank of ice that lay across the site's entrance and drew to a halt beside a ring of small boulders.

Leaving his passengers in rapt contemplation of the panorama, he set tea to boil, unpacked a heavy tent from the sled and slotted two support poles into a long beam of timber that served as the main ridge brace. When the frame supported the double-walled canvas, he carried boulders to secure the guy ropes and then lugged more to weigh down the ground flaps. Unbidden, the girl came to his aid, shifting the heavy stones without undue effort.

Odette, who had never seen a large tent put up so fast, helped him to arrange food boxes and cooking equipment on a sheet of plywood just inside the entrance.

Paddy poked his long nose through the flap, his impatience manifest at the delay. 'Expecting bad weather, are we?'

Jack smoothed down a caribou rug. 'Impossible to tell. We don't want to be caught out in the open.'

A few more minutes and it was done. He led them towards the weir, explaining the layout of the settlement and patiently obliging Paddy's repeated demands for clarification. At last they stood expectantly in front of the den entrance. Paddy stood well back on the other side of the stream, scanning the scene with quick little jerks of the head. His gaze kept returning to the wide ramp of shelving rock that led from the weir pool to the base of the den mouth.

'Well now, we may be looking at a *naust*.' Paddy's cautionary tone reminded Jack of his admonishments to over-hasty students. 'The Vikings often use natural features as slipways for boathouses. There are some very good examples in south-west Norway that give us references for comparison, although their structures have the benefit of unlimited supplies of wood. Some *nausts*, unlike this one, are very big, designed for large sea-going warships.'

79

Odette interrupted the lecture. 'Aren't we missing something, Paddy? This encampment is a ready-made haven. The ship's shallow draught allowed the Vikings to pull it up the stream and beach it. There's only one reason they would go to the trouble of putting it in a permanent structure.'

Paddy's bursts of cerebration were expressed in small puffs of steam from his nose.

'Good point. I'm getting your drift, my dear. Go on.'

'Well, the short summer gives them a three-month window of opportunity to look around before the sea freezes. But they decide to dig in for the winter. They found something that caught their interest.'

'Or they were weathered in and decided to make the best of it.' Jack nodded at the hummock of ice barring the exit.

Paddy looked fretful. 'Damnably difficult. It's worse than I thought.'

Jack, standing beside him, tried to spot the focus of his concern.

Odette explained. 'The rock pile complicates things enormously. First of all, the falling rocks disturb the original setting and then your family of wolverines starts distributing harpoons and God knows what through the structure.'

Jack felt he was being reproached. 'If they hadn't, we wouldn't be here today,' he pointed out mildly.

The girl frowned, offering him a glimpse of an altogether more professional mien. 'If this site is to be investigated,' she continued, 'anything that's found has to be recorded in three dimensions and compared with its immediate surroundings for radioactive background, acidity and suchlike. Loose stones make that almost impossible.'

Paddy was poking with a steel pick between two rocks. 'We also have a problem with earth,' he pronounced heavily. 'There's none to speak of, which is a great pity. In Greenland you can count on a good foot of soil and find the Viking story about six inches down – rubbish dumps, bone, dead carrion flies, everything. What we really need are artefacts sealed in layers of deposits, not lying around haphazardly.'

Jack suspected they were getting hung up on technicalities. 'I don't see the problem,' he confessed. 'Either it will turn out to be a Viking site or it won't.'

A sigh escaped Paddy. 'And the lame shall be made to walk and the blind to see. Dear boy, our digs in Scotland came under the heading of worthy but dull. This site, on the other hand, could set the archaeological world ablaze. We'll be under a microscope, trying to convince a lot of very sceptical people. The standard of proof will be ferociously high.'

Both Paddy and Odette were shivering, he noticed. With promises of warm food, he led them back unresisting.

The tent was chilly, despite the Coleman stove's glowing rings. Odette unfolded a bedroll and set out warm nightclothes in her curtained-off third of the tent, savouring the delicious odour of cooking.

Jack called out to her. 'There's arctic char if you prefer. It's like salmon, but it doesn't have the calories you need to stay warm.'

'What are you having?'

Jack grinned to himself. 'A broth called *kuvilak*, which means pouring warmth on your feet.'

'It smells like just what I need.' She parted the curtain and sat on the end of her sleeping bag, still chilled to the bone.

Paddy rummaged in his rucksack. 'Now, Jack, I'd like to take a peek into your treasure trove with this cunning little contraption.' He extracted a small laptop and a long, semi-rigid coil. 'God bless the Japanese. It's an eye on a stalk. I won't tell you which branch of medical science it's derived from, but it's proved a godsend for probing the bowels of ancient buildings.'

Jack examined the small lens at the tip of the probe. The last foot was flexibly jointed.

Paddy switched on the computer and plugged loose wires from the coil into its side. Suddenly, a wide-angle picture of Jack's face sprang into sharp relief on the screen. He noticed a bright light recessed behind the pinhole lens.

'Neat, eh?' Paddy looked smugly content. 'The computer stores the images digitally, of course. But the real beauty of it is the directional movement. Look at this.'

The final length of the probe swayed like a snake as he manipulated the laptop's joystick.

Jack voiced his doubts. 'The battery's going to drain rapidly in this cold.'

With a magician's flourish, Paddy produced a couple of additional items. 'One adapter, to be rigged to the electrics of your snowmobile. And one heating shroud, to keep the little beast warm.' He secured the transparent plastic covering in a snug fit over the laptop, zipping the airtight seal. The picture, Jack saw, remained crystal clear.

'It has a tiny heater motor that circulates warm air inside the cover. Rather like those electrically heated socks I keep hearing about. I could do with a pair if you've any to spare, Jack.'

'I've got something better.' Jack dipped a ladle into the simmering broth and filled three mugs. 'Cheers.'

Odette felt the life-giving heat of the liquid course through her body. It ricocheted from her toes to her cheeks, creating the effect of standing before a roaring fire. Her whole body zinging, she experienced a rush of strength.

'God, that was bloody delicious. What is it?'

Looking at her glowing face, he hadn't the heart to tell her. 'Beef and fish stew,' he lied, pouring her another libation.

Paddy, who knew seal when he tasted it, flashed a grin.

After dinner Jack rode the snowmobile up the stream. This time the boulder refused to budge and he had to run a lasso from the machine's tow bar to break the ice seal.

'May I?' Paddy wedged his head and shoulders into the entrance, his short legs presenting the comical illusion of a human projectile crawling into a cannon. After a quarter of an hour of squirming and huffing, he emerged in deep thought.

'This rock cut is most interesting. It lends a very powerful air of authenticity. Even if the original materials have decomposed, we might expect to define the structure by its anchor points on the rock face.'

With the laptop adaptor rigged to the idling snowmobile, Odette fed the long probe into the hole while Paddy monitored its progress on the computer screen. The picture, at first too dark, could be enhanced via the keyboard and eventually resolved into a sharp image of the den's interior. The floor was not level, as Jack had supposed, but consisted of a series of shelved rocks. He noticed the wolverines had packed the cracks with smaller rocks, although they had not succeeded in creating a comfy refuge. They would have been forced to squeeze under a sharp boulder protruding through the roof, he saw.

Jack recognized the scrap of hide and slivers of bone he had touched near the den mouth but as the probe snaked forward, the floor was revealed to be disappointingly bare. Odette, under Paddy's direction, made several careful sweeps before he picked out something at the back of the cave. It was another tunnel, slanting downwards.

'Good,' Paddy exclaimed. 'Now that explains where our Viking loot is coming from. Either it's an escape tunnel, or it leads to another den. Let's have a look down there, my dear.'

'No can do. The lead's not long enough. We're at its furthest extent.'

'Hold it.' Jack was certain he had caught a dull gleam among some small stones. He turned to Paddy. 'Can you come left a fraction? There, can you see it?'

Paddy stared at the screen. 'Impossible to say. I'm going to try nudging those stones aside.' The picture lost focus as he manipulated the joystick, inclining the probe head downwards. Then they were looking at a curved object, encrusted with green blisters.

'A bracelet?' Odette ventured.

'Too big. Brass for certain. I've seen something like this before. I'm thinking of Oseberg for some reason. Let's see, in 1904 an excavation beside the Oslo fjord discovered the most sumptuous burial hoard from the Viking age. Yes, the Oseberg collection includes beds, oil lamps, farming tools, buckets. . . . That's it, buckets!'

Odette snorted delicately. 'It doesn't look like a bucket, Paddy.'

'Of course not. Viking buckets were made of wood, very much like oak casks without the lid. They were bound in brass hoops, which, if memory serves, were made in Ireland. That, my dear, is a fragment of a bucket hoop.'

To Jack's surprise, Paddy leapt up and pounded him on the back. 'Jack, you fell into a shit hole and came up with the gold watch and chain. Oh, pardon me, my dear. Look, I'm freezing, do you mind if we repair to our chambers?'

Fortified by boiled pork chops, Paddy's mood grew more festive, and then abruptly serious. 'Jack, there's no doubt this site has the hallmarks of becoming the only other authenticated Norse site on the continent. If it's proved to be older than the Newfoundland settlement we're looking at a sensation – the Vikings' first landfall in North America. It will open up the whole of north Baffin Island and the North-West Passage to archaeology. Academics who have been in denial for years about the Vikings' Arctic travels will have to rewrite the history books.'

Paddy held up a gloved finger in caution. 'We now face some important decisions. On our side there's the immediate question of protocol – who carries out the excavation, who pays for it and so on. What we need from you is to tell us what the local reaction will be.'

Jack had already considered some of the implications. Strictly speaking, the site was hallowed ground. Family histories were still bound up with the Place of the Old People, where so many had faded away into ghosts. 'I think it would depend on the size of the excavation. If it's confined to the rock pile, I think people would consider it, given some cast-iron guarantees. But if they think you're going to lay one finger on the whalebone houses, you can forget it.'

Paddy's face fell. 'That's a great pity. Because it's not unreasonable to suppose that our Vikings occupied the houses we see here, or rather their antecedents.'

Jack was keen to impress on them the narrow timeframe imposed by the Arctic summer. 'Freeze-up is in mid-September, so you'd better get your skates on.'

Paddy shook his head firmly. 'No question of doing anything this year. Too much to arrange.'

'In that case you'd better mount a guard on the site.'

He told them about Karlsson's persistent interest in the harpoon and its provenance.

'Paddy, you said this could be a sensation. Once the word's out, there'll be nothing to stop people helping themselves to trophies, even rocks and stones.'

Paddy's face was a study of dismay. 'But I thought this was a sacred site.'

'It is, and the local people will respect it. But in summer we have tourists wandering far and wide. This is quite a popular campsite for hikers and kayakers.'

'Jaysus.' The imprecation was torn from the scholar. 'Then we'll have to move like streaks of greased weasel-shit, begging your pardon.'

They agreed on a two-track strategy. Paddy and Odette would clear procedures from Oxford while Jack made overtures on their behalf in Snowdrift.

Paddy was snoring like a drain pump and failed to stir as Jack slipped into his outside gear. The low sun was obscured by cloud, creating a bluish twilight that allowed him to find the trail easily. It led away from the rock fall to a granite outcrop overlooking two of the whalebone houses.

It was a steep climb, but the handholds came back to him and soon he was seated below the skyline. Satisfied that he had a clear view of the tent and the den entrance, he drew a white tarpaulin around his neck and gathered the folds at his chest. He was invisible.

This perch had always been his sanctuary, a place where he could ignore his mother's angry summons to bed. Then his stepfather would shout threats into the night and eventually both would retire into the tent, leaving him in shivering defiance.

He watched the den entrance, trying to analyse his gloomy forebodings and seeking a weak link in the chain of coincidences that had led him to this lonely vigil. He concentrated on the key that had unlocked the cave's secret. What were the myriad permutations of chance that a Viking spear would be dug up by wolverines, save a man's life, be preserved in a walrus's blubber for two years, poison three hunters and then find its way into the hands of the one man who would be sufficiently interested to discover its source? And what game was Karlsson playing? It was as if an unglimpsed wheel of fate was driving the cogs and ratchets of a complex mechanism towards a preordained conclusion.

And this was only the beginning, he realized. A stream of consequences would flow inexorably from today's visit, impacting on family histories and changing this site forever. The nature of an archaeological excavation was to destroy the very history it set out to record.

A figure was moving in front of the tent. He recognized Odette, probably attending to a call of nature. He turned away.

It had been his nightly duty to bring the family's food here after the evening meal as a precaution against hungry bears. He would suspend the meat bag on a pole stretched across a deep basin in the rock. A bear's hunger could overcome its good sense and send it toppling fifteen feet into the huge trap. His stepfather, Aglukark, had conceived the idea.

He looked down the basin's sheer walls. The floor was covered with deep snow. He remembered his stepfather spearing a trapped bear from the basin's rim.

A muffled noise made him turn. The girl was following his tracks. Irritated, he watched her approach the foot of the outcrop until she was looking up directly at him but failed to spot his outline.

'Up here.'

She made light of the climb and dropped down beside him.

'Here, this will keep the wind off.' Unprotesting, she allowed him to wrap the tarpaulin around her. The silence stretched between them.

'I hope I haven't been too much of a pain.' She did not sound too contrite.

'I wouldn't say that. It's difficult for outsiders to understand there's a different logic to living here. It turns their values upside-down.'

'What do you mean?'

'Well, the icy wastes that give southerners the heebie-jeebies are a wonderful boon to people here. Snow and ice provide them with fast transport, building insulation and a platform over the sea to hunt the big mammals. Most people dread the summer because it makes travelling difficult and dangerous. Their lives are not ruled by day and night, but the best time for hunting. I suppose the biggest cultural difference is that people here live from day to day. They don't plan their holidays, or know what they're going to do when they're sixty-five.'

Odette shifted. 'It's odd, to read the newspapers you'd think that all Eskimos are falling down drunk, like the Aborigines. What you said is true: the people I've met here don't seem like that at all.'

Jack nodded. 'Then it's probably not true of Aborigines, either. The people here have got their act together. Most small communities have gone through the alcoholic bends trying to get from the Stone Age to the Internet age in one generation. We still get a few teenage suicides: kids see southerners having a great time on TV and then their parents turn round and tell them they're not real Inuit. But families have survived because they're strong.'

'How do you mean?'

'They help each other. Maybe the father does a stint on an oil rig, the daughter works in the store checkout, the son does casual labour and the mother makes gloves. They pool their earnings to subsidize the harvesting of animals.'

'Sorry, you've lost me. Why does hunting need to be subsidized?'

'Before you put one foot out the door you need basic equipment. A snowmobile and sled cost about fifteen thousand dolars, a tent's a thousand, a heater's four hundred and a two-way radio with antenna comes to nearly three thousand. Everything has to be replaced every four years. Add petrol at eighty dollars a day, ammo and food.'

'You admire these people,' Odette prompted, tempted to exploit this chink in his diffident air.

'Yes, I do. They don't brood over their failures and defeats. They shrug their shoulders, make it into a joke and move on. You only get confidence like that when you've survived for centuries with little more than snow and stone, bone and skin.'

Odette switched tack. 'But you were an academic. Don't you ever get bored here?'

Jack smiled at the ludicrous proposition 'No, there's more to interest me here than there ever was in England. The job doesn't end at five. I'm part policeman, part social worker and half-a-dozen other things.'

'More interesting than writing about Neanderthals?'

He was surprised she had seen his article in *Archaeology Now*. 'I was going to submit something on the subject myself, but you stole my thunder,' she explained.

He tried to recall the details.

'You suggested how *Homo sapiens* and Neanderthals might have co-existed, instead of humans trying to wipe out an inferior competitor,' she prompted.

'Oh, yes, the Tunit paradigm.' Jack grinned ruefully. His theory had not gone down well.

'Weren't the Tunit the little people in Eskimo folklore, so small their sledges were pulled by lemmings?'

'Oh, they were real enough.' Like the Neanderthals, the Tunit were evolution's losers, destined to become extinct – although they survived long enough to have fought pitched battles with the Vikings, he recalled.

'The Tunit were the first Eskimos to come from Siberia, now known as the Dorset Culture,' he said. 'Then in about AD 1000 – the time of the Vikings' arrival in Greenland – the Tunit began to be overtaken by a more advanced culture based on whale hunting, named the Thule people. They're the real ancestors of modern Eskimos.'

'And everyone assumed the Tunit were killed off by the newcomers, just like the Neanderthals?'

Jack noticed Odette was shivering, and pulled the tarpaulin more tightly around her.

'Well, that's the curious thing. In all the folk stories about the Tunit, there's no mention of open warfare between the two groups, but rather cooperation. In a way, the tales are paradoxical. They say things like, "The Tunit were stupid, but they taught the Inuit many things". The little people apparently didn't know how to build boats or use dogs for sleds. But they're also described as wise master craftsmen who showed the Inuit how to make bows and other implements.'

'And you think there's a lesson there?'

Jack nodded. 'It's a more useful way of looking at Neanderthals and modern humans. The loser is always stereotyped as stupid, but we know the Neanderthals were anything but.'

Odette laughed. 'My article would have made a nice end piece to yours.'

Jack caught a note in her voice and felt a pang of guilt. 'I was droning on. What were you planning to write?'

Odette sighed. 'Just a knockabout piece, really. Do you remember that report about London taxi drivers growing larger brains by memorizng all the city's streets? It got me thinking about a seminar on map-making I went to. One delegate had been collecting Bushman place names and was astonished by the mental maps these hunters and old people carried around in their heads.'

Jack could see where she was going. 'Bushmen have larger brains than normal, right?'

'Not just Bushmen, but Pygmies, Eskimos and – interestingly – Neanderthals, which seems to upset everyone. It conflicted with the old "Neanderthals-are-stupid" line, so they argued that a larger brain was an adaptation to the Ice Age. But of course that doesn't work for Bushmen and Pygmies.'

'Whereas it's simply a development of spatial memory among hunter-gatherers,' Jack murmured. It was a clever bit of reasoning, all the more so because the answer was hidden in plain sight. He began to view Odette with increased respect.

'Big brains weren't enough to save the Tunit,' he reflected. 'Perhaps they interbred with the Inuit, who are still praising the beauty of Tunit women.'

'Are you married?' Her question was delivered with forensic detachment.

'Let's say the local girls are very obliging.'

His flippant reply was clearly designed to close the subject, but Odette pretended to be intrigued. 'I've read that Inuit sexual morality is quite liberated.'

'Absolutely true. The women just give it away. An honest working whore would starve to death in Snowdrift.'

Odette lapsed into one of her thoughtful silences. After a minute or two she stirred. 'I think I'm going down. But I want to thank you for looking after us. I hope we can come back. Snowdrift gives me a strange feeling. It's like coming home.'

Jack watched her descend. 'Yes, I know,' he murmured.

CHAPTER 13

THE OFFICE WAS open when Jack arrived at 9 a.m. He had ferried Odette and Paddy to the airstrip the previous evening and now he could postpone the backlog of paperwork no longer.

'HMV called,' Levi said. 'He sounds pissed off.'

'Nothing new there, then.'

If Masters, his touchy superior in Iqaluit, had never bridled at the nickname His Master's Voice, it was not altogether surprising: his Christian name was Kermit. Jack sighed, anticipating another querulous remonstrance for his absences.

It was a longstanding bone of contention. Masters was a throwback to the Yellowknife bureaucracy that had governed the entire Northwest Territories like a colonial fiefdom until the Eskimo region of Nunavut had sheared off in 1999. Drawing a short straw, Masters had been reassigned to the new Inuit homeland in the east. Jack pictured his plush office at the department's new headquarters in the island's capital town.

Despite the recent emphasis on putting the Wildlife Department at the service of the people, Masters clung to the tradition that an officer's place was at his desk, concentrating on administration and paperwork. Fortunately, Jack's statistical facility kept Iqaluit bombarded with a stream of documentation that bought him time to play a more pragmatic role out on the land. Desk-bound officers filled him with contempt.

He got through to Masters' office and heard the phone picked up at the first ring.

'Hello, Kermit. What can I do for you?'

'It's too late for that, Walker.' Masters' voice carried a triumphant note, and Jack groaned inwardly. 'We've had a serious complaint from Mr Sverker Karlsson, who is with me here.'

So that's where he went, Jack thought. Karlsson had checked out of the clinic and left by plane.

'Tell him I apologize for saving his life.'

'Walker, you can't joke your way out of this one. As a public servant you know it's a disciplinary offence to act as a guide in a trophy hunt, not to mention neglecting your duties in Snowdrift.'

Jack wondered where this was leading. 'Is that the best you can do?'

'By no means. How does criminal negligence sound to you? Mr Karlsson has described in disturbing detail how your failure to provide covering fire forced him to defend himself and end up being seriously injured. He's talking about pressing charges.'

Jack almost laughed. 'Do me a favour. Why would I do that if I had to go hand-to-hand with a bear?'

Masters cut him off. 'Mr Karlsson has no recollection what happened after the bear attacked him, but that's irrelevant. The bottom line is that you're formally suspended until a disciplinary hearing two days from now, which you're instructed to attend.'

Jack replaced the receiver thoughtfully, remembering his boast to Karlsson. He was not well paid; it was the package of free housing, snow machine, boat, Land Cruiser, clothing and equipment that lent him the appearance of affluence in an impoverished society. His earnings as a freelance journalist were no more than intermittent, and the exorbitant costs of the High Arctic had made deep inroads into his savings. He was an orphan and Wildlife had given him not just a home but a base at the heart of a community where he could pursue his own ruminations.

Dismissal left two possibilities if he decided to stay in Snowdrift: a subsistence existence or setting himself up as an outfitter and guide. The village's trickle of tourists could not sustain such an operation even for a couple of summer months, so he would be forced to move south.

'*Ajurnamat*,' he murmured. Maybe it wouldn't come to that.

'Don't say it can't be helped.' Jonas materialized through the workshop entrance. 'That kind of attitude is why nothing gets done around here.' The small Inuk was wearing a green jumpsuit today, complemented by a matching Bushline cap with fur-lined earflaps and green rubberized boots. His mournful expression presaged more bad news.

Jack held up a hand. 'Don't you start. I've just been suspended.'

As he explained Masters' accusation, Jonas puffed himself up into a picture of outrage. 'Don't those assholes realize the job you've been doing? You've won a lot of respect here, Jack.'

'Have I?' His friend's remark caught him by surprise. His thoughts shifted to the coming hearing. 'Fuck 'em.'

'Haven't you heard of hubris, Jack?'

'Sure. It's a delicious Greek starter made from chickpea and served with pitta bread. Is Lila making some?'

Jonas permitted himself a faint smile. 'Hubris, not hummus – overconfidence that invites disaster.'

'Oh, I forgot the paprika. No hubris worth its salt is served without a sprinkling of paprika. Now get your teeth round this.'

Jack outlined his discovery of the Viking site and the purpose of Paddy's visit. As he began to list the excavation's requirements, Jonas exploded. 'You're crazy. We don't have the manpower or the tents for that kind of operation.'

'We'll find them. Jonas, a discovery of this magnitude has irresistible momentum.'

'Yeah, straight to the bankruptcy court.'

'If it's proved to be a Viking foothold in North America, we could be looking at hundreds of tourists. We have to see this as a future investment by the community, because if we turn our backs now it will be taken out of our hands and given over to outside contractors. We might as well wear Mickey Mouse outfits and become curiosities in someone else's theme park.'

Jonas shook his head. 'Aren't you forgetting something? The community's first gotta decide they want something like this. They could throw it out, just like that national park idea the government was so keen on. I put a lot of work into that.'

Jack mentioned Karlsson's interest and spelt out his own fears that the site might be desecrated by souvenir hunters.

Jonas took a deep breath. 'Look, you know how things work here. The hamlet council will have to chew it over and they might even hold a referendum, but the guys who take the real decisions are the elders. You'll have to speak to them. Why not start with John Ulayoukuluk? He was in the land chain talks for years and people have a lot of respect for him.'

Ulayoukuluk must be close to eighty, Jack estimated. By virtue of his hunting skills, he had emerged as a born leader long before the Eskimos settled in villages or created politicians.

The elder lived in a wooden house indistinguishable from its neighbours on Snowdrift's highest terrace. Jack did not knock, which would have been discourteous, but pushed open the outer door and stamped the snow from his boots until he heard a muffled response from within.

A tall, stooped man, his hair still untouched by grey, beckoned him into a neat sitting-room, lined with family photographs, that reminded Jack of Scottish fishermen's homes he had visited in Peterhead.

'You'd like some coffee? Good.' The patrician tones of Ulayoukuluk's fluent English reminded Jack that this man had spent seventeen years patiently negotiating the world's biggest land deal with southern politicians. As if reading his thoughts, the old man took down a framed photograph and offered it ruefully for inspection. It showed him with a small Eskimo delegation, photographed in London's Piccadilly Circus.

'I sometimes felt I knew the streets of Ottawa and European cities better than my own village. When I returned I was virtually a stranger here. I live quietly now. After all, who wants the opinion of an old man?'

It was an invitation to state his case and Jack talked without pause for half an hour, feeling the weight of his host's steady gaze upon his face. Out of respect, he spoke in Inuktitut, imparting neither spin nor embellishment to the story, and when it was finished he experienced a profound relief that the matter was out of his hands.

Ulayoukuluk's face remained impassive as he pursued a perplexing digression. 'You know, when I was six my father took me to the Hudson's Bay store at Pangnirtung to buy a muzzle-loader. The manager said the price was a pile of furs to the height of the rifle, but my father didn't have enough. It was a hard winter, hard for my mother dying of TB, but we hunted and trapped enough pelts to buy the rifle. The gun was first-class, and when my father died three years later it became mine.

'In 1938 I lost it over the side of a boat and went to replace it at the same store. I remembered the exact number of furs my father had paid for the rifle, but, of course,I took a few more because I didn't want to be humiliated in the same way. The manager was very polite and explained that the old model was obsolete. From a display case he took out the new rifle, which was much longer. Of course, I hadn't enough furs.'

The old man wheezed mirthlessly. 'I never forgot that lesson in how the white man does business. He didn't give us this land, we had to bargain for it even though we are an unconquered people. Now you are asking us to give up some of it to encourage the white man's conceit that he discovered a country that we, the Inuit, were already occupying.'

Jack outlined his ideas on how the project could benefit the hamlet. In the short term, he conceded, it would generate only menial jobs such as supply drivers, maintenance workers and polar bear sentinels. Success held out the prospect of a skilled local workforce to service a tourist industry that would encourage young people to return to the community. He stressed the importance of the hamlet retaining control, perhaps in partnership with a southern consortium.

Ulayoukuluk listened patiently until the end, and then composed his thoughts. 'We must balance the economic benefits against two questions. First, how will this affect our food chain? The slopes above Ituquvik are summer feeding grounds for the Cape Hooper herd. Second, we must be sure that the status of the land doesn't revert to Crown title. At present, the site is designated as wholly Inuit-owned land, with subsoil and mineral rights. These give the community a share of any objects found by the archaeologists.'

This cogent analysis brought home to Jack the complexities of the undertaking. At least the old bird had not refused outright. Indeed, he promised to give it more thought and speak to a few others.

As he rose to leave, Ulayoukuluk motioned him back in his chair and looked at him keenly. 'You know people are saying your stepfather is still alive?'

'Aglukark alive?' Jack saw the floor falling away into a black void. Sweat pricked his arms and back. He was barely conscious that the old man was still talking.

'You know how these stories start. Someone sees a raven with a white feather that reminds them of your stepfather's tame bird. Someone else finds an old-style trap line in the mountains and suddenly the dead have come back to life. Superstitious nonsense! But of course, you were there, you tried to save him.'

An image of Paulie's leg-hold trap whirled through Jack's mind in a torrent of confused thoughts. Suddenly aware of an expectant pause, he struggled to understand Ulayoukuluk's question. 'It was all I could do to get out myself,' he managed to say. The room was stifling.

To his relief, the old man was rising to his feet, signalling the end of their meeting. His parting words were kindly.

'You make out a good case. If the community agrees to your proposal, they may want someone to liaise with the *qallunaat* on a daily basis. I'm too old for that sort of thing. We'll need a young man who can represent our best interests.'

On his return to the office, Jack tried to tease out the subtext of the conversation. The mention of his stepfather and the offer of a liaison job seemed to have been subtly linked.

What if someone knew the truth?

Winter was spitting from its grave as he reached the far side of Victoria Sound, but the wind at his back permitted him clear vision down the tunnel of white blips enfilading his headlight beam. He parked the snowmobile and sled on the shore, removing his rifle, a spade and a gas lantern before proceeding stealthily up a shelving incline. He cursed the rivers of snow that raced like phantoms across the ground, obliterating fresh tracks. Nevertheless he circled around to make a careful inspection before approaching the mound.

Since his return to Snowdrift, Jack had avoided his stepfather's outpost camp, consigning it with a trunkful of memories to a mineshaft of mental oblivion. It was located thirty miles down the fjord, between the village and summer hunting grounds. He felt foolish carrying the rifle: it was an explicit admission that beneath his curiosity pulsed an irrational fear.

The wooden cabin was almost subterranean, sunk into a six-foot trough in the permafrost that was now filled with a snow bank extending to the pitched roof. Using the spade, it took him nearly an hour to cut a trench and by the time the door stood exposed he had discarded his parka.

At his touch, the door swung open and after a moment's hesitation he stepped across the threshold. The gas lamp's powerful glow threw into bleached-out relief a single, unkempt room with clear evidence of previous occupation. The layout was as he remembered – a fixed oil stove in the centre, three spring beds with cotton mattresses, a large table with four chairs and a kitchen shelf bearing a few pots and pans – but somehow smaller.

The door's crash made him whirl. Heart hammering in his chest, he stood immobile and watched spectral fingers of frost reaching across the wall from the doorjamb. Turning, he squatted beside the stove to check the fuel level and, finding it nearly full, was transfixed by a thought. During the past thirteen years the cabin might have passed into other hands, in which case he was trespassing, even though no Eskimo would question a traveller's presence in his dwelling.

It also occurred to him that if the hut had not found a new owner there could only be two explanations: respect for the dead, or a belief that Aglukark would return.

At first, his inspection yielded no clues: apart from the rudimentary kitchen equipment the room seemed bare. Then his eye fell on a small cupboard fixed at chest height on the wall. From inside he removed two objects and laid them gently on the table. Thirteen arctic winters had laid no blemish on the inlaid mother-of-pearl of his mother's hairbrush. Tangled in the bristles he saw a strand of the golden mane that Elizabeth had groomed with religious zeal each night.

The *Rupert* annual had not fared so well, its cover creased across the familiar picture of a little bear with yellow check trousers and scarf. In slow motion he opened the book and read the inscription in a childish hand: *John Walker, Christmas 1982.*

Driven by intuition, he strode across the room to stoop beside the large bed. Flush with the wall, his hand encountered a medium-sized suitcase that offered resistance as he lugged it onto the mattress. At the release of its catches, the lid popped open, enveloping him in a cloud of familiar, cloying perfume. The case was brimful of his mother's clothes.

He backed away slowly and sat on his bed, bereft of thought. The illusion stole over him that he was looking down on an ancient edifice that, after centuries of guarding a tomb, was responding to intrusion by triggering mechanisms of trickling sand and moving blocks of stone inside hidden shafts. These were, he realized numbly, the sensations he was experiencing within himself, except that the doors and shutters were opening to admit the interloper.

Now the past shrieked in his face.

His earliest memory was of his father carrying him on a visit to the mine and hugging him reassuringly as he quailed from the tumultuous sounds and pungent smells of the workings. Ned Walker was a retiring and indulgent man, an engineer and geologist from Cornwall who enjoyed his son's company, reading him stories, imparting his drawing skills and keen to foster the boy's understanding of the Eskimos' conquest of the ice.

Even by then, Jack realized, his father was approaching middle age, married to a woman twenty years his junior who had long since ceased to love him. Elizabeth was a highly strung yet striking woman who ruled her husband and son with a steel lash. She had been fostered by a strict couple in the Surrey village of Outwood who inculcated in her harsh Biblical tenets, enforced by the adage 'Spare the rod and spoil the child', that vied with her sensual nature. Her existence became a battle to dominate and control her world.

For a while, Jack remembered, his parents' rows seemed to abate after the family moved from the mining settlement to Snowdrift. His father's friendship with Aglukark, an Eskimo who lived permanently out on the land, led to a series of memorable weekend excursions. Living under canvas, watching whales from the floe edge and travelling into the mysterious hills, captivated Jack and set free his imagination. But Elizabeth's rancour returned with alarming vengeance and Jack noticed his father began to spend more time at the mine, often returning with whisky breath.

As Elizabeth's behaviour drove her husband away, she made greater efforts to enforce Jack's craven obedience and unquestioning love. These he felt impelled to deny her, for the sake of his self-respect and through dogged obstinacy. Then she would beat him. Jack's father could never have raised a hand against him, but his mother rewarded each rebuff and hesitant compliance with a merciless thrashing on his bare buttocks. He never gave her the satisfaction of crying out or revealing his feelings, for to do so would surrender his individuality.

Jack sometimes wondered if Elizabeth was slightly mad. Her decision to move in with Aglukark seemed to him insane, a view he did not hesitate to voice, with the usual painful consequences. He felt keenly the injustice done to his father and, by extension, to himself. He began to rebel more openly and the whippings increased.

Jack hated Aglukark for usurping his father's place in ways he was only beginning to understand. He burned with anger and shame at the sounds of the nightly lovemaking in the adjacent bed. Looking back, he wondered if this was their main attraction, rather than a misguided evangelism that drove Elizabeth's attempts to convert an avowed pagan. Aglukark was charismatic and Elizabeth's feisty beauty made her a trophy that enhanced the healer's reputation. His mother was not the first European woman to fall for a native.

Learning that the Eskimo was a medicine man, Jack ridiculed his diagnostic techniques as mumbo jumbo. Aglukark used several rituals for identifying the cause of sickness. One involved lifting a rock on a piece of sealskin rope and asking questions of a spirit. If the rock felt heavy, the answer was no; if light, the answer was yes. Jack bought a yo-yo and conducted loud conversations with it.

Aglukark's vocation had certain compensations. The outpost camp was a beacon to a steady trickle of ailing visitors from Snowdrift, and during the summer months travelling families made a point of calling in to exchange gifts and gossip. Then an air of normality descended and Jack felt he belonged to an extended family of cousins and friends.

At first, Aglukark had reacted with bemusement to Jack's defiance, displaying Eskimo patience towards a wilful child. But the revelation of his father's suicide drove Jack to a new level of hostility that threatened to disrupt the houshold. In an attempt to break his spirit, Aglukark made the boy run behind the sled and denied him food until he had caught his quota of seals. Jack's response was to raise the stakes by courting hardship and self-punishment. He would fast, not sleep, and disappear for long periods during which he would walk for days in the hills and across the ice.

He always returned for Soosie. Aglukark's daughter by a previous wife possessed the beauty of a young seal and a bright spirit that, by degrees, was being crushed under Elizabeth's tyrannical regime. Inevitably, the two youngsters turned towards each other. The two-year difference in their ages cast Jack in a protective role. They spent most evenings playing cat's cradle, working string into elaborate patterns of running caribou and upright bears while Jack made the figures come alive with invented stories.

As Jack matured physically, his mother became prone to violent tantrums. Exercising the hawk-like vigilance of a puritan, she took to creeping up on him at night and snatching away the covers if she imagined that carnal thoughts were keeping him awake. She stripped off his pyjamas and laid into his buttocks with a cane. Jack endured such beatings with stoical detachment.

Soosie's developing figure inflamed Elizabeth's possessive instincts, goading her to extend the same punishment to the girl after she had finished with Jack.

By the age of 14, Jack had experienced only three winters of formal schooling in Snowdrift since his departure to Aglukark's outpost camp seven years previously, staying at a church hostel in the village. Many hunters exercised the right to take their children out of school for the spring and summer hunts, and Aglukark was no exception. Like others, he hunted for meat and needed Jack's burgeoning skills and strength.

When summoned home after the Easter term, Jack found things had changed. His mother had given birth to a baby boy after prevailing on Aglukark to go through a formal marriage ceremony. The shaman had agreed with bad grace, believing the white man's god to be an instrument of Eskimo enslavement, and now bitterly regretted his capitulation to Elizabeth's viperish tongue. The atmosphere in the cabin became sulphurous, with Jack and Soosie trapped in the crossfire.

The two adults increasingly vented their frustrations on the teenagers throughout the ensuing year, relieved by their absences at school. Aglukark collected them as usual for the Christmas break, but sent them back on foot when he discovered Jack had left the remaining thirteen dollars of their joint allowance at the church hostel. The thirty-mile walk to Snowdrift would have presented little hardship to Jack if he had not been forced to carry Soosie on his back for long stretches. It was minus 30° and blowing snow when they set out and after four hours they were hit by a storm while crossing the inlet. By digging a hole in the snow and wrapping Soosie in his caribou parka, he kept her alive for two days until a snow-mobile passed by.

One day Jack returned from one of his lone excursions to find Aglukark embracing Soosie on his lap. He had never offered violence to his stepfather before but reacted to the sight instinctively, delivering a blow to the face that almost broke his hand.

Despite Soosie's protestations that nothing serious had occurred, Jack had reached a crossroads. He pondered the two common Eskimo strategies for dealing with serious anti-social behaviour. You could sometimes disarm tormentors by rendering them a valuable service that put them in your debt. If they persisted, you moved away. He rated both as impractical, in the latter case because he could not abandon Soosie.

There was a third, more dire option, when survival itself was at stake. Jack tried not to think about it.

He started. The moaning wind had swung around to blast open the door and, he saw, deposit a growing snowdrift on the cabin floor. Leaning down, he trailed a glove across the floor planks. Dirt. Someone had brought the previous summer's grit into the cabin on their shoes.

Before leaving, he paused by the door, nagged by a sound. In the flailing draught, the clinking noise returned. In the shadow of an alcove beside the door he saw them. They hung in clusters by their chains from a line of nails. Aglukark always kept a score of traps. Jack counted them: only eight remained.

CHAPTER 14

HIS TAXI DRIVER at Iqaluit Airport was a loquacious French speaker from Montreal who had envisaged rich pickings in the capital of Baffin Island when it became the administrative centre of the new Nunavut territory. Judging by his dour tones, it hadn't worked out like that.

'You can see a class system among the Inuit that never existed before. Those with government jobs and those sleeping six to a room.'

Jack grunted. The plane's delay meant he was already late for his inquisition. The car's heater was on full blast even though the driver wore a trapper's hat and heavy parka.

'Yes, *incroyable*. Salaries come down and rents go up. We now have a soup kitchen: that was unknown before. People always had enough to eat.'

Jack gazed at the snow-banked streets and high-rise buildings, noting the pace of change since his last visit six months before. The town was a construction site, with new estates creeping like tendrils over the gentle hills.

The Wildlife and Fisheries building looked as desolate as ever. Jack tipped the driver a dollar and pushed through the door. Ignoring the girl receptionist, he made his way to his former office, to find Bill Richardson placing coloured pins in a wall map. Bill had been stationed at Rankin Inlet: he had evidently come in from the cold. His handshake was warm, his eyes clouded.

'Jack, I hope you've got a good pension plan. They're loaded for bear and they want the skin and claws too.'

'Good, they can have them.'

Bill nodded to a waiting-room across the hall. 'I'll tell them you've arrived.'

The room had a single occupant, a well-tailored non-native who leaned back on the sofa with crossed legs, his face buried in the *Nunavut News*. At his entry, the man lowered the paper. It was Karlsson.

'Sverker the Berserker. How's the toxophily? Shot anyone recently?'

The Swede seemed disconcerted by Jack's genial tone but instead of sitting in stiff silence he seemed anxious to talk.

'Look, Walker, I don't want you to lose your job.'

'You've a funny way of showing it.'

Karlsson spread his hands in a conciliatory gesture that exposed a red weal on his wrist, a legacy of his mauling. 'This hearing could be halted now if I withdraw my complaint.'

'Go ahead. No one's stopping you.'

The Swede shook his head ruefully. 'What am I to do with you? You say you are not interested in money. What can I give you?'

Jack contemplated the man thoughtfully. 'I've a certain sympathy for the congenitally bewildered, Sverker, but it must have penetrated even your skull that the harpoon is not mine to sell. Strictly speaking, it belongs to the estate of Inuk Charlie or the community of Snowdrift, which is a matter of probate.'

Karlsson swatted his remarks away. 'Keep the harpoon. I don't want it.' He paused, weighing his words. 'I know what you and your Irish professor are planning. I want you to stop it.'

Jack was intrigued. 'Why?'

'There are . . . factors you don't understand. If you did, you would realize it is in your own personal interest to heed me.'

Jack shrugged. 'Sorry, it's out of my hands. Nothing's a foregone conclusion. The hamlet council will have the final word.'

'They will listen to you. I have researched you, Walker. An Oxford man, impeccable qualifications, fluent in Eskimo and a respected member of the community – who better to advise them?'

'What should I tell them?'

'Say an excavation will cause nothing but trouble.'

Jack smiled dismissively. 'Trouble's an old companion. Go away and blackmail someone else, chum.'

The Swede appeared to be on the point of saying more when Bill arrived to say the tribunal was ready.

In the corridor Karlsson tugged at his sleeve. 'For the sake of your family,' he began, but Jack pushed past him.

The three-man disciplinary panel sat at one end of a large table that almost filled the conference-room. Jack recognized the freeze-dried features and suspiciously red cranial fuzz of his boss, Kermit Masters, who was conferring with the Inuk head of personnel and another senior Wildlife executive. Ranged along one side of the table were three non-native men and an Inuit woman whose demeanour and clothes proclaimed their powerful status.

It's a kangaroo court, Jack thought, taking a seat.

The chairman, a slim Inuk of fastidious appearance, tapped his pencil and addressed Jack. 'I'm Robert Koonoo, head of personnel. This is a preliminary hearing to establish the facts concerning serious allegations made against you. Do you understand the nature of those allegations?'

Jack looked at Masters, who raised his eyebrows mockingly. He ignored the question. 'For the record, sir, I wish to state that I have received no written notification of the charges against me, nor have I been invited to submit my response. Perhaps Mr Masters can enlighten us why these basic formalities have been ignored?'

Anticipating the objection, Masters' smooth reply began to cover the extraordinary gravity of the charges when the chairman cut in primly, 'The procedures are quite in order. This hearing has been called only to establish the facts. Please answer the question.'

'No, I don't understand the allegations.'

Koonoo tapped his pencil. 'Let's try again. Shall I put the charges to you, Mr Walker?'

'Go ahead. I'm interested.'

They were brief, amounting to unprofessional conduct and neglect endangering life.

Karlsson was invited to give evidence. Adopting an air of wounded gravitas, he outlined the events leading up to the incident, coaxed and questioned by Koonoo.

'Please describe what happened when your bow malfunctioned.'

Jack smothered a laugh.

'At first I was paralysed by shock. I looked over to Walker, expecting him to fire, but his rifle wasn't even raised. He just looked at me with the same supercilious expression you see on his face now. I should mention that he was not standing where I expected, but had retreated behind the sledge, putting me between him and the bear.'

'What did you conclude from this?' Koonoo prompted.

'Perhaps he wanted just to frighten me. But then the bear charged and I realized I would be forced to defend myself. Even then I believed Walker would fire, but he didn't. I threw a harpoon, injuring the bear quite badly, I believe, but it didn't stop and I was obliged to use my knife. Then the bear seized me and I don't know what happened next.'

It was a convincing performance, Jack had to admit.

'You say Mr Walker showed animus towards you from the outset?'

'Correct. He constantly denigrated Scandinavians as barbarians and Swedes as slave traders. In another setting, his comments would be classed as racist.'

When Karlsson had finished, Jack was granted a cross-examination. He stood up and produced a notebook.

Long ago, Jack had realized that the steps a man most feared were the most crucial, even if the direction was unclear. As a Mountie, he had prosecuted dozens of cases and had learned to invest his court appearances with the impersonal yet daunting cadences of authority.

He turned to the Swede. 'Are you an experienced hunter, Mr Karlsson?'

'I suppose so, yes.'

'Can you name the Big Five trophy animals?'

'Of course. Rhino, elephant, Cape buffalo, leopard and lion. I've shot them all.'

'Thank you. Do you think the polar bear should be included in what is called the "grand slam"?'

'Yes, I think most serious hunters would agree. It's the greatest prize.'

'Did you intend to export the skin to Sweden?'

'Yes, of course. It's quite legal to do so.'

'Tell me, Mr Karlsson, if someone else had shot your bear, would you still have wanted to take the skin home?'

Karlsson could see where the question was leading, but was obliged to answer. 'Probably not. It would not be honourable.'

'No? Are you an honourable man, Mr Karlsson?'

The Swede sent an appealing look to the panel. Koonoo nodded. 'I can't see where this is going.'

Jack wasn't quite sure, either. He was distracted by the sight of a European, still wearing his parka, gesturing to him from the doorway.

He raised an index finger and, catching the chairman's nod, went over to the man, who was clutching a Jiffy bag. He gripped Jack's hand.

'Hi. Jeff Sparling. Sorry to barge in. I just got in from Pond. Doc McPherson said to be sure you got this.'

Jack tore back the packet's sticky seal and fished out McPherson's note. After a moment's swift perusal, he grinned. He was going to enjoy this.

He resumed his place and addressed Koonoo.

'Just a couple more questions, sir, and then we can all go home. Mr Karlsson, are you aware of the penalties for perjury?'

Koonoo's patience was wearing thin. 'This is not a court of law, Mr Walker.'

'You're right, of course. But anything said before witnesses in this room may have a bearing on legal proceedings pending elsewhere.'

The chairman looked baffled. 'What legal proceedings? Are you threatening the witness, Mr Walker?'

'Criminal proceedings, I'm afraid, sir. I trust you've no objection to me taking a recording.' He had turned on the small dictaphone at the start of the hearing, in case he eventually ended up before an employment tribunal. Now he placed it on the table before him. Its red eye drew the appalled stares of the panel. They were powerless to refuse, Jack knew: the disciplinary code spelt out an employee's right to take an aural record.

Masters leaned forward, his face flushed. 'This is a typically insubordinate attempt to intimidate the panel, Mr Chairman,' he blustered. 'Look at him. He's a disgrace to his uniform.'

Jack turned back to his accuser. 'Were you wearing gloves when you handled your bow?'

Karlsson looked puzzled. 'On the left hand, yes. On my right hand I wear a loose leather tab that can be folded up to protect the string fingers.'

'Last question. Could you tell the tribunal if you have seen these before?'

Jack reached into the Jiffy bag and removed a transparent medical sachet. He placed it on the table before Karlsson. The Swede stared at the bullets, thunderstruck.

Without waiting for a reply, Jack continued, 'Isn't it the case, Mr Karlsson, that to ensure that only you and no one else would be credited with the bear kill – what you call the greatest prize among trophies – you unloaded my rifle, thereby endangering not only your life, but mine as well? Why else would my bullets be found inside your coat pocket?'

Karlsson's expression was thunderous. 'That's absolutely ridiculous,' he snapped.

'I'd caution you not to handle those,' Jack said. 'They could be exhibits in the criminal prosecution I mentioned earlier.'

Masters erupted. 'This is a farce. The bullets prove nothing. They could come from anywhere.'

'I'm afraid not,' Jack pointed out mildly. 'They were removed from Mr Karlsson's pockets by Susan Taggart at Snowdrift Nursing Station when she tagged his personal effects. Doctor John McPherson had reason to suspect the state of mind of a patient who had just attacked a polar bear, so he confiscated them without appreciating their significance.'

He held up the sachet and inspected the contents. 'I crimp and pack my own cartridges. Anyone in Snowdrift can identify these as mine.' The Winchester's standard .30-.30 ammunition was ineffective at shooting caribou at more than 100 yards' range, obliging him to use a heavier grain. 'And I think a simple forensic test will prove they were handled by Mr Karlsson.'

He wondered how far he could push his luck. 'Leaving aside the question of malicious libel for the moment. . . .' The panel watched mesmerized as he patted his pockets absent-mindedly before retrieving a sheaf of papers. 'I'm sure you gentlemen would like to see photocopies of the statement I made on the incident to Sergeant James Elias of Snowdrift RCMP on the day I evacuated Mr Karlsson to hospital. You'll be familiar with the breaches of the Wildlife Acts, but I'd be happy to explain the criminal issues.'

The panel members silently accepted the folded affidavits. Jack was determined to retain the initiative during the endgame. 'Of course,' he said diffidently, 'the tribunal would have been spared embarrassment if Mr Masters had bothered to elicit an explanation before pursuing this hearing.'

Masters, he noticed, had turned the colour of his hair.

Jack had not finished. He patted his dictaphone. Its red light gleamed unwaveringly. He held the panel's full attention. 'Which brings us to my earlier question. Mr Karlsson, do you understand the penalties for perjury?'

The Swede tore his gaze from the recording machine and stood up. With all the dignity he could muster, he strode to the door.

'Oh, one more thing, Sverker.' The big man froze, refusing to look back.

The Hollywood line was irresistible. 'I wouldn't leave the country just yet.'

The raven hooked its claws on to a telegraph wire, whizzed around once and threw itself into the sky, where it flapped about before returning to cackle from its perch. Jack watched its antics bleakly from the waiting-room window. Jonas was right, he thought. Pride before a fall. I've spread the hubris too thick.

A disciplinary hearing normally ruminated for weeks before delivering judgment, but not a voice had been raised when Jack invited the panel to retire and consider their verdict. He remained puzzled by the alacrity of the department's response to a rich man's complaint.

When Sullivan, the taciturn panel member, slipped into the room he had a feeling he was about to find out. He knew the man by reputation as a fixer, one of the Irish mafia from Yellowknife.

Close up, the executive was small and sweaty, exuding menace and unctuousness in equal degrees. 'OK, Jack, you've had your fun. Done your dirties and rubbed our noses in it. Sure, you'll get an apology with all the trimmings. Kermit's going to be twitching on a hotplate for a while. But I want an assurance that you're going to drop this criminal business against Mr Karlsson.'

'Who is he?' Jack held Sullivan's gaze.

'A very big cheese in construction. He could roll over you.'

'He didn't. You mean he could roll over you.'

Sullivan sighed. 'OK, facts-of-life time. Karlsson Construction is a big player in Nunavut. Forget all the bullshit about Inuit building quotas: we need outside contractors and Karlsson gets the job done, on the nail. There's no way the powers-that-be are going to let him be arraigned, or given one iota of bad publicity.'

'It may be too late for that.'

'What do you mean?' Sullivan paled.

'Nothing sinister. You know how it is, Ted. When a criminal report goes into the system, word leaks out. I've taken a couple of media calls and pleaded ignorance.'

Something recalibrated behind Sullivan's eyes. 'All right, you've got us over a barrel with our pants down. What do you want?'

What do I want? Jack wondered. He harboured his own doubts about prosecuting Karlsson. The publicity could frighten off trophy hunters, upon whom many communities depended.

'I want to save the government some money,' he replied.

'Good, good.' Sullivan was actually rubbing his hands together. Then his face fell. 'You want Masters sacked?'

'No, I'd miss our friendly chats. Think polar bear tagging for a moment, Ted. At present the government pays over a hundred and twelve thousand a year on helicopter charter fees. The hunters' association of Snowdrift will do the same job for half the cost, say sixty thousand. Of course there are other incidentals. . . .'

Sullivan beamed. 'Let's say seventy thousand.' He grasped Jack's hand in his sweaty paw. 'Deal.'

The reconvened hearing was short and to the point. Koonoo recited a prepared text while Masters' fixed stare burned a hole in the table.

'We find the charges against Jack Walker to be unfounded and ill-conceived. We sincerely apologize for any stress or anxiety this inquiry may have caused. Furthermore, the department undertakes to conduct an urgent review of complaints procedures in the light of deficiencies brought to light at this hearing.'

A man cannot be too careful in the choice of his enemies, Jack thought.

CHAPTER 15

OUTSIDE, THE RAVEN was gone. With a jaunty stride, Jack set off towards a book store in the Arctic Ventures building, but then he stalled on a street corner and found himself examining the back of an envelope. Iqaluit had no street names, and Anna Algona had supplied him with a description rather than an address. Soosie's house was a good half a mile distant, he reckoned.

As he walked past the new government buildings and luxury apartments, his euphoria seeped away. Large-scale government had little relevance to Eskimos who still related to small family groups, he reflected. He had once met John Amagoalik, revered as the father of Nunavut, and had been stirred by his words: 'We're not trying to break up Canada. We're trying to join Canada.' But the monstrous apparatus that was clanking in place to mesh with the global economy seemed dangerously out of scale with ordinary people's needs.

The house was in a near-derelict neighbourhood. Jack checked the number and paused. It was odd, he thought, that after imagining this moment for thirteen years he felt detached.

At last, his knock was answered by a young Inuit woman whose face seemed to have been designed for chopping wood. Searching her features, Jack could find no match with the profile he remembered.

'I'm looking for Soosie Aglukark,' he said.

'She's not here.'

Jack switched to Inuktitut. 'I'm an old friend, hoping to see her before catching my aeroplane.'

Recognizing his northern dialect, the woman mellowed. Soosie would be home at in a quarter of an hour. He could wait.

He went into a small lounge and stood by the window, inspecting each ornament in the room for evidence of Soosie's touch. He recognized his calm as the kind he experienced during a caribou hunt. At length the outer door banged. Silence. He was looking out the window when her reflection swam abruptly into focus.

She had slipped into the room and stood contemplating him silently. He took in the trim figure in jeans and an embroidered leather waistcoat, then his gaze flew to her face. Soosie's upturned nose and lustrous eyes had always reminded him of an inquisitive seal pup, but now her sleek features were touched by maturity and, he realized, a sad beauty.

Without thinking, he went to embrace her, but her outstretched hand stopped him. It was a formal handshake that became a gesture for him to sit. She remained standing.

'What do you want, Jack?' She continued to regard him solemnly.

Unable to reply, he heard within himself the hollow sound of a retreating sea.

'Isn't this call rather belated?'

He had to put words in the air. 'Thirteen years is a long time.'

She weighed the statement and, finding it threadbare, let it fall to the ground between them. Gently, she crossed her arms.

'I heard you came back to the north four years ago, Jack. You were in Yukon, then here in Iqaluit and now Snowdrift. Didn't they teach you to write postcards at your private school?'

He could find no response.

'Maybe you were ashamed to tell your English friends you had an Eskimo stepsister who eats whale fat? I guess a native in the family didn't look too good in the Mounties either. So tell me, Jack. Why now?'

He felt a caul of misery tighten around him. What could he say? That people believed her father was still alive? That he didn't want her to come to Snowdrift? That she was the only person capable of understanding what he had become?

The lie proclaimed itself the moment he spoke. 'I heard you'd applied for a job in Snowdrift. I wondered if there's anything I could do.'

She let the silence stretch between them and then sighed impatiently. 'Thanks for dropping by, Jack, but I've got work to do. Please give some warning before you think of coming again.'

He stood awkwardly, but she was gone. Held by the force of his self-loathing, he looked at the doorway blindly, praying she would reappear. He was unprepared when she did, stumbling across the room to put her arms around him. 'I've missed you for so long, Jack,' she whispered. He held her tightly, feeling sobs shake her frame.

I'm like a ghost, Jack thought, living on borrowed time. He felt sorrow giving way to the old guilt. He had given no thought to Soosie's future when he killed her father.

Aglukark's murder was not premeditated – at least, there was no point at which the details had been carefully formulated, Jack told himself. He had seen an opportunity and then exploited a statistical likelihood that, even if the truth was revealed, could not be laid at the door of a 15-year-old. This calculation had not diminished the guilt he carried throughout his life.

The opportunity had arisen during a halt. The family, more divided than ever after Jack's display of violence, were travelling by sled to the spring-time seal grounds at the far end of Victoria Sound. At Elizabeth's insistence, his stepfather had bought a new snowmobile with his outpost subsidy. Jack, consigned to driving duties, looked back to check all were aboard and saw Aglukark retrieving an object from the ice. One foot, Jack noticed, was encircled by a coil of the tow rope. Without hesitating, he pushed the throttle to maximum.

The snap of bone and Aglukark's cry were almost simultaneous. The shaman was flung across the ice like a doll, landing badly on the side of his head. Elizabeth had been hysterical, cradling the baby and screaming at Jack while Soosie looked on, wide-eyed.

Aglukark's leg was broken in two places, he noted with grim satisfaction. The shaman drifted in and out of consciousness, prompting Elizabeth to demand that they pitch camp there and then. No Eskimo would have chosen the site. The proximity of cliffs topped by heavy snow cover made it a potential death trap in spring, when warmer temperatures created unstable layers of ice and snow. To compound the danger, the spot was known for extreme winds.

Jack should have said something. For all Elizabeth's attempts to master Inuktitut and adopt Inuit ways, her land skills were negligible. His intention had been merely to incapacitate his stepfather for Soosie's sake. Yet as he studied the darkening sky, another possibility uncoiled in his mind.

Soosie helped him to secure the main tent and settle her father on a bed of furs. It was not difficult to rekindle a blazing row with his mother that allowed him to stalk out, aggrieved, with Soosie. He led her 200 yards on to the fjord ice, where, with practised skill, they began to construct an *iglu-viga*.

It took them less than an hour. Jack selected a snowdrift deposited by a single storm and inscribed a large circle on the ground. Using a long saw, he cut out trapezoid-shaped blocks of snow from within the circle, leaving a sunken interior. With Soosie standing inside to support the rising structure, he built an ascending, inwardly leaning spiral, finally adding a keystone-shaped linchpin at the top that made the unit self-supporting. While he cut a low entrance facing away from the prevailing wind, Soosie scooped up snow shavings to fill the cracks.

They settled down in sleeping bags, watching the glow of the stove and listening to the rising wind. Aglukark had sometimes appealed to Sila, the weather spirit, to bring calm skies but he had no incantation to summon a ferment. Jack remembered his entreaty to Sedna, the half-woman, half whale, who governed the animals from beneath the sea. It was a potent spell that compelled killer whales to drive terror-stricken narwhals into the shallows. Jack's scorn for his stepfather's incantations had surrendered one summer before the spectacle of thirty small whales beached upon a single shore. Now he addressed the same invocation to Sila. Send your worst, he prayed.

It came all too soon, a massive wind that made the snowhouse shudder and wrung an alarmed cry from Soosie. Ordering her not to move, he snatched up the snow saw and ran outside. Bent double, his back to the icy blast of air that threatened to pluck him off his feet, he cut new blocks and began to build a second outer wall to shield the *igluviga*.

At first he was aware of a muffled rumble behind him and, as he turned, it became a roar. He watched appalled. What had begun as an avalanche was now a river of snow gushing from the cliff tops as the plateau's covering was stripped by the violent air flow. White spume, fifty yards across, cascaded in an arc on to the ground far below. The tent had vanished.

Looking around, he found Soosie standing transfixed. She gave him a penetrating stare.

'I'm sorry I never wrote.'

Soosie looked up at his troubled face. 'It's nothing that can't be mended,' she replied softly. Taking him by the hand, she led him down to the lounge.

Tentatively, they laid out the jigsaw pieces of their lives. Jack skated over his time in England and forced a smile from her with his account of arresting a drunken truck driver in Dawson.

Soosie told how she was dispatched below the tree-line to a mission school in Yellowknife, the capital of the North-West Territories and an Indian tribal centre where Inuit were not welcomed.

'Most of the kids were Dogrib Indians. I called them Doglegs. You can imagine how popular I was. When they finished beating me up it was the turn of the nuns. They found out my dad was an *angatkuq* so naturally it was their duty to drive out the pagan devils.'

Jack was rapt, marvelling how a self-effacing girl had become this confident, articulate woman. After Yellowknife, Soosie went on, she studied for a sociology degree in Toronto. 'I could never get used to the people or the heat. There was no ice or seals. I just wanted to come home.'

Then a long spell of social work in Pond Inlet had led to a more responsible position in Iqaluit. 'I'm working on a domestic violence programme. Have you seen those posters, 'Think before you hit your loved ones because they love you'? It's terrible, Jack. It's as if people are standing on two ice floes, tradition and modern life. It's OK if they can keep balanced, but too many are falling through. Sometimes it seems suicide is the only control people have over their lives.'

Jack caught the note in her voice. 'And it's getting to you?'

Her face hardened. 'We never had these problems in the old days, but now we're in the trap of the *qallunaat*. People were stupid to believe the whites would go away when we got self-government. The politicians told them, "If we make mistakes we will have no one to blame but ourselves." Instead, there are more white people than ever, building nice homes for themselves and running everything. Until we get rid of them, we can never sort out our problems.'

Feeling awkward at her change of tone, Jack made sympathetic noises. As if sensing his embarrassment, Soosie bowed her head so that long wings of glistening hair brushed her cheeks. 'I'm drowning, Jack. It's like holding back the sea. I want to go to a smaller place where I can make a difference.'

'Like Snowdrift?'

She shook her head. 'I applied for a job on impulse, but I had second thoughts. You never got in touch, so I guessed you wouldn't want me around. There's another vacancy in Cape Dorset.'

Jack felt like a man with a newly restored limb only to be threatened with another amputation. He thought of all the things he wanted to say and how trite they would sound. They vied with other thoughts. Would Soosie reveal his secret? How much did she understand about his part in her father's death?

Soosie watched the play of emotions on his face. Eventually he faced her squarely, his conflict resolved.

'Soosie, come home.'

She drove him to the airport in her tiny Chevy. They hugged at the departures gate. He felt somehow lighter.

CHAPTER 16

THE ANNOUNCEMENT OF a public meeting had given outlying families little notice to abandon their spring camps, but the school gymnasium was three-quarters full. Jack looked across the seated assembly, noting a good turnout by hunters and elders. It would be the old tug-of-war between tradition and progress, mirroring Inuit ambivalence about the modern world, he guessed. Although the aim of the meeting was to reach a consensus, the issue exposed a jagged fault line in the village. He could sense Jonas quivering, seated bolt upright, in the adjoining chair.

The chairman of the hamlet council kicked the meeting off with a dry outline of the archaeological project. Matthew Taqtu had made his money working on oilrigs in the Beaufort Sea – a status reflected by his gold inlays – and although still in his forties he sat on the elders' panel in juvenile court. He affected not to notice two children who noisily played tag in front of his table; no one was bothered. Taqtu stressed the safeguards and guarantees that would be put in place. He called on the economic development officer to give his assessment.

Jonas, in a spruce suit enhanced by half-a-dozen pens and pencils in his breast pocket, made no attempt at an objective evaluation. 'Do you remember how Nunavut was going to make us all millionaires?' he demanded. 'We dreamed about that pot of gold Ottawa promised us, a "compensation kitty" of one and a quarter billion dollars. We'd already put in our orders for new snowmobiles and holidays in Florida.'

The audience's laughter was tinged with remorse.

Jonas pressed on. 'Well, it turned out to be baloney. The money was tied up in a trust fund and even if you parcelled it out, everyone would end up with fifteen hundred dollars a year – half the cost of an HF radio.

'Nunavut passed us right on by. What became of decentralization? Government ministries were relocated to other communities, but they said Snowdrift was too remote. Other settlements struck fat deals with mining companies,but what happens here? Snowdrift's mine closes down.'

Jack noticed that his friend's oratory was lifting him up on his toes. Jonas stabbed the air with a pencil. 'Here's the bottom line. It's called the poverty line and by any Canadian standard this community is below it. The bulk of our livelihood comes from the land, because we can't afford to buy meat in the store. After the 1972 anti-sealing campaign, our average incomes went from fourteen thousand dollars a family to zero in a year. We've come up with alternatives, but we're going under.'

Ostentatiously, Jonas folded up his notes. 'I'm asking you to look at this project as a short-term economic proposition. It isn't going to make us millionaires, but it will give us jobs. The *qallunaat* need supply drivers, construction workers, cooks, maintenance men and translators. We'll set up a commercial arm of the Hunters' and Trappers' Association that will give equal shares of the profits to all. The wolf's at the door and we don't have the luxury of walking away.'

Jonas sat down to a smattering of applause. Jack patted him on the back, suppressing his reservations at such a naked appeal to self-interest.

An elderly man hoisted himself up and fixed the chairman with rheumy eyes. Jack recognized him as John Ulayoukuluk's brother, Philip. His strong voice filled the hall. 'Hainiliak has said the wolf is at the door. When I was a young man, I hunted wolves, but they were too smart to be caught in traps or stone dead-falls. So we made a bait, which was kind of cruel. As cruel as the wolf. We took a small strip of whale baleen, sharpened it at both ends and folded it like a spring until it was frozen solid. Then we hid the sinew inside a piece of blubber and left it where a wolf was sure to eat it.

'Inside the wolf's stomach, the spring warmed up and straightened out so the pointed ends cut the flesh and made it bleed to death. It was a trap no wolf could escape. So we have to look carefully at what is before us today. Is there a spring inside? If the *qallunaat* find what they are looking for, many southerners will come to see it. They like to drink alcohol and walk wherever they want. Can we control them? That is all I have to say.'

Another aged voice chimed in from the back of the hall. 'If we live on money alone we destroy ourselves and the land. Money makes people greedy, it makes them take advantage of each other and separates the young from the old. Our ancestors taught us something: they didn't understand economics but they understood sharing.'

A murmur of approval lapsed into several seconds' silence that was broken by a man speaking Inuktitut in rasping tones. 'I was listening to *naalaut*, the machine to hear things from. The radio said the white men like to steal the bodies of native people from graves and put them in houses for people to look at. How can we know they will not take away the bodies of the old people from Ituquvik? Can the striped one tell us?'

People were looking at him, Jack realiized with a start. The man's derogatory term, *pukitalik*, referred to the striped trousers of Mounties.

Was that how they still saw him? He noticed the Revd David Kalluk smiling at him encouragingly. It gave him an idea.

'There's been a lot of talk about wolves today,' he began. 'I'm sure the vicar will correct me, but I seem to remember that Saint Francis of Assisi met a wolf once. He spoke to it and reformed it. And you know what? The wolf apologized for its ways, and for the rest of its days it ate grass. Maybe that's what we should do – grow some grass and sell it.'

The idea of grass surviving at these latitudes convulsed his audience with laughter. Jack thought quickly. The trick of his polemical articles was to put forward the adverse proposition first. 'Before Nunavut, every idea that came into this community was brought from outside,' he said. 'With self-government, people won't accept any concept from outside without the community taking the decisions.

'It is right to be concerned about how this plan will impact on tradition. Can jobs be weighed against damage to the environment or greater distance between the young and old? These are questions to be raised a long way down the road, when we know the result of this limited excavation. Then is the time to hold another public meeting to decide what should be done.'

Going into detail, he explained how the contract drawn up by Jonas locked the archaeologists into protecting and restoring the site. The ancient habitations would be fenced off; any violation would trigger penalty clauses and instant closure of the project.

Time to wind up. 'The Inuit had good mentors, their elders. If there was an obstacle, they looked at ways of getting around it. But this is just a bump on the ice. No one's going to fall through a crack.'

His rhetoric won a long round of applause, after which the debate became desultory and the chairman brought the meeting to a close. No vote was taken; a decision would emerge via the elders.

David Kalluk was waiting for him at the exit. 'I hadn't realized you were so up on your saints, Jack. It was a good parable, and it was clever of you to let people work out the bit you left out.'

'What's that?'

The vicar laughed. 'The Lord helps those who help themselves.'

Odette Blanchard lived in that grey hinterland of east Oxford between Iffley Road and Cowley Road that had become a rookery of first-time buyers and impoverished students. The expedient purchase of a spacious semi in the unfashionable quarter allowed her to retain a weekend *pied-à-terre* in her old London haunts.

This geographical division accurately reflected her two lifestyles: filial duty in London and a career in Oxford. A small flat in Belsize Park allowed her to keep an eye on her increasingly eccentric mother in a nearby semi.

Marie-Yvette Blanchard had paid, packed and followed her civil-engineer husband to hydroelectric projects around the world until he died in his early fifties, leaving his wife and daughter a handsome sum and the mental outlook of displaced persons.

As a student at St Hilda's, Odette had been marked out by a gift for lateral thinking that made interesting connections across cultures and geological time. Remarkably, history and archaeology were still seldom combined as a unified discipline, and her insights had established her as a coming star at Paddy's informal lectures.

In was not her intellect that had attracted the head of her faculty. Tender and astute, Jon Hall still had the looks of a young Roman senator blessed with a flopping mane of black hair. It was a story of Machiavellian betrayal that still left her with cold fury. Claiming to be concerned about the marriage of a senior colleague who was conducting an academic flirtation with a visiting female professor, Jon had prevailed on Odette to phone the wife anonymously with a warning that something was going on. Instead of saving the marriage, her call had primed its destruction. When the senior colleague moved to a new posting in Canada, Jon had appropriated his job and then his wife, who turned out to be young and extremely attractive. Odette's reaction, prompted by her French genes, had been violent: she had hit him with his own cricket bat. The bruises had kept him away from work for a week.

The reckoning came soon enough. Doors closed and her funding dried up; as Paddy was fond of saying, academic patronage was of truly Tudor proportions. Paddy had been one of the first scholars to establish an independently funded research office outside the university, and when he took early retirement and emeritus professor status two years previously he needed an organizer and site director to pursue his projects full-time. Odette fitted the bill perfectly.

The betrayal still hurt. She didn't think of herself as promiscuous, rating loyalty above looks and intellect, but was forced to concede she now raised the bar to a level that few men could clear so that she probably seemed sardonic and standoffish.

Hands-on archaeology was proving to be more of an intellectual challenge than she had imagined. Paddy's choice of 'hot' sites put her at the cutting edge of medieval history, where her facility at reinterpretation made her a welcome contributor to *Archaeology Now*.

A week after her return to Heathrow, Snowdrift still held her in its enchantment. A village in a time warp, isolated in the endless snows and populated by kind people leading meaningful lives. She envied Jack's sense of belonging and the ease with which he walked through the Looking Glass into the Eskimo world. He seemed to have three personalities, switching from English understatement to Canadian bluntness and then to the quick-fire humour of Inuktitut. She remembered him waggling his fingers to enact an episode that reduced Simon to helpless laughter, something to do with a helicopter and a bear.

Jack's description of summer tugged at her: flocks of fulmars and kitti-wakes wheeling over thousands of whales whose mottled skins coiled like serpents through the arctic waters. Which was why she was pulling out all the stops to get the excavation under way. The obstacles were daunting. A wholly British expedition was a non-starter. While Italy, France and Germany could mount such long-range undertakings, British overseas archaeology had withered under government neglect over the previous twenty years. The funds could be found, but not immediately.

An international collaboration, on the other hand, offered diplomatic and cost benefits. There were Canadian and American sensitivities to appease, which meant both countries would have to be brought on board.

Paddy almost danced a jig on receiving Odette's first nugget of informa-tion: Cornell University was fielding an archaeological team at a pre-Dorset site on the Arctic Coast. 'You darling girl. Cornell's the only US university doing Viking and medieval archaeology. Their man Professor Klein's an old Trinity colleague: he'll want a hand at the card table. Well done!'

After this outbreak of high spirits, Paddy assumed his most gnomic mode, vanishing to London with a muttered explanation about 'back chan-nels' and 'big men'. Odette thought his terminology unfortunate, but if anyone could finesse the deal it was Paddy, she thought.

No sooner had he departed than Jack phoned. His tone was different, almost carefree. It was a short conversation to the effect that the hamlet council had agreed to the excavation, subject to stringent conditions that he was listing in a fax.

It was a long document, formulated as a contract that revealed canny negotiating skills. Odette whistled. It called for a flat payment of $40,000 to the community and stipulated rates of pay for local labour on the site, plus resupply costs by sled, air and boat. Each mode of transport would give way to the next as the ice broke up. The food and fuel bills were the highest Odette had encountered, reflecting astronomic air freight charges in the High Arctic. Factoring in the ravenous appetite of the American team, she prepared a breakdown of the figures and e-mailed them to Paddy.

After four days, he returned triumphant. Cornell had agreed to divert seven students from its Arctic Coast dig, including an engineer skilled in operating heavy-duty plant. On the Canadian side, Parks Canada and the Royal Ontario Museum were providing academic ballast, their proprietorial instincts tamed by fear of upsetting native sentiment in the new Eskimo homeland. An Irishman at the helm would be the ideal compromise, they concurred.

Crucially, Paddy had tapped a cornucopia of funds. Retaining control of an excavation meant controlling the purse strings, and he had located an independent source of prodigious generosity. For decades the Norse Foundation in London had muddled along, producing an annual magazine of dubious quality and distributing modest sums to small archaeological projects. For the past two years, however, new management and Scandinavian backing had transformed the foundation into a major player. Paddy's contact at Canada House had made the introduction and the rest had been plain sailing.

One aspect of the meeting left him slightly perplexed. 'They imposed one condition,' he reported to Odette. 'They want to send out their own moderator. A referee! Can you imagine? It's highly irregular, but a small price to pay, I suppose.'

They set in a provisional start date of 29 May, a slender ten days away. Mobilizing to the short deadline would impose a crushing weight, resting mostly on Odette's shoulders. 'Never mind, my dear. Think of it as ten days that—'

The telephone's insistent summons cut him off. Odette answered it, listening for several minutes before pulling a face. 'It's *The Times*. They're writing an article about the expedition. They want to know why you're trying to prove the Vikings sailed to China.'

'Holy Mary, Mother of God!'

Jack found an incoherent fax from Paddy, scrawled by hand, waiting for him at home at midday. The accompanying *Times* article was a half-page spread, cut down to two A4 sheets. Beneath the banner headline VIKINGS TOOK THE FAST BOAT TO CHINA were graphics depicting a horned Viking warrior, a longboat, an inset panel and a large map with arrows snaking from Norway to China via Iceland, Greenland, Baffin Island and the North-West Passage.

'*The Vikings planned to use America as a stepping stone to China according to a sensational archaeological find that rewrites the history of the New World,*' the article began.

The discovery of a Viking site beside the North-West Passage, the fabled short-cut to ancient Cathay, showed that the Norsemen intended to sail across the top of America and reach China nearly 300 years before Marco Polo.

In seeking a western route to the Orient, the Vikings have presented the first evidence of their cartographic understanding that the world was round, anticipating European geographers by centuries.

Jack groaned. Skimming through the article, he found its source in the tenth paragraph. 'According to the Swedish daily newspaper *Stjäna*, a British expedition led by Patrick O'Connor, emeritus professor of Norse history and archaeology at Oxford University, will seek to prove the Vikings' Chinese connection.'

Karlsson had wasted little time, he realized, feeding the story to one of his papers and adding a spin that would prove irresistible. The Chinese angle was inspired, he had to admit. *The Times*'s stringer in Stockholm had picked it up and flashed it to London, where it had been rehashed and padded out. It could be the start of a feeding frenzy, he realized.

He found Paddy quoted briefly towards the end. His defensive statement did not amount to an emphatic denial: '*It is conceivable that the Greenland Vikings were aware that the North-West Passage was a migratory route for Eskimoan peoples. But their precise motives must remain pure conjecture until we have had a chance to evaluate the site.*'

Jack glanced at his watch. It would be 7.15 a.m. in England, but he doubted that Paddy would be enjoying the sleep of the just.

He wasn't. Paddy let out a string of apoplectic oaths. 'This is a very damaging piece of mischief, Jack. No scholar in his right mind would give any credence to it. It makes us look like amateur buffoons. I must get a correction printed.'

'That's not how it works, Paddy,' Jack demurred. 'The hare is out and the press will run after it, whatever you do. The trick is to split the pack by releasing another hare that's just as plump and juicy. Eventually most of them will pursue the second quarry because we'll be there marking the way.'

'Yes, I see. What sort of diversion did you have in mind? Does Odette have to dress up as a belly-dancer?'

Jack had already sketched out a plan. 'Look, I know *The Times*'s features editor. I'll offer him the real story. Personalizing it will carry more clout than the dry views of academics. While we've got people's attention, we explain the expedition in its proper context.'

'You think they'll drop all this China nonsense?'

'Not entirely. Once it's in the media's fossil record they'll feel bound to keep trotting it out. It's up to us to keep the initiative.'

'Good. I'll sleep easier for that. Oh, Maeve asks how cold it is there.'

Jack looked out across the bay. 'It's a sweltering 15° below. Better pack your summer clothes.'

CHAPTER 17

THE WOLF TROTTED in a straight line across the sea ice between two points of land. The luxurious tangle of white guard hair at its throat stood out sharply in Jack's binoculars. He could see the stiff winter tufts of hair sprouting between its footpads, protection from the ice.

Some instinct prompted him to glass the slopes ahead, where the flicker of legs betrayed a small caribou herd on the run. Moving the glasses higher, he detected three sets of sharp ears protruding above a tumble of rocks. The lone wolf was driving the herd into an ambush.

He felt unsettled by the scene for some reason. He slipped a camera strap around his neck and edged the snowmobile forward, keeping the engine note low. Unconcerned, the wolf stared at him over its shoulder, allowing him to approach within thirty-five yards until the camera's whirring auto-winder sent it loping forwards.

'Good hunting,' he murmured. There would be a den nearby, he guessed. Tundra wolves were less territorial than their cousins below the tree-line, but the pack would be working to support a litter of perhaps seven newborn cubs ensconced on a sandy lookout.

He swung the machine around and set a course for the mine. The workings had opened in 1974, sixty years after an English prospector discovered heavy deposits of lead and zinc beneath a mountain known as Nasallugannguag, in tribute to its hat-like shape. The company had pulled out in the late 1990s, leaving an empty settlement haunted by a few Inuit.

The fierce winds that tore through the camp had given rise to a curious architecture of curved exterior walls that lent the miners' houses the accidental appearance of igloos. They were clustered around a large steel complex that had once cradled a school, post office, health centre and government offices.

It was this outer shell that interested Jonas Hainiliak. Professor O'Connor's wish-list called for living-quarters and a permanent structure to protect the archaeological site after it had been breached. The complex's metal panels, together with their inner scaffolding, could be reassembled in shapes of variable geometry.

Under the direction of four construction workers, loaned by the public housing office, twenty Inuit laboured to unbolt sections and load them onto a mobile crane and trailer, hired from the PWD.

Jonas was nibbling a sandwich from a packed lunch as Jack climbed up beside him in the crane cab.

'Hi, Jack, I reckon we're going to lose this lot through the sea ice.'

Jack grinned. 'That's the spirit. Doesn't anything ever depress you?'

Jonas regarded him blankly. He was wearing a bright yellow ensemble today, with matching helmet.

'Quit worrying, Jonas. The ice hasn't started to candle yet, but you're pushing it close. Another week and the leads will be open. You'll have this pile of junk down there inside a couple of days.'

'And we won't see it again until freeze-up. That's what's worrying me, Jack: we don't have a boat big enough to ship the crane back. You know what the hire charges are for three months? That's a very inefficient use of plant.'

'Sure, but it's someone else's money.'

Jonas's mouth tightened so that the tips of his moustache almost met under his chin. 'That's the point: it isn't. We haven't seen a cent of the Norse Foundation money. I had to raise a loan on their promises. If the nutty professor wasn't your friend I'd call off the damn circus now.'

Jack frowned. 'I'll chase it up. There's something else we should think about. We may be receiving a visit from the gentlemen of the press.'

He had already fielded several calls from newspapers eager to follow up *The Times* story. The British media were reluctant to be dislodged from the North-West Passage angle, while the Americans had latched on to the aspect of continental discovery that stroked their own national preoccupations.

'Could this site be older than the Vinland site in Newfoundland?' a New York journalist had demanded. Jack wasn't prepared to hazard a guess, attempting to explain the margin of error in radiocarbon dating. 'So it could be the oldest Viking site in North America,' the reporter concluded perversely.

Other calls followed a similar pattern. Most wanted to send staffers immediately. Jack's insistence that there would be little to report and less to photograph until Paddy's team arrived was not believed. Many would be packing their bags right away.

Jonas slumped at the hideous prospect unfolding before his eyes. 'The hotel's full. How're we going to deal with them?'

Jack patted his knee. 'Here's where you recoup your bank loan. Put up some luxury tents with heaters and charge them double. Open the village hall as a press room. These aren't back-packers and tree-huggers who bring their own biscuits. Newspaper expenses are limitless, as long as you keep giving them receipts. *Tukisiviit?*'

'Sure. Thanks, Jack. I hear Soosie's coming back.'

'Yeah, she's staying with me for a few days until the nurse's house becomes vacant. She's flying in this evening.'

'You think that's wise?'

Jack glanced at his friend. 'Wise that she's coming back, or that she's staying with me?'

Jonas began playing with the cab's control panel. 'There's a lot of talk about her father. He's meant to be walking around and you two are getting together. It seems strange.'

A red light throbbed on the dashboard. Jack switched it off. 'What are people saying?'

Jonas sighed. 'Before he died, Aglukark is supposed to have made a prophecy. He said that one day a hole would open in the ground. Out of it would pour a wave of happiness, followed by a wave of misery. Then people would turn back to the old religion and his spirit would be there to guide them. Baloney!'

'So where do Soosie and I fit in?'

'As his helpers, I guess.'

Soosie arrived like a conquering general. '*Tavva vugut*! Here I am!' she cried. Apart from the decorum of her outfit, a traditional white tunic of embroidered wool, Jack had difficulty connecting this effervescent spirit with the sombre woman of recent memory.

'Oh, stop the car, Jack. There's Auntie Rose. I'll only be a moment.'

She ran into the arms of a matronly figure amid cries of mutual delight. Bemused, he halted for two more joyful reunions on the short drive from the airstrip. He wondered what Jonas was fretting about.

No sooner had he carried her suitcase to her room than she was off again, promising to return for dinner in two hours' time. He was slicing caribou steaks with a crescent-shaped *ulu* blade when the phone rang. It was *The Times*. They wanted another thousand words. 'Great stuff. It's scheduled for the front.'

Another ring, this time an irritating NBC interviewer who stuck resolutely to his list of ill-informed questions.

'You have a good day,' the presenter said at last.

'Sorry, I've made other arrangements.'

Taking the phone off the hook, he finished preparations for the meal.

Soosie breezed in, sniffed the cooking appreciatively and leaned against the sink. 'It's so nice to have a big brother taking care of me again.'

'I see. Madam must give me a list of her culinary and cleaning requirements.'

She watched him pensively. 'Jack, what's happened to Snowdrift?'

He reached for a saucepan. 'How do you mean?'

'Well, on the surface it's the same sleepy old place. I've been away for thirteen years and people ask me if I've had a nice holiday.' She laughed. 'But it's going to the dogs, literally. The dog population's going up and the youngsters are leaving as quickly as they can.'

Jack examined a tiny store cauliflower for mould. 'It's the same all over the world, Soosie. The kids head for the bright lights, leaving behind the middle-aged and the old.'

His stepsister stirred impatiently. 'Yes, girls maybe. But a certain number of boys always went hunting with their fathers so they understood the Inuktitut way of life. That doesn't seem to happen much any more. And a lot of the men only go hunting at the weekend.'

Jack grinned. 'You've been talking to the women. They don't want the menfolk underfoot every day. But you're right, Snowdrift is going through hard times. People can't afford to hunt if there's no market for animal by-products. But we've got plans to change that.'

Gesturing her to the table, he carried the plates over. 'Do you remember Ituquvik?'

She pulled a face and Jack suddenly glimpsed the little girl he remembered. 'The Place of the Old People? I always felt terrified there.'

He filled her in on the excavation, sketching the possibility of a tourist bonanza that could stop the exodus from the community and perhaps attract skilled people to come home.

She looked at him silently for a few seconds, then dropped her gaze. 'Jack, I know you're doing your best for the village, but have you thought this through?'

'What do you mean?'

Soosie toyed with her fork. 'I'm just thinking aloud, but isn't this plan another *qallunaat* solution to an Inuit problem? White people believe that money and economic structures are the answer to everything. I saw that in Iqaluit and the results are devastating. People aren't happy; they're miserable. Tradition is the only thing that keeps them sane, and when that's gone, they're lost.'

Jack thought she was being a little melodramatic. 'This isn't Iqaluit. And people are more resilient than you think. Remember the old days, when they grabbed whatever was on offer and made it work for them? They traded furs for saws and shaped the steel into *ulu* blades that were better than their copper ones. Rifles and skidoos meant they would never go hungry again.'

Soosie contemplated him sadly and dipped her head. 'Maybe you're right, Jack. I'm probably still suffering from big town sickness.'

They sipped their wine, allowing small talk to bridge the chasm of time. Absently, Soosie ran a finger around the rim of her wine glass, stirring a low, moaning resonance.

'Jack, people are saying they've seen Father.'

He grinned. 'I'm convinced I saw Elvis in Iqaluit; he was loading a dump truck and singing *Winter Wonderland*. No one would believe me.'

'What would you do if he came back?'

'I'd tell him about my amazing dancing chickens and become his manager.'

'Not Elvis, silly. I mean Father. What would you do?'

Searching her face, he could read no calculation beneath her curved lashes. Yet the question was loaded. He wondered again how much she remembered or understood of the events preceding Aglukark's death.

'I'd probably take him straight to hospital. After thirteen years he'd have a pretty bad case of frostbite.'

'Father never felt the cold.'

It was true. He caught a mental picture of Aglukark hauling a fishing net from an ice hole with his bare hands.

'Do you still hate him?'

He needed to know where this interrogation was going. 'Do you?'

Soosie bowed her head, the twin streams of her black hair cascading over her eyes. 'He wasn't a bad man, Jack. He became a healer to help people. He was always warning them about white people but he married a *qallunaat* who made him crazy like her. When Father disappeared, I felt my life had been stolen from me. I still do. If things had been different maybe I'd be working in a check-out now, but I'd have a husband and children instead of patching up other people's sick lives.'

There was nothing he could say. Instead, he fetched a book from the study and placed it before her. 'I went back home,' he said. 'Apart from Elizabeth's clothes, it was virtually all I could find.'

She opened the cover slowly. 'The little bear. I loved it when you read me Rupert stories.' She smiled wistfully. 'Go on, Jack, read me a story.'

He inspected his watch sternly. 'No, you've had too much excitement for one day. Little girls have to get their beauty sleep or they turn into witches. Go on, I've got one or two things to do.'

'A date?'

He shook his head. 'Nothing like that.'

Soosie folded her arms and inspected him quizzically. 'Do you have a woman, Jack?'

An honesty session between siblings was not something he was ready for. 'There's no one,' he said, falling back on a stock answer. 'I'm probably too selfish to share my life with anyone else.'

Soosie, he could see, was not going to be fobbed off. 'I can't believe that,' she said. 'You're a handsome man, Jack. Most women would kill to have you as a boyfriend. I know I would.'

He felt himself flush.

Soosie folded the book slowly and stood up, hugging it to her chest. 'I always dreamed we'd run away and you'd marry me. Don't look so shocked, we're not the same flesh and blood. But life always turns out differently.'

She took the dishcloth from his hand and put a consoling hand on his arm. 'Poor Jack. We'll just have to find a woman for you. Good night.' She stretched up and kissed him on the cheek before turning towards her room.

Turning to the washing-up, he felt pleasantly confused. He had been alone all his life but never lonely. Now the void was filling up, he ached.

That night he eschewed the fixed routines by which he hunted oblivion, closing the curtains and switching off the HF radio. When his head touched the pillow, the black rock of sleep rolled over him.

He spent the afternoon showing Levi how to log hunting yields on the computer, determined that his assistant would be a fully fledged Wildlife Officer when the Inuk returned to Coppermine in eighteen months' time. The sooner the department's dinosaurs were replaced with native staff, the better.

Returning home, he was struck by the welcoming aura that seemed to envelop the house since Soosie's arrival and he suppressed a pang of disappointment at hearing no sounds within. Without thinking, he pushed open the bathroom door and was a pace inside when he detected a presence behind the frosted glass of the shower stall. With a muttered apology he turned quickly to leave, but Soosie's voice arrested him.

'Is that you, Jack? Stay, I need to talk to you. When are you going to Ituquvik?'

He moved outside the doorway to answer, but the sudden roar of the shower spray forced him back inside to make himself heard.

'The Professor's team arrives the day after tomorrow,' he shouted, studying the pattern of the floor tiles. 'I have to take them down to the site the same day.'

Soosie adjusted the jet spray to a more tolerable level of background noise. 'So how long will you be away?'

Jack noticed a bar of soap had skidded beneath the stall and he carefully slid it back with his foot. 'It's a day's journey and then I have to settle them in. The answer is I don't know. Could be three days or a week. Why do you ask?'

'Well, I've been promised a house, but it may be a little while.' Soosie began humming a snatch of tune. 'Do you mind if I stay here until you get back?'

Her silhouette, he noticed, was slowly moving in time with the song she was singing. He recognized it dimly as a ceremonial chant. 'Of course not. You're welcome to stay as long as you like. You don't regret leaving Iqaluit?'

It was strangely pleasant chatting like this, listening to Soosie's snatches of song and watching the shadow play of her shower dance. He felt drugged by the warmth of the room which seemed to suffuse his limbs and made his face burn. He was concentrating on framing a reply to something she had said when the glass pane swung back and she stepped out wrapped in a red towel.

'Wait,' she commanded, and came to stand before him. 'I think you've been sick, Jack,' she said softly. 'You need healing.' He went to move away again but something held him fast. He searched her intense face uncomprehendingly.

'Do you remember when Elizabeth used to beat us?' she murmured, her arms meekly by her sides. They stood, inches apart, for an age. Then his arms went around her and he buried his face in her perfumed hair.

The next morning his inept attempts at making scrambled eggs left him mopping a shell and its yolk from the floor. The egg had cost a small fortune and his mother would have made him pay dearly, he remembered. What had happened last night? Somehow Soosie's singing and humming had led him into an unsuspected realm of emotion. No, it wasn't that, he recalled. It was the thrilling shock of her imitating Elisabeth's shrill voice when she used to thrash him, laced with Soosie's profanities and obscenities as she drew out his ecstacy.

His mother, he acknowledged, had twisted something inside him that blocked a normal response to women. He still associated sexual feeling with the pain of her beatings. Soosie was somehow bound up with the process. Self-punishment and self-denial had been his response to Elizabeth's sadism. Killing Aglukark, Elizabeth and her baby had reinforced a cycle of guilt and self-punishment. He had simply closed a door in his mind to carnal thoughts and gathered together some positive traits to mould an acceptable persona. He had tried to let women down gently; he supposed they thought him gay.

He had the eggs under control, but not his thoughts, when Soosie took her seat at the breakfast-table. She looked clear-eyed and demure.

'About last night,' he began.

'Don't say a word, hurry up!' she ordered with mock severity. 'You promised we'd look for *tuugaalik* today.'

They took a packed lunch and rode for two hours to an open polynia of clear water on the fjord platform where fierce currents prevented the ice from forming.

It had been Aglukark's self-proclaimed duty to sing in the first whales of summer at this spot. Soosie and Jack had always relished the occasion's suspense and mystery. Narwhals, whales with a spiralling sword, were tempted by some instinct to leave the open waters of Lancaster Sound and swim beneath the ice down Victoria Sound. Those which failed to locate breathing holes at ice cracks and polynias drowned in the attempt. The early pathfinders were critical to the mass arrival of narwhal family groups several weeks later. When they hadn't come, hunters starved in the old days.

'*Ajaijaa, aijaijaa,*' Soosie sang. It was a song of joy, addressed to the sea spirit Sedna. She spread the arms of her powder-blue cloak like a butterfly.

Jack found himself thinking again of Elizabeth. She, like Sedna, had been a cruel mother. In one story of the creation of sea mammals, Sedna was discovered having sexual relations with a dog and was banished to an island. In attempting to escape, she clasped the side of a boat, but her stepson rewarded her cruelty by cutting off her fingers, the joints falling into the water to become seals, walruses and whales. Now she reigned beneath the sea, a sometimes glimpsed half-woman, half-narwhal, her long tresses curled into the whale's corkscrew horn.

He recognized that Soosie, by intuitively re-enacting the moments when his desire had been frozen in adolescence, had found the exact note of resonance that made his emotional locks spring upon. He knew his body was over-ruling his reason and that physical infatuation was not to be confused with other feelings. Incest was not a sound basis for a relationship, a small voice counselled. There was no consanguinity in a legal sense, but it bothered him that he still thought of Soosie as his sister. Was it the reason for his attraction?

All his reading of anthropology and human affairs had left him adrift. Surrendering his independence went against his nature, yet he supposed that sex was a kind of insanity that had no place for logic. And wherever this passion led, he and Soosie would have to live with the consequences. Incest was not unknown in Inuit families, so stepsiblings who shared a bed would raise no eyebrows, he supposed. Everybody loves a lover, ran a song his father used to play on the record player. But if things went wrong, he and Soosie could not avoid each other in such a small community.

He knew next to nothing about her. He had read somewhere that women made the first move in most relationships and there had been something contrived about the bathroom scene. And then there was her attitude towards the dig. In one breath she praised and encouraged Jack for helping the community, anxious to know all the project's ramifications; in the next she was bad-mouthing the project behind his back. Soosie's contrariness was part of her appeal, one moment affectionate sibling, the next sultry lover.

'*Alianait, alianait,*' Soosie intoned, beseeching Sedna to send forth her creatures.

Jack thought of the misery his mother had released. As if reading his thoughts, Soosie joined him beside the sled, out of the bite of the wind. 'Jack, people are grateful for what you and Jonas are doing.'

'Really?' The scent of her hair was intoxicating.

'You're offering them something to look forward to, something that might change their lives. I just hope it lasts.' Before he would ask what she meant, she jumped up and ran a few paces. 'They're coming, I can feel it.'

Jack could see nothing, but Soosie's instincts had always been uncanny. 'Maybe we're too early. It's not yet *maniit.*' In June, the egg month, people would go out to gather bird eggs, the rivers would run and pods of *tuugaa-lik*, the horned whales, would arrive.

'Quiet. Look. . . .' Soosie's gaze was focused on a pressure ridge about a quarter of a mile away. A faint crack connected the ridge to the polynia.

As they stood in silence, she linked an arm with his. Abruptly, her inspection switched to the small gash of furrowed waters before them. She smiled.

A seven-foot sword broke the surface, followed by a loud blurt of expelled air and a miasma of fine spray that hazed the creature's mottled back and the heart-shaped flukes of its tail. For a few moments the sixteen foot narwhal lay inert in the narrow basin, like a submarine recharging its batteries, before tilting its horn to the sky.

'He can see us,' Soosie whispered.

'No, he's looking for a sky map to read the way forward.' Low cloud sometimes reflected open leads ahead in dark patches, but today the overhead vault was a peerless blue.

With a final salute of its sword, the whale arched its body length in a glide beneath the ice, leaving a swirl in its wake.

Jack hugged her. 'Well done. You've saved Snowdrift for another year.'

She gave him an enigmatic look. 'Not yet.'

CHAPTER 18

THE ENGINE'S SIGNATURE tune was unmistakable. The Yamaha 540 had oil injection and a loose piston ring that was trying to flail the snowmobile to death. It coughed and died.

'Come up,' Jack called.

Jonas, resplendent in a silver jump suit, appeared at the top of the stairs, nodded to Soosie and helped himself to coffee.

'You have some objection to answering the phone, Jack?'

'Yes, it's a religious thing. I've become a hunter and Trappist.'

Soosie, in sparky mode, giggled and dabbed marmalade from a corner of her mouth. She was wearing patterned jeans and a plaid shirt, her hair drawn into a single plait.

The Inuk glanced at the shadows under their eyes and sat awkwardly at the breakfast-table. 'Damn bloodsuckers wanted to break your door down last night. Said they needed words, not grub.'

'The gentlemen of the press?'

'Gentlemen is right. They all had to file stories the moment they left the plane. Half of them didn't have cold-weather gear. They froze their asses off doing interviews with anyone they could find in the street. Then their cameras jammed and they demanded a shop selling graphite lubrication. Where they hell do they think they are?'

'On a freebie, for as long as they can stretch it out. How many?'

In his agitation, Jonas began rearranging the breakfast things. 'Ten, and it's not a pretty sight, Jack. Nearly had a riot on my hands when I showed them the tents. I thought handling the press was going to be your job. I cut them off at the pass by promising you'd see them at nine in your office.'

Jack thought quickly. 'OK, I'll take them off your hands. But do me a favour, will you?

'Sure.'

'I want them out of town tomorrow when the team arrives. Can you set up a press charter for a North-West Passage flight? You know the sort of thing – the Amundsen sites around Gjoa Haven and the Franklin graves on

Beachey Island. Charge them a hundred dollars a head and they'll jump at it.'

'OK. Any news from your nutty professor?'

Jack smiled. 'He's linking up with the American team at Iqaluit and they're flying up to Resolute. They arrive here midday tomorrow and I want to get them down on the ice straight away.'

'Right.' Jonas rose, paused at the door, thought better of it and left.

Jack followed him a few minutes later. He stooped to kiss Soosie but his lips only brushed her turning cheek.

The press had made themselves comfortable in his outer office and he took a moment to assess them while he stamped his boots and hung up his coat. A good number had evidently purchased standard blue parkas from the local Co-op and Northern Stores. They were not frontline correspondents serving a news agenda, he noted with relief, but star feature writers who had mastered joined-up writing. Such skills made them no less predatory.

Naturally, their demands were impossible: each wanted an hour's interview with him followed by immediate access to the site. Grudgingly, they accepted his compromise of seeing three at a time from non-competing newspapers and stood meekly when he spelled out the ground rules on drink and harassing villagers. As he expected, their anger at a three-day delay before visiting Ituquvik dissolved at the prospect of an air tour of the North-West Passage.

His first session was with a studious Canadian, a brusque Brit and an American woman with brittle brown hair who complained about the washing facilities.

The woman insisted on going over the events in his *Times* article. 'You wrote that it was easy for Vikings to travel from Greenland to Baffin Island. What did you mean, exactly?'

'Look at this.' Jack unpinned a sheet from a wall board and placed it before them. It showed the coasts of the two islands joined by dozens of zigzag lines.

'There's Baffin Bay, a stretch of sea about two hundred miles wide between Greenland and Baffin Island. A few years ago we tracked the movement of East Baffin polar bears, using radio collars and satellites. We were trying to identify the bear population, but we discovered that a surprising number of females move back and forwards between the two islands in winter.'

The three journalists leaned forward, suddenly alive to the implications.

'My God,' the woman said. 'You mean each of these lines is a polar bear? Some of them cross over several times. Are you saying the Vikings actually walked across the ice to North America?'

'No, not at all, simply that the difficulties of such a journey have been exaggerated.'

The woman persisted. 'But it's theoretically possible?'

'Nomadic Eskimos could follow a polar bear anywhere, including moving ice. But the experts claim the Vikings lagged behind the Eskimos in survival skills and technology. I can't disagree with that.'

The trio left, content, carrying photocopies of Jack's chart. The dominant character in the next batch was a genial writer from a London broadsheet with a clear brief to rehash the glorious exploration of the North-West Passage.

Jack groaned. 'If you're looking for British heroes, you've come to the wrong place.'

The writer was intrigued. 'You don't think explorers like Frobisher and Franklin were heroic?'

'Heroes make up their own history when there's no one around to contradict them. It's called myth. You probably grew up reading about brave Mounties mushing through the northern snows, but did any of you hear of the Native Specials?'

The journalists returned blank looks.

'If you talk to some of the old people, they'll tell you a different story. The Native Specials were the invisible guys who kept the Mounties alive when they were so cold they refused to get out of their sleds. The Specials had to undo their flies when their hands were frozen.'

The Brit was the only one using shorthand. 'Go on,' he urged. 'What's your point?'

'The point is that your famous British explorers are a bit of a joke around here. Most of them never bothered to learn the language and even when they had an interpreter they often couldn't understand him. As a result, they were frequently starving, lost and dependent on the Inuit to save their hides.'

'You mean they never asked for directions?'

Jack shook his head wearily. 'They were British officers who believed the local people were ignorant savages. When they did bother to make contact, it paid dividends. In 1822, Sir John Barrow was astonished when a woman named Iligliuk drew him a detailed map of Winter Island and the mainland, showing a crucial shortcut through the North-West Passage. He's the only explorer I know who credited an Inuk with a major discovery.'

The Brit frowned. 'So you think the Inuit were unfairly left out of history?'

'Sure. Ask anyone in Snowdrift who Joe Panipakuttuk was and they'll tell you he was responsible for the first complete transit of the North-West

Passage in 1944. It had never been done before in one season. He showed Henry Larsen how to steer south of heavy ice that was blocking M'Clure Strait. There are books and exhibitions devoted to Larsen, but you won't find Panipakuttuk's name on any roll of honour.'

'What happened to him?'

'Larsen dumped him with his family and seventeen dogs on Kerschel Island and left him to make his own way back to Pond Inlet.'

An elderly American spoke up for the first time. 'I read your article about how the site was located. I'd like to do an interview with the Eskimo who found the spear.'

Jack could see no objection. 'Sure. Make Marcus famous.'

Sam coaxed the hotel's Suburban people-carrier into life and kept it idling beside the airstrip in its own cloud of steam. The Tuugaalik's owner could smell business.

'These guys are bringing Christmas early. I got reservations backed up to next year.'

Jack waved ineffectually at the fumes of the Ukranian's cigar, which occasionally spluttered like a sparkler. With more rolls of fat than a baby seal, the manager's face was an impending landslide of blubber that was anchored by the root system of his beard.

Sam and Marie usually closed the Tuugaalik in October and sat out the winter in Medicine Hat after a fortnight in Hawaii. It was no secret they had been thinking of selling up.

'Soon you'll have to pay them to stay away,' Jack responded, only half listening. He was gauging the ominous banks of low cloud that laid siege to the village. A steady breeze was keeping the elevated ground clear, but the melting ice sheet had produced a low overcast that hovered over the fjord.

'Tell me, Jack, is this Viking business a flash in the pan? Jonas says we might need a second hotel.'

Jack looked at him. 'Jonas?'

'Yeah, he's got a structure plan. Reckons if this thing is as big as the Viking site in Newfoundland we'll need a development strategy. Visitors' centre, new hotel, tourist shops, Viking trail, all those good things.'

It was news to Jack. 'Let's wait and see what the excavation turns up.'

Sam turned up the heater. 'From what I hear, you've found enough already. A lot of folks want to cash in and now is make-your-mind-up time. They can't wait. Orders for big stuff like construction must go in soon to catch the Sealift.'

The Sealift freighter from Montreal made its annual visit to Snowdrift in September, the narrow window of opportunity before freeze-up, Jack remembered. Among his earliest memories were scenes of pandemonium as wide barges ferried housing materials and the occasional vehicle from the Sound into the small bay. 'Where would they find the money?'

'Most families have something stashed away from the good years. Let's face it, there's not much to spend it on here. Plus, they've got relatives down south who can put their hands on some. Forget all that stuff about the dependency culture: if there's action in the offing, the Eskimos want a piece of it.'

'It's too early to start playing Monopoly,' Jack cautioned. 'Let the professor have the final say.'

On cue, a distant boom reverberated within the van. Jack cracked open his window and watched the Twin Otter approach. Both men held their breath as the plane began its kamikaze run at the mountainside, then banked at the last moment and plunged towards the narrow strip.

Paddy was first out, his short frame topped by an outsize sheepskin cap worthy of a Klondike prospector. A furious energy propelled him across the gravel to where Jack was standing.

'Good to see you, Jack. You're looking well. Now, we're all present and correct. I take it we're travelling to the site today?'

'There's lunch at the hotel and then we can leave as soon as you like.'

Paddy nodded briskly. 'Good, good. As quick as possible, if you please.'

He turned back to shepherd his charges into the reception hut. Jack counted seven students and caught a wave from Odette, realizing he had missed her glowing smile.

Within half an hour they were attacking impacted-rubber steaks in the hotel's dining-room while Sam danced attendance on them. The students had opted for a trestle table, leaving the grown-ups to confer among themselves.

After a few bites Paddy seemed to slump, distractedly rubbing his eyes. 'I can't seem to shake off this jet-lag,' he apologized. 'My blood sugar's all over the place. I think I need a nap.'

Jack had a quiet word with Sam, who nodded and led the professor to a newly vacated room.

Resuming his seat, Jack noticed Odette had done something to her hair. The flowing renaissance look had given way to a longish Paris bob, emphasizing the lines of her neck. She was more striking than he remembered. 'Welcome back to the land of the meat eaters,' he said.

Ruefully acknowledging the provocation, Odette glanced down at her steak. 'I wasn't always a vegetarian,' she sighed. 'I suppose I'll get used to it again.'

Lowering his voice, Jack explained the necessity of avoiding the press.

Odette agreed with surprising fervour. 'Jack, you wouldn't believe the fuss this story has created in Britain. It's open season, believe me.'

'The media?'

'Worse. As Paddy says, academe likes nothing more than pulling the wings off flies just to hear them buzz. It hasn't quite got to that, but they think they've got Paddy in a jam jar and they're queuing up for the entertainment.'

'They're attacking him directly?'

Odette shook her head and Jack observed the way her hair swung and settled back neatly into place. 'That's not how it works,' she said. 'Anyone who comes up with controversial findings always poses a threat to networks of patronage. A few important figures violently disagree with the proposition that Vikings traded directly with North America, not to mention their presence in the North-West Passage. They've got their surrogates to do their dirty work.'

'Sounds serious.'

'It is. They began by writing papers in journals, which the press picked up. Now they're putting up opponents on television and in the media. And the tragedy is that truth is always the first casualty. To date Paddy has been very careful in what he says. If we give them an opening, the heavyweights will move in.'

Odette relinquished her struggle with the steak and put down her utensils in disgust. 'I haven't told you the worst news. You know this project is contingent on the approval of a referee?'

Jack nodded.

Odette critically inspected the large glass of indeterminate purple juice before her and took a tentative sip. 'It's highly unusual, and naturally we assumed it was just a formality. The Norse Foundation people have just written to Paddy, naming their man. It couldn't be worse. They've appointed Tuan Fingest and he's arriving here this week.'

The name meant nothing to Jack. 'Tuan?'

She speared a piece of gristle. 'His real name's Sir David Fingest – buffoon, pedant and grand inquisitor. Paddy knows him of old. He made his name in the 1950s when he was a special adviser, still in his twenties, to one of the Malay sultans. He found an ancient city-state in the jungle that managed commerce across the Malay peninsula from China to the Middle East. It was something of a coup at the time, and he's been trading on it ever since.'

Odette laughed incredulously. 'After Malaysia's independence he converted to Islam and became a grand young man of Far East archaeology. Paddy says that if you can bring yourself to picture a startled bird wearing a sarong, squawking on about Malay folklore in the strangled vowels of an eighteenth-century squire, that's Tuan Fingest.'

'So why should he worry us?'

'Paddy says he's a dangerous parasite. He latched on to Viking studies about thirty years ago and he's had his hooks into Paddy ever since. He's obsessed with procedure and methodology. According to Paddy, he's basically a technician who lacks any real understanding of the human culture behind artefacts. If he analysed the contents of a present-day rubbish bin in New York, it would never occur to him that the householder might spend time watching television or going to a concert. That sort of tunnel vision has earned him a reputation as a fastidious scholar.'

As she spoke, Odette studied Jack, conscious that something had changed. The imperceptible clouds of thought that rippled across his face had vanished, she realized. In their place was a calm, more assured look that was almost playful. She sighed heavily.

'Remember what I said about networks of patronage? Most of the opposition to this project has come from Fingest's acolytes. And he is the man who can close us down.'

Jack was bemused. 'Am I missing something? Why would the foundation send someone to close you down before you've even started?'

'Elementary, my dear Walker. It's a set-up.' Odette opened a small red notebook and laid it on the table. 'I've been doing a little checking up on the Norse Foundation. Until recently they were muddling along, handing out the odd grant and sliding towards penury. When they became awash with cash two years ago, everyone assumed it was lottery money or an American backer. Well, it was neither. Does the name Karlsson Industries ring a bell?'

Jack felt he had been sucker-punched. The big Swede was evidently a better tactician than archer. After failing to remove him as a player, Karlsson had devised a more elaborate means of sabotage. 'Come into my parlour, said the spider to the fly,' he murmured.

Odette nodded. 'They rolled out the red carpet and we obligingly walked in. Now they can just pull the rug from under us.'

Another aspect puzzled Jack. 'Odette, you said it was a set-up. How could Karlsson have anticipated this situation two years ago?'

'We don't know that he did. By all accounts, he's genuinely keen on Viking excavations and funds a number of projects in Scandinavia. It's just this one he's set against. And he's left us with a ball and chain.'

Jack stopped listening and made to get up. Soosie had entered the hotel lounge and was making her way towards their table. Slipping into Paddy's empty chair, she wrinkled her nose at the rejected steak on Odette's plate and turned to Jack. 'I need to get some posters made up. OK if I use your office computer?'

Before he could open his mouth she launched into a quick-fire burst of Inuktitut that excluded Odette. 'Can you believe it, Jack, there's no domestic violence programme here and from the stories I've already heard they desperately need one. It's no good printing posters in English, they have to be in Syllabics. Can your computer handle that?'

'No, but you can draw it up by hand and use my photocopier.' Conscious of Odette's discomfort, he raised a hand to pre-empt Soosie's next outburst. 'Soosie, this is Odette Blanchard, who'll be the site director at Ituquvik. And this is my sister, Soosie, who's sorting out our welfare problems.'

Soosie did not let his omission pass. '*Step*sister,' she corrected, hugging Jack's arm and looking at him with mock adoration. 'The mayor's given me a consulting-room in the hamlet office,' she continued, as if the interruption had not occurred. 'I've told him I need something bigger and he says he'll talk to the doctor about getting some quarters in the nursing station.'

Odette, he saw, seemed bemused by this display of rudeness. 'I was just talking to Odette about a problem that's cropped up in the dig,' he said.

The two women examined each other impassively for a long second and then, as if synchronized, their gaze switched expectantly to him. His neck prickled as he also registered the stares of the construction workers, who could not hide their delight at finding themselves in the company of two such eye-catching women, one apparently straight from a Paris salon, the other exuding a sleek sexuality.

Summoning a winsome smile, Soosie turned to Odette. 'You must be very clever. I always wanted to do something like archaeology, but I seem to have an allergy.'

Odette raised an elegant eyebrow. 'Oh, what's that?'

'Dirt. When you've grown up on the land, you never want to go through that again. Jack's just the same, aren't you?'

He started. A sudden vision of Odette naked save for the red ski socks Soosie had worn last night was scrambling his thoughts. 'Come again?'

A seductive smile touched Soosie's lips. 'He hates being dirty, don't you, Jack? He's always taking showers, but for some reason he can never find the soap.'

He held the cough that threatened to erupt in the back of his throat and inspected his watch urgently. 'We have to rouse Paddy if we're going to keep to schedule,' he said hoarsely. 'Sorry, Soosie, time and tide.'

She rose from her chair. 'Just what are you digging for?' she asked Odette.

The Anglo-French woman inspected her nails before answering. 'Oh, victory,' she said.

Soosie nodded, as if confirming something. 'There is no victory in the ground, only death,' she observed, before leaning across and pecking Jack on the cheek. She rose and offered her hand to Odette. 'I'm so glad to meet you. Please feel free to drop in on Jack and me whenever you like. Our bathroom is always yours.'

Jack walked Soosie to the door. 'She's a pretty girl, but not your sort,' she said.

He watched Soosie walk away with a swaying stride, placing her deerskin mukluks confidently on the scoured gravel. Turning round, he found a Paddy similarly absorbed. 'A vision of loveliness,' he pronounced, sounding refreshed. 'Now, I take it Odette has told you about the nasty condition lurking in the small print of our contract.'

'Tuan Fingest?'

Paddy took his arm and steered him back to Odette while uttering a stage whisper, 'It gets worse. If we fail to impress Fingest sufficiently, the foundation's financial obligations cease forthwith. We – that is to say our partnership with Snowdrift – will be left with the expense of restoring the site, removing the equipment and paying the team's expenses.'

Jonas had racked up a small fortune hiring the plant and tents, Jack reflected. 'The ice won't be firm enough to get the heavy equipment back until October, so we're stuck with it. What are the options?'

Paddy buttoned his cardigan. 'We'll just have to pull a rabbit out of the hat.'

CHAPTER 19

MOST OF THE snow cover was gone from the land, exposing rank animal bones and discarded objects that would be picked up from the streets in the coming days. The archaeology team walked out onto the slippery bay ice, looking businesslike in their orange neoprene buoyancy suits and rubber waders.

'If your sled goes into the water, remember it floats,' Jack instructed. 'Stay with the sled and we'll fish you out.'

'Just try to save the grub box,' grunted Benny, whose wife had spent the morning packing sandwiches for the team. He and two other drivers formed a human chain to transfer luggage from the back of the Suburban to the four twenty-four foot *qamutiqs*.

Jonas came to watch, delicately keeping his feet out of the melt water. With an embarrassed air, he pushed a small box into Jack's hands. 'Don't left the bears get these.'

'What are they?'

The Inuk's anxious face spilt into a grin. 'Lila was making flapjacks. She thinks you don't eat enough.'

Jack was touched, guilty that he had decided to spare Jonas the worry of knowing the ruinous odds until his return. After reassuring himself that Odette and Paddy were seated in relative comfort on a sponge seat, he opened the throttle.

It seemed to Odette that she was in a speedboat. The sled's runners carved a wake through several inches of slush and melted water on the ice platform beneath them, sending up sheets of spray that cascaded onto the tarpaulin she shared with Paddy. Wisps of fog reached down from a thick, grey ceiling. Ahead, visibility was reduced to fifty yards.

Inexplicably, Jack was half-kneeling on the snowmobile seat, his other foot planted on a running board. Looking around, she saw the driver behind in a similar stance. With a shock, she realized they were poised to leap off. *Nom de Dieu!* After a few minutes, the precaution became clear when she spotted a three-foot lead of black water ahead of them and felt the sled surge forward. She saw Jack's snowmobile fly through the air and crash down on the far side, followed immediately by the sled's jarring impact. Sailing over the crack, she glimpsed open water between the four feet deep walls of ice. She shivered and took a tighter grip on a rope stretched between the sled's flexing sides of plywood.

Jack glanced back over his shoulder and grinned.

'Jack's enjoying himself,' Paddy shouted.

He's certainly been enjoying something, she thought. The passive tracking of his gaze had switched to active. She had seen that look before in men's faces at the start of an affair, when their hunger communicated itself to other women. The exchange with Soosie had left her feeling challenged and confused.

'Only another five hours,' Jack shouted.

A wide ice-crack snaking into the distance proclaimed the approaches to Ituquvik. The rushing melt water of the valley stream had carved deep gashes in the steep ice mound at the shoreline, creating a series of treacherous gullies.

Jack walked up the incline for an inspection. It was too dangerous for the snowmobiles to climb. 'No go. You're going to have to get out and push,' he announced.

Perching on unsteady footholds, he helped the students to haul and shove each sled across the ravines to the stony beach, where they collapsed gratefully.

The work crew had made a good job of fencing in the whalebone houses, leaving a central access road on which the mobile crane was parked. Higher up the valley, a flat section of land was occupied by an encampment of tents, over which a metal shroud had been constructed. It looked neat and competent. An octopus of electric cables extended from a throbbing generator hut.

Paddy beamed appreciatively. 'Be it ever so decadent, there's no place like home,' he murmured. 'I wonder where everyone is.'

'Shush.' Odette pushed back her hood and listened. Above the rushing of the stream, she could hear voices. 'It sounds like singing.'

The party advanced towards the encampment and stopped outside a large tent, suddenly embarrassed upon recognizing the murmur of a prayer. After a few seconds the flap was raised and a hand beckoned them inside. A burly Inuk in a dog collar came forward and shook Paddy's hand. Odette recognized him as the violinist at the barn dance.

The clergyman turned to Paddy. 'Hello, Professor. I'm David Kalluk. We're holding a service of blessing for your great enterprise. We've just started, so you're welcome to join us. Won't you all come in?'

Odette blinked away the sun's residual flashes. In the gloom, she saw a dozen Inuit facing the front, patiently waiting for the service to resume.

The clergyman returned to his place before them. 'Let us say the prayer that the Lord taught us,' he began. '*Atatavut qilamitutit atti isumagisiaq-taull.*'

Odette felt humbled by the intensity of those around her, their eyes tightly clenched, hands pressed together as they intoned the words. There was an element of fear in this abasement, she realized. For the first time, she glimpsed the true nature of the environment she had entered – one of sudden and random death. To her surprise, Jack assumed the same posture of intense genuflection.

Kalluk paused a moment, contemplating his congregation. 'The Bible tells us that Adam and Eve were the first people. But they came to a world that was already old with history, with the history of its creation by a Creator.

'When the first human beings refused to recognize this history, problems started for mankind. Then the Bible becomes a tragic story of those who ignore the relationship between the land, the Creator, and the human race. They were chased out of the location they called Paradise and became the first displaced persons.

'The people who died in this place where we stand never made the mistake of forgetting that connection. They honoured the land and the Creator. We ask the Lord to look down with compassion and love upon the souls of those buried here, and to take any unquiet spirits to His bosom. We also ask for His blessings on the work of Professor Patrick O'Connor and his team in this place.'

Afterwards, Jack took the clergyman aside. 'What was that about unquiet spirits, Dave?'

Kalluk studied his boots. 'Oh, the usual thing. People are worried about disturbing the graves here. Someone said they saw a ghost. They thought a service might settle things down.'

'Any ghost in particular?'

The Inuk looked up. 'Aglukark, I'm afraid. He seems to be flavour of the month. I wouldn't worry. I once read people kept seeing Butch Cassidy decades after he died. I guess they wanted to.'

Jack found Paddy inspecting the rock fall with feverish impatience.

'What's the plan, Paddy?'

'To satisfy our grand inquisitor Fingest, we have to do things by the book, which means three distinct phases. First, a complete televisual recording of the tunnel and boulders, during which we retrieve any objects of interest. Then we remove the rocks, one by one, cataloguing their position on a three-dimensional grid and by camera. I've promised your friends that everything will be restored to its original order. Lastly, of course, an excavation of any cultural layer that may exist underneath.'

'You're not worried about the tunnel collapsing?'

'I've given thought to that. We have some clever expansion tubing we can feed into the holes to provide rigid support. But moving these stones is going to be like that Chinese game with chopsticks. Any undue movement will disturb the rest and possibly damage artefacts trapped between the surfaces.'

After a late supper, Jack took his leave, promising to return with Fingest in two days' time.

Paddy grasped his hand warmly. 'I don't suppose you could arrange for the Tuan to fall down an ice crack? No, I suppose not.'

Odette accompanied him down the slope to his snowmobile. The service had left her curious.

'I hadn't realized the Inuit took religion so seriously.'

Jack folded back the engine cowling and checked the leads. 'They were already more Christian than most people when the first missionaries arrived.'

'Is that why they became converts?'

'It depends who you talk to. Some elders say the shamans were cruel and unreliable. Others say their religion was systematically destroyed by missionaries like the Reverend Edmund Peck.'

'Are there still shamans?'

'It's not something people talk about.' He closed the cowling and pulled the starter toggle experimentally.

'You're in a hurry to get back, Jack. I can't say I blame you.'

She looked forlorn, a stranger in this desolate landscape.

'Sorry,' he said. 'I've got to find some way of keeping the hacks off your back for a few more days. Then I'll show you the floe edge, if you like.'

'I'd like that.'

Freed from the sled's burden, his machine leapt away. She stood in a pool of water, watching his silhouette recede into the murk. She recalled a corny line from a Clint Eastwood movie: 'If he looks round, he's interested.' At the limit of her vision, she saw him raise a hand.

Rushing through the fog, he had the impression that time was reeling backwards. The dead now stalked the land and his adult caution had regressed to teenage infatuation. Behind him a skein of history was unfurling from a hole in the ground. For reasons he could not explain, all these events were converging on some point in the past.

His gaze flickered restlessly over the cracks ahead while his mind wandered far away. Again he considered the possibility that his stepfather was still alive. Aglukark had always seemed indestructible. Two sorts of hunters emerged from Jack's ledger of harvesting yields. There were those who caught one beluga and a couple of caribou a year, if they were lucky. And there were those, like Aglukark, who consistently brought in animals against all the odds. Aglukark always set off with an empty grub box, so if he didn't catch anything he went hungry. It was a mindset that allowed him to make light of enduring hours beside a seal hole, even in a biting wind. His spirit was harder than the elements, and he never quit.

If Aglukark had tunnelled out of the snowfall, how far would he have got with a broken leg? Jack reflected on Inuk Charlie's feat of endurance. But Aglukark had no dogs, he remembered. Had he hitched a ride on a passing snowmobile? Jack's version of events had gone unchallenged so perhaps the shaman's rescuer had been sworn to secrecy.

Why had Aglukark remained silent all these years? He must have settled in another community where he was unknown, Jack reasoned. Why return now if not to denounce his stepson? The timing seemed connected to the discovery of the Viking site. What had Jonas said? Aglukark had prophesied that a hole in the ground would bring forth a wave of misery that would usher in a return to the old religion. Then why was Aglukark's 'ghost' frightening people away from the site? He also remembered Jonas's comment that people supposed he and Soosie were Aglukark's 'helpers'.

Soosie. Their relationship was stalled in the bedroom. It was mind-blowing, unimaginable and delicious, but there was something askew about it. Sex was not something people switched on and off in the bedroom. Instinct told him that an afterglow should pervade their waking lives, so it hurt to be apart. At some point, self was subordinated to love. Yet he experienced no such feelings. Naked Soosie in her red ski socks was a schoolboy's fantasy. What had be been thinking of?

To his surprise, a pick-up was parked outside his house. He pushed open the door and made a loud show of stamping the snow off his boots.

'Jack, come up here quickly!'

Not again, he thought. On the journey he had mapped out the calm discussion he would have with Soosie, letting her down gently. Instead, she was pushing him into a showdown. He stood indecisively in his unlaced boots, tempted to leave.

Another urgent summons. 'Jack, it's important!'

He recognized a new inflection in her voice and reluctantly climbed the stairs to find the living-room door open, framing a curious scene. Soosie was kneeling beside a recumbent figure on the sofa, around whom several people were grouped. She was chanting in a husky voice while executing a flowing gesture with her hands.

Jack stepped into the room. He recognized the prostrate form as Isaac Igloolik. Clustered around were his anxious family. In his three years as mayor, Igloolik had established a reputation for cheery competence. Now his face looked ashen and imploded, dark bruising encircling his closed eyes. His ragged breathing was punctuated by snores.

Shit. Heart attack, Jack thought.

'Jack, take off your shirt.' Without looking around, Soosie beckoned to him impatiently. 'Just do it,' she ordered.

Conscious of the family's stares, he unbuttoned the shirt and offered it to Soosie. She pushed it away.

'And now your vest.'

Wondering what she had in mind, he pulled the long john thermal top over his head.

'OK, what now?'

At last Soosie looked at him. To his alarm, her eyes were ablaze and slightly glazed, as though entranced. It was not a trance, he realized, but some kind of hyper state. Her whole body language emanated a transcendent authority.

'Help me to lay him flat,' she instructed.

Together, they levered the mayor's limp body upright and lowered him to the floor, so that he lay on his back. Working swiftly, Soosie unzipped his parka and opened his shirt. Then, taking a pair of scissors, she cut through his vest and peeled it back.

'Get me a straight glass.'

Perplexed, Jack fetched a whisky tumbler from the kitchen.

'Lie on him.'

Jack stepped back. 'Now, look—'

Soosie silenced him imperiously. 'He's dying. There's no time. Lie on him sideways.'

Gripping Jack's arms, she steered him into a position at right angles to the body. He felt himself pushed down and manoeuvred until his left breast was in contact with the mayor's left pectoral muscle. Then he felt the cold rim of the glass as it was inserted between their two bodies. To accommodate it, he was forced to support himself with his arms.

'Don't move.'

The overhead light suddenly expired, leaving the penumbra of a small table lamp. Jack gasped as Soosie's weight came down on his back, driving the glass rim into his chest. The pain to his heart was so intense he thought he would pass out. Maintaining the pressure, Soosie began to sing.

The pain and the singing seemed interminable. By flexing his arms, Jack established a tolerable threshold of discomfort. He looked down at Igloolik's haggard features, willing his own heartbeat into the stricken man.

At first he thought it was his imagination when the mayor's pallor changed imperceptibly. And, despite the glass base clamped to his chest, he seemed to breathe more easily. With a shock Jack registered that Igloolik's eyes were open, focused on the singer above him. Then he felt the weight lift from his back. Simultaneously, Igloolik shifted as if to push him away.

Jack rolled over, pressing a hand to his burning chest, and watched the impossible unfold. Supported by Soosie's hand, Igloolik rose unsteadily to his feet, his gaze locked on her face. Smiling, she began a sinuous dance in which the movements of a seal were unmistakable. The man's relatives, unbidden, broke into the rhythmical clapping of a drum dance, the women's voices blending with Soosie's song. Shakily at first, Igloolik made a few steps then he, too was dancing and laughing, never taking his eyes off the girl.

'Marie, come.' At Soosie's beckoning, Igloolik's wife allowed herself to break the invisible thread between healed and healer. Shyly, the little old lady in a headscarf took up the seal dance, enacting the movements she had learned as a girl. Soosie slipped away to a chair, leaving the couple dancing together.

Jack needed a drink. He poured a small glass of Hennessy and stood at the door, watching the boisterous party. The mayor seemed none the worse for the experience. He clapped Jack on the back, making him wince.

'That's one heck of a girl, Jack. I feel like a boy again.'

Even when Igloolik took his leave, he insisted he was fit to drive. 'First time an empty glass ever made me feel good.'

Jack found Soosie seated in the kitchen, subdued and staring at the wall.

'Why did they bring Igloolik here?' he asked.

Soosie shrugged. 'The nursing station is closed for a few days. I guess they thought a social worker would know what to do.'

'How did you?'

Soosie looked down at her hands. 'I don't know. It seemed the obvious thing: to get the heart beating evenly.' She shivered. 'I'm going to be ill now.'

Jack looked at her with concern. Her eyes were smoky with tiredness, like burnt-out bulbs.

'You mean you've done this before?'

'A couple of times. Not like this. There was a girl with appendicitis once. We were miles from anywhere. It just came to me what I had to do. I took a knife and operated on her. Afterwards I couldn't believe what I had done.'

'Did she recover?'

'She was fine.'

Another question formed before he consider its implications. 'This ceremony, how did you learn it? Did your father teach you?'

He found her reponse shocking. 'Does it surprise you that Father was educating me? He was passing on his learning, which is more than I can say for your crazy mother and her Bible. Stupid doesn't even come close.'

Jack felt the barb penetrate and grate inside him. Scooping up his thermal vest, he looked at her. 'Sleep,' he commanded gently.

It was a bad dream and, since he couldn't push it away, it was a relief to surface to the sound of his name being called. He recognized Paddy's tones of shredding patience through radio static.

'Sorry to call this late, Jack. Something's come up.'

'Yeah? Shoot.'

'That rabbit I talked about. I think we've found one.'

'Sorry, you've lost me.'

Paddy chuckled. 'The rabbit that a magician pulls out of a hat. The rabbit that will save our bacon. With me?'

'Sure, a nod's as good as a wink to a blind horse.'

'Without mixing our metaphors too much, suffice it to say that Odette has found something that may convince our grand inquisitor. And I'd like a journalist on hand to witness his epiphany. Can you arrange that?'

He reflected for a few seconds. The press had been promised a visit to the site two days hence. They might agree to a pool reporter sending them an earlier dispatch.

'Consider it done, Paddy. Anything else?'

'That's it. Odette sends her love.'

CHAPTER 20

TUAN FINGEST WAFTED into the small arrivals hall with the air of a colonial panjandrum adept at rising above the discourtesies of a vulgar populace. This impression was accentuated by the archaeologist's great height and a cranial tilt that permitted him to inspect the world from behind a beak-like proboscis.

Jack watched, entranced. Paddy's splenetic description of the grand inquisitor had not done the man justice. The 'Tuan' resembled an exotic jungle bird, caparisoned in a coloured patchwork of furs that hung almost to the ground. This resplendent garment, the focus of incredulous stares from Inuit passengers, was surmounted by a tapering head inset with a pair of beady, red-rimmed eyes and topped off with a tufted coxcomb of white hair. He looked in his late seventies.

Jack stepped forward. 'Sir David?'

For a moment Fingest's pale eyes rested on him. Then he felt something pushed into his hand. 'Good chap. Just the two bags.' The great man turned away.

Jack inspected his palm. A fifty-cent tip. Stifling a grin, he collected the luggage and rejoined Fingest. He touched his cap. 'Just follow me and I'll be right behind you, sir.'

In the car, Jack introduced himself properly.

'Yes, yes. The chap who found the spear. Well, drive on.'

Fingest answered enquiries with the utmost parsimony. Yes, he would take lunch. No, he did not require an overnight rest.

At the hotel, Jack was glad to note the media's absence. Sam seated them at a table by the window, raising his eyebrows to Jack. They ate in silence, the Tuan carving his beef steak into small squares with meticulous precision.

At last he delivered a pronouncement. 'This tea tastes like elephant urine.'

Irreverently, Jack wondered if there had been elephants in colonial Malaya and whether this signalled his approval of the tea. 'Yes, we try our best,' he replied conversationally. 'The closest we can manage is musk-ox, I'm afraid.'

The pale eyes reappraised him. 'Musk-oxen are not endemic to Baffin Island. Nor, I dare say, are Vikings.'

Jack wondered what he would think of the rabbit.

Fingest would take no lessons in travel etiquette, climbing into the covered sled with practised economy. Jack lashed down his monogrammed bags and winched the ropes securing the petrol cans. Last, he slung the Winchester across his back. He moved off gently, enjoying the afternoon sun.

After two stops, Jack spotted a cluster of figures far to the right. A family grouped around a snowmobile. He veered off the track.

A tall, lean Inuk in his early thirties looked up. His intelligent features reflected the amusing irony of his predicament.

'*Asujutilli.* Trouble?'

'Yeah. The crankshaft nut's cracked. No spares.'

Jack stooped under the engine cowling and hand-tested the nut. It loosened a quarter turn.

'Nasty,' he murmured. 'I once heard how someone fixed this.'

'It needs a weld.'

'This guy said he filed a groove around the nut, then held it in a C-clamp and bound it with heavy wire. It stayed good for a month.'

The Inuk turned the idea over in his mind. It was a neat solution. He nodded his thanks. His wife brought steaming mugs of tea and a plate of doughnuts.

Tuan Fingest accepted his alimentation graciously. Children gathered around the old *qallunaat*, fascinated.

The Inuk removed the nut and hunkered down beside the machine to examine the thread. Jack joined him and offered his hand. 'I'm Jack.'

'Yeah, Jack Walker. I remember you. Hi, I'm Barnabas.'

'Barnie Auyuittuq? Hey, you were two grades higher than me in school. Where'd you disappear to?'

Barnabas's short account of himself was a modern parable of the Arctic: leaving school at 15, two years of hunting with his father, then a job in Iqaluit. Now he was a building inspector.

'My first time back in eleven years. My kids never saw the floe edge before. They love it. Lots of beluga and narwhal down there. But the ice is safe for only a few more days. I don't want my family here when it breaks up.'

Jack chewed the doughnut thoughtfully. 'You ever work for Karlsson Construction?'

'No, they've got a bad name for safety. People get hurt all the time. They say Karlsson is crazy like his old man.'

'Crazy how?'

Barnabas held the nut up to the sky. 'He cuts corners, then sacks workers without pay. A bully with a temper. Like his dad at Snowdrift mine.'

Jack was intrigued. 'His father worked at Snowdrift?'

'No, Ove Karlsson owned the mine.'

'Wait a minute. Karlsson's father owned the mine? I never heard that.'

'This was way-back-when. He only showed his face a few times. That way he could order lay-offs when the ore price went down. My dad was sacked and said he'd never go back.'

Jack felt a chill down his spine. He didn't believe in coincidences. They were piling up.

Barney nodded down the trail. 'You visiting the floe edge?'

'No, Ituquvik. You pass by there?'

'Sure, the scientists' camp. You better hurry.'

'Yeah?'

'They won't be there long. Looks like they're packing up.'

'Shit.'

The Tuan permitted Jack to support him on the steep approach climb. Leaving the old man to catch his breath on the crest, Jack hurried forward. The site was abuzz with activity. Men were removing fencing and a section of aluminium sheeting dangled from the crane. Several roofing panels had been stacked to one side.

Jack spotted Simon Inuksaq and caught his arm. 'What's going on?'

The bullet wound on the hunter's forehead crinkled with perplexity. 'The professor gave the order last night. Said we had to cut our losses before break-up.'

Jack stared at him. 'I spoke to him last night. He didn't mention it to me.'

'Here he is now.'

Paddy strode towards them, his expression sombre. Walking past, he murmured a greeting. 'Jack, you've a smile as thin as a crack in a teacup. Mum's the word, now.'

Paddy approached Fingest, raising his arms and letting them fall expressively. 'My dear David! You've come all this way and now I feel I've brought you on a fool's errand.'

Fingest regarded him balefully, his gaze shifting to the unmistakable signs of the camp's abandonment.

'I think I'll be the judge of that.'

'Yes, of course. But it's just a formality, I'm afraid. It's not the real goods. Fool's gold, just like poor Martin Frobisher's. There's enough egg on my face to make an omelette. Still, least said, soonest mended.'

For a few seconds Fingest was lost for words. Suddenly the appetizing prospect of closing the project and demeaning O'Connor in various journals had been wrenched from him. 'No,' he managed to stutter. 'That will not do at all. I require a full explanation.'

'And you shall have one.' Paddy fussed around him and took his arm protectively. 'Come into the warm and all will be made plain.'

Fingest shrugged him off and followed him into the grub tent clutching his tattered dignity. From the doorway, Jack spied Odette and wandered over. The sun had already darkened her skin.

'You and Paddy are playing a dangerous game,' he remarked.

She pushed a plate of food into his hand. 'Our game is poker. We're very good.'

A silent truce reigned during the meal, leaving Fingest to his thoughts and the careful dissection of boiled caribou.

At last Paddy cleared his throat. 'Well, now, David, I owe you an explanation. Or perhaps an apology would be more apt.'

Fingest patted his lips with a handkerchief. Under his judicious glare Paddy seemed to falter. 'Well, as you know it has always been my belief that the Greenland Norse made regular visits to the North-American coast. Unfortunately, little evidence for such landings exists.'

'None at all, in point of fact.' Fingest could at least exact some satisfaction from his enemy's humiliation.

'Sir David is right,' Paddy acknowledged heavily to the room. 'A fundamental problem bedevils such investigations. The Norse occupy Greenland for three hundred years or more and then disappear mysteriously. Disease, climate, whatever, that doesn't concern us. When they leave, the Inuit loot their property and carry it away. Norse artefacts are scattered all over the Arctic. Any find can be ascribed to looting or trade.'

The grand inquisitor peered over steepled fingers. 'What is your point?'

A long sigh escaped the Irishman. 'I'm afraid what we have here is another Renik Island.'

'A Thule site?'

'Near enough. You remember in 1982 Paul Mander began an excavation on a small island in northern Ellesmere. It was an obvious Norse gateway, very close to Greenland. He turned up a treasure trove of Norse finds – ship rivets, knife and spear blades, chain mail and carpentry tools – all powerfully indicative of a Viking presence. But one ugly little fact destroyed a beautiful theory.'

Fingest's cockscomb jerked in affirmation. 'They were found in the ruins of Thule winter houses. Radio carbon dating suggested an earlier Norse occupation, but nothing could be proved. Contaminated evidence.'

The Irishman removed his spectacles, peering around myopically. 'That is exactly our situation, David, I regret to say. Contaminated evidence. We start with a Viking cornucopia: a spearhead, an iron rivet, a comb, some brass coopering and I dare say much more will emerge. These held out the promise of a pristine Viking naust. But, alas, there is now incontrovertible evidence of Dorset occupation.'

'What evidence?'

'A wooden carving in the Dorset style. What would the Norse be doing with such an object? We know they never collected Inuit souvenirs.'

Fingest frowned, digesting the implications. 'I warned against this sort of eventuality from the outset. But where is your authority for closing the excavation?'

From inside a plastic folder Odette produced a sheaf of documents. 'This is our contract with the hamlet of Snowdrift,' she stated. 'The terms specify that all work will cease in the event that the site proves to be ancestral. Of course, strictly speaking the Dorset people weren't ancestors to the modern Inuit, but I don't think they'll appreciate the distinction.'

'I see.' Fingest's mood was souring again. 'I'd better see this carving.'

'Well, now, that might be difficult.' Paddy replaced his glasses carefully. 'It has been left *in situ*.'

'*In situ*? Where, exactly?'

'It's located at the end of a tunnel, in what we call the lower den. It's quite inaccessible. Unfortunately, I suspect the viewing equipment has been dismantled.'

'I want to see it!' Fingest glared at him.

Odette coughed diplomatically. 'It's only a matter of reconnecting a few leads, Paddy. If Sir David doesn't mind waiting a few minutes. I'm afraid you'll have to wrap up warm again.'

The party crunched outside, Jack following pensively.

The tunnel, he noticed, was now covered by a large tented awning that was open on one side to avoid disturbing the permafrost beneath. Inside, a television monitor had been set up within a protected booth. Odette explained the remote scope technology while fiddling with wires and sockets.

The picture sprang up crystal clear. Jack took up a position behind Fingest, who had drawn up a chair close to the screen and was scrutinizing the image closely. Jack could make little sense of it. The small camera head was evidently tilted up towards a wall of the lower den, where a flat, black object was wedged between two rock cornices.

'Can't see a thing,' Fingest complained.

Paddy glanced over to Odette. 'A close-up, please, my dear.'

Zoom magnification threw a disturbing visage into sharp relief. It was evidently the central section of a mask, about five inches wide and a foot long, Jack judged. The crude representation of an anguished face had been lent a more sinister cast by the dark wood. The twisted features put Jack in mind of Edvard Munch's painting *The Scream*. The mouth was a round hole.

'As you see, a Dorset fright-mask.' Paddy's tones were pained. 'Probably made for some shamanistic ceremony and therefore doubly out of bounds to us as grave goods. Very similar to the example found in Avalayik Island off northern Labrador, wouldn't you say, David?'

Fingest ignored him, staring fixedly at the mask.

'Haunting and quite exquisite,' Paddy rumbled on absently. 'There was nothing benign about their hocus-pocus.' He sighed. 'Well, if you've seen enough, we must get this equipment into boxes. Odette, I think you can turn it off now.'

'Wait.' Fingest pushed his chair back and squinted fiercely at the screen. 'I want a closer look at the mouth.'

The picture wobbled before resolving on the lower face. Fingest jabbed the screen. 'There! Do you see?'

Paddy leaned forward, frowning. 'I'm not sure I do. What are we supposed to be looking for?'

'Good God, man, there are none so blind. . . . The circular indentation around the mouth: it's not carved, it's been compressed.'

Mystified, Paddy bent forward again. His tone was grudging. 'Well, yes, perhaps. But I don't see. . . .'

'Now look at the chin. It's asymmetrical and there are signs of charring. The edges have been burnt and then fallen away. Miss Blanchard, maintain that focus and range up slightly higher, please.'

The top of the mask juddered into view. Fingest was now confident of himself. 'See the charring on top? And note the straight sides: planed, not broken. Look closely at the eyes and nose: they appear to be roughly hewn, but that is an optical illusion caused by the wood grain. Grain and perhaps pitch.'

'What are you saying, Sir David?' The voice came from a tall figure standing to the rear with a group of students. Jack recognized Tom South, a big hitter from *The Washington Post* whom he'd had shipped down the previous night.

Fingest hesitated, as if weighing the implications. He took a deep breath. 'This is an elementary error I had not expected even from you, O'Connor. Your mask turns out to be a ship's plank that has been in a fire. But two things tell us it is no ordinary ship's plank. First, what you took for the mouth is a rivet hole. The round indentation was caused by an iron washer.'

'A rove?' Paddy looked thunderstruck.

'Second, the so-called chin has been worked down to a feather edge. Does that suggest anything to you?'

'Scarfing?' Paddy ventured weakly.

'Exactly. We know Norse shipbuilders had difficulty obtaining planks of sufficient length, so several pieces were joined or scarfed together. The ends were shaped to overlap each other and then were riveted together.'

South spoke up again. 'Could it be driftwood from Greenland picked up by Eskimos, sir?'

Fingest frowned. 'Most unlikely. Such a long immersion would cause wormholes, and there's no evidence of that. Besides, Greenland has its own tidal trap for driftwood. No, what we are looking at is prima-facie evidence of a Viking shipwreck or landing in these waters.'

He turned to Odette. 'Can we retrieve the plank?'

'No problem, Sir David.'

The grand inquisitor rose majestically and a flustered Paddy hurried to pull back his chair. 'I don't know what to say,' he gabbled. 'It's a monumental discovery.'

Nose high, Fingest preened himself. 'Lucky for you. That pile of bric-à-brac you're accumulating is entirely circumstantial, you know. The ship's strake takes us into the realm of the probable.'

'Us?' Paddy looked more bewildered than ever. 'I thought you wanted to close us down?'

An awful neighing sound escaped the old man. Jack looked up with concern. Fingest was laughing. 'Heaven forfend. No, I'm just beginning to enjoy myself.'

Paddy beamed. 'Then I believe this calls for a bottle of Margaux I've been saving.'

'I think not,' the visitor demurred severely. Then he relented. 'Well, perhaps a drop.'

Jack watched as Paddy disengaged and the American journalist sidled up to take his place beside Fingest.

'You were taking a risk, Odette.'

Jack felt the force of her sparkling gaze. 'Nonsense. It was something that Paddy once said. Catholics know that a man who proclaims his atheism too loudly is a soul who desperately wants to believe. We merely gave Fingest something to believe in.'

'Let's hope his faith survives.'

'Oh, it will. Fingest fights his battles from an armchair: he's never found anything of archaeological value in his life. That business in Malaya was an inspired guess that others verified later. Now we're going to make him an immortal. A multi-media hero.'

'Is the plank real?'

Odette looked shocked. 'Oh, it's real enough. It had Paddy fooled for about two minutes. Then he remembered the only Dorset fright-masks he'd seen were two thousand years old. That's a thousand years before the Norse era in the Arctic. It made no sense.'

'Hence the sting.'

Paddy had overheard the conversation and leaned close. 'What is the saying about an ungrateful daughter and a serpent's tooth? Jack, I'm going to ask you a favour. Odette has been pestering me for a day off. A touch of cabin fever. She's tired of playing Snow White to the seven dwarfs. Can you show her the floe-edge tomorrow? She thinks you made her some such promise.'

Jack had forgotten.

CHAPTER 21

THE BEAR LAY fully elongated on its belly, calmly contemplating murder. A ten-footer, Jack estimated, silently passing his binoculars to Odette. Snow glasses pushed back, her remarkable indigo eyes were framed in a soft balaclava of blue wool.

'What's happening?' she whispered.

'Just watch.'

The bear had chosen its elevated ambush site with care. Its perch, a huge block of ice, sat at the extremity of the fjord ice where it was sheared off by the open waters of Lancaster Sound. The bear's nose protruded above a fifteen-foot drop to the sparkling waters of deep green-blue below. Several times it tensed and gathered its rear quarters before subsiding into patient watchfulness.

Suddenly it launched itself, a huge white malediction suspended for a split second in the classic diving position, arms extended.

In the same instant, the ghostly shape of a twelve-foot beluga whale surfaced below in a fine mist expelled from its blowhole.

The predator's front paws, bearing its 1,200 lb weight, slammed into the white whale's spine.

The beluga sounded in a white explosion, its flukes sweeping up for the dive.

Jack sensed the bear's miscalculation. It had missed the vulnerable spot behind the blowhole. Instead of breaking the whale's back, it was forced to straddle its prey like a bronco-buster. Roaring with frustration, teeth buried in the beluga's neck and claws clamped to its sides, the bear rode its bucking mount into the depths below until they dissolved into an opaque blob.

There could be only one winner. Unable withstand the roaring pressure in its head, the bear eventually bobbed up like a white floe and swam nonchalantly back to the ice edge.

Jack lowered his spotting scope. 'You're lucky to see that. Not many people have.'

Odette looked pained. 'I'm not sure I wanted to. Is the whale badly injured?'

'No, but he'll always carry the autograph. Each time the beluga sounded, the bear clawed a zigzag either side. Quite a few small whales carry marks like that. They look like a read-out from a cardiac test.'

It had been an hour's ride through fog and slushy ice to the floe edge, enlivened by the occasional seal diving down its hole. Then a pencil beam of sunlight had poked through the overcast and the murky curtain was wrenched aside.

Now they walked to the water's edge to be greeted by a cacophony of splashing, gurgling, blowing and snorting.

Odette couldn't contain her disbelief. 'There must be seventy.'

In disciplined pods, narwhals surfaced and dived in unison, displaying the full length of their marbled bodies and elegant tails. Young males, moving in separate formations from the matriarchs and their offspring, parted the waves with their six-foot spiralling tusks. Adults casually brandished ten-foot swords.

Odette stood spellbound. Even in an orange survival suit she looked striking. Her height and slimness imparted an unfathomable grace to her natural beauty. She pulled off her balaclava, and swung her hair. Jack tried to account for the brilliance of her eyes and teeth.

As if conscious of his gaze, she turned towards him. 'What do they use the tusks for?'

'Opening letters is the best guess. Even the Inuit don't know. Courtship rituals, herding shoals of cod, maybe something connected with their sonar. Do you want to hear what they're saying?'

He lowered a microphone into the water and fitted earphones over her head. Her eyes widened and she sank into a crouch, mesmerized.

'Behind all the clicks there's a sound like an incoming artillery shell.'

'That's a bearded seal. Look, belugas.'

There were dozens of them. Frolicsome and filling the air with their fluting harmonics, the creamy white creatures were living up to their reputation as the most skittish of whales, dubbed 'sea canaries' by early sailors.

In companionable spirit, harp seals entered the ring formed by a sea-borne ruff of pack ice. A fly-past of ivory gulls was followed by flights of fulmars, black guillemots and arctic terns.

They ate sandwiches perched on the sled, gazing at the chocolate-swirl patterning of cliffs in the near distance. On the other side, the floe edge stretched into infinity, disappearing into the blur of the far coast, forty miles distant. It was 15° below, yet a blazing sun made the temperature seem pleasantly cool.

At last Jack broke their reverie. 'Is Fingest still behaving himself?'

Odette smiled. 'He and Paddy have reached a secret concordat. They both agree the Vikings weren't the first to discover North America. Paddy insists it was the Celtic hermit monks whom the Vikings encountered when they first arrived in Iceland. He rests his case with an Irish ecclesiastical writer named Dicuil.'

'And Fingest?'

'He swears it was the two Scottish scouts who went with Leif Erikssen to Vinland. If they hadn't discovered grapes and wheat, he says, the Vikings would never have tried settling in America. He quotes chapter and verse from the *Hauksbok*. It's quite comical.'

Jack squatted to prime the Coleman. 'I hope he doesn't confide that theory to the press. They're arriving today.'

'No, he's quite taken with that *Wash-Post* chap. He's singing like a bird.'

It occurred to Jack that Karlsson had been a shade too subtle in choosing Fingest to do his dirty work. The archaeologist's opposition to Paddy had turned out to be professional, not corrupt. He wondered what the Swede's next move would be. 'How long do you think this dig will take?'

Odette shrugged. 'Dig is the operative word. We may not have to. We've already examined the tunnel pretty thoroughly. Removing the rocks will be tedious but won't take that long. A week, maybe. Paddy's keen to get the basic story as soon as possible.'

Jack frowned, distracted. Another mystery was being elaborated, stone by stone, without making any sense.

Odette sipped her tea, studying him. 'Jack? Something's worrying you.'

He found himself telling her about Karlsson's father, another piece in the jigsaw puzzle.

'Too many coincidences. Ove Karlsson owned the mine where my father worked. Karlsson's son turns up out of the blue and seems to know the significance of the spear before I do. After failing to buy or bully me into co-operating, he plans an elaborate scheme to stall the excavation.'

He omitted the ramifications of Aglukark and his prophecy.

'Maybe there's something in Aladdin's cave he wants.'

Jack shook his head. 'I think it's the other way around. Something he wants to stay buried, something he fears. Its discovery would compromise him in some way.'

Abruptly Odette stood up, hugging herself. 'I'm cold. I took my gloves off to eat and now my fingers are like icicles.' She looked at him appealingly. 'Would you, please?'

'Sure.' He slipped off his mitts and took her hands. They seemed cool rather than cold, and he squeezed her knuckles experimentally. To his surprise, she returned the grip and stepped forward, laying her head on his shoulder.

'That's nice,' she murmured, closing her eyes against the blazing sunlight.

Jack stood awkwardly, feeling like a dog chosen as a backrest by a cat: any move he made would be the wrong one. A tingle ran through his limbs and the sun felt warm on his back. He studied the minute pores of Odette's skin, the way her sculpted cheekbones and jaw-line set off her wide mouth. From inside her turtleneck jumper peeked a knotted silk Hermes scarf that seemed like a glaring reproach. This, and the subtle perfume rising from her hair, hinted at cultural evenings and restaurants that had no place here.

He pulled away mentally. He didn't believe he was being measured up for the glass slipper or that the golden coach and horses would be along soon. Instead, looking up, he spotted a snowmobile approaching, its rider waving vigorously. Even at a distance, he recognized Simon Inuksaq's machine.

He took Odette's arm. 'We've got to go.'

The girl glanced up, confusion flaring in her eyes. She seached his face then followed his gaze to the ice on which they were standing. A hairline crack, only two inches wide, snaked from her left boot to the water's edge twenty feet away. As she watched, its crusted lip gaped open. They walked briskly to the snowmobile through gelid pools of surface water.

Odette stepped into the sled and arranged a tarpaulin over herself. 'Are we in any danger?'

Jack flipped up the snowmobile's bonnet and glanced at the leads. 'The ice sheet's beginning to flake off from the edge. It's the start of break-up. Don't worry, we'll be OK.'

His reassurance seemed at odds with the urgent bow wave thrown up by Simon's front skis. The Inuk pulled up a few yards off and thumbed the cutout button. 'Your engine OK, Jack?'

Jack dropped the cowling. 'Yeah, just checking to see if the propeller's working.'

Simon pushed back his hood and grinned. 'Ebb tide and a south wind, always good sailing weather.'

'Tell Odette about your sailing holiday.'

Simon acknowledged her with a shy nod and gestured out to sea. 'Three years back I was stranded on a large floe with some families. The wind and tide were like today. We left our tents and stuff behind but some hunters had a bit of whale meat and *maktaak*. We were floating for a week, but we kept calling on the radio and a helicopter picked us up. I found my snowmobile about a month later on a little island. It was kind of funny.'

Odette tried to picture the near-tragedy. 'What if there had been no helicopter?'

Simon shrugged. 'I guess that's when you know who your friend is.' With a cheery wave, he fired his engine and pulled away.

She watched Jack haul back on the sled's bindings. 'What did he mean?'

He grunted and turned to her. 'When all the food's gone, you eat the sealskin bindings of your sled. There were fifty-four people on the floe with Simon, so they were soon going to be pretty ravenous. That's when you find out who your friends are.'

Odette didn't get it. 'Why?'

Jack mounted up and reached for the toggle. 'Because your real friends won't eat you.' He pushed hard on the way back. Too hard. At a bifurcation in the ice he gunned the engine to leap a four-foot gap but a ski caught the lip, corkscrewing the machine sideways and throwing him from the saddle. A split second later, the sled slammed into the snowmobile's rear and Jack glimpsed Odette tumbling to one side.

Scrambling up, he saw her fall had been broken by a pile of slush, but she lay awkwardly.

'I'm all right,' she said breathlessly. He could see she wasn't. 'It's my stupid knee,' she complained, clutching her left shin.

She allowed Jack to unzip the inside leg of her storm trousers and examine the impact point on the jeans she wore beneath. He found no blood. 'There's no flesh wound, so it's a pulled ligament or a sprain. It was my fault. I should have been more careful.'

'Kill your speed, not your passenger,' she admonished sternly. 'If you think I'm getting back in that sledge, you can forget it.'

Jack saw she was serious. 'OK, you can ride with me. But let's dry you off, first.'

Gently, he lifted her in his arms and deposited her on the sled's foam seat, where she dug out a towel from her bag.

He glanced at the snowmobile lying on one side, its rear light smashed. Loosening the sled's bindings, he slipped out the tent's stout ridgepole and walked over to the snowmobile. The machine was much heavier than a motorbike, but yielded to the beam's leverage until it toppled back into the upright position with a crash. Three pulls of the toggle established the engine had not flooded. He ran the snowmobile forward and aligned it with the sled.

He turned to see Odette watching him. 'All aboard the *Skylark*. Shall I carry you again?'

She smiled. 'As long as it's not a fireman's lift.' She reached up and clasped his shoulders while he lifted her. She barely winced when he lowered her astride the saddle.

Jack retrieved the foam seat and slipped it beneath her. 'There's very little suspension, so hold on tight. And you'd better wear these.' He handed her a pair of goggles.

He set off more sedately, gauging Odette's reaction at the faster approaches to ice cracks, but she showed no distress, gripping him tightly. It was a good feeling.

He walked through the camp looking for Paddy. The party of visiting journalists had been evacuated to a beach landing strip, leaving a buzz of excited indignation in their wake. In the kitchen, he found Benny dourly contemplating stacks of unwashed dishes. The big cook rubbed his empty eye socket distractedly.

'Can you believe it? This photographer buys himself an old-time bow and arrow in Snowdrift and he wants to take my picture holding it. Offers me thirty dollars.'

'Very generous of him. Did you beat him down?'

'He says I have to strip down to some leather underpants for the photograph. I said, "Mister, you've got us confused with Dogribs. We dress up, they dress down." You know what he said? "Never mind, nobody's perfect".'

Paddy was hunched over a small table in the Finds Office. Blindly, he fumbled to remove an optical device from an eye socket and discover his spectacles on his forehead before recognizing his visitor.

'Ah, Jack. Look at this, will you? Veritable jewels in a swine's snout, as the Bible says. Or perhaps a wolverine's snout would be more apt.' With a flourish he folded the cloth back to reveal a dozen tiny rock fragments arrayed on a paper sheet. Jack made out yellows, ochres and slate grey among the dull colours. 'Precious stones?'

'More valuable than you can imagine. Jasper stones, the fingerprints of the Vikings, no less. Not quite DNA, but the next best thing.'

'Are they ornaments?' Jack asked.

'Fire-starters!' the archaeologist exclaimed with the air of a lottery winner. 'Jasper is the flint-like stone that the Vikings strike with steel to make sparks and light their fires. These turned up when we sieved through the spoil outside the tunnel. Dear God, think what archaeology could do with trained wolverines.'

Jack pinched a jasper fragment between his forefinger and thumb, holding it up for inspection. The orange chip was coarse and lustreless, unlike flint.

'You mentioned fingerprints?'

'Well, now, jasper's quite rare. The stones' origins can be identified by comparing their trace elements with materials in regions where jasper occurs naturally.'

The technique, Paddy explained, was known as Instrumental Neutron Activation Analysis and had proved useful at the so-called Vinland site in Newfoundland. By comparing jasper artefacts with geological samples from sixty different source areas, the site investigators had came up with three different sources of origin.

'Two were no surprise – western Greenland and western Iceland. Can you guess the third?'

'Ireland?'

'Too obvious. One fragment appeared to be from north-central Newfoundland, about a hundred and fifty-five miles south of the Viking site at L'Anse aux Meadows. This was hard proof that the Norse were exploring down the northern American coast and what they called Vinland may have encompassed quite a large area. Just imagine the story our own little fire-lighters can tell.'

Jack considered the ramifications. 'If there's no Newfoundland stone in your batch, the Vikings came here first, so this site could be one of their first land-fall in North America. On the other hand, if there is such a stone, this site is ruled out as early Viking because they'd already explored to the south.'

Paddy looked pensive. 'You're right. One stone could sink us, but a Viking site would still cause an earthquake.'

'What does Fingest think?'

Stroking his nose, Paddy folded a cloth over the stones. 'Think? He doesn't. The Tuan's brain has the cutting edge of a rotten *pisang*, which he kindly informed me is Malay for banana. These stones would only confuse the poor eejit. What the eye can't see the heart doesn't grieve over. Mercifully, Sir David is joining the rout back to dry land, where he can posture to his heart's content.'

Jack filled him in on Odette's mishap, quick to put his fears at rest. 'She's lying down now. But she should have that knee examined professionally. I thought I'd take her back to Snowdrift with me on the plane, if you can spare her for a couple of days. I need to do some research on our friend Karlsson.'

Jack also outlined the chain of coincidences connecting the Karlsson family with Snowdrift.

'Long odds,' Paddy growled. 'Never trust a Swede, my auntie said. Mind you, she married a Protestant. Look after Odette and yourself. I wouldn't want anything happening to my two favourite people.'

Jack's appearance on the beach with Odette in his arms, followed by Benny carrying her suitcase, raised a mocking cheer from the journalists. A photographer tore up a handful of paper and threw it as confetti before realizing he had shredded three precious receipts.

As they boarded the Twin Otter, Odette smiled up at Jack's discomfiture. 'I really must get a bearer. It does allow one to make an entrance with a bit of style, don't you think?'

Jack exchanged a look with Benny. The Inuk's dead eye winked.

CHAPTER 22

THE NURSING STATION receptionist informed them that Nurse Taggart was absent and would return from her prenatal visit in an hour. Drugged by the building's warmth, Odette insisted on waiting alone.

Jack walked to his office, offering a prayer that the local Internet service provider was still in business. It was. When the computer had struggled to life, he went into Google and entered Ove Karlsson's name. Of the twenty-four references, the most promising appeared to be the English language site of an independent Swedish newspaper, depicting a family tree of the Karlsson dynasty's business interests.

He whistled silently. Mining and construction were shown as minor subsidiaries in an empire that encompassed steel, banking, vehicle plant, publishing, electronic goods and television stations. The diagram noted: *In 2004, the firms controlled by the Karlsson family accounted for nearly 30 % of the market capitalization of the Stockholm stock exchange, including six of its twenty biggest companies.*

Depressing an icon labelled *Family History*, he read that the conglomerate had been founded in 1935 by Ove Karlsson. Like many businessmen in 'neutral' wartime Sweden, Ove had been complicit with the Third Reich in hiding German industries under the cloak of Swedish ownership and Karlsson Industries had emerged from the war greatly enriched, like many other Swedish concerns. In 1946, US State Department officials had estimated the approximate value of German holdings in Sweden as $105,300,800, second only to Switzerland with $250,000,000.

The phone cut through a tumult of thoughts. It was Jonas, sounding like a dog with two tails. 'Jack, I'm glad I caught you. I'm at the hamlet office with the mayor and the hamlet council. We're going over the structure plan and I thought you'd be interested.'

He frowned. 'You're counting your chickens before they're hatched. You could end up with egg all over your face.'

Jonas's tone became mollifying. 'Hold on, Jack. It's only contingency planning. The cut-off date for Sealift orders is early August. That gives us a little while to work things out. Isn't that reasonable?'

Jack lifted his jacket from the chair. 'OK, I'll be right over.'

The council chamber had been fitted with parquet flooring, a roof of wooden inlay and, to emphasize the consensual nature of local government, was dominated by a large round table around which the council members were grouped.

He recognized the mayor, evidently fully recovered from his thrombo. Isaac Igloolik shook Jack's hand. 'I heard about the good work you're doing, Mr Walker. You and your sister are a credit to the community.'

'Soosie?'

'Yeah, I'd like to co-opt her on to the council. She's got a good handle on our social problems and she's making quite a stir. We need a young woman's voice – gotta move with the times. Mind you, she's dead set against all this and I think she's right.' He gestured to an array of documents on the table, over which Jonas presided nervously.

Jack picked up a résumé and read it through. He nearly choked. Jonas had really pushed the boat out. His development plan called for the construction of five four-star hotels, a new civic centre that would serve conventions, a fully staffed hospital, a visitors' centre displaying artefacts from the archaeological excavation, a Viking Trail through a newly desig-nated national park and the recreation of a Viking village showcasing crafts, skills and foods of the Viking era. He stopped reading when he got to a mention of wheelchair facilities for a Snowdrift Dome and shook his head incredulously.

As if reading his thoughts, Jonas hurriedly began his pitch. 'I know it's a lot to take in all at once. But, believe me, this is quite a modest proposal when you look at the Viking site in Newfoundland.' He passed around copies of a handout before reciting from it. ' "L'Anse aux Meadows is the only authenticated Viking site in North America. It was discovered by Helge Ingstad and his wife Anne Stine in 1960 and is now a UNESCO World Heritage Site and a National Historic Park." '

In a conductor's gesture, Jonas held up a commanding finger. 'Listen to this. The site attracts approximately four hundred thousand visitors a year, who spend in the region of six hundred million dollars on travel and tourism, of which two hundred and sixty million is spent in Newfoundland. The number of four-star or superior facilities has risen from two to nearly thirty. You can see the sort of stuff they have – civic centre, Viking Trail, visitors' centre and so forth.'

The mayor sat down and glowered at him. 'You didn't mention this when we agreed your short-term job-creation project. Then, the wolf was knock-ing at the door. Now you want us to build a new town.'

Jonas beamed. 'Like I said, this is modest. We're not suggesting anything on the scale of Newfoundland. I had a look at what they've done in Pangnirtung, down the coast from here. It's a pretty village, about twice our size, which gets a lot of visitors to its national park. They highlighted a main problem. They didn't have the infrastructure to welcome all the tourists that wanted to come.'

Matthew Taqtu, the council chairman, interjected. 'I know Pangnirtung. The people there didn't want to be disturbed so they kept things small-scale. There is another problem you haven't mentioned. Tourism is seasonal, so what do we do with all the new hotels and buildings for the rest of the year?'

Jonas folded his arms. 'You have to understand what a World Heritage site means. Snowdrift will belong to the world, which will beat a path to our door for reasons we will probably never understand. The *qallunaat* are hungry for Viking history the way we are for *maktaak*. Look at the press interest we've had. Look at the Newfoundland figures. Even if we get a fraction of that, we're talking about serious money.'

'And where does the development money come from?' Taqtu demanded.

A new sheaf of photocopies sprouted in Jonas's hand. 'Obviously, Parks Canada would take responsibility for the archaeological stuff, the visitor centre and the national park. I've had a favourable response from the investment consortium Nunavut Tunngagik Inc and several banks listed here.'

An obvious flaw in Jonas's scheme for world domination had occurred to Jack.

'It's a remarkable plan,' he ventured guardedly. 'But tourists can reach Newfoundland on the highway, not to mention cruise liners and ferries. None of those are relevant here. We're going to need 737 airliners to bring in the numbers you're talking about. How are you going to land jets on our little airstrip?'

Jonas reached for a large-scale map. 'I'm glad you asked that, Jack. The old mine company surveyed a site twenty-three miles out of town during the 1980s boom, before mineral and oil prices dropped through the floor. Of course, we'll need a road.'

This admission touched off an intense debate on the danger the road and tourists might pose to caribou migrations. Jack had to admire his friend's nerve as Jonas trotted out suggested guidelines for protecting hunting areas, calving grounds, nesting sites, estuaries and sacred sites.

With equal insouciance Jonas brushed aside concerns about an influx of southern workers. 'Sure there's a shortage of skilled people in Snowdrift. So we put them on a training programme and bring in southerners on short-term contracts to run things in the meantime. Then our guys take over; it's normal practice. And we hold the strings all the time.'

Jack glanced at his watch, worried about Odette, and made his excuses.

He had the sense that support was running in Jonas's favour, with only the mayor and a couple of others against. Lottery fever.

Slipping into Jonas's office, he called the nursing station, to be told Odette would be at least another hour.

At the entrance of the hamlet office, he paused and looked across the village, taking in the church, the stores, the fire station and the old Hudson's Bay Company store. Little had changed since his birth. In the distance, hooded figures moving slowly across the ice increased the illusion of a preordained continuum.

The thought of Jonas's plan ripping the scene to shreds filled him with dismay. Did tradition count any more to poor people taunted by television images of the sweet life? Yesterday, he would have said yes. The dollar signs flashing in the councillors' eyes had left him uncertain. Perhaps it was not his place to judge. Whatever the outcome, he resolved to stay neutral.

Suddenly reminded of wartime Sweden and his unfinished business, he walked back to his office. It took him a couple of minutes to crank up the Internet again and work his way back through Ove Karlsson's file to the underscored word Vikings.

Karlsson had evidently been a keen amateur archaeologist who funded excavations in Sweden and on the Danish peninsula. He had also, Jack read, visited Greenland and South America to pursue his 'theories of Viking expansion for which he was ridiculed by many experts.'

Jack had to scroll down through two pages of text for further enlightenment: *He continued to believe, until his death in 1999, that the Norsemen had sailed southwards beyond Vinland to Mexico and plundered the Toltec Empire, accounting for its collapse in the twelfth century.*

A nutso from the same tree, Jack thought. Like father, like son. Then he saw the next line: *Ove Karlsson continued to assert his conviction that proof would emerge one day, of the Vikings' journeys to the Orient through the North-West Passage.*

A hook sank into his stomach. He read the sentence again, to be sure. Laid out before him were the bones of a conspiracy. Jack listed them on a sheet of paper.

1.   *O.K. believed Vikings navigated NW Passage.*
2.   *Was ridiculed for beliefs.*
3.   *Owned Snowdrift Mine.*
4.   *Viking site found near Snowdrift.*
5.   *Discovery would vindicate O.K.*
6.   *O.K. had means to plant fake evidence?*
7.   *Son desperate to stop excavation.*

The thump of his outer door brought him back to reality. An ancient figure shuffled in, his dour features twisted with indignation. Red Addams was not in a mood to observe formalities.

'Jack, I've only lived here fifty-nine years and I've held my views back because I'm a white man. In all that time I've worked for my living and not asked for a cent – not like some I could mention that sit around collecting welfare cheques. Now I'm hanged if they're going to hand everything on a plate to those people without a thought for folks like me who built up this community.'

Jack was mystified. 'Don't hold back, Red. What's biting you?'

The fuel-dump manager struggled to find the words. 'You saw the structure plan at the hamlet council meeting. It's all over town. Just tell me why there's no mention of my new gas station?'

Jack took a deep breath and opened the door. 'Out!'

Odette greeted him with a guilty smile. 'I feel like a fraud. I was sure it was the ligaments I tore skiing, but all it required was a stocking support. And I made you suffer as a beast of burden.'

Jack helped her to walk down the nursing-station ramp to where his Land Cruiser was parked. His efforts at conversation sounded lame to his own ears.

Odette looked at him with concern. 'Is something wrong? You're not ill, are you?'

'Trouble at mill. I'll tell you when we get home.'

At the porch, she leaned on his arm and mounted the steps slowly. Jack could sense people in the house and made a noisy show of removing his boots before mounting the stairs. Two elderly women and a teenage girl with a child were ranged on seats around his living-room. Greeting them politely, he made reassuring gestures for them to remain seated and looked around.

'She's in there,' said the girl, nodding to his study.

He pushed open the door cautiously, to see an old woman sitting in front of his desk. Behind her stood Soosie, holding the woman's arm in both hands, as if weighing the limb. When she saw him her expression became closed.

'Hello, Jack.'

'What's going on?' he asked. It did not come out as he meant.

Soosie's face clouded. 'I didn't think you'd mind. These are just some people who thought I could help them.'

He turned to inspect the group in the living-room. 'Help? I don't understand. What sort of help?'

Soosie shrugged impatiently. 'You know what happened with the mayor.

Word got round and sick people came to see me for advice.'

He had a suspicion of what lay behind her dissembling, but pressed on. 'Why don't they go to the nursing station?'

Her look of impatience deepened. 'Come on, Jack. Not everyone wants to tell white people their problems.'

'So they've come to see an *angutkuq*. And you're their new shaman now, right?' But Soosie was looking past him at Odette, who was supporting herself on the rail at the top of the stairs. She leaned forward and addressed her patients in Inuktitut. 'See, Jack has found himself a nice white girl!'

Odette looked puzzled. 'Look, I can book into a hotel. I don't mean to be a nuisance.'

Soosie's eyebrows rose. 'Oh, you were planning to stay here with us? That will be cosy, won't it, Jack?'

He felt misery competing with a stirring anger. 'Soosie, behave yourself,' he murmured. 'You'll have to pick up some social skills if you're joining the council. The mayor said you've been creating quite a stir.' He glanced around at Soosie's makeshift surgery. 'Now I know what he means.'

'You're right, Jack.' Soosie glared at him. 'The first thing I'm going to do on the council is to get them to throw out that stupid idea of your friend Jonas. Do you realize what it will do to this community? Have you seen what drink and greed have done to Cambridge Bay and Iqaluit? Well, I have. The *qallunaat* have brought us nothing but misery, but now you and this woman have opened the door to more of them. Why should you care? You're foreigners.'

With peremptory gestures, she began to usher the visitors from the house.

He took her arm gently. 'There's no need for that.'

She pulled free and strode towards her bedroom. 'No, Jack, it's time for people to choose sides. I've just chosen mine. The mayor's made a house available for me, so I'll leave you alone with your girlfriend.'

As the house emptied, he and Odette sat stiffly on the sofa without meeting each other's gaze. Jack couldn't escape the suspicion that Soosie had engineered the break, so what had their passion been all about? Relief mingled with the hurt of her cutting rejection.

When the front door banged shut he rose to busy himself in the kitchen. 'Sorry about that,' he murmured. 'Soosie gets a bit possessive at times.'

With brittle lightness, Odette dismissed the apology. 'It's none of my business. I really think I should book into the hotel.'

'I wouldn't advise it,' he said. 'There's a fresh crew of construction workers staying there and they can get a bit boisterous.'

Odette inspected her nails, frowning at the cold's ravages. She wished she had prised more than an abridged account of Jack's background out of

Paddy. It seemed such a horrific story that she hadn't found the courage to raise any aspect of it with Jack.

He brought a tray of coffee and sat beside her. 'Odette,' he said heavily, 'there's something I have to talk to you about.'

Oh God, I'm not ready for this, she thought. To her relief and then consternation he outlined his suspicions regarding the Karlssons. She listened carefully and then put down her cup.

'I've got two comments,' she said. 'The first is that old Father Karlsson was a complete fantasist. It's almost inconceivable that the Vikings could have reached either Mexico or China.'

'Why's that?'

'It's quite simple. Their settlement in Greenland was too small to mount such expeditions. Their total population amounted to less than five hundred men, women and children. The main reason they withdrew from the Vinland base in Newfoundland had nothing to do with hostile natives. It simply put too much strain on their manpower and resources. That's why Paddy was so upset by the newspaper articles. No one would credit a voyage to China.'

'You said almost inconceivable.'

Odette tugged a stray lock of hair. 'That's true. Not all the westward expeditions set off from Greenland. There were a few from Iceland and even Norway, but they tended to come to grief because of the distances involved.'

'And your second point?'

Odette smiled mischievously. 'A hoax would be child's play.'

Jack looked to see if she was joking. She wasn't.

'Seriously, I could do it myself. I'd start by getting some bits of Viking ship timber of the right age. They're stored in plastic bags in the basements of museums such as Dublin and York, which are so understaffed that no one would notice if you helped yourself.'

'Odette, you amaze me.'

'Be more amazed. Then I'd put my hands on a few bits of iron bloom – you know, the little metal globules from a furnace – as evidence of some iron working. Throw in a few ship's rusty washers, add a pinch or two of cinder or charcoal . . . *et voila!*'

'That's all that's required for a hoax?'

She nodded. 'It's unusual to find a lot of artefacts even at major sites. At Ituquvik we've already turned up almost as many artefacts as they did in Newfoundland during forty years of excavation. Paddy's worried that it all seems too good to be true.'

Jack posed the outstanding question. 'Do you think our site is a fake?'

'Well . . .' Odette chose her words carefully. 'The convincing thing about our site is the way it came to light. No one went looking for it. A local man stumbled on a harpoon or spear and you, a disinterested public servant, did the rest. It's just how the Dead Sea Scrolls were discovered.' For second she looked distraught. 'Jack, think what it will do to Paddy's reputation if it all goes pear-shaped.'

They fretted at the puzzle. Somehow lunch passed them by and they eked out the afternoon on bannock slices until six o'clock, when Jack set about making dinner and Odette retired to take a bath. Despite her conversion to arctic food, he decided to spare her the caribou tongue reserved for special guests.

Emerging from the kitchen with a meal of thinly sliced steak and vegetables, he felt the plates develop a wobble in his hands. Odette was wearing cut-off jeans that encased impossibly long legs and a Marseilles-striped T-shirt that forced him to revise his beanpole image of her. Never having seen her in anything more revealing than a thick jumper, he felt he was in the presence of a stranger. Lightly applied make-up highlighted the graceful lines of her jaw, a sharp bone structure and skin that seemed to glow.

She was amused by his tongue-tied reaction. 'I hope you don't mind. For weeks I've been wearing layers of thermals, jackets and furs. It's such a relief to feel free.'

He suspected she had been brooding on Soosie's behaviour and was relieved when the question popped out casually. 'Your stepsister seems to get upset very easily. Was she always like that?'

Jack leaned back and shook his head. 'No, she was a very uncomplicated kid, sweet and obliging. She went to the university of hard knocks.' Under Odette's gently persistent questioning he recounted a version of the family tragedy that air-brushed out most of his own role and left no loose ends for her to speculate on.

He imagined Paddy had given her the bare bones of the story. Even so, she looked stricken, reacting with concern as if the events had happened in the recent past. 'So you and Soosie have lost both sets of parents? How terrible.'

'It does seem a bit careless, but it's an occupational hazard of Arctic life. There are quite a few orphans in every community. Most families in this village have adopted one or more children, but it's no big thing. Kids aren't personal possessions up here, they belong to everyone.'

Mistaking his long silence for pained recollection, she tried to put him at ease by coaxing out some details of his life in Yukon. 'Did you wear a red uniform and a guide's hat?'

He pulled a face. 'I wasn't the sort of Mountie you see on the screen. It was mostly police work and dealing with domestic disturbances – pretty thankless work. You'd go to a house where a man is beating his wife and when you'd pulled him off, the wife jumps on your back and takes a swing at you. She really loves him! A few days later she probably shoots him.'

'Give me an example.'

He racked his brain. 'There was a disturbance at a trailer park – a truck driver with a drink problem who had broken a couple of his wife's ribs.' He could recall the tight face of a little blonde woman. 'She begged me not to put him in jail because she had two children and would have to go on welfare. So I gave her some advice. I suggested that the next time he came home drunk she might tell him that when he went to sleep she'd get her revenge.'

Odette's eyes sparkled. 'What happened?'

Jack grinned wryly. 'Nine months later I was called to the house with an ambulance. The husband was screaming that both his arms were broken. "I want that bitch charged", he shouted. His wife told me, "Officer, I just did what you told me. I said that if he hurt me or the kids, I'd get him when he went to sleep. Last night he slapped me around real good, so I took my son's baseball bat and hit him hard on one arm and when he hollered I hit the other arm".'

Odette put down her glass to control her laughter. 'Did she end up in court?'

'We all did. But the judge worked out what happened and let her off. Nothing was heard from them again.'

She was smiling at him, he noticed, with an expression that mingled fondness and reluctant pride for a wayward child. Dozens of men must have been transfixed by that look, he thought. Absurdly, it pained him to imagine it focusing on anyone else.

CHAPTER 23

A CACOPHONY FROM the street drew him to the rear window of the lounge where he had been sleeping. He recognized the sound of a Rolling Stones record blaring from the house opposite. It had been unoccupied during renovation work, which made the sight of a crate of whisky on its porch all the more puzzling.

As he watched, two women in their thirties lurched up the steps and knocked at the half-open door. Recognizing them as villagers' wives, he felt his guts lurch. They were welcomed inside by two thickset men wearing decorated moose-hide jackets, new jeans and cowboy boots. Construction workers.

Jack had witnessed the scene too many times elsewhere to guess what the outcome would be. The women had probably left their husbands drunk at home. Drawn to the whisky like flies to jam, they would spend the night in the house and there would be hell to pay tomorrow. Recriminations, domestic violence and perhaps court appearances. Everything he had described to Odette and perhaps worse.

'Jack?' Odette stood at the door in a dressing-gown.

'Just a little local difficulty.'

He found Jim Elias's number and waited while it rang at the Mountie's house.

'Jim, sorry to bother you this late, but we've got a domestic, just across the road from me. There's whisky, construction workers and wild, wild women. They're married, so stand back for the fireworks.'

Elias sounded bored. 'Hang on a moment, Jack. Those construction boys have got special clearance for the booze. There's no law against holding a party.'

Jack's face hardened. 'Now you listen, Sergeant. You either stop it now, or you'll have to clear the mess up in the morning.'

He could hear Elias's yawn. 'If they're creating a public nuisance, just tell them to pipe down. You used to be a Mountie. But remember, you don't have any rights.'

Jack replaced the phone. He returned to the lounge to find Odette at the window. The music swelled louder and three other women, supporting each other on unsteady legs and giggling, entered the house. He recognized Molly and Ningyooga.

Jack turned back to Odette. 'I'm sorry,' he said. 'I've got to pay a neighbourly call.'

'Must you? They can't be doing any harm.'

Jack spelled it out for her. 'The husbands of two of those women are friends of mine. They're on a hunting trip and after what I think will happen they'll wonder why I didn't do anything.'

He dressed quickly and lifted his Wildlife parka from its peg downstairs. Zipped and laced, he sauntered across the street. He had never entered a bar with a gun or a baton for the simple reason that he placed no value on his own life. It was, he dimly acknowledged, a form of penance for his murders to lay himself open to injury. Yet, remarkably, most hardcases and drunks mistook his folly for fearlessness and found themselves listening respectfully to his deep, reassuring voice.

Jack mounted the porch and pushed the door slightly ajar, receiving the full blast of *Dancing in the Street*. Configuring the standard layout of public housing, he reached down inside the door and yanked out a socket of wires. In the pulsing silence, he pushed the door open wide. Two men, faces blotched with anger, loomed towards him. His glance took in three other men, seated with women on their laps and holding glasses.

'Sorry, boys, got to close down the party. You know why.' Speaking in reasonable tones, he stepped into the middle of the room so that he was a dominant presence rather than an outsider appealing to their better nature. He raised his cap to the ladies respectfully. 'Hello, Ningyooga, Molly. I was just speaking to Jimmy and Clyde the other day.' Shame-faced, they picked up their bags and scuttled past him, followed resentfully by the other women.

The men were now all on their feet but seemed unconcerned by the women's departure. They smiled at each other. Jack put them in their late thirties to mid-forties, noting builders' muscles bulking over their beer bellies. He kept talking calmly. 'OK, boys, better be getting back to the hotel now.'

The largest of the men, a bulldog with a moustache, stepped towards him. 'You've got it wrong, faggot. You're the one that's leaving. Wildlife has no business here.'

Keeping it light, Jack watched the others' eyes to see if this was their ringleader. The loudest was seldom the most dangerous. 'You're wrong,' he said mildly. 'Wilful cruelty to animals. Section two of the Wildlife Act carries a six-month jail sentence.'

'What the fuck you talkin' about?' Bulldog inched forward.

'I'll show you.' He grabbed the tape deck lead and plugged it into the wall socket. The banshee voices of Mick Jagger and David Bowie hammered the walls. The men looked at each other uncertainly. After ten seconds he ripped the lead out and cupped his hand to his ear. The plaintive howling of sled dogs floated in through the door. 'Do you hear those poor suffering animals?'

Two of the men guffawed. 'He's got you there, Stan.'

Bulldog-Stan swung at him. Jack had been expecting it and swayed back, waiting for the man's head to follow through before unleashing a practised clip to the side of his temple. As Stan crumpled and fell sideways, Jack stepped into the ring of men and looked hard at them.

'Time to go home,' he ordered.

In the same instant the lights went out. Jack found himself on the floor and felt boots thudding into his guts and back. Someone from outside had crept up and hit him in the back of the head. Opening his eyes, he found himself looking between the legs of his assailant to the open door, where a spectral apparition in a billowing cloak hurtled towards him. His attacker's boot went back again.

'What do you say now, shit-face?'

'Goodnight,' Jack croaked.

He heard the wood crack on the man's skull and watched his knees buckle. Then the men were flinching back in alarm as an avenging fury burst in on them, screaming challenges and wielding the greater piece of a two-by-four beam. Odette was dressed only in a flimsy nightgown, her breasts, tendons and musculature sharply outlined by the cold and her murderous intent.

'*Which of you bastards wants it first?*' she shouted, drawing back the cudgel.

The men took one look at her and fled. Jack saw that his attacker and Bulldog were still on the floor, clutching their heads.

'*Out!*' he bellowed. They left, staggering.

Jack zipped Odette into his parka. 'What took you so long?'

She looked at him and then burst into laughter. Her shivering gave it a hysterical edge. 'I saw that man sneaking round the front of the house and I had to do something. Then I remembered your Yukon woman. I wrapped myself in a blanket but it came off as I was running across the road.'

'Yes, I saw. We all did.' It had been an athlete's burst of speed, he recalled.

Odette gave him a reproachful look. 'What did you say that so upset them?'

Jack was wondering about that. 'I read them the Riot Act, but the wildlife statutes don't have quite the same ring.'

They both heard a faint scuffle from the bedroom. Jack motioned Odette back and quickly opened the door. He clicked on the light.

Karlsson was sitting on a settee, smoking a cigar. He looked up sheepishly.

Jack leant against the door. 'Well, well, my old friend Sverker. Why didn't I guess? All in a day's work for Karlsson Construction, I suppose. You set this up?'

The Swede flicked a speck of ash from his trousers. 'Walker, I now realize it was foolish to try to intimidate you. It's time for the truth. I will lay all my cards on the table and you'll see that I have been sparing you considerable anguish.'

Jack ignored him. He was outraged that this man's scheming had drawn Odette into the casual violence of his bully boys.

'On your feet,' he said softly. When Karlsson looked away in disdain, as Jack knew he would, he hauled the businessman upright in an arm lock, spun him round and ran him into the wall. As he bounced back, Jack pushed him into a chair. It happened so quickly that Odette couldn't understand why blood was pouring from Karlsson's face.

'This is our sponsor?'

Jack nodded. 'Construction's a dangerous business. Even the boss should always wear a helmet.' He looked down at Karlsson clutching his face with one hand and staring in disbelief at the blood on the other.

Jack glanced at Odette. 'Mr Karlsson and I are going to have a talk. Why don't you go back to the house and get warm?'

She shook her head. 'I'm staying. You might need me to beat someone else up.'

Karlsson's lips had ballooned and he found difficulty expressing consonants. Tears of pain had given his sea-green eyes a reddish tinge. 'There was no need for that,' he lisped. 'I told you I was going to give you the truth. But you won't like it.'

'We're listening.'

They allowed him to soak a towel at the sink to staunch the bleeding and collect his dignity. He began to describe his father's interest in archaeology and his 'enthusiasm' for the theory of Viking navigation of the North-West Passage, but Jack cut him short. 'We know about that. What else?'

The Swede felt his nose tenderly. 'About six months ago, I made a complete inventory of my father's private collection. It is quite unique and very valuable. I realized that certain items were missing. Then in my father's papers I came across a plan for a deception.'

'A hoax,' Odette corrected.

'Yes, a hoax.' Karlsson nodded bitterly. 'The details were not clear, but I could see he had done something in the Snowdrift area. When I heard of the spear's discovery it seemed like confirmation: it was one of the missing pieces from his collection. But there were other, more sensitive items that may now come to light.'

Jack frowned. 'More sensitive?'

Embarrassed, the Swede searched for another euphemism. 'They were unauthorized acquisitions.'

Jack laughed. 'I think Sverker's trying to say they were stolen – taken from excavations his father helped to fund. Perhaps from Greenland?'

Karlsson dabbed the bloodstains on his shirt with a towel corner. 'You are only beginning to understand the problem. Some of the items were from other countries' collections and they are now listed as missing on websites that show them in photographs. If they come to light in your excavation, my father will be seen as some kind of criminal.'

The damage to the family's business interests would be devastating, Jack guessed. 'So why are you telling us all this?'

A triumphant look suffused the Swede's bloody face. 'Because your father was involved in this deception.'

'I don't believe you.' The idea of his father handling stolen loot seemed ludicrous to Jack.

'Yes, your father, Ned Walker, engineer and geologist at my father's mine. It's written in my father's own hand. My father provided the means but the idea was your father's and he carried it out exactly thirty years ago.'

'Rubbish.'

The Swede appraised him keenly. 'I wanted to spare your feelings, but now I don't. Your father was a drunk and my father was a persuasive man. But Ned Walker was the one who chose the site and carried out the work. With a friend of his, a young native man. Some kind of witchdoctor, my father wrote.'

A creeping numbness weighed down Jack's limbs. 'Aglukark?' His step-father.

'I believe that was his name.' Karlsson leaned back and laced his fingers together. 'Good. Now all the cards are on the table. It's time to make a deal. We both want to protect the reputations of our fathers. And we don't want their sins to be visited on their sons. I take it Miss Blanchard agrees?'

The look she shot at him made him touch his mouth nervously.

He resumed with more caution. 'We are fortunate to have Miss Blanchard on our side. As site director, she is the first to be aware of any finds, even while still in the ground. We must count on her to remove anything that should not be there. Anything that links my father – correction, our fathers – to this deception.'

Odette shook her head. 'Who said I'm on your side? And how can I remove items if I don't know what I'm looking for?'

Reaching beside the bed, Karlsson lifted a briefcase and removed a file of photographs. He handed them to Odette. Most were faded monochrome, interspersed with a few colour photos.

'My God,' she exclaimed. 'There are skeletons here.'

Karlsson rose wearily from the bed and, gaining Jack's nod of permission, made for the door. 'Yes, too many family skeletons,' he said. 'We just have to put them back in their closets.'

They stood in silence by the window and contemplated the glowing icescape, reluctant to surrender to sleep. Jack felt a tingling sensation inside him, a loose, careless dreaminess. Something shimmered in the air between them. 'Thank you for coming to save me,' he said.

Odette's luminous eyes contemplated him solemnly. 'About Soosie,' she reminded him softly.

Jack looked at her steadily. 'It's a complicated story that belongs to the past.' He paused. 'Tell me about you.'

Her face and body went quite still and in her eyes was an enigmatic expression – amusement, tenderness and something else. 'I will one day, if we get to know each other better.'

As if it was the most natural thing in the world, Jack reached out and cupped her cheek in his hand. 'Why don't we?'

Time slowed to the speed of flowing honey.

He awoke to find her curled around him, a sweet smile on her dreaming face. Looking down at her, he marvelled at the grace of the life force packed into such a slim vessel. After the tenderness of the last few hours, his crude antics with Soosie left him feeling ashamed.

They lingered over a late breakfast, filled with the languor of their love-making.

'So that's a Yukon Kiss,' Odette remarked, pouring a coffee. 'Now I know how you kept order on the wild frontier.'

'It was also called the Barman's Goodnight,' Jack confessed. 'They swore it sobered up violent customers faster than liver salts. Any medical examiner could see they had walked into a door.'

'You brute.' Odette gave him one of her lingering smiles of indulgence that he wanted to capture and store away. 'Do you believe what Karlsson said about your father?'

Jack frowned into his tea. 'No, I don't.' The truth was, he remembered little about his father other than his gentleness and humanity. A thought struck him. His swift repatriation to England had offered him no opportunity to examine his father's papers. He didn't even know if they still existed. Perhaps Alice would know.

Odette insisted on accompanying him. To her surprise, numerous people greeted the couple as they walked through the hamlet. A group of teenage boys clapped her and punched the air with delight. The night's escapade had done the rounds.

'How long were you running around naked in the street?' Jack asked.

She blushed and changed the subject. 'Are we really meeting your aunt?'

Alice had rented her house to the Walker family and became their housekeeper, he explained. Now she was the hamlet's most skilled glove and bootmaker. 'She only has to look at your hands and feet to know the exact size.' Gossip held that she exercised the same gift for judging the dimensions of other male appendages.

They crossed a piece of waste ground in the centre of the hamlet, where a few men were repairing their sleds after the ravages of winter travel. Jack acknowleged a wave from Jimmy Okadlak who was screwing a long strip of impacted plastic to a runner.

They found a short, stout woman in a blue headscarf behind a sixteen-foot high skinning frame on which a polar bear skin was stretched. 'He made a mess of this one,' she muttered, nodding to five pinpricks of sunlight glinting through the hide. Bullet holes. 'Damn sports hunters.'

'Aunt Alice?'

Instantly he realized his mistake, recognizing Alice's sister, Mary. She took a moment to recognize Jack, then hurried forward with a delighted smile to hug him. 'Johnny! Why did you never come to see us?' She stood back to examine him with sparkling eyes. Noticing Odette, she bobbed her head.

'Mary, this is a friend from the scientists' camp. We've come to ask Aunt Alice something. Is she around?'

The old woman looked at the ground, confused. 'Alice always said you would come to visit her. She kept some of that crowberry cake you liked. But I guess you were too busy.'

A premonition twisted inside Jack. 'Can we see her?'

Mary's face slumped. 'We buried her back in April. I was told you were down south when we held the funeral.'

All the grief he had frozen inside him threatened to flood his chest so that he turned away, full of bitter self-reproach. He felt Odette's hand pushed into his, squeezing tightly and his thoughts returned slowly.

'Mary, we were hoping Aunt Alice might have kept some papers of my father's. Perhaps they were in a box.'

The woman crinkled her eyes and looked down at her feet. 'Box. A box,' she muttered. 'She left some things, but no box, I think. Wait, please.'

While they waited silently, Odette studied the bronze mask that Jack's face had become, unable to read his distant gaze. After only a quarter of an hour Mary returned, bearing a small tin chest. She placed it in Jack's hands with a forlorn expression. 'Mister Ned was a nice man, real nice. I am still sad for him, Johnny.'

Odette watched Jack lean down to embrace the small woman and whisper something to her. When they parted, they were both smiling.

CHAPTER 24

THE IRISH HAD an expression, he remembered. 'Let's stop going on about the present and get on with the past.' Jack guessed some Inuit felt the same way. Their greeting, *asujutilli*, 'Is it yourself?' was a pure distillation of Irishry. Which was perhaps why they took to Paddy so readily. His thoughts were drifting.

The chest, unadorned and no larger than a medium-sized biscuit tin, sat unopened on the kitchen table. He tried to recall the story of Pandora's box. She had released all the ills of human life to punish mankind for the theft of fire. Or was it Zeus? Jack's rule had been to let the past stay buried; it was how he got through the present.

Odette watched the clouds of thought flit across his strong face. 'Aren't you going to open it?'

It was not locked and the hasp hinged up easily, followed by the curved lid. The contents were a sad summation of his father's life: two neat piles of documents and small ledgers surmounted by a 45 rpm extended play vinyl record in a red cover. Jack handled it gingerly; the Firehouse Five Plus Two were his father's favourite Dixieland jazz band. The record sounded like a continuous party and had always represented the essence of happiness to Jack, its brash music interspersed with ribald laughter and women's screams.

'Do you remember it?' Odette strained to catch his reply.

'It was a party I always wanted to go to.' Except that the jolly firemen turned out to be a wild bunch of Disney animators who were moonlighting in their spare time, he recalled.

He was not sure whether his father had kept a personal diary, but there was none here. Sifting through the legal records of work, insurance, marriage and the birth of Ned David Walker, Jack revised his opinion: his father had led an uncomplicated, decent life that many might envy today.

He took out the thin notebooks. Karlsson had said the hoax was carried out exactly thirty years ago, nearly two years before Jack's birth. He located the correct year and turned the pages slowly, baffled by the abbreviated details noted in his father's small, precise handwriting. They recorded three basic sets of information: his work schedule, holidays and appointments.

By the time he reached July, the dust was making Odette sneeze. A cryptic entry on 13 August caught his attention. Ned Walker had noted: '10 a.m. J. Ulay. Ituq.'

Jack's bruises throbbed painfully: here was confirmation his father was involved. He tapped the page thoughtfully. 'This is it. Dad mentions our site, Ituquvik. But it's a mystery why he would discuss it with an elder called John Ulayoukuluk. I can't see him being involved in any dishonesty.'

'Jack.' Odette took his hands. 'I have to tell Paddy about this. He's expecting me back and he does still pay my salary. I can't tell you how lovely it's been here with you, but. . . .'

She was saying goodbye, he realized with panic. They had barely had time to discover they liked each other, let alone discuss their future – or if they had one. He searched her slim face for the meaning behind her words; perhaps he had served his purpose and, like a bearer surplus to requirements, she was letting him go.

Yet, incredibly, he could see the same anxiety reflected in her beautiful eyes. 'I'd like to come back, if you'll have me,' she whispered. She opened her mouth to his kiss and clung to him.

The insight that came to Jack was not flattering. Throughout his life, he had discarded friendships and possessions as dangerous encumbrances that could reveal aspects of his character he wanted to conceal even from himself. Soosie and Aunt Alice were only the latest. The expediency was really cowardice, he realized. If he let this moment pass, he would face a future of what-ifs. To keep Odette, he would have to tear up his rulebook.

'Dodge won't be the same without you,' he said lightly. 'Neither will I. I'm coming with you. Whatever Paddy decides will have to be squared with the community and I'm meant to be their liaison man.' He didn't want to think about Jonas's reaction to the collapse of his grandiose strategy.

He disengaged gently from her embrace and reached for his cap. 'I'll ride up to the airstrip and see if there's a resupply flight to the site. And I want to see Ulayoukuluk about his meeting with my dad. I'll be back in about an hour.'

He took the quad-bike. The elder was not at his house, nor at the Co-op where a neighbour directed him, so he rode to the airstrip and arranged to hitch a lift on a VIP flight that afternoon.

Jack made several more enquiries before spotting the stooped figure emerging from the school. Ulayoukuluk seemed pleased to see him. 'Let's go inside and talk. I know there's a classroom free.' He led the way to a door marked 'Computer Studies' and ushered Jack through. They both took seats at desks.

The old man gestured to the banks of computer screens. 'I've been learning the Internet. Everyone talks about the generation gap and blames the young, but the elderly must make an effort, too. Unfortunately there's a literacy problem with my age group, so two others and myself have been elected to set an example. You would think the system could cope with Syllabics, which is only another form of shorthand, but no doubt that will come.'

The Inuk's shrewd gaze rested on Jack. 'Now, what do you want to discuss?'

Respect for the man led him into a circular explanation that could offer no offence.

Ulayoukuluk grasped the point immediately. 'You are asking me to remember a meeting I had with your father thirty years ago on the subject of Ituquvik. I'm afraid I can't. Can you remember what you were doing thirty years ago?'

Jack grinned. 'I wasn't born.'

The elder nodded and his face took on an introspective cast. He's holding something back, Jack thought. He pressed a little harder. 'Perhaps he told you he planned to do something there?'

Ulayoukuluk seemed puzzled. 'But you were his son. Surely he would have told you?'

'I last saw him when I was six. I don't remember much about him.'

The elder's perplexity increased. 'And yet you came to tell me about the Place of the Old People.'

Jack shrugged. 'There's no connection.'

After a long silence, Ulayoukuluk seemed to reach a decision. 'I'm going to tell you something. It was your father's secret and you're entitled to know. But it was my secret, too, and I want your word that you won't repeat a word of it without reference to me.'

Jack nodded. 'Agreed.'

The old man sighed. 'What is no secret is that in the 1970s, the whole of the Canadian North was staked out for minerals. The Arctic is rich in gold, diamonds and bauxite. What is less well known is that the mining companies agreed to put exploitation on hold, pending the outcome of native land claims. They figured correctly they could strike more favourable deals with local communities than with the federal government. Of course, no one knew the talks would stretch out for so long.'

His frail hand made an elliptical gesture. 'I'll cut a long story short. I had two meetings with your father. The first time, he told me in confidence that he had located gold-bearing seams at Ituquvik.'

'Gold?' Jack struggled to comprehend.

Ulayoukuluk ignored the interruption. 'He was the mine company's geologist and owed them a duty, but he was also raising a family in Snowdrift and he wanted my advice. I shared his fears: we'd both seen the gold rush in Yellowknife and the terrible effects on everyone, natives and non-natives. It was a monster that destroyed family life. So we swore to each other to say nothing.'

Jack was overcome by relief and a swelling sense of pride. 'And the second meeting?'

'It was about a year later. Your father said he was worried that the gold stratum would eventually be discovered, perhaps by some amateur geologist. He told me he had a plan that would protect Ituquvik. He described it as a safety mechanism which, when activated, would reveal something more precious than the gold itself, but with less destructive effects. He didn't give me details, but I trusted him. It was only when you came to see me that I realized what he had in mind.'

Jack had to admire the elegance of his father's thinking: one treasure concealing another. Even if the gold seams were identified, the area would remain inviolate as a historical site. But perhaps his father had not reckoned on the explosion of tourism in the past thirty years or Jonas's vaulting ambitions. He couldn't imagine what Jonas would do with a goldmine.

He frowned. 'Did my father mention his boss at all?'

Ulayoukuluk closed his eyes for several seconds, like a resting bird. 'Yes, that was the strange thing, I recall. The Swedish mine owner had a bad reputation as an employer. I met him once – a rich man, unpleasant. But your father said he had this man's support. I asked myself why such a person would not take profit from this discovery.'

Perhaps his father had kept back his discovery of gold and simply identified Ituquvik as the most plausible refuge for a Viking ship. Something else nagged at Jack: his stepfather's possible involvement. 'Did my father mention Aglukark in this connection?'

The former land negotiator shook his head. 'Frankly, I was surprised by their friendship. Aglukark was making his reputation as a campaigner: he wanted a truly independent Inuit homeland in which no southerners would be welcome. A few people felt like that and your stepfather had a small following, but he was no politician. I think perhaps your father was a little naïve.'

Not just naïve. The ugly word 'cuckold' sprang into Jack's mind. His father had held out the hand of friendship and Aglukark had stolen his wife.

He looked at the old man. 'I'm afraid Dad's safety mechanism is coming apart. It may be difficult to keep the truth hidden, but I'll do my best.'

The old men nodded. 'That's good enough for me. I hope you are your father's son.'

CHAPTER 25

THE MALE BEAR worked at the block of ice with its teeth and claws, pausing every few minutes to rise to its full height and sample the air with a swaying motion of his head. The predator's keen nose confirmed that his prey remained on the ice shelf where he had sighted it earlier. Satisfied with the block's dimensions, the bear slipped down on his stomach and began to nudge the heavy sphere forward with his head and paws.

The intended victim lay sunning itself close to the water's edge more than a hundred yards distant. Weighing a ton, the walrus possessed a wicked pair of three-foot canines capable of inflicting mortal wounds on any attacker, including killer whales and polar bears. The animal was also equipped with exceptionally acute smell and hearing.

The walrus possessed only two weaknesses: poor eyesight and a narrow, vulnerable skull. The bear had factored both into its strategy.

Aglukark watched the drama unfold with keen appreciation. It was a supreme demonstration that the spirits of animals and men were interlinked. In the distant past, he reflected, bears had shown the Inuit this way of stalking seals and walruses while remaining invisible. Hunters still used the technique, pushing forward white screens until the moment to rush forward with harpoons. The *nanuq*'s method was more precise.

The bear was taking infinite care, pushing the heavy ice ball forward a few feet at a time across the surface melt water before subsiding on its belly in tense stillness. Forty yards away, the basking walrus fanned itself with a flipper, its back turned to the danger. For several minutes the ice block became lodged on an arm of ice rubble until the bear understood the problem and skirted round it, using its huge claws for traction.

The final act had arrived. Aglukark watched the bear gather its rear quarters and place its forepaws under the ice block, while clamping down securely on the sphere with its long muzzle. In a prodigious display of strength and speed, the bear reared up and wielded the mace above its head. Only a pace separated the predator from smashing the skull of its prey.

In the same instant, Aglukark uttered a grunt-like 'oogh' sound that carried to both animals. The startled bear looked up and the walrus, alerted by the danger signal, awoke with a roar and jerked round in a slashing movement that opened its attacker's unprotected stomach. The walrus stabbed twice more before making its way to the water in a rapid humping, shuffling motion, leaving the bear on its back, clutching its chest spasmodically as it choked on its own blood.

Aglukark turned away, pleased with the entertainment and this demonstration of his power over events. It was a good omen, an apt metaphor for the human drama he was helping to shape. Atsiluaq would be proud of him, he thought. The shaman recalled again how, when the world was new, the prophet Atsiluaq had looked into the future and warned the Inuit of what lay in store. In his mind he heard the words of the prophecy revealed in the great shaman's song that had introduced a word that the people had not heard before – qallunaat, meaning literally 'high brows', or white men. Atsiluaq was remembered for his second song, in which the shaman described a lustrous red cloth fluttering in the wind. Sure enough, the High Brows had come to the north and the two predominant symbols of their power were both red – the Canadian flag and the ensign of the Hudson's Bay Company.

Aglukark still felt anger at the enslavement of his parents' generation. He had been born on a week's trek to the HBC store at Pond Inlet, the sled loaded with furs to trade for bullets, knives, blankets and a few groceries. By his father's account, when his mother cried out with her labour pains he built a small igluviga for her, but minutes after the birth she was walking ahead of the sled carrying the new baby in her parka.

Supplying the Bay with products became the pattern of his childhood. The opening of the trading post at Snowdrift in 1947 had eased the family's travels, but the welcome was no less frosty or demeaning. The Scottish High Brows paid in aluminium tokens which could be traded for items kept behind the counter, after which the family was directed to an unheated outer room where they counted themselves fortunate to receive a mug of warm tea and some hardtack before being dispatched into the wilderness to harvest more fur and ivory.

The prophet's warning had done the Inuit no good: the Bay and the church had blinded them with tricks. All slaves became dependent on their masters, Aglukark reflected. His own prediction would have a more salutary effect. Which is why it had suited him to be thought dead for the past thirteen years while he hid in the obscurity of the capital's outlying slums.

The sayings of dead prophets carried far greater potency than those of the living, as he was coming to appreciate. Now people thought they saw his ghost and were repeating his revelation: out of a hole in the ground would come a wave of happiness, to be overtaken by a wave of misery.

The meaning of Ituquvik's secret had not been evident when Ned Walker enlisted him in a seemingly foolish venture. It was a deception, the miner had explained, to protect the community. But, at the last minute, Ned had seen a fatal weakness in the plan that would bring shame on everyone, he warned.

In a dream that night, the shaman had been granted a glimpse into the future. He saw a plume of dark haze arising from Ituquvik that twisted in the sky and settled in coils around Snowdrift, bringing despair, destitution and a final understanding of how the Inuit had been betrayed into embracing modern ways. From such disillusion, he realized, a new order might be constructed to restore the old religion, songs, dances, myths and histories of his people.

Perhaps the spirits were directing him, for what at first seemed like self-interest had assumed surprising purpose. The lust of Elizabeth, Walker's wife, had matched his own; her screams had sharpened his own desire. Taking a *qallunaat* woman as his own had burnished his charisma as a healer, bringing as many visitors prompted by curiosity as those suffering from sickness.

Even the irrational defiance of Elizabeth's boy, Jack, had played a part when the marriage was flaking like black ice. The avalanche had rid him of a harridan and planted the seeds of his own immortality. Soosie was his own flesh, to do with as he pleased, but incest was a grave crime in the eyes of *qallunaat*. It explained Jack's violence towards him and he had to assume that, should he return publicly, the boy would report him to the authorities to counter the shaman's accusations of attempted murder.

Despite a broken leg, Aglukark had managed to tunnel out of the mass of snow, then conceal himself aboard the last of the rescuers' departing sleds and make his way back to the outpost camp. When the bone healed, he began the interminable trek south, taking his pick of outlying shelters that lay abandoned along his route despite the inducements of the government's outpost camp programme.

It took him nearly a year to travel to Iqaluit, where there was appreciation for his skills among the displaced and impoverished people on the capital's outskirts. His accidental reunion with Soosie had come three years before when she was summoned on an errand of mercy to the squatters' camp where he was living. Destiny had returned to him not only an intelligent daughter, disillusioned with the white-men's ways, but a loyal disciple.

He recalled the evening she arrived with news of a commotion in Snowdrift: the radio said that a walrus harpoon had led to a valuable historical discovery at Ituquvik. Until that moment, Aglukark had been content to warm his soul before the embers of his prophecy, resigned to his own death before time brought about its fulfilment. Ned had impressed on him the need to let time do its work at the site. The sudden confluence of events, with his stepson's prominent involvement, made the prospect of intervention almost too sweet to contemplate.

In the distance, the bear lay motionless, a raven pecking at its eyes. Aglukark approached the rock opening with caution. The cave's proximity to Snowdrift was a risk to be weighed against the need for fresh intelligence. Sensing a visitor's presence within, he ducked quickly under a rock overhang. The woman had been sleeping, lulled by the warm primus stove, and stretched out a hand to pull him down on the blankets.

It was his Soosie.

They were alone in the terminal and no passengers emerged when the plane swung its tail around and cut its engines. Jack lifted Odette's bag and took her arm.

'The big-wigs are paying Paddy a visit.'

Odette pulled a face. 'Perfect timing. I don't know how I'm going to tell him.'

As they crossed the gravel apron, they saw the grizzled pilot descend and check something beneath the near wing. Jack recognized him and touched his cap.

'Hi, Harry. Wings coming off again?'

The thin, laconic Newfoundlander acknowledged him gruffly while squinting up at a manual fuel register. He scratched his beard with a glove. 'Damn gauge went down on me last week. She was fine on one engine, but taking off again was something else. Better get on board now.'

The plane was full and they made their way down the narrow aisle to settle in two adjacent bucket seats at the rear. Jack turned to Odette and gestured to the passengers. 'We've got the Nunavut premier and the Canadian Culture Minister flying with us, plus a TV crew. I hope Paddy's got the red carpet out.'

Paddy had laid on the next best thing. A sturdy wooden ramp with hand ropes now bridged the steep incline between the beach and a bank of the stream. The Irishman stood at the top, glad-handing each arrival with effusive charm.

'Odette! Jack! Heavens be praised!' In a stage whisper, he added, 'As soon as I'm shot of this nonsense, we've work to do.'

They left him to it, idling away the next two hours in the grub tent until Odette grabbed Jack's hand and led him to her quarters. The room was snug and warm, protected by metal shielding.

'I think I've come over all faint,' Odette said, holding a hand to her forehead. 'I may have to lie down.'

Jack drew her to him.

A shuffling outside made them spring apart. A cough preceded a gentle knock on the door. Jack opened it.

Paddy made no attempt to hide his delight at their discomfiture. 'Marvellous. Just marvellous. Just remember what they say, Odette: you begin by sinking into his arms and you end up with your arms in his sink.'

Odette blushed and Jack laughed. Then he remembered the grimness of their mission and made Paddy sit down. He heard them out to the end, his expression of bafflement succeeded by outrage, shock and finally denial.

He leaned forward earnestly. 'You have to understand I'm in too deep to back out now. I'm told the Canadian Prime Minister is visiting next week and I've been nominated for a Gold Medal of the Royal Geographical Society.'

Jack couldn't believe it. 'Can't you just say you were mistaken?'

Paddy shook his head. 'You don't understand. I've made the cardinal sin of crowing too soon in the media. The magnitude of such incompetence will leave me a laughing stock and perhaps drummed out of the profession.'

Odette's harsh tone surprised both men. 'Then I resign here and now.'

Paddy raised his hands as if warding off a blow. 'No need for that, my dear. I've put myself badly. Let's look at what you've told me. We are given to understand that Jack's father and this Ove fellow conspired to bring about a hoax. But where is the evidence? It's all circumstantial.'

Jack didn't grasp the point being made. 'What more proof do you need?'

'Jack, I always thought you were one of my brightest students, but you disappoint me. This so-called hoax lies under several hundred tons of rocks and boulders which have been sitting there for as long as anyone can remember, according to reliable sources. It's not physically possible to insert fabricated evidence at the surface level. Don't you see? There was no hoax.'

He watched her direct the lifting operations and issue orders to her adoring band of seven dwarfs. An aura seemed to shimmer around her long-legged figure and flare out from her orange safety helmet.

It was a cumbersome and yet delicate process that required each boulder to be jacked up a few inches and a steel harness secured around it before the mobile crane hoisted its burden and trundled away to deposit it, carefully labelled, at a site further up the valley. Three cameras fixed to permanent mounts recorded the position of each stone. After each removal, a student hastened forward to vacuum the newly exposed surface with an electrical filter device.

In the mid-morning break she wandered over to him, clapping dust from her heavy work gloves. 'I think Paddy may have a point,' she said. 'You'd have to be a mole to insert anything in there.'

'Or a wolverine.'

Odette smiled at him. 'Well, let's suppose there was a hoax. The three people who carried it out are dead. Why didn't they make sure it came to light so they could reassure themselves that everyone was taken in? The discovery of a Viking site here would vindicate old man Ove's theories.'

Jack had been wondering about that. 'Perhaps they were storing up some satisfaction for the hereafter.'

That evening they strolled up the valley and climbed one of the mountain foothills. Here, the tundra had become a lush meadow, sprouting pale cream aven, arctic heather, saxifrages, poppies, diaspensia and a host of other plants. Rock blooms of lichen added to the palate of vivid colours.

To Odette, it was like looking down on a coral reef. She stooped in delight. 'Are those dandelions? And buttercups?'

Jack picked a mountain aven and showed it to her, twirling the cup-shaped dish of petals. 'The Inuit call it *malikkat*, because it follows the sun around the sky. See this dish? It reflects the sun's rays into the centre of the flower.'

Odette was transfixed by a display of fluffy willow catkins. 'They're so beautiful.'

Jack stood behind her, holding her shoulders lightly. 'Pussy willows. The hairs are transparent, taking sunlight down the shaft to warm the body. The hair of polar bears does exactly the same. That's why they overheat so easily.'

Odette mocked him with large eyes. 'Pussy willows and overheated bears?'

They wandered back, hand in hand.

Later that night, she traced a faint scar on his forehead. 'Playground fight?'

He laughed. 'I can't remember. Probably a sled accident.'

She pursed a moue at him. 'I wish you'd tell me about growing up here.'

He made an effort. 'I suppose it was like being on a farm. Instead of milking the cows you'd go out and get a seal or put down a net. You didn't have to struggle to get a tractor started, just sort out the traces of a dog team that thought they were kittens with a ball of wool.'

He ran a hand lightly along the swell of her hip. 'Tell me about your name. Wasn't Odette a Resistance heroine in the war?'

When she looked down and said nothing, Jack had the feeling he had blundered on to consecrated ground. 'It doesn't matter,' he said.

'No, I'll tell you. I don't think my parents realized how hard that name would be to live up to. To most people there is only one Odette, a shining heroine, even if they can't quite remember what she did. Of course, my parents admired her and it was the highest compliment they could give to their daughter.'

Jack felt stricken to see tears glint in her eyes.

'Until I was fifteen I took it for granted, like being named Marilyn or Ava. Then I saw a television film about her. Her name was Odette Brailly. She was a French girl of nineteen who married an Englishman and then moved to London. She volunteered to go back to France as a radio operator, but she was betrayed and taken to a Gestapo prison for interrogation.'

Her eyes took on a distant look. 'They tortured her for a long time. She was branded in the base of the spine with a white-hot iron. They pulled out her toenails with pliers, but she refused to talk. So they sent her to the women's camp at Ravensbruck.'

Jack took her hand gently in his. 'But she survived?'

Odette gripped his hand and smiled sadly. 'Yes, she survived. She was awarded the George Medal for bravery. But her story haunts me. It's silly, I know, but I feel unworthy.'

He cradled her to sleep in his arms, listening to the music of the valley stream.

CHAPTER 26

B Y THE FOURTH day, the rock pile had been reduced to a few boulders and flattish slabs, revealing a base that sent Paddy into transports of joy. Confounding all expectations, he was rewarded with a cultural layer eighteen inches deep.

'Jack, we have been singularly blessed. Permafrost, sand and clay have conspired to create the perfect conditions for preservation. Clearly, the river flooded during the summer months and the sediment was swept into this natural trap where it combined with the subsoil and was frozen.'

While Paddy rattled on happily, Jack's gaze was drawn to a remaining boulder, on which the bench slot he had originally noticed was clearly exposed. Excusing himself, he knelt down and inspected it closely. It did not seem to have been chiselled, as he first thought, but rather gouged out. He wondered what Viking implement could have cut the rock so cleanly.

With the end in sight, the lifting operation acquired a fresh vigour. Even the Inuit, who had treated the whole exercise as another *qallunaat* folly to be indulged, crowded around and offered to help. The ice was still firm in the fjord's higher reaches, and a steady stream of drivers continued to deliver supplies.

'I saw a picture of Vikings,' Simon Inuksaq told Jack. 'They had horns, like cows.'

Benny laughed. 'They were the first cowboys.'

'One time, I saw a cow, down south,' Jimmy Okadlak volunteered. 'It was a pretty stupid animal. It let me walk right up to it. I got its mess on my boots. Maybe these Vikings with horns were stupid people, too.'

'Yeah,' Jack said. 'Shit for brains.'

They all held their breath as the last slab was lifted clear. Only Paddy was permitted to enter the vault, treading gingerly in his rubber boots. He squatted down to mutter a lengthy commentary into a tape recorder. Then he retreated carefully and beckoned his team around him.

'The area that interests us is quite small, about eight feet by twelve. There's a thin layer of sterile sand on top that's been disturbed on one side by the wolverines' digging. Protruding through the cultural layer are pieces of timber, which I suspect are bearing elements for the collapsed roof.'

Paddy looked around the circle of faces, his intense air impressing on them the seriousness of their task. 'The procedure is quite clear. First, we construct a wooden frame to support the sides, before removing the sand. Then we have to melt the frozen cultural layer. As you'll recall, the maximum thaw rate is about four to five inches a day and this will turn the upper layers into a morass of water and mud. That will have to be cleared away carefully and any artefacts recorded and removed.'

He smiled at them reassuringly. 'Remember, if we do this correctly, you'll all be written into the history books.'

In the afternoon, Odette joined him on their daily walk. To Jack she appeared stressed. 'An excavation like this would normally take two seasons,' she fretted. 'Every stage has to be written up and I'm afraid we'll make technical mistakes that everyone can pick holes in.'

Jack decided not to confide his own forebodings. He stopped suddenly. 'I've lost track of time. What date is it?'

She looked looked at her watch. 'Thirtieth of July.'

The worry stayed with him and as soon as they returned he made for the communications tent. Raising Jonas on the squawk box was like getting through to a spirit in a séance.

'Sorry, Jack, I've been kinda busy. I hear you fine.'

'Have you ordered the Big Dipper and the fairground yet?'

'Oh, I get you. The orders go in any day now.'

'So the hamlet council backed your plan?'

'Yeah. And no thanks to your sister. Soosie's been getting people riled up like a cloud of blackfly. She got a seat on the council and the ear of the mayor. She wants him to scrap the structure plan.'

Jack stared thoughtfully at a television screen displaying a 3D grid of the rock pile. 'What are the chances of that?'

'Zero. Eighty per cent of the council wants my scheme to go through.'

'Jonas, do me a favour. Hold back on those Sealift orders and don't sign any contracts for a few days, until you hear from me.'

'Jesus, the closing date for both is 2 August. That's only three days, Jack, and there's no refunds. Is something wrong down there?'

'No, just dandy. I just want to be sure there's no egg coming your way.'

'Will do. Over and out.'

Jack turned back to study the rock configuration on the computer screen.

The imminent arrival of the Canadian Prime Minister brought out the stage blarney in Paddy, who practised his diplomacy on cooks and students alike.

Above the cultural layer Odette had supervised the construction of a light plastic chamber, pumped full of hot air, in which small teams sweated in rotation.

When Jack ducked in to check on progress, he saw that two days' thawing had reduced the upper coating to a layer of thick, black slime that had to be scraped out with trowels and then run through a filtered sluice. Several pieces of timber and planks had been borne away to be catalogued.

'It's like waiting for the creature from the black lagoon,' Paddy confessed. 'Whatever's down there – and I'm counting on something significant – will be plain enough tomorrow.' The thought contorted his features with worry lines. 'What a day for the PM to drop in.'

Jack tracked Odette to the finds tent. She zipped up the entrance flap and embraced him. 'You're quite a discovery, Jack Walker. Can I label you and take you away for examination?'

The sculpture of her cheek fitted warmly into his hand. After a while he nodded to the polythene bags of artefacts. 'Anything in there you recognize?'

'From Karlsson's photographs? Not really. They're just bits of wood. You don't really think there's a chance of that now?'

Jack took her hands. 'I wouldn't hold your breath. I think I know how the hoax was done.'

She stared at him.

Then he told her.

The pup squirmed desperately in his hands and made pitiful barks that pleased the shaman. It was a sound no mother could resist. Aglukark had cut a length of thin fishing twine and now he slipped the noose around the pup's flipper and secured it firmly before lowering the tiny seal into the breathing hole.

A fox's recent digging had alerted him to the pup's presence in the lair. Some instinct of self-preservation drove baby seals to dig several small tunnels where they could hide in safety while their mother was absent hunting fish or fleeing a predator that threatened the lair. Few predators were fooled. After enlarging the oblique shaft dug by the fox, he had seized the pup's soft body, still coated in its white fur.

The mother seal would be circling not far away, Aglukark knew. Her own instincts committed her to an unwavering sequence that would bring her directly to his harpoon. There! He felt the line plucked from his hand as the seal responded to her floundering baby's barks by snatching it in her mouth. He raised the harpoon and waited for her next pass. She would return for a visual check of the lair, a manoeuvre that required her to turn over and present her belly uppermost.

It took no more than a minute. A tiny wave in the dark waters signalled her run and he thrust down hard, feeling the harpoon impale the creature. Bracing against its dying struggles, he reflected on the fatal power of love. When the loved one was in peril, the protector discarded all caution and became easy prey. Among humans, the selfless impulse to rescue was even more powerful. It was a fitting death for Jack.

The elegance of Jack's nemesis revolved in his mind. Even sweeter than the prospect of revenge for his young son, who would have carried the healer's spirit into the future, was the thought of returning to Snowdrift. Age, he had to concede, was taking its toll and his life in the shadows was proving more arduous than it had once been. Knowing the Inuit habit of compromise and reconciliation, he was tantalized by images of being welcomed home and playing a leading part in the renaissance of traditional values.

His daughter endorsed the prospect. Only Jack stood in his way. His stepson had tried to kill him once and might do so again, or use his authority against him. Soosie had identified the bait that would draw Jack to his death.

It took him twenty minutes to dissect the adult seal and place the chunks inside a sack. It was hot work and the blood excited the dogs whose irritating clamour was compounded by the pup's pathetic barks. He retrieved the harpoon, crossed to the seal hole and skewered the baby seal before tossing its body to the dog team. When they had finished he whipped them forward, halting every fifty yards to throw down a piece of meat and, for good measure, sprinkle the ground with fluid from a stoppered bottle. The bladder contents of a young female polar bear in season would be irresistible.

Then nature would take its course.

They awoke to a murky day of swirling overcast that sent tendrils of damp cold stealing into the camp. Before breakfast, they followed the stream to its mouth and looked out at the fjord's ominous ceiling. This point marked the new floe edge, a shelf now less than three feet thick that bordered the fjord's open waters.

Jack estimated the visibility at fifty yards. 'The Premier's due at eleven. It might have cleared a bit by then.'

Odette breathed into the fur patch on the back of her glove and held it to her face. She had put her hair up in a French style. It gave her a brisk look that matched her words. 'There's work to do, PM or not.'

The cold was illusory: a warmer nocturnal temperature had boosted the air heater and accelerated the thaw rate, so that a dipstick lowered into the cultural layer showed six inches of black slime. By Paddy's calculations, only four inches of permafrost lay beneath. Impishly, he could not resist donning rubber gloves and exploring the mud by hand, his face turned up blindly like a safe cracker.

His exclamation brought Jack over.

'Jack, Odette, there's something here. If it's what I think it is, we have proof of a smithy. Good God, it's shifting. It's just lying in my hands below the surface.'

With infinite care, he lifted out a heavy object and placed it beside him. It appeared to be a cracked and crudely shaped piece of stone. Odette played a small hose over its outlines and Paddy uttered a small grunt of triumph.

'There! Do you see the kaolin clay baked to the surface? This is part of a small furnace. The Vikings pack these with pre-roasted bog iron and layers of charcoal. The metal drains off at the bottom. Once the firing is complete, they smash open the stone frame. Only a very small quantity of iron is produced, so most likely this is used to make new boat nails.'

Paddy looked around at his jubilant team. 'Let's get to it, my fine fellows.'

In the next hour, the mud yielded up further treasures – three clenched nails, two split washers, five wooden boat pegs, a fragment of a stone lamp with a small oil hollow pecked in its top, and a small hammer head. The most intriguing discovery was a set of chain-mail rings.

Odette was obliged to set up office in the finds tent to list and bag the stream of objects. Jack saw she was checking each item against Karlsson's file of photographs.

He dropped his voice. 'Playing snap?'

She frowned. 'It's so difficult to be sure. Yes, a lot of these objects are on the missing list, but they're pretty indistinguishable – nails, washers, smelting equipment. Here's a picture of a broken furnace, but our piece seems to be broken in a different way. Perhaps it cracked later.' She sighed. 'If there was a hoax, it may only come out in the chemical tests or radio-carbon readings.'

The shattering roar of a helicopter startled them both. Jack took her arm. 'We're on parade.'

A large machine landed on the beach and several minutes passed before a small security detail satisfied themselves that no risk was posed by assassins or terrorists. Paddy welcomed the Prime Minister at the foot of the aircraft steps, dwarfed by the tall politician.

Eric Renouard paused at the top of the ramp to be introduced to Odette, bowing his head and plainly enchanted by her metropolitan French. Jack registered the rugged features of a working man, at odds with his snappy attire, as the Premier shook his hand. Noticing his uniform, Renouard's smile broadened. 'You know, my father was with the Wildlife Service back in the fifties and sixties. I miss those times. My father worked with animals and I became a politician. I sometimes wonder if it's so different.'

With Jack and Odette trailing as a guard of honour, Paddy escorted the Premier on a tour of inspection. At last they faced the plastic tent, through which hunched figures could be seen working, and Paddy explained the latest phase of the operation.

'The level of mud is so low that the artefacts are making it impossible to scoop it out manually. So we're using a small pump to drain off the organic sludge.'

Jack noticed that figures inside the tent were standing up and reacting with agitation. A student hailed Paddy respectfully. 'I think you should see this, sir.'

Holding back the tent flap courteously, Paddy beckoned his visitor inside. Jack and Odette followed.

The excavation area was now littered with objects, many clearly recognizable through their black coating. Jack's sweeping glance took in a boot-shaped anvil, a chisel blade and a pair of iron-working tongs, but the gaze of everyone present was locked on a sinister shape in the centre of the detritus. A rack of ribs, protruding knees and finally a skull, open-mouthed in a rictus of death, left no room for doubt. The bones had collapsed under the weight of matter pressing down upon them, but it was plainly the skeleton of a young man.

Renouard was the first to break the tense silence. 'Congratulations, Professor. You have made history and I'm proud to be here to see you do it.'

Paddy seemed to paddle in a pool of pride before leaning forward to inspect the skeleton. 'I think this gentleman met with an unfortunate accident,' he pronounced, pointing to crown of the skull, in which a flat, triangular hole was evident. 'A Dorset arrow or a falling-out among shipmates. The story is probably here in the mud, so we must treat this as a crime scene.'

Jack glanced at Odette, who shot him a look of dubious confirmation and slipped away. As he watched Paddy fussing around the corpse and lapping up Renouard's compliments, he recalled Jonas's little lecture on hubris. It was no longer a matter of egg on faces, he thought: there was a shit storm coming.

It was a student who spotted it. The pendant had been concealed in the glutinous slime around the corpse's neck, but the dull links caught his eye. Remarkably, a small dousing of sterile water revealed a clear face of bronze, on which a decoration was incised. Paddy hunched over it, squinting and muttering.

Jack saw the blood leach from Paddy's face and the strength leave his legs, so that he nearly tipped into the black pit. With a visible effort of will, the archaeologist stood up and engaged the Prime Minister in further pleasantries before firmly ushering him outside.

Paddy caught Jack's arm in a trembling grip. 'We're banjaxed,' he whispered. 'Ove Karlsson was too greedy. He wanted to kill two birds with one stone. He wasn't content with placing his Viking site in the North-West Passage as a signpost to China, but he has to give our skeleton a Toltec memento from Mexico. He might as well have put a sombrero on his head and left him holding a pair of maracas.'

Jack made directly for the finds office and found it empty. Lying open on the desk was Karlsson's catalogue, showing the photograph of a skeleton. The skull was pierced with a small, triangular hole. Under the title 'Ornaments', he found the Toltec brass pendant in the South-American section.

He checked Odette's quarters and the meeting-room before heading for the grub tent, where he was surprised to find Benny in a chef's hat and white coat.

'I never cooked French food before,' the Inuk confessed. 'I don't have any frogs' legs. You think he'll go for some *maktaak*?'

Jack grimaced. 'Have you seen Odette anywhere?'

Benny jerked a roasting fork towards the upper valley. 'I think I saw her heading for the ladies' cabin about ten minutes ago. You can wait for her here, if you want.'

Five minutes passed before Jack got to his feet and thanked Benny. 'I'll just go and check on her.'

He strolled up the valley, trying to work out how the chips would fall. Disaster for Paddy, disgrace for Jonas and bitter disappointment for those villagers who thought an end to the years of struggle was in sight. He himself would probably relinquish the trust he had worked for. The only winner was Soosie, riding her celebrity as a healer and now a politician whose warnings had been spectacularly vindicated.

The ladies' cabin was sited at the higher end of the encampment, in front of the relocated boulders. As its sole visitor, Odette loved the pristine condition of the shower and toilet. Noticing the door ajar, he knocked and, hearing nothing, looked inside.

He made a thorough search of the camp for the next ten minutes, enlisting Simon and two students in an increasingly urgent hunt, but had to concede defeat. Odette had disappeared.

Paddy, in subdued mood, was bidding goodbye to Renouard when Jack interrupted them and explained the situation. The Irishman's distress at Odette's peril eclipsed any other torment he might be experiencing.

Renouard frowned. 'I'm sorry, but I have to go. The pilot says we may not get off in this fog if we leave it any longer. I'm sure the young lady will turn up. There's nowhere for her to go.'

As a search and rescue officer, Jack was prepared to commandeer the Prime Minister's chopper if necessary, but he put it as a polite request. 'Sir, there's a chance she's fallen into the water, in which case she won't have long to live. It's vital that we make a visual sweep along the shoreline in the next few minutes. Do you mind?'

Renouard nodded his assent and urgently summoned his pilot. Meanwhile, Jack briefed Jimmy Okadlak to lead a search team out on the fjord ice and instructed Simon Inuksaq to scout up into the foothills with three hunters. Benny offered to take the camp's outboard inflatable to search down the fjord.

Jack ran to the helicopter and strapped in beside the pilot, a small, wiry Saskatchewan who did not conceal his doubts. 'Won't see much in this shit,' he complained.

The chopper flew as low as the pilot dared, but the cloud base was stuck fifteen feet above the water and the bulky machine could not penetrate the murk without forcing the pilot to fly blind. Jack strained his eyes, seeing only hallucinatory shapes in a thick vapour that seemed to churn in sympathy with his stomach. They returned after half an hour.

He stayed calm, drawing on the experience of past rescue missions to quell the rising tide of panic that threatened to overwhelm him. Reluctantly acknowledging he couldn't detain the Prime Minister any longer, he thanked Renouard and bade him farewell.

One by one, the search teams returned empty handed. 'There's a thin trail in the hills, but the light's not good,' Simon reported. 'Maybe it was made by caribou.'

It gave Jack an idea and he cursed himself for his stupidity. Accompanied by Simon, he returned to the ladies' cabin and together they scoured the surrounding ground. At a gesture by the Inuk, he hurried to squat beside him.

Jack strained to catch Simon's murmur. 'Small tracks. Look, a lady's boots.'

Barely visible, the prints led away from the camp and towards the cluster of boulders. After only ten paces, however, they came to a stop in midstride.

Thoughtfully, Simon traced the last footprint with a finger and looked at Jack.

'She was taken.'

CHAPTER 27

ODETTE WAS BENT almost double under the load of stinking seal meat, her breath rasping at the steep climb. There was a gloating quality to the man's look that disturbed her more than the physical humiliation she was enduring as his pack horse. Once again she stumbled over the frolicking dogs.

'Look,' she gasped during a brief halt, 'do you realize you'll go to prison for this?'

When he rested his gaze on her, she thought his irises twitched, as if to spin. 'No,' he informed her mockingly. 'No dead men in prison.' She thought about that.

They had crossed the inlet without seeing a soul before abandoning the sled and climbing this mountainside. All the dogs carried loads, slung pannier-style across their backs. Her own burden of meat was secured by a single rope that cut into her upper chest and shoulders, yet she was reluctant to rest in case the sweat of her exertions caused her to chill. It was a few degrees above freezing, but the steady wind scythed through her leggings.

The trembling of her limbs was uncontrollable by the time they crested a ridge and looked up at a bulging glacier slick with melt water.

'I'm not going up that,' Odette protested.

Puzzlingly, her captor produced a knife and began cutting long tufts of guard hair from his caribou skin jacket. Crouching down, he tied a thin swatch of hair around each of his boots and gestured for her to do the same. Her first attempts at tying the knots were defeated by the paralysing cold in her fingers and, while she fumbled, a sickening realization dawned. They were going over the glacier.

Aglukark pushed her forward. The woman still adopted a defiant posture that barely concealed her pain. Surprised by her strength and violent resistance to her capture, he had seized her hand and cut the palm with a knife to subdue the wildness in her and although the cold had staunched the bleeding, over the past few hours the wound had become swollen and raw.

She looked at him with narrowed eyes. It was, he thought, the look of a trapped wolf – an expression that showed no fear but rather a dangerous patience and he resolved to watch her closely. Yet doing so filled him with a secret well of pleasure that owed nothing to her looks, for she was undernourished and unattractive to him.

No, his gratification came from the knowledge that this was Jack's woman and his stepson would burn with the pain of her loss before he met his own terrifying death.

The woman's capture had not gone smoothly. He had never known a female to strike a man's face with her fists or bring her knee up into the groin, but in the end his knife had been persuasive and she had stumbled ahead of him obediently, gripping her hand and cursing him. Having taken the precaution of laying two false trails, he was able to disturb their spoor with practised skill, but not so carefully that a skilled hunter would be deceived for long. Someone like Jack.

For his escape trail he had chosen an inaccessible caribou path that led along the cliffs for two miles before it plunged to link a series of narrow, descending ledges on the crumbling rock face and finally dropping to the inlet's beach. Pushing the woman into the waiting dog sled, he crossed to the fjord's far side under the dark folds of overcast. Concealing the sled beneath rocks had consumed a precious two hours, but experience told him the fog would last another day. It was long enough.

Odette plodded up the ice slope, surprised by her boots' traction on the treacherous surface. She studied her captor surreptitiously. He was old, but stronger than her and robust enough to shoulder a heavy backpack from which, puzzlingly, the handle of a carpenter's saw protruded. He had also revealed an ingrained cruelty in the way he had used his knife. For the moment she shelved the mystery of his identity or purpose and concentrated on escape. Two facts were indisputable: she could not have outrun the dogs on the fjord ice and now there was nowhere to hide.

Mental images of flooring the construction worker with a two-by-four were supplanted by the memory of Jack running the Swede into a wall. Odette smiled grimly. She was looking forward to Jack's vengeance.

He knelt, eyes closed, and fought down the sense of failure that welled within him as he forced his brain to think. The faint scintilla of a trail had led to this rugged upland above the cliffs, but the mossy tundra had given way to an expanse of loose, sharp stones that held no imprint nor yielded any clue. Odette had been missing now for five hours.

Jack's instincts overpowered all reason to tell him Aglukark was behind this abduction. The certainty had gripped him in the second that Simon had voiced his opinion, followed by another realization that hit him like a physical blow. His stepfather had left a signature visible only to Jack, as if to taunt him. The business of the discontinued footprints was one of the shaman's tricks of the trade, easily executed but a source of awe to the credulous. Aglukark had been adept at making objects vanish and reappear, like any cheap conjurer.

With equal conviction, he acknowledged that he would be ridiculed and lose control of the search if he revealed that he was hunting a ghost. It was he, after all, who had reported his stepfather's death in an avalanche.

In Yukon, Jack had been called in on two abduction cases and he knew the sliding scale of survival would soon tip into the zone of maximum peril. If there was a sexual motive – and Jack was stabbed by the memory of Aglukark embracing his daughter on his lap – Odette's chances of remaining alive beyond forty-eight hours would become progressively slim. Revenge as a motive conjured images too graphic to contemplate.

Abduction meant an extended search and Jack had been touched by the willingness of the drivers, cooks and manual workers to put themselves under his command. Strictly speaking it was now a police matter, but the necessary land skills in unfamiliar terrain were outside the Mounties' competence.

Wearing his search and rescue cap, he had borrowed Paddy's satellite phone and rousted the pilots' controller at Resolute Bay. He waited impatiently for their OK before turning over his authority to Jonas.

'I'll be lucky to have any kind of job,' his friend lamented. 'Do you know the penalty charges we've racked up on freight and loans? There's talk of skinning me alive, and these folk in town know how to do it.'

Paddy was equally distraught but found less sympathy than he expected from Jack. In a bout of confession worthy of a Chinese cadre, Paddy berated himself for self-delusional stupidity that came to an abrupt halt at the sight of the skeleton's pendant. 'It had all the appearance of a trophy from the Middle East, but then I looked closer and nearly wet my trousers. I could see it was ancient Mexican. Of course, some of the other knickknacks we found are listed in the record of Ove Karlsson's kleptomania. Well, he's put my career on a slow boat to China.'

Jack frowned. 'Did anyone else identify the pendant?'

The archaeologist scratched his head. 'Well, no.'

'There's your answer. Give out the explanation you offered to Fingest, say it's a Dorset site full of Norse souvenirs. Close it down, restore the boulders and bury the skeleton with all due ceremony as a native person. Then go home and forget it.'

It occurred to Paddy that this hard-faced man might have lurked perpetually beneath Jack's genial facade. 'You say you know how the hoax was done?'

It was a sleight of hand obvious to any mining engineer, Jack explained. But his father had made a tiny mistake. He demonstrated the ploy on the computer. Calling up three-dimensional imagery of the rock fall, he used the cursor to define a keystone at the bottom of the pile and slid it out.

'Before this boulder was removed, the rocks resting on it were lifted a couple of inches and braced exactly the way you did. Ove Karlsson had arranged his Viking skeleton and collector's items in a metal palette that he filled with local sediment and then left to freeze. My father simply inserted the ice palette with a forklift truck and carefully eased out the supporting tray. Then he replaced the original rock with a shorter one.'

Paddy's eyebrows took on a life of their own. 'What alerted you to this . . . skulduggery?'

Jack leafed through a pile of photographs. 'This one. The rock that persuaded both of us the site was a *naust*.' He pointed to the groove. ' "Strongly indicative of Norse bench design", I think you said.'

Paddy's head came up aggressively. 'Well, it is.'

Jack let the photograph fall on the table in front of Paddy. 'All it's indicative of is that my father wasn't too good with a forklift truck. One of the prongs gouged the rock.'

Paddy lowered his head into his hands.

Jack blinked. Lost in thought, he had been staring blindly at the stone-strewn terrain and his eyes had made a connection that eluded his conscious brain. The tops of the stones held no footprints, but what about underneath? Curious, he put his weight on a small rock under his hand and it rolled it slightly. Picking it up, he studied the light screen of sand beneath. A small, crusted rill of sand marked the rock's movement. Few of the stones were flat, he noted, making them prone to disturbance. Carefully, he removed a stone that he had not touched; here, the sand was undisturbed. When he stepped on a third stone, the fresh impression beneath was sharply defined.

He began working outwards, painstakingly lifting stones and studying their resting places. He kept at it for an hour and a half, crawling forward with an obsessive concentration that, he was only too aware, was consuming precious time, until finally he turned up a recent smudge, then another. The third stone's depression left no room for doubt about Aglukark's direction: he had headed for the cliffs. Jack set off at a run.

He found the caribou path two miles ahead at the point where it cut through a narrow fissure in the rock and descended in a series of dizzying jinks to the beach a thousand feet below. The wind that blasted at him over the lip of the cliff sent tattered clouds racing overhead towards a scrap of blue sky. Below, the ferment barely ruffled the low-lying blanket of vapour muffling Victoria Sound.

Jack stared down at the indistinct jigsaw of ice, trying to project himself into his stepfather's mind. Travelling along the near shore was not an option as it remained a busy supply route to Ituquvik, he reasoned. Aglukark would have been obliged to cross over to the more inhospitable shore and then climb into the mountains.

Jack needed a snowmobile. Turning back, he retraced his route at a fast, loping pace. Ignoring the cutting pain of his rifle and knapsack straps, he imagined Odette's fears at the ordeal she had been pitched into. He had barely mentioned Aglukark to her, so her abduction would seem utterly bewildering.

Another agonizing thought intruded: what if his stepfather convinced her of Jack's efforts to kill him with the snowmobile and then murder his own mother and stepbrother? Whatever excuses Jack offered, she would never see him in the same light again. At all events, she would demand an explanation when this nightmare was over. The permutations of his shame seemed limitless.

He thrust this selfish speculation aside and resolved to tell her the truth, whatever the consequences. His priority was rescuing Odette. Her life force gave him hope: she was a fighter. Hold on, he prayed. Hold on.

The glacier seemed endless. In places they had to skirt crevasses and traverse ice buttresses that spanned vertiginous chasms. The walking surface was sheeted with melted water, but in other parts the ice was pitted and dry, cutting the dogs' paws.

Odette, spurred on by her captor's peremptory gestures, wondered where it was all leading. Rape? Murder? After cutting her with the knife, the man had offered her no further violence, indeed he seemed to treat her as a piece of inconsequential baggage. Was she being punished for disturbing Ituquvik, a sacred site? On the other hand, this juvenile drama could have been scripted by Karlsson, whose ploys had a habit of misfiring, she reminded herself.

She staggered to a halt at an ice bridge and watched the man lead the dogs across. At the mid-point they broke into a furious chorus of barking until the man shouted a command that had them slinking across, their tails between their legs. He summoned her with an impatient motion.

Odette approached the brink, averting her eyes from the drop, and concentrated on the slender span. Only eighteen inches wide, it was the narrowest she had yet crossed but it had the virtue of being only half-a-dozen paces in length.

She stepped forward firmly, careful to keep her heavy load balanced, and was halfway across when a movement tugged at her peripheral vision. For a split second, her gaze raked the depths on her right, capturing the image of a thirty-foot deep vault of ice in which a large animal was trapped.

Her concentration snapped back to the bridge and she ran the last few paces to the safety of firm ice, where she threw herself to the ground. Unexpectedly, the man helped her to ease the rope off her shoulders and release the seal meat from her back, indicating with the palm of his hand that she should rest.

'There's a polar bear down there,' she said in disbelief.

The man looked at her quizzically and again she had the impression that his irises twitched, as if they were about to spin. '*Nanuq*,' he pronounced with satisfaction. 'It is hungry.'

With the strain of the rope released from her chest, Odette breathed deeply but caught her breath as she watched the man performing an incomprehensible ritual. From his backpack he extracted a carpenter's saw, two wooden rods and a hammer, which he carried back over the ice bridge. At the far end he made a vertical cut about three feet deep with the saw and then, inching backwards on his knees, began sawing a line beneath the surface of the bridge. This cut was made at an oblique angle.

The man took infinite pains in his work, glancing down occasionally at the bear, which moved its head from side to side with a distracted air. The man hammered and sawed and then hammered again, until the purpose of his exertions became clear to Odette, chilling her stomach.

The top of the bridge was now a loose wedge of ice, resting on a base that slanted towards the right and was secured only by two slender rods. Anyone stepping upon it would be tipped into the vault with the bear. It was a trap for pursuers, she realized. This whole escapade was not about her, but about Jack.

The man had his back to her, preoccupied with obliterating traces of his work with a knife. Without hesitation, she ran at him silently, distilling all her strength and hatred in the effort. Her plan was to push him over the edge, but before she reached him he swivelled lightly and faced her with the knife. She did not falter, counting on a screamed challenge to confuse him, but in a disarming move he stepped towards her and seized her wounded hand, twisting it with such brutality that red-hot needles shot up her arm and dropped her to her knees. Still applying the pressure, he led her unresisting back to the dogs.

Aglukark turned and inspected his handiwork with pleasure, reflecting once again on the fatal entrapments of love. His trail of seal meat had captured the bear's attention, but the real lure had been the fragrant urine of a female. A large bag of scented meat, suspended tantalizingly just out of reach, had been the bear's final downfall. Bears never learned. Neither did humans: Jack, too, was driven by a lover's instincts and soon he would be

TRAILS TO HEAVEN   201

thrown into the bear's company, both enraged to be deprived of a mate. There was no doubt which one would prevail.

Aglukark hoped his stepson lived just long enough to appreciate the refinements that had gone into his death.

The machine bucked like a living thing in his hands and he wondered what Benny had been putting into it. Barbecue sauce? The cook's borrowed Yamaha was confounding its years with an upper register of speed that lifted the leading skis into aquaplaning mode, making the snowmobile difficult to steer and raising a sheet of water that obscured the trailing sled from Jack's sight when he glanced behind. The overhead canopy pressed down as thick as smoke, muffling the engine's snarl and blotting out his forward vision beyond fifty yards.

He had taken up the trail at the foot of the cliffs, where unmistakable marks of a dog sled on the land-fast ice narrowed the parameters of the search. If Aglukark had taken a boat and braved the waters of Lancaster Sound, he could have vanished into the northern hinterland. But a sled limited his options to crossing the fjord ice and seeking concealment in the mountains buttressing Victoria Sound.

The physical demands of controlling the machine did little to quell the shrilling note of panic that rose within him as images of Odette broken, raped or dead, strobed his thoughts. His speed was suicidal. The flooded ice pan he was crossing had remained unbroken for several miles and the odds that he would hit an open lead were compounded by an instinct, based on no more than a tingling in his inner ear, that the floe was on the move. He could drive straight into open water. But logistics, as much as urgency, dictated such folly: beneath him lay nearly a foot of melt water and a critical velocity was required for the heavy machine and its ponderous sled to break the liquid's turgid embrace.

Let the dead remain dead. Jack was only half aware of the debate going on at the bar of his conscience. An insistent voice declared that no one would miss Aglukark, who had surely forfeited his right to remain with the living. Another counsel pointed out the rationale of such a brutal solution: Jack wanted to escape the consequences that would arise from Aglukark's testimony. The deaths of his mother and little stepbrother could not be dismissed lightly.

He could picture his stepfather's trial on a charge of kidnapping. The courts' policy of extending leniency and rehabilitation to native people would probably mean nothing worse than a six-month jail sentence followed by Aglukark's return to the community. Whereas Jack could incur murder charges.

Was there a moral justification for murder? The Bible said not, but there

were enough precedents in Inuktitut lore for killing someone who threatened your survival. He recalled a man who went berserk and killed eight
people in a camp. Fearful of what he might do to their families if they went
out to hunt, the other men in the camp had surrounded his snow house and
shot him inside. In another case, a terrified camp had drawn lots to kill a
woman who blew her breath of madness at them, tore down their tents and
threw rocks at them.

Jack could think of half-a-dozen such examples but none, he scourged
himself, equated to what he had done. The blood of his mother and her
baby stained his hands indelibly. There could be no understanding or
forgiveness for what remained a mortal sin in the eyes of the Church.
Adding to his torment was that he couldn't remember what exactly had
triggered his behaviour. Did bullying parents merit death at the hands of a
rebellious teenager? Had Soosie really been sexually abused, as he believed,
or was Aglukark's behaviour part of some initiation ritual? He had no real
legal defence.

The machine slammed down on a protruding shelf of ice and a moment
later he felt it swerve to the right as a towrope parted. He cut the throttle
and cruised to a halt. The cliffs behind him lay out of sight and he took a
new bearing on the fjord's invisible far shore, another two hours' travel by
his estimate.

As he waded across to the sled, a thought checked him. What if he had
read it all wrong? The débâcle of Ituquvik and Jonas's scheme had stemmed
from his own naïvety and now he was responding blindly to yet another
impetus. Was a quite different agenda being elaborated here by someone
else? Karlsson? Why was he so certain it was Aglukark?

Slewed to one side, the sled stood proud of the water on an ice ledge. It
had taken a pounding and he stooped to check the bindings. That was when
he saw the dog's ear by his foot. It had been severed cleanly in one stroke,
leaving a thin crust of blood. Something flickered down Jack's forehead and
he shivered. As a child, he had seen his stepfather slash the ears from errant
dogs with his whip. He knew of no one else capable of such mistreatment.

He retrieved the towrope from the icy water and fixed it to the tow-bar.
Selecting reverse, he backed onto the ledge of dry ice and accelerated off
its firm surface to jerk the sled into motion.

After only 300 yards a change of light on the surface ahead prompted
him to halt again. Before him lay open waters. Waves at the foot of the ice
platform told him the floe was moving quite fast. He circled around and
drove slowly along the edge, scouring the translucent grey light for a
glimpse of another floe. He debated whether to ditch the sled; it was now
a dangerous encumbrance that could hold him back in the precious seconds
afforded by the manoeuvre he planned. On the other hand, it would serve

as a life raft if the Ski-doo went under, buoyant enough to support Benny's machine as it dangled at the end of the towrope. He decided to take the risk.

The rank smell of a male seal reached him before he saw its dark shape looming in the fog. The animal reclined on top of a wall of ice moving inexorably towards him at a closing speed that he calculated would cause the two floes to collide in less than half a minute. The turbulent water roared a song of death. He circled around to leave himself a thirty-yard run-up, measuring distances. It would be tight: the colossal impact of the two masses would throw up a pressure ridge of ice and so he had to leap the gap while open water still separated them.

The seal looked up and dived. In the same instant he pushed the throttle with his thumb, gently at first and then at full depression. The machine seemed to crawl for an age before it found its grip and suddenly he was airborne, knowing he had misjudged it as the lip of the approaching floe was still an impossible five yards distant but the ice wall kept moving to meet him and he crashed onto solid ice with the sled still in tow before the lips of the floes came together with a juddering kiss.

It took him more than two hours to reach the far shore and he was shaking with the machine's vibrations when he beached the sled and cut the engine. Ignoring his cramped limbs, he paced along the land-fast ice, spotting crablike indentations that signified hauling dogs, and followed them to the buried sled. Aglukark's lack of subtlety was puzzling. Subterfuge had bought him perhaps seven hours, but now he had abandoned caution and was travelling on foot with a woman who would slow him down.

Jack glanced up at the cliff face. Twenty years previously a Vancouver-based travel agency had chosen this spot to bring in tourists for whale-watching weekends, flying them to a small airstrip atop the cliff and accommodating them under canvas. In its zeal, the firm had cut a crude, slanting track down to the beach before discovering that narwhals and belugas preferred more sheltered waters. With extreme caution, he inspected the beach in both directions before satisfying himself that Aglukark's dogs had taken the cliff track. The melting surface had obliterated any human footprints.

He ran the figures through his head, calculating that the snowmobile could halve Aglukark's lead, especially if his stepfather had taken the glacier route. The critical factor was Odette. Even if she did not resist the pace set by Aglukark, her strength and fitness would count little against the dehydration that sapped ill-adapted Arctic travellers. Soon she would become a liability.

He unhitched the sled and, from long habit, transferred Benny's radio and aerial to the snowmobile. Last, he checked that his Winchester, loaded with hard points, slid easily inside its damp leather scabbard: shrinkage of the hide had cost several hunters their lives when seconds counted.

With a mental apology to Benny for the damage he was about to inflict, he ran the machine up to the narrow path and inched forward, climbing steadily. At the first bend the Ski-doo nearly toppled. Here, the ice had become slush and the drive track scrabbled at the rock, trapping the lead skis against the rock face and swinging the machine's rear over the edge. A surge of anger lent him the strength to seize the front with both hands and wrench it round. It became the pattern of his ascent, forcing him to dismount at each corner and repeat the manoeuvre, so that by the time he reached the summit his gloves were torn and bloody.

The dog tracks led unmistakably towards ascending rock where he could not follow, so he swung left along a stretch of smooth stone that wrung a scream of protest from the skis, praying his recollection had not failed him. Just as he remembered, a thin tongue of solid ice drooped down from the glacier to lick the far edge of the airstrip. Jack headed for it, deaf to the machine's agonized shrieks.

Once reunited with its natural element, the snowmobile seemed to fly up the slope, accelerating on the corrupted ice and clawing desperately for purchase on the glass-smooth sections. Jack threw caution aside, focused on maintaining uphill speed even if it meant throwing the machine at obstacles to gain the slingshot traction that hurled the ungainly vehicle across gullies and over splintered sections. As he climbed, the ice sculpture and the ride grew wilder, until a jarring through the handlebars and a flapping ski brought him to a standstill. A glance showed a bolt had torn out of the left steering ski.

Jack estimated that in the half-hour since leaving the beach he had travelled nearly seven miles, reducing Aglukark's lead substantially. The ride, he realized, had shaken loose his thoughts of violent retribution and replaced them with a more sober introspection. The bottom line was he could not bear the idea of Odette being a witness to his third murder. Better to arrest Aglukark and face the consequences. The air base at Resolute could have a helicopter out and tracking in half an hour, while he acted as sweeper on the ground. Between them, Aglukark didn't stand a chance.

The prudent course now was to report his position and the direction in which his stepfather was heading. Or he could repair the ski in the Inuktitut manner by shooting a new hole for the bolt in the soft metal. Rejecting both options, he grabbed his knapsack and began to run.

After only 200 yards he drew up short to examine a profusion of paw marks that milled around the approach to an ice bridge. Puzzled by a lingering animal smell of acute pungency, he glanced down beside the bridge and saw the bulk of an animal. A bear was looking straight at him, crouched on all fours. He drew back, assessing the risk, but the bridge looked firm and posed no greater hazard than he had faced a hundred times.

Keeping his eyes fixed on the surface ahead, he stepped onto the narrow span, hearing the hoarse breath of the animal below and a quickening of its movements. At his third pace, gravity seemed to switch poles as his footing tilted, the knapsack in his hand swung out to the right and he found himself falling into the vault below. In the same instant, a thought overrode the glimpsed horror that awaited him: he had no rifle.

CHAPTER 28

CRAMP SEIZED ODETTE'S calves and then her knees before racking the tired muscles of her aching back. It was hours since she had chewed a sliver of ice, for they had veered off the glacier to cross a rocky ridge to this bowl in the mountains and now the effects of dehydration were crippling her. Feeling the first pangs of headache, she stopped to remonstrate with the man, but to her surprise he gestured for her to unload, this time not offering to help, so she slumped down and eased the rope over her head.

When she looked up, he had vanished. A rummaged movement in a cleft in the rock announced his emergence, pulling a large canvas bag. She watched him assembling the beams and walls of a two-man tent, aware of her exhaustion and the clamouring question of sleeping arrangements.

He led her to the rock opening and pushed her inside. Beyond a hanging tarpaulin, she saw, was a low cave with rugs and a stove.

'You sleep here and you cook,' he announced.

'I am not your bloody cook.' She uttered the words with slow deliberation, only to see him smile.

'Then you do not eat.'

There was no answer to that. Except there was, she realized the following day. A prisoner's first duty is to make things difficult for their captor, she reminded herself, before carrying the five-litre can of naphtha cooking fuel to her 'rest room' a short distance from the cave and pouring it between the rocks. Perhaps he would be forced to leave for more supplies.

'No fuel,' she announced that evening. He inspected the empty can, sniffed its sides and seized her bad hand. Instead of inflicting more pain, he led her inside his tent and made her sit on the floor while he chopped up and crushed a white plant before spreading the paste onto the livid wound in her palm.

The reason for the gesture became plain in the morning, when he pointed to the hillside and made a gathering motion with his hands. Odette saw he meant the tussocks of arctic heather and she spent the next two hours pulling sheets of the tough, leathery plant from the tundra. The high resin content of the stems generated a very hot flame that quickly heated the man's improvised oven of flat stones. Her act of resistance had merely earned her a daily stint of manual labour.

Not quite. The chore provided cover for hoarding food against the moment when an opportunity to escape might occur. On the second day she discovered a cache of piled rocks. Scraping back the top slab, she was horrified to see the pale corpse of a young woman, perfectly preserved and bound tightly in a hide. The man materialized behind Odette and to her relief he looked surprised and even shocked. Not one of his victims, then. She tried to visualize how disease, hunger or an accident had snuffed out this young woman's life, compelling her family to move on.

In the presence of death, thoughts about Jack's fate were unavoidable. Refusing to admit the likelihood that he had died in the bear pit, she forced herself to imagine other scenarios which accounted for his continued non-appearance. She owed it to him, and to herself, to stay strong.

Aglukark felt alarm at the body's discovery and with an effort suppressed the voices that rose within him, warning against the proximity of a dead stranger to his camp. In life, women's unclean menstruation could disrupt the harvesting of animals, but in death their unquiet spirits could invoke worse. He would have to propitiate this woman's *iriraq*.

'Give me your watch,' he ordered Odette. Interpreting her hesitation as disobedience, he grasped her hand and unclipped the metal strap. Bewildered, she watched him disengage the dead girl's arm from the shroud and slip the watch over her wrist.

It had been a present from her lover Jon, a Tag Heuer worth £1,500 but small recompense for his treachery. Guilt pricked her unawares at the thought of all the grave goods she had taken from the dead in the name of science. It felt good to give something back. She watched the man offering a prayer over the grave. 'Rest in peace,' she murmured.

That night she discovered that the heather made a soft base for her sleeping fur. She puzzled over the man's intentions, wondering whether his actions were governed by a schedule that was heading to some kind of resolution. She took comfort from recalling each day that she had known Jack and the subtle changes she had noted in him. To her dismay, it was becoming more difficult to picture his face.

He was falling. It was a twenty-five-foot drop and Jack knew he would probably break his legs but in the frozen elapse of time a possibility sparked by his unconscious mind made him throw his knapsack behind the bear. Confused by this second threat from above, the animal had barely turned to savage the bag when Jack's boots thudded into its back. As the bear reared up, he sank his fingers into its fur and hung on, straddling its broad girth with his legs.

Winded, he gave a moment's thought to his pocketknife but the price of relinquishing his hold was death so he desperately scanned the prison's confines as his enraged mount attempted to dislodge him, roaring and hitting the ground jarringly with its front paws. Frustrated by this tactic, the bear shook its fur violently, as if shedding a coat of water, and Jack felt himself hurled across the vault to connect with an ice wall. He took the impact on his shoulder before falling awkwardly to the ice floor. A couple of ribs felt broken.

He closed his eyes, stunned, and waited for the end. Incongruously, he had a mental image of the two posters on his office wall. 'Curl up! Play possum!' one instructed. 'Fight back!' said the other. He lacked the strength to do either.

After seconds had lengthened into a minute, he opened his eyes and realized the bear was as shocked as he was. It was tearing apart his satchel with its teeth, eyeing him warily and clearly working itself up for a charge. Jack shivered, but realized the cause was not fear alone. Melt water had soaked his trousers and a freezing draft was turning his legs to ice. He groped behind him, expecting to feel the wall's solidity but instead his hand encountered an icy airflow. Ducking down, he saw a a two-foot deep fissure and heard rushing water far below.

The bear chose that moment to attack, barrelling forward and delivering a massive swipe of its paw to the threatening interloper. Jack felt a pulverizing blow to his back that propelled him like a cork through the shaft. He glimpsed a kaleidoscope of lights and experienced the sensation of being airborne before he collided with something solid and was then falling vertically until the breath was smashed from his body.

He returned to consciousness slowly, registering an internal audit of pain and damage that he was reluctant to face. Experimentally he flexed a few muscles and registered that his legs were useless.

Water dripping on his face revived him enough to open his eyes and peer around in the spectral light. He was jammed on a ledge overlooking a parabolic wall of ice, slick with water, that curved downwards for 200 feet before it vanished into darkness. Far above him stretched a sheer ice surface that offered no escape.

Jack mouthed a simple prayer for Odette's safety, striving to subdue the agony of losing her with memories of their short time together. He also thought of his mother and her dead child, resigning himself to the judgment he had spent his life postponing. Then he fumbled with leaden hands to pull up his hood as protection and, like a seal, slipped over the edge.

*

Odette vomited. She had boiled the moss campion after chopping its large taproot into more digestible form, but her empty stomach rejected the bitter soup. She longed for the taste of bread, sugar, even meat.

Le Conard, as she had dubbed the bastard contemptuously, had not brought back any game for nine days. The small stock of groceries had been consumed long since and her attempt to hoard scraps of meat had earned a new punishment. Le Conard always hobbled her during his absences; now she was permanently bent over by a short chain that shackled her right wrist to her left ankle. Weakness forced her to adopt a painful crouch that made even cooking difficult.

For the first time she contemplated her own death on these slanting planes close to the sky. It did not seem such a bad thing, except that she had been stolen from loved ones. Injustice and the imagined pain of others – Jack, Paddy and her mother – inflamed her anger. With all her waning strength, she cursed Le Conard.

A blob detached itself from the wall and coalesced with another wobbling shape. In his intermittent spells of consciousness, Jack had watched the Jelly People and tried to make out the indistinct words they addressed to him. Inuit folklore told of a timid race of human creatures who lived on the ice, rarely glimpsed because their bodies were translucent and defined only by a faint aurora. Several elders claimed to have seen them.

They seemed to be kind. He heard their whispers when they gently touched his wounds and fed him soup. He dreamed a recurring nightmare of finding Odette but she looked right through him, not hearing his words.

One morning he woke up to find Jonas seated beside him. 'You had concussion,' the Inuk told him. 'You were beat up pretty bad but you'll be OK.' Jack went back to sleep.

When he awoke, he saw he was in a tent with an Inuit family. Jonas handed him a mug of tea and answered his befuddled questions patiently. 'You have these folks to thank. They were crossing the glacier and their dogs started barking. They hauled you out from a crevasse.'

Jack shook his head, puzzling it out. 'No, that's not right. I was hundreds of feet down.'

Jonas grinned. 'The knees of your wind pants were all worn through. I guess you crawled and came out lower down the slope.'

'How long was I out?'

'These people reckon nearly two weeks. Their radio was out so they waited for their son to come in a boat. He got through to me.'

For a moment Jack was touched that his friend had overcome his fear of leaving town to make such a dangerous voyage. Then the import of his words struck him. A fortnight! He struggled to sit up. 'What about Odette?

Has she been found?'

Jonas shook his head. 'They called off the search. Jim Elias says there's no proof she was taken. She's just down as a missing person.'

Sensing that something was being held back, Jack grasped the sleeve of his friend's parka. 'What's going on?'

Jonas looked down. 'There's a lot of changes. Your sister is deputy mayor. I guess people were kinda disappointed. They believed all that stuff I told them about hotels and tourists. Instead, the community owes a lot of money.'

'So?'

Jonas looked embarrassed. 'Your sister and the mayor want to close the primary school.'

'Why would they want to do that?'

'They say children should be out hunting and learning land skills with their fathers.'

The thought of Soosie on a fundamentalist mission to turn the clock back to the dark ages filled Jack with gloom. It was a clever idea: school was partly responsible for the decline in hunting. It also brought white teachers into the community. Jack could imagine the agenda Soosie had in mind.

He noticed Jonas kept clasping his parka pocket uncertainly.

'What else?'

Jonas sighed. 'Your sister made out a complaint against you.' He took two envelopes from his coat and handed them across. One was stamped with the crest of the RCMP. Jack ripped it open and read it incredulously. It was a formal summons, signed by Sgt James Elias, compelling John Walker to surrender himself immediately to answer a charge of murder. It made no sense.

'Who am I supposed to have murdered?'

His friend shrugged. 'Soosie says you killed her father.'

'Aglukark?'

His unhappy silence was eloquent confirmation. It seemed to Jack that steel bars were clamped across his shoulders. He took a deep breath and closed his eyes. 'Do people believe this?'

Jonas glanced at him sideways. 'They don't know what to think. She's the deputy mayor and a lot of people listen to her. She warned everyone what was going to happen.'

Jack considered the implications. Suppose Soosie and her father were working in league but out of touch with each other. Had his own reappearance led Soosie to assume that he had killed Aglukark? In which case she had cut her losses and was trying to neutralize Jack as an obstacle to her political ambitions. His tortuous thinking produced another startling conclusion: Soosie had effectively locked out her father from ever returning to Snowdrift. Aglukark, she must be claiming, had died under an avalanche engineered by Jack.

His head swam. The second letter was from the Wildlife Department, to the effect that he was suspended, pending legal action. He swore.

He declined Jonas's offer to take him back, but accepted a rifle and two packs of cigarettes. 'What shall I tell Elias?' the Inuk wanted to know.

Jack tore up the letters. 'Tell him he can discuss the matter with Aglukark when I bring him in. And if he doesn't resume the air search I'll make sure he loses his badge.'

That evening he managed to sit up and take an inventory of his injuries. Two cracked ribs were tightly strapped and gave him little pain. Both knees, his right thigh and left elbow were still heavily bandaged. His leg muscles were atrophied from disuse, as he discovered when he tried to stand.

Wincing with the effort, Jack staggered out of the tent with the help of a harpoon. He emerged onto a whaling beach, strewn with the vertebrae of narwhal and beluga, that looked out on to the ice-free waters of the Sound. Five weathered tents were huddled down against a blustering wind that strained the guy ropes and threatened to pluck them from their securing rocks. His gaze fell on a solitary figure seated on the pebbles outside a tent, oblivious to the spray and volleying wind. The man was beckoning to him.

Jack walked over and lowered himself slowly beside him, noticing the man's extreme age and deathly pallor. 'Hello, I'm Jack Walker.'

Accepting a cigarette from Jack, the man chuckled. 'You can't guess my name.'

Studying the ancient plates of his face, Jack was tempted to try Rumpelstiltskin.

'When I was born, my mother looked at me and gave me my name – Little Piece of Cooked Meat.' The elder sucked in the smoke appreciatively. 'I was luckier than a man I know. His mother called him Nice Little Behind.'

Jack forced a chuckle. He glanced up. 'Will the weather clear, grandfather?'

The old man nodded. 'It is the same each year. Three, four days of wind and then calm, but people worry just the same that the whales will leave. It is a good thing about age, your long memory. I don't have so long. Six months ago the doctor said I was dying. Cancer. I told my family I was not going to die in town and I came here to wait for them. I told them, `If I'm dead, bury me but don't be sad.'

'So you've been here by yourself for months?'

'Not so alone. I think about my parents and old friends. Their spirits visit me and sometimes we talk. I saw Aglukark with his sled and dogs but he didn't look dead to me.'

Jack stopped him. 'You saw Aglukark? Where?'

Little Piece of Cooked Meat waved a hand along the fjord. 'I went to hunt for a seal. I was cutting up the animal at Qajaq Point when I looked over the rocks and saw him coming down the mountain with his dogs.'

A tic fidgeted on Jack's cheek. 'How did you know it was Aglukark?'

The old man stared at him. 'I know. I saw the way he whipped the dogs. I heard his voice. There was a good wind that day. That's why his dogs didn't smell the seal.'

'When was this, grandfather?'

'Mmnn.' He sucked a tooth. 'Must be the time of that hamlet meeting I heard about. A few days later, maybe.'

A week before Odette's disappearance. Jack struggled to his feet.

CHAPTER 29

AGLUKARK COULD NOT understand it. The mountain had always been a larder stocked with game, but his traps and snares failed to take their harvest of hares, foxes and lemmings. He knew caribou herds to be fickle, yet even fish avoided his nets and no bird crossed the sky. Prayers and blood sacrifice failed to lift whatever offence he had given. He thought of the young woman's grave.

A solution glared at him, fraught with complications. He would have to fetch fish and whale meat from the inlet, a full day's return journey. Yet he could not transport enough to keep the camp supplied for long. Some of the dogs had fox sickness and it was spreading in the pack. They could not be relied upon to carry much and neither could the woman.

His stepson must be dead, he reasoned, for there had been no pursuit. Why had Soosie not sent word to him that he could return, as they had arranged? His mind turned to the question of the woman's disposal. He studied her. How thin and dirty she looked, but still dangerous. She had served her purpose and yet he found himself unable to comply with Soosie's insistence that she be killed. He had never taken a human life directly, which only invited misfortune. But his luck could not get much worse. Kill her or abandon her?

Aglukark reached for his knife.

Sheets of spray, hurled aloft into the wind's slingshot, flailed the boat like grapeshot as it dug through the waves. As though a colossus was tipping the inlet like a bath, its disturbed water sloshed to the narrow end and rebounded with renewed violence. Jack was drenched and partly blinded by a waterfall cascading from the cabin roof to the open deck, yet he was experiencing a murderous calm.

The old man had lent him his twenty-four foot Winnipeg Lake Boat, ill suited to bad weather but its shallow draught allowed him to hug the shore unseen for the five-mile passage. Deep gorges split the drear coast of barren cliffs that betrayed no movement to his vigilant eye. He ran the boat into a sheltered spot and cut the engine. Checking the grub-box, he found it bare except for a rusty leg-hold trap and a bag of fish.

Qajaq Point had been named in the kayak era and although the Inuit had long since abandoned such craft in favour of larger, sea-going boats called *umiak*, Jack spotted several ancient kayak-rests of piled stones that confirmed the veracity of the original place name.

To a modern generation, the place was known as High Heaven in memory of its rubbish dump. The mine authority had selected the spot at a sufficient distance from its settlement to diffuse the evil pall of smoke from food scraps, industrial waste and rubber tyres that burned night and day like a scene from Dante's Inferno. The name had been self-evident to anyone within a five-mile radius: *it stank to high heaven*. The company had rehabilitated the site when it pulled out, but the name had stuck.

Through his rifle-scope, the foothills showed a tracery of animal paths to the mountain above, with no obvious human trails catching his eye. The fall line was marked by a river gorge that boomed with the violence of swollen melt water and he opted for a parallel route of sufficient distance not to deaden his sense of sound.

He shifted the scope to the darker slopes above, to see a moving object swim through his vision. As the image steadied, his breath checked.

Someone was descending.

Aglukark was tired and flustered. The killing had been necessary but unpleasant and he could not escape the presentiment that fate had turned against him. It was not mere chance that no animal allowed itself to be taken, although he had never failed to show respect to the parting spirits of game.

Several times he stumbled on the steep, rocky ground. Starvation was not a bad thing, he reasoned. A period of purification would enable his voice to reach his *iriraq* and reverse the malediction placed upon him. It was a curious thing: he could dream for others but not for himself; it was the way for all healers but that did not stop him trying to look into the future.

Which is why he mistook the object as a hallucination. It sat on the ground fifteen yards ahead, defying all logic and reason. He crouched down instantly, scanning the hillside for an explanation, but the empty slopes taunted him. A few swift strides and he squatted again, studying the conundrum.

A trap with a fish in its jaws. A fresh arctic char, he noted, and a rusty leg-hold device not unlike one of his own. The realization was punctuated by a click behind him and he turned to see a figure rising from a hollow. A white man.

'*Asujutilli atalli.*'

It was Elizabeth's boy. The disobedient child had become a vengeful man, he saw, looking into a pair of eyes as cold as the steel of the rifle that prodded his throat. Evidently he had killed the bear.

'Where is the woman?'

Aglukark shrugged and looked at the crystalline sky. He was ready to die. But the thought of Jack killing him again made him retreat to an inner place where he might patiently find a way of turning the situation to his advantage.

When his stepson repeated the question Aglukark searched his voice for weakness but finding none, deigned to answer. 'If you are talking of your mother, you know the answer. She lies in a cold grave, where you sent her.'

Jack pressed the rifle further into his neck. 'You know I don't mean Mother.'

'You have her wildness.' Aglukark nodded, unperturbed by the gun's pressure. 'You killed my son and now you come to threaten me again. A child learns from his father to accept the order of things, but not you.'

'You were no father to me.' Jack checked the bitterness that threatened to spill over.

'Nor was your own father. What sort of man kills himself and leaves his son?'

Jack realized Aglukark was goading him into anger but he couldn't let the taunt pass. 'He lost the will to live because you stole his wife and his son. I will ask you for the last time: where is the woman?'

'I don't understand you, boy. What woman do you speak of?'

Jack had not thought through this part in his improvised plan, but the urgency of the situation brought an answer from which one side of him recoiled. He had once read that it was an infallible method used by the French in Algeria for extracting information. The technique was listed in the annals of infamy.

Circling his captive with the rifle, he bound his thumbs together behind his back and marched him towards the river. 'You told everyone you could talk to the fishes, *attali*. Now we'll see if they taught you anything.'

Aglukark lurched backwards, believing he was about to be thrown into the river, but Jack anticipated the move and went with it, pulling him to the ground beside the bank. Lying on his back, the shaman watched curiously as Jack emptied the contents of his satchel and selected a small towel. Aglukark still had no idea what was intended when the towel was knotted securely over his face.

Jack's tone was conversational. 'I'm going to drown you for one minute. Then you're going to tell me what you have done with the woman.'

The satchel nearly wrenched itself from Jack's hands and stitched a line of fire across his ribs when he dipped it into a cataract of water. Carrying the bag to the recumbent figure, he poured carefully, ensuring the entire towel was wet before allowing the freezing water to gush over his captive's face. The thick cotton puckered frantically and Aglukark twisted sideways but again Jack was ready for him, stepping on his shoulder and holding him firmly until the bag was half empty.

He undid the two top knots and pulled the towel off Aglukark's gasping features.

'That wasn't so bad, was it? The next time will be two times worse. Tell me where the woman is.'

Chest heaving, Aglukark croaked something and then tried again.

'I do not know what you mean. Leave me in peace.'

Seeing his implacable gaze, Jack fastened the towel again. The exertion was making him feel faint. This time he emptied the satchel's full contents and Aglukark's struggles intensified towards the end.

'That was two minutes,' Jack informed him. 'Next time will be four.'

Aglukark had found a reservoir of strength that kept his mind detached from his drowning lungs, Jack saw.

'If you want to kill me, do so.'

Jack forced himself to think of Odette and repeated the procedure with two satchel-loads. This time Aglukark's choking features were distended with effort, but his resolve remained intact.

Eight minutes could be fatal, taking Odette's whereabouts with him. Jack's other self watched, appalled, as he filled up the satchel again. He knew he was approaching the point of diminishing returns, but the heaviness of his limbs told him he had no time to be merciful.

After six minutes, Jack felt the body go limp. Setting his jaw, he poured for a further minute and then removed the towel. The bloated face was slack, the chest immobile. Turning him over, Jack pumped his back and was rewarded by a spout of vomit and water.

When a moan escaped Aglukark, Jack levered him into a sitting position and left him to splutter and cough while he refilled the satchel. At the sight of the slopping bag, the shaman nodded. He fought for the breath to speak. 'Dead.'

Jack seized him by the coat and looked hard into his eyes. 'You killed her?'

With a resigned expression, Aglukark shook his head dazedly. 'No. Too weak.'

Fighting back despair, Jack persevered. 'Too weak?' What do you mean?'

'No animals. No food.' His gaunt frame lent credence to his words.

'Where?'

'A camp. Below the mountain cliffs.'

Jack took stock. His stepfather was in no state to lead him there, but his tracks would be not be difficult to follow. He levered the waterlogged man upright and supported him slowly down to the beach, where he made him sit while he trussed his arms and legs tightly with the sled's bindings. Securing the rifle across his back, Jack limped up the trail.

The metal glowed red-hot and Odette cried out. She could taste blood in her mouth and knew she could not last out much longer.

Le Conard had given no signal of his intentions. One moment he was lost in thought at his usual lookout spot, then a knife had appeared in his hand and he was striding towards her. Paralysis surrendered quickly to the instinct of self-preservation. She scanned the ground but no weapon presented itself. Think, she told herself. Seize his knife hand, even if the blade cuts you, and kick him between the legs. No, the trap chain linking her wrist to her ankle allowed no such latitude. She would have to use her teeth. Bite the hand or throw herself at his legs. Get him on the ground.

Aglukark passed her without a glance and walked towards the dogs. Squatting down, he fondled the lead dog beneath the jaw and, as it arched its neck with pleasure, the shaman pulled the head back sharply and slashed the offered throat with his knife. Seeing him repeat the procedure with another dog, Odette edged away.

When at last the whimpering and cries fell silent, she steeled herself and took a firm grip on a sharp-edged stone. But Le Conard had begun assembling a collection of tools and possessions on a hide, which he folded and secured with twine until she recognized the large bundle as a backpack. He was leaving.

Almost as an afterthought, he walked over to her, the bloody knife in his hand. In her enforced crouch, Odette watched his boots approach until only a couple of paces separated them before she launched herself at his legs, the stone drawn back to cut him. She felt the manoeuvre defeat itself from the moment her legs jack-knifed back, pulling her chained wrist down and twisting her body so that she sprawled at Le Conard's feet.

An instant later she felt his hand clamp around her jaw, holding her immobile. She was not going to plead. Instead she sent him a look of scalding hatred. Once again his irises twitched but his expression was tinged with pity at her decrepit condition.

'Jack has no need for you now,' he said. 'Better to die.' Then he stood up and, after carefully checking her iron shackles, turned his back. She watched him shoulder the heavy backpack and begin the long descent.

Too dazed to experience relief, she was driven to obey her gnawing hunger pangs. The idea of eating the dogs turned her stomach. She crabbed awkwardly across the hillside to her food cache and felt despair at the paucity of her hoard. Choosing a stringy meat scrap, she chewed it thoroughly while storing the remainder in a bag. It would last a few days, if she travelled in sensible stages.

Now she needed her watch to regulate her stops and keep track of time, but could not face the prospect of retrieving it from the young woman's corpse.

Her next priority was freedom of movement: she could never make the journey bent over like a crone. She had examined the chain many times and now she inspected it again. Both hinged manacles were of solid steel, adapted from an animal trap and secured by solid key mechanisms. Every link was welded except the two large outer ones connecting the chain to each manacle, but these were of a much heavier gauge.

Odette searched the camp until she found a short, pointed stanchion of forged steel. Placing its tip on one of the chain's central links, she used a rock to hammer the other end while sitting awkwardly on a boulder. A dozen blows made no impression on the link's shape or its weld, but cracked the rock in her hand. Several variations of this method, using other improvised tools, proved equally futile and left her close to weeping.

She had pushed the thought of fire to the back of her mind, but it was the only remaining option. She shuffled over to the crude oven. By experimenting, she discovered she could produce a small, intense flame in the aperture between four flat rocks. Flinching at the prospect, she would have to heat the large, unwelded link adjoining her ankle manacle in order to make it malleable, while simultaneously prising the link apart with two levers. The stanchion and a steel tent peg both fitted neatly inside.

Odette blanked out her mind and held her foot close to the flame. She had removed her boot, knowing it would be incinerated, relying for protection on a thick strip of bearded sealskin that she slipped inside the manacle and wrapped around her foot. Within seconds it began to smoke. The glowing heat of the rocks, compounded by the proximity of the flame, sent excruciating pain up her leg and through her brain. Biting the inside of her cheek, she waited until the link glowed red, its heat passing into the manacle around her ankle, before she inserted the two levers and pushed in different directions. The link resisted.

Suddenly aware that the steel picks were burning her hands and her foot casing was on fire, she screamed and threw desperate strength into the levers. The link began to bend.

Moaning with hurt and rage, Odette swung her body sideways and plunged her foot and both hands into a plastic basin of cold water. It was one commodity she was not short of. She clenched her eyes shut, knowing that the acrid smell in her nostrils was her own burnt flesh.

There was no time for self-pity, she admonished herself, slipping out the bent link from the manacle. Le Conard might return and her slender supply of meat put her in a race against the clock. For half an hour she replenished the cold water until her swollen blisters seemed to stabilize. The manacle remained clamped to her ballooned ankle, but the sole of her foot was unaffected and she could at least walk.

It would be foolhardy to follow Le Conard's descending route, she decided. Better to strike out along the present contour and hope to find a way down to Victoria Sound through the complex of valley systems.

With unsteady steps she set off across the mountain.

The tough hide of Aglukark's soles had laid a clear trail and Jack prayed every painful step of the ascent, pausing every hour to lie on his back in an effort to rally his draining strength. All the joints in his body proclaimed their imminent seizure. His stepfather had lied to buy time, he repeated to himself.

The smell hit him in nauseating waves. An aura of death hung over the camp. Even when he saw the bodies of the dogs, their throats slashed, he continued to cling to the belief that she had survived. His hopes soared when he found her sleeping quarters and detected telltale signs of her presence, but the scene bore out Aglukark's story. He sniffed the cooking pot and winced. Moss campion, starvation food.

It took him an hour of searching the hillside before he found her body in a stone grave. One glance at the Tag Heuer watch on her sun-darkened wrist, visible through an opening in the shroud, confirmed his worst fears. She looked so peaceful, curled up in the permafrost's embrace, that he could not bear to disturb the hide that bound her or gaze at her face.

The earth came up to meet him and he lay face down, eyes open, as his frozen grief burst in a flood. The inner thing that had sustained him with its cold blue flame was suddenly extinguished and his link with the world hung broken. All feeling left him and he could sense his spirit departing, too, along a half-remembered trail. He longed to stay beside this meadow, living quietly until he, too, sank into its folds.

A raven came to inspect him after he had not moved for three hours. His trance kept reality at bay until urgent messages reached his brain, piercing his tearing sense of loss.

In the recess of his mind fretted a sense of something forgotten. Aglukark.

Little circulation remained in Aglukark's wrists or feet but his senses were still alert, so he stiffened when he heard the noise behind him. It seemed that only a few hours had elapsed since Elizabeth's boy had left, which was puzzling. His heart leapt when he placed a meaning on the shuffling paces that approached with such hesitation – perhaps Jack had injured himself falling from one of the treacherous crevices on his ascent. The shaman remembered the knife still in his pocket, undetected.

Then he felt a cold nose pressed into the back of his neck.

He screamed.

Screaming was a mistake. If Aglukark had played dead, the *nanuq* might have lost interest. Even rotting whale carcasses, the polar bear's habitual fare in the summer months, smelled better than this foul man-thing covered in dead hide. But the shaman's cry of alarm triggered a predatory instinct that sent it into attack mode.

Aglukark watched in horror as the beast seized his boot in its mouth and pulled violently. He resisted in a grunting tug-of-war before the boot was torn from his foot, bringing the exultant realization that his leg bindings were severed. While the creature toyed with his boot, he scrambled upright, arms still bound behind his back, and began running along the shore.

He was concentrating on avoiding sharp stones when the monster caught up with him and delivered a blow that sent him sprawling. He got up and ran a few paces, only to be struck down again. The *nanuq* was playing with him, he realized helplessly. This time he had the presence of mind to curl up. Eyes clenched shut, he felt the animal's hot, foul breath on his face as it sniffed him. Without warning, he found himself plucked into the air by razor claws and smashed to the ground. Dimly conscious that both his arms were broken, he felt the beast's teeth sink through his thigh and grate against the bone. Something burst inside him. The last thing he heard was a crack.

The effort of the descent nearly defeated Jack. His waning concentration led him to the lip of a vertical drop, where he realized he had left behind his satchel and rifle. Cutting through his disorientation, the river's distant boom restored his sense of direction.

At last he could see Aglukark on the beach. His stepfather lay at an odd angle, one leg thrown out. The other leg was gone. His body bore the unmistakable marks of a polar bear's teeth and claws. Aglukark had suffered the fate recorded in the coroner's original verdict of death.

EPILOGUE

JACK WAS THINKING of trees and his next posting. Around the Great Bear Lake, birch and spruce trapped snow in deep drifts that required a tandem hitch to pair off sled dogs through narrow trails, he reminded himself. He had packed his snowshoes. There would be wheeling constellations of migratory caribou, in numbers unimaginable in the High Arctic, which found refuge in the sub-arctic forests, together with an unfamiliar bestiary of ermine, lynx, beaver and muskrat. Wolverines, of course. And in the forest, the Indians.

A different life. He was only beginning to understand what he had lost. His brief weeks with Odette had allowed him to glimpse for the first time what he might have become, a complete human being. The intellectual shell with which he had protected himself now seemed hollow and in sloughing it off he had reverted to an earlier, more vulnerable state of being, unsure of his place in the world.

The bay was quiet this evening, the air sweet, the scarred boats nuzzling the shore. From his window he scanned the bay entrance once again and fell back into his reverie. His return with Aglukark's body had lit a Chinese cracker whose reverberations could still be heard. Charges withdrawn, Jack's reinstatement by Wildlife and disciplinary action against Jim Elias that would put him back on traffic duty in a southern town.

Odette's spirit had been at his side, walking him through her funeral service and the unavoidable demands on his attention just as Jack had once shepherded other trauma victims in his days as a Mountie. He felt disembodied, with the clumsy light-headedness of a drunk.

His meeting with Soosie had been strained and brief. He found his step-sister packing at her house behind the fire station. She turned and greeted him with a forced smile.

'Jack! I'm so glad you're safe.'

'Are you?' He regarded her coldly. 'Is that why you're leaving town?'

She shrugged. 'I found politics doesn't agree with me.'

'Neither will a prison cell. You falsely accused me of murder. Instead,

221

your father abducted an innocent woman and let her die. He tried to kill me as part of some half-baked plan he cooked up with you to go back to igloos and barter.'

Soosie folded her arms. 'You have no proof of that and you never will.' She smiled winsomely. 'I was understandably mistaken about Father's death, but so were you, remember? And aren't you forgetting something, Jack? I saw you break his leg and kill his family by camping under those cliffs. An innocent woman and a child. I'd be careful before you start throwing accusations around.'

'That was a long time ago.'

'True,' she nodded emphatically. 'But there's no statute of limitations for murder or attempted murder. And I can remember it as clearly as if it was yesterday.'

'So you set out to punish me.' He recalled her bavura performance in the bathroom. 'You chose a strange way of doing so.'

A steely look twisted her features. 'Yes, I wanted to fuck you to death, but decided that was too good for you.'

An idea was running backwards and forwards in his mind. 'You thought you could sign me up to your mad crusade,' he said slowly. 'When that didn't work, you decided to get rid of me. You wanted to bring your father back, but I stood in the way. Isn't that right?'

She let her arms fall and gave him a measured look. 'Look, Jack, you've lost Odette and I've lost my father. Isn't that enough tragedy for one family? Why not leave it at that?'

Jack couldn't let it go. 'What did you think you were doing here trying to go back to Year Zero? What was worth Odette's death and my own? You know there was never any halcyon Inuit age, just starvation and early death. And you wanted to cut people off from what spared them all that. Why?'

Soosie closed her suitcase lid and stared at him with naked venom. 'I won't waste my breath because you wouldn't understand, Jack. Don't you realize you're a *qallunaat*? Oh, you've picked up a few native tricks to impress your white friends and you do some good impressions, but nobody's fooled. You were a Mountie and now you're another kind of policeman. Enjoying a white-man's privileges isn't enough – you need a badge to display your superiority and to show us savages the error of our ways. It's people like you who are holding us back.'

Without answering, he walked past her and let himself out. Her barbs had found their mark, and they hurt.

The phone rang. It was Jonas.

'You all right, Jack? A guy just called in from ten miles out. He got a visual sighting on the boat but he can't raise them on the squawk box.'

'OK, thanks, Jonas.'

Odette's mother was insisting on the body's return to England. The Revd David Kalluk had firmly ruled out Jack's participation in Odette's retrieval and dispatched Simon and Benny on the mission. Jack was reassured by their gentle manner when they had set off by boat towards High Heaven three days previously. Since when their radio had been out.

Escorting Odette's coffin to a southbound airliner at Resolute would be his last duty before taking up his new post. He wished she could be left where she lay. High Heaven was a more peaceful setting than London could provide. In spite of everything, Aglukark had shown a rare spark of decency by burying her in the rock cairn, tightly wrapped in a caribou hide. It was strangely at odds with the way he despatched the dogs, Jack reflected. Nor had his stepfather stripped the expensive Tag Heuer watch from Odette's wrist.

In recent days Jack had come to see himself as others must – a human fire-ship who burned everyone he touched. While busily blaming others, he had failed to identify himself as the true malediction in their lives. His father had put a gun to his own head, his mother and stepbrother had died at his instigation, he was the reason for Odette's capture and death, and he had left Aglukark as bear bait. It was he who instigated the Viking fiasco and pursued the project until the hamlet was deep in debt. The truth was that he was bad luck, a walker, and everyone knew it when they looked at him. He had to remove himself from their gaze.

He was leaving some amends. Jonas had been about to build a new Titanic from the wreckage of the last one when Jack had intervened to revive an idea they had previously discussed to restore the hamlet's finances. By pooling hunters' surpluses of fish, meat and whaleskin *maktaaq*, he argued, and converting the old Bay warehouse into a refrigerated storage depot, they could market 'country food' throughout Nunavut. The figures impressed Jonas: by the third year they could be turning over $150,000.

Jack looked wearily at his watch. They should be arriving soon.

At last he spotted Simon's boat turning through the chicane of rocks at the bay's mouth and he slowly made his way downstairs, picking up a harpoon to lean on. He was touched that Paddy had telephoned to offer him a job, but they both knew Odette's ghost would hover like a reproach between them and Paddy had accepted his polite refusal without demur.

At least Paddy was off the hook. 'I misjudged my profession, Jack,' he reported sombrely. 'People are ready to tear your eyes out over a misplaced comma. But it seems that an archaeologist who puts up his hand and says, `I've made an honest mistake' is not only forgiven, but applauded even.'

Jack took the long route past the Hudson's Bay Company building and around the church before beginning the walk down. He was surprised to see that Simon's boat had not cut back, but sent out a powerful bow wave. Wrong boat, he thought. There were three people on deck, not two. Why were they waving?

Jack rested on the harpoon while he took out his pocket scope and squinted. A slender figure, supported by Simon and Benny, was alighting stiffly on the shore.

Strength drained from his limbs. His heart lurched in his ribcage, his belly seemed to be sinking and sweat prickled on his skin. He stopped breathing.

In the glass, a radiant smile trembled.

He dropped the harpoon and ran towards the bay.